EVEN HIGHER THAN EVEREST

For Jeanetta.
& Lottie !

Enjoy this saga !

Love & thanks

George Almond

George Almond

21. Sept. 2019

ISBN 978-1-78222-624-6

Book design, layout and production management by Into Print
www.intoprint.net
+44 (0)1604 832149

FOR ALL THOSE WHO ASSISTED THE AUTHOR
ON THE LONG JOURNEY OF THIS STORY

AND TO THE MEMORY OF ALL THOSE WHO
DEFIED THE STORMS OF THE HIMALAYAS ON
THEIR WAY TO THE HIGHEST PEAK

AND ESPECIALLY TO LUCY HOUSTON WHO
UNDERSTOOD THAT GREAT WEALTH MUST BE
SHARED WITH DESERVING CAUSES

'At 12.50, just after I had emerged from a state of jubilation at finding the first definite fossils on Everest, there was a sudden clearing of the atmosphere, and the entire summit ridge and final peak of Everest were unveiled. My eyes became fixed on one tiny black spot silhouetted on a small snow-crest beneath a rock-step in the ridge; the black spot moved. Another black spot became apparent and moved up the snow to join the other on the crest. The first then approached the great rock-step and shortly emerged at the top; the second did likewise. Then the whole fascinating vision vanished, enveloped in cloud once more.'

Statement of Noel Odell, support climber and last man to see the climbers Irvine and Mallory alive. June 8th 1924

Characters in order of appearance

Colonel Blacker	Initiating a flight over Everest
Percy Etherton	Planning the operation
Garland Ross	Reuter's journalist in USA
Ralph Blumenfeld	Editor of the Daily Express
John Buchan	Author and mountaineer
Arthur Hinks	Royal Geographic Society
Donal Ryan	Bloodstock trainer
Lady Lucy Houston	Heiress extraordinaire
Willie Graham	Lady Houston's lawyer
Jenny	Company secretary
John	Lady Houston's chauffeur
Torrance	Steward on the Liberty
Lord Peel	Committee member
Marquis of Clydesdale	Chief pilot
Neil Jacobs	Foreign office staffer
Colonel McCleod	War office cartographer
Cyril Pitt	Bristol engineer
Burnard	Westland Chief fitter
Barkas	Film Director
Sydney Bonnett	Cinematographer
Frazer	Camera technician
Marco	Radio officer on the Liberty
Air Commodore Fellowes	Expedition leader
Eleanor Fellowes	Supernumerary and wife
Flight Lieutenant McIntyre	Second Pilot
Duchess of Hamilton	Clydesdale's mother
Shepherd	The Times correspondent
Mrs. Munro	Housekeeper at Kinrara
Captain O'Brien	Skipper of Hannibal airliner
Raja Banaili	Host to the expedition
Maharaja Shere Jung	King of Nepal
Tom Smith	Estate Manager
Sally Smith	Domestic manager
Sergeant Greenwood	RAF Sergeant

1. Tiger Hill, India – February 1932

PERCY ETHERTON WAS STAYING AT the Governor's residence in Madras when the telegram arrived. He was enjoying breakfast at the time and chose not to open the envelope until he'd finished. Telegrams generally offered grim or welcome news and finally, when he was ready for either eventuality, he had slit open the envelope.

> PERCY. I HEAR YOU ARE IN INDIA! I INVITE YOU NEXT THURSDAY FOR LUNCH AT GRAND EASTERN IN CALCUTTA? AFTER A CURRY WE CAN TAKE OVER-NIGHT EXPRESS TO WEST BENGAL FOR A WEEKEND IN THE HILLS. HAVE SOMETHING IMPORTANT TO DISCUSS SO PLEASE DO COME. RSVP SOONEST – BLACKER.

The cool air of the foothills was a tempting attraction, but for Etherton the prospect of spending time with Colonel Blacker had to be the real clincher. In any case, how could he decline an invitation from this particular friend, his former fellow officer on the Western Front? Etherton had cabled his confirmation immediately via the operator in the Governor's office.

Now a week later, after 1500 miles of constant rail travel, a superb fish curry and a sleepless night on the overnight leg from Calcutta, Etherton was calling on resilience when he alighted at Siliguri. Here, in the busy township beside the Mahananda River, he and Blacker had transferred to the hill train of the Darjeeling Himalayan Railway. It would take them, climbing and cork-screwing all of fifty scenic miles to their destination.

Once under way, Etherton began to relax. The three day marathon was nearly done and he realized with amusement he was still none the wiser. Nothing of importance had been mentioned to date so he wondered if he'd been lured into all this merely for a lungful of fresh air? Such motivation would be unusual for a man like Blacker who sat opposite. The Colonel was engrossed in a Penguin paperback while totally ignoring their passage through the tumbling foothills. Though renowned in Britain and India for deeds of action rather than words of jumbled substance, Blacker had so far provided no details whatsoever.

For an hour, the locomotive thrust against steep gradients and multiple reverse zig-zags, all attributed to highly skilled engineers, but then Etherton began to sense an inconsistency in the train's spasmodic progress. Or was it his imagination? Either way, he wasn't surprised when, after looping around Agony Point, the hill train convulsed and shuddered to a halt.

As soon as the screech of brakes faded, a lively debate began. Some passengers accused the famous loop for straining the engine while others suggested a sacred animal might be blocking the track? Both were fair assumptions, thought Etherton, as he stood up to look from the window. He saw no holy cows ahead and behind lay only the lethal coil of track poised over a forested chasm.

'Whatever the reason,' he remarked, 'I can think of better places to break down.'

Colonel Blacker glanced up from his book. 'A runaway here would bring plenty of agony. So if the train slips, Percy, don't hesitate to jump.'

'Good advice,' agreed Etherton. 'The only option.'

Fortunately this survival tactic was not put to the test. Instead the hill train held to the track with the tenacity of a stick insect while the jibber-jabber of its crew floated away on escaping steam. Soon enough, news arrived with the chai-wallah, an elderly Behari, who came shuffling through the carriage with tea and biscuits. The wheels were wedged, the man reported, while engineers repaired a valve. It was most regrettable and he advised the passengers to take their comfort from the great and truly wonderful Indian gift of patience.

Both Blacker and Etherton knew all about time in the sultry turmoil of the sub-continent, so they paid for their tea and took the wallah's advice. After a few sips, Colonel Blacker fitted a monocle to his right eye and returned to his book leaving Etherton to resume making notes in his diary, a much easier task on a stationary train. They both ignored the odd puff of smoke that invaded the carriage, driving out the dominant scents of tropical foliage and burning dung.

Half an hour ticked by. Then Colonel Blacker closed his book with a loud snap. Etherton could see how his friend's self-assurance had bloomed with years of military service and yet there were no hints of grey in the Colonel's raven black hair, eyebrows and mustache. Blacker's eyes, darker than shotgun barrels, added a cautionary gravitas to their owner. This was a man who relished confrontation.

7

'So you've finished?' Etherton enquired. 'I find Thirty-Nine Steps is one of his best.'

Blacker's fingers drummed on the book's cover. 'And I agree. John Buchan has filled the Scottish highlands with pure mischief. A gripping tale to be sure.'

'And you quite enjoy a bit of mischief yourself,' added Etherton.

Blacker raised an eyebrow allowing the monocle to swing free on its cord. 'And what do you mean by that, Percy?'

Etherton gestured at the commotion outside. 'Because, my friend, you've failed to say exactly what I'm supposed to be doing here? Now marooned in West Bengal on a train going nowhere?'

'You can't blame me for that,' protested Blacker. 'But yes, Percy, you deserve an explanation and I promise to tell you tomorrow.'

Etherton's origins were in the sweeping downland of West Sussex where people were generally affable and compliant. It was clear that Blacker had something in mind, an objective for this long pilgrimage and Etherton, an accomplished career diplomat, knew he had little to gain by insisting. 'Very well, then. Tomorrow it is.'

'But I'll offer you a clue, Percy. You can think of my grandfather.'

'Your grandfather?'

'Yes, Valentine Blacker who died a hundred years ago out here in India.'

Etherton struggled to find a link. 'He died in a duel, so you've told me, after challenging a fellow officer?'

The Colonel leaned forward to blow a fly from the biscuits before taking one. 'Yes, that's all true and the scrap was a stupid idea considering the outcome, but at least he managed to kill his opponent.'

'So, a pyrrhic victory for both men?'

'Yes, I suppose so,' said Blacker. 'My grandfather then commanded the National Survey of India. His men fixed the trig points with theodolites, chains and what-have-you. In fact, his death almost scuppered the mapping of the subcontinent though ultimately, the survey was delivered.'

Etherton had no chance to comment. Up ahead, the locomotive sounded like thirsty hounds panting after a long chase. Next came a silence and then a bright squeak from its whistle. The valve troubles were over and the hill train lurched forward to resume its climb. With renewed momentum, everyone felt inspired as the locomotive fired smoke pillars into the sky, honking defiantly at the gradients ahead.

Within an hour, the hill train reached the village of Ghoom, at the highest elevation of any station on India's extensive rail network. Here they disembarked and took a pony tonga to the settlement's guest house. After traveling for so many hours, it was time for a break.

Next morning, well before sunrise, they were on the move again. Slipping from the guest house into the darkness they found their guide waiting with three saddled ponies. In the dim glow of a kerosene lantern, they checked the saddle girths and mounted to adjust their stirrups. Then they were off, following the guide at a fast trot on the track that led to Tiger Hill.

At first the trail held to the contour before rising between thick clusters of rhododendron and verdant undergrowth. A prowling tiger would regard this as perfect territory, thought Etherton. He had heard that a professional hunter had shot the man-eating tigress who once terrorized the hill. Everyone was safer now, the guide explained, as they rode on, passing wood gatherers, several sadhus and a snake catcher.

Such vagaries of life on the road were standard fare for both men. They had rapidly discovered the need for resilience and adaptability in the bloody quagmire of the French battle front. Here they had become close friends and somehow, against overwhelming odds, they had survived the slaughter until the Armistice in 1918. Blacker had then joined the Corps of Guides for further military service in India's tribal territories while Etherton, a less combative individual, had taken off on a trek of 10,000 miles across Asia before accepting a diplomatic posting in Turkestan.

Now as his pony trotted obediently in line, Etherton realized that, apart from that rather obscure clue on the train, he was again wondering what devilish reason could Blacker provide for all this activity? However, he had been promised an answer today.

In a glade just below the final ridge the guide drew rein, advising his clients to continue on foot. Etherton dismounted to follow Blacker who was still limping thanks to a wartime air crash. The injury was rarely mentioned and did little to deter the Colonel as he pushed on ahead through the shards of early sunlight cutting through the trees.

Some yards from the ridge, Blacker stopped and turned. 'Can you wait a moment, Percy? I'll go on ahead. Just to be sure.'

Ready for a breather, Etherton held back willingly enough while Blacker vanished into the dewy bushes. But why, he wondered, was caution so necessary? Perhaps the man-eater had left behind a litter of cubs?

Blacker's shout came soon enough, cutting crisp and clear over the chorus of jungle birdsong. 'Come up, Percy! I now have something to show you.'

When he joined Blacker on the crest of Tiger Hill, Percy Etherton understood immediately. Across the northern horizon was the most spectacular vision Etherton had ever seen. Stretching high, wide and seemingly afloat on a foreground of dusky foothills and deep valleys, lay a display of snow-clad mountains with a multitude of glaciers and dazzling slopes. The whole vista was glistening in the orange blaze of dawn.

'My God! That is beautiful!' Etherton said. 'Just the best! That *really* is the Himalaya, the pearls on the throat of India.'

Blacker raised his hand towards the parade of white peaks as if he was introducing guests at a party. 'There you see the world's finest. First lies the massif of Kanchenjunga beyond Darjeeling. Then, out to the West, you can make out the razored profile of Makalu with Nuptse close by. Out there at the back is the most famous of all, trailing that thread of banner cloud. Some call her Chomolungma, but I'll settle for Everest.'

Etherton had seen the highest of all mountains on several previous occasions, but today the peak broadcast her famous aura with the dawning light across the entire panorama. Was this the answer to the clue on the train? 'And Everest was discovered thanks to your grandfather's survey?'

Blacker grinned. 'Oh yes, he played his part. And now, Percy, here's my plan. I want to finish what he began. I intend to go up there.'

Etherton stayed silent. Watching the lone spume of cloud that drifted from the peak, he wondered how to play this? A trot up Tiger Hill was easy for a man like Blacker, but an ascent to the highest summit on Earth had to be ridiculous. 'I'm not clear about this,' he finally admitted. 'Are you going to climb up there?'

'With a leg like mine? I'm not bloody daft, Percy!'

'Then I'm sorry, I don't understand.'

'It's quite simple,' said Blacker. 'It's thirty years since the Wright brothers began it all, but only now has aviation evolved to the point when we may actually fly over Everest.'

Etherton's gaze wandered from the distant range of mountains down to the folds of shaded ridges and valleys below. From Tiger Hill to Everest seemed a very tall order. 'So you're planning to fly there?'

'If the new Pegasus 650 horse-power engine from Bristol Aviation can be fitted to a Westland biplane, then flight at 35,000 feet is feasible. Assuming tests are successful, I shall mount an expedition. Flying as observer, my photographic survey can only add to my grandfather's legacy.'

Thousands of square miles of uninhabited land lay before Etherton's feet and he preferred to keep good friends alive. 'Assuming you survive a flight with a single engine over such unwelcoming territory.'

'I'll keep ticking till they call my number.' Blacker raised a dismissive eyebrow. 'Well, you've seen the target, Percy, and I'd be honored if you'll agree to join me in the enterprise.'

Etherton had an immediate concern. 'Do remember I'm no aviator. I much prefer keeping my feet on terra firma.'

'And that's fully understood,' said Blacker. 'I'm not expecting you to go up. But such a major undertaking calls for someone with your diplomatic and leadership skills to put it all together – on the ground.'

The enormity of the challenge held an undeniable, almost irresistible, appeal for Etherton. Nor could he find any plausible reason to refuse such a unique offer from this friend.

'My thanks for the compliment,' he said. 'I am interested, but only if we both agree that such a flight is feasible.'

Blacker's right hand shot out to seal the agreement. His smile was as bright as the tiny reflection of the Himalayas that blazed across his monocle. 'Yes, Percy, it's all feasible. Just a few bits and pieces to resolve, then as easy as doing circuits around Bristol aerodrome.'

'Or tying knots in a tiger's tail?' Etherton's quiet comment went unanswered. He stared at the distant ranges on the skyline where the finger of banner cloud still beckoned enticingly. 'So where and when do we start?'

'We go back to the ponies. Back round Agony Point. Back to Calcutta, onto a ship and back to London. And there,' said Colonel Blacker with a dark grin,' we'll find all the answers.'

2. Lake Placid, New York – February 4th 1932

THE PEOPLE OF MANHATTAN CAME to another range of mountains early that day. The assault began before first light when the temperature was zero and the Adirondack peaks remained hidden by a strata of veiled mist hanging over the valleys of Lake Placid.

Police trucks, public service and catering vehicles were the first to show, preparing for the public who began arriving as the mist dissolved into bleak sunlight. Soon, the combined clamor of slamming doors, rehearsing bands and public address systems rose between the forests to dissipate in a sky of flaxen blue.

After parking their vehicles in the special zones, newcomers were obliged to cover the final stretch to the stadium on foot. For most of them it was a good way of warming up after the long drive from the city. Among the crowd now tramping over the packed snow, one young woman was clearly in a hurry.

She was on her own and moving with a stride that never faltered. Slipping past the hot dog stands with their sweet aroma of frying onions, she dodged through lines of excited school children, overtook dawdlers and pushed on until she was forced to stop at a pedestrian crossing. Here a traffic cop, noting her urgency, waved her over. For that he received a smile and a wave from gloved fingers as she moved on again.

Striding forward, she peeled back her coat sleeve to check the time. She could still make the appointment, even if half Manhattan was out to hinder her progress. Nearing the stadium, the throng grew ever more frenetic with famous faces adding to the febrile anticipation. Hollering and glad-handing in the latest winter outfits from Saks and Bloomingdales, everyone had come to see Governor Franklin Roosevelt launch the 1932 Winter Olympics.

Competitors from seventeen nations would soon fight for gold, silver and bronze on the sculptured runs and rinks around Lake Placid. Their contest would dominate the media and no aspiring journalist could ignore such an event. With a Reuters press pass tagged to her shoulder bag, Garland Ross sped on to capture her exclusive story.

Much earlier that day, Garland had rummaged through her wardrobe for a suitable outfit. Most of the women in the crowd were snug inside the pelts of silver fox and mink but such luxuries were well beyond her means. A Burberry coat, blue roll-neck sweater, scarf and flannel slacks were all Garland had found to protect her from the daggers of the Arctic wind.

The plan had developed over Christmas in her rented apartment on the Upper East Side. Here a colleague had mentioned knowing Jack Shea. The speed skater was tipped for gold and would be competing before his home crowd. Garland had sensed a hot story and an exclusive, though brief, interview with Shea had been arranged.

Garland was to meet the athlete outside the Press Enclosure. For ten minutes, she would ask about Shea's views about taking the Olympic Oath on behalf of the USA. With his quotes in a tight report for Reuters, her career could only benefit. Now she trod cautiously over a patch of unsalted sheet ice.

From nowhere came a crashing blow that sent her down to land with a thump on her back. Lying on the ice, it took a few moments to catch her breath. She found herself staring into the face of a middle-aged woman who was sprawled beside her and groaning.

Garland got unsteadily to her feet. She bent down. 'You ok?'

'Dumb question,' came a snarl. 'You knocked me down. I swear to God you did!'

'I don't think so. It was the ice. We went down together.'

Around them, feet were shuffling as crowd pressure built. The woman was moaning louder. 'Goddammit, I've busted my arm. I can feel the bone.'

The woman's arm did look odd. 'Someone get a doctor!' Garland yelled. 'This lady's broken her arm.'

Garland considered this rude but injured stranger. Should she abandon this unfortunate soul? Probably not, she decided. Unwinding her scarf she placed it below the woman's head and took off her coat to cover her. Wearing just her slacks and sweater Garland squatted down beside the patient. 'Don't move. I can hear an ambulance coming.'

The Olympic organizers had planned for such emergencies. A Chevrolet ambulance arrived with its siren howling. Seconds later the casualty was hoisted inside and rushed off to a first aid clinic.

Still dazed, Garland recovered her clothing and resumed her hurried walk. She had almost certainly missed the appointment with Jack Shea. On reaching the Press Enclosure, she learned that the athlete had left to take his prestigious role in the ceremony.

Without trying to conceal her disappointment, Garland waved her pass at the gatemen and headed directly to the refreshment area. She felt chilled, bruised and resentful. The accident certainly wasn't her fault. As she stood at the bar, slush began dripping from her coat and her scarf. One of her gloves was missing and when she caught sight of her reflection in the back-bar mirror, her dark chestnut hair was a crazy mess. And all thanks to a frigging awful, selfish woman.

'Just a guess, young lady, but you need a strong drink.'

Another stranger now stood beside her. He was raising his fedora hat as Garland turned to see a lively gentleman in his sixties wearing a cashmere overcoat. His voice was deep, his manner easy and gracious.

'A strong drink? Sure, we'd all like one of those, but there's this little thing called Prohibition, remember?'

The man shrugged. 'Not where I'm from.'

Garland took another look. Was he a banker, an impresario? He might be Jewish, Armenian or Greek? She smiled. 'Hot coffee's just fine. Thanks anyway.'

A barman pushed two cups of steaming coffee across the bar. As she stirred in milk and sugar, Garland saw her new acquaintance pull a hip flask from his pocket. With a playful wink he unscrewed the cap and tipped a measure into his coffee. 'I saw what you did back there. Was she a friend?'

'No. I never met her before. Just an accident.'

The stranger hesitated. 'Looked to me you were being helpful. Surely that deserves a slug of Jameson's to fire up your coffee?'

Garland glanced around them, then held out her cup. 'OK. Thanks. I don't know what happened, but it sure cost me a good story. I was just about to interview Jack Shea.'

'Shea, the skater?' He poured whiskey into her coffee. 'Losing a scoop like that would be a pain in the ass.'

Garland drank and felt the whiskey warming all the way down to the bruise now forming around her coccyx. 'It was horrible. I'm sure I heard her bone snap.'

'That's tough. Bones heal but news always keeps a-coming.'

So he was a journalist. 'Got any leads?' she asked. 'I'm with Reuters at the moment, but I don't want that forever.'

The public address crackled with a final call to take seats. In the Press

Enclosure hacks and correspondents wound up their conversations and set off to their positions. When the announcement finished, her companion said. 'You were asking for ideas, Miss...?'

'Garland Ross. From Ohio, but based in New York. And you, my knight with a shining hip flask?'

The stranger laughed and slid a card from a silver case. 'You and I are neighbors. I'm from Wisconsin originally but these days I'm the managing editor of the *Daily Express* in London.' Further crackling issued from the public address system as he placed the card firmly in her hand. 'You have my number. Feel free to contact me if you ever cross the pond. Just ask for Ralph Blumenfeld.'

The exchange, or perhaps the illegal liquor, had revived Garland's spirits. She popped the card into her purse. 'You were right. I did need that Irish medicine.'

'Works every time,' said Blumenfeld as they left the Press enclosure to hear whatever Roosevelt might have to say.

3. The Alpine Club, London – April 1932

FOR JOHN BUCHAN, CELEBRATED AUTHOR of The Thirty-Nine Steps, it would be a day of many meetings. The former war correspondent and politician had left his country home near Oxford early to catch the fast train to Paddington. Here a taxi whisked him to the offices of *The Times* newspaper for interviews about his latest novel.

Buchan had long accepted that an author's lifestyle and personal reflections were all grist for the publicity mill. He rattled off his comments with easy humor, posed for photos and thanked everyone for their interest. Afterwards another cab returned him to the West End, to White's Club in St. James.

Arriving after noon, Buchan left his coat, hat and briefcase with the porter and went to meet his host Lord Peel in the members' bar. This dignified gentleman came from an illustrious family of public servants and under a previous Tory government, he had served as Foreign Secretary, dealing with countless politicians and governors in the distant provinces of the Empire. Lord Peel's detailed political knowledge had always intrigued Buchan. Over glasses of dry sherry they agreed that trying to govern a nation suffering great economic depression was never an easy matter but the Labour Government under Ramsay MacDonald was making a right mess of it.

Lord Peel suggested they should have lunch as he had something else to discuss and he understood Buchan was on a tight schedule. Once in the dining room Lord Peel came to the point. 'You know my daughter Doris is married to a certain Colonel Blacker?'

'Oh yes, I'm aware of that. And I believe you have two grandsons?'

'Couldn't wish for finer boys.' Lord Peel was proud of his family. 'No, this concerns a most unusual proposal. Over dinner last week, my son-in-law, the Colonel, sought my advice about an expedition he wants to set up. He has just returned from India touring the foothills of Bengal with his old chum Percy Etherton. I imagine you've heard of him too?'

'Yes, indeed,' said Buchan. 'One of our greatest adventurers.'

'Well, guess what? They want to fly over Mount Everest. If successful, they believe the flight would advance British engineering, aviation science and man's understanding of the natural world. So what do you make of that?'

Buchan admitted he knew little about aviation and the practical requirements for such a flight. Lord Peel explained that engine and aircraft companies in the West Country were assessing these technical factors, apparently with some success. Promoting Britain's industries was an enticing target, especially in these dire times and Lord Peel clearly supported the proposal. 'Blacker's quite up to the task. No doubt about that.'

Buchan promised to think it over and to deliver his opinion within the week. He then rose to thank his host and left the club taking a cab to Foyle's Bookshop in Charing Cross Road.

Here the author had agreed to spend an hour signing copies of his work. before his next assignment at Lime Grove Studios to meet with executives of the British-Gaumont Picture Corporation. They had hired Alfred Hitchcock to direct the film of his *Thirty Nine Steps* and a creative confab about the draft screenplay continued till 6 p.m. when Buchan finally left to return to the West End. The conference had not pleased him. The screenwriters were intent on reducing his plot-line to the minimum, removing the essence and subtleties he had taken months to install. Recalling the generous fee he had received for the film rights, Buchan had capitulated with a wry smile.

He paid off the cab in Berkeley Square and continued on foot through Mayfair's splendid arcades to his final appointment. As he walked, his thoughts reverted to lunch with Lord Peel. The scheme to take an aeroplane over Everest presented a thrilling opportunity.

But first things first, he thought. How would such a venture appeal to potential backers? Wall Street's nose-dive in 1929 had destroyed so much wealth that many investors were facing financial hardship of their own. This fact of life worried him.

The author soon reached Savile Row. The street, famous for its tailors, was also the location for the Alpine Club, headquarters of the world's climbing fraternity. It sat above the premises of a tailor who wondered why otherwise sane men, when near any mountain, often became overwhelmed with a mad desire to scramble and haul themselves to its peak? The tailor even mentioned the risks of vertigo, frostbite, crushed bones or death to those who passed his door to go upstairs.

Members of the Alpine Club came from diverse backgrounds. Many were from the Armed Forces, others from sheep farms in Wales, Scotland and the Peak District. Among the assembly that evening, Buchan soon recognized

17

the climbers Ruttledge, Noel, Norton and Smythe who were preparing to challenge Everest in 1933. Arthur Hinks, Secretary to the Royal Geographic Society, was also present. Prone to irascibility, Hinks was nevertheless a ferocious champion of exploration on all continents. How would he react to the concept of Himalayan flight?

Buchan himself loved a vertical challenge. Having climbed in the Alps, he had baulked at the Himalayas, believing their altitude was beyond the limitations for a man of his age. Now that his eligibility for the post of Governor General of Canada was under discussion, Buchan confined his climbing ambitions to the Rockies. Even so, while he listened to the club announcements, his thoughts returned to Lord Peel's scheme. Though aviation was only of passing interest to many climbers, the expanding technology of air travel had thrilled the world. Buchan barely listened as other members outlined their own expeditions.

When the meeting broke up he sidled over to Arthur Hinks to suggest a nightcap at The Red Lion pub around the corner. Soon, they were at the bar with pints of London Pride discussing the evening's events. Did Ruttledge have a realistic chance on Everest? Which route would his climbers take? 'And tell me,' Buchan asked. 'What's the latest thinking on Mallory and Irvine?'

The mystery had baffled the world since 1924 when the two mountaineers had disappeared in a fist of cloud close to the peak. Hinks blew a contemptuous snort towards the ceiling. 'There is no news. Either the poor devils made it to the top – or they didn't? We only know for sure that they have never returned.'

'Might an aerial survey provide any clues regarding their fate?'

'What's that supposed to mean? How do you find clues at that altitude? Besides, aerial photography doesn't extend that high, as far as I'm aware.'

'I realize that,' said Buchan. 'But with close-up photographs of the summit zone, we might find some clues. If either climber had made it there, surely he'd have left a pile of rocks or a spike in the snow?'

'Do you really think airmen might find answers up there?' Hinks asked.

'Yes. And I know of pilots who are willing to go that high. They just might find a sign of conquest in their aerial photographs. It's a long shot but the opportunity exists.'

'Long shots and Everest make bad bedfellows. You remember that crazy

American, Roscoe Turner?' Hinks drank some beer. 'The damned fool wanted to fly into the headwind over Everest. With zero ground speed he would leave his machine to a fellow pilot, and then scamper down a rope ladder onto the peak to claim the mountain. It was the most fanciful nonsense the RGS was ever asked to consider.'

'So tell me, Arthur, would the RGS consider any serious plan to photograph Everest and its approaches from the air?'

Hinks gazed at his receding beer. 'I imagine such an idea might be constructively received. Photography and geography are close cousins, aren't they? We'd need to see the details.'

Buchan was running short of time. 'I'll make some enquiries and tell you what I learn. Anyway, my thanks, Arthur. Must dash. Last train to Oxford in thirty minutes.'

The discussion had been a good bonus at the end of his busy day. Buchan hurried to the cab rank on Regent Street. He had nothing to lose. He decided he would meet Colonel Blacker and Percy Etherton and take it from there.

4. The Savoy Grill, London – May 1932

IN THE SECOND WEEK OF May, as spring arrived to cheer the northern hemisphere, Garland Ross handed the keys of her Manhattan apartment to the landlord and took a train to Quebec. Here she boarded a liner of the Royal Mail Service for a tourist class voyage to Southampton. Though Garland didn't know it when she walked up the gangway, the vessel's name carried an omen for her future. The name on the liner's bows was *Empress of Britain*.

The five-day ocean passage was calm and free of storms and errant icebergs. Garland remained in her pocket-sized cabin to read magazines and books between visits to the dining areas and promenade deck. Most evenings she contemplated the whale-grey emptiness of the Atlantic, asking herself if this career move was such a good idea? She had promised her mother and sister in Ohio that it might amount to a year in Europe, but she would return for sure. She would write each week so they had no need to worry. With only enough savings to sustain her for a few months, she had to shift the gears in her life. To pastures new, she had told friends and family. Her misgivings became more frequent when the liner was over half-way across the ocean. By then, of course, it was far too late. So what the heck?

From Southampton's Ocean Terminal, Garland took a train to London where she rented a room in a small Kensington hotel with switchboard and message service. As soon as she had sorted out her bags, she put in a call to Blumenfeld's secretary at the *Daily Express*. She was in town, and when might she meet the editor?

After Blumenfeld's suggestion at Lake Placid, it was pure optimism that had carried Garland over the pond. At twenty-nine years of age a girl was entitled to search for the odd nugget of luck? This was still her conviction as she adapted to London, finding the city rather ponderous and sullen after the rip and curl of Manhattan.

On the second day, the editor's secretary telephoned to ask if Garland was free for lunch that day? Mr. Blumenfeld would see her at the Savoy Grill at one o'clock. Garland went to work on her make-up, aiming for a no-fuss look. With a print summer dress and cream high heels but hatless, she felt ready to face the world. When she first met Mr. Blumenfeld, she'd been crazy haired and covered in slush. She needed to show some improvement in her attire.

As she stepped out from her taxi at the Savoy, the façade of the hotel with its uniformed doormen gave a shot to her confidence. This was more like Manhattan. The Grill's maitre d' guided her into the busy restaurant to the table where Ralph Blumenfeld was already eyeing a menu. He was in a dark suit with a blue tie and a yellow rose in his lapel. With a courteous bow, he stood to welcome Garland as a waiter readied her chair. 'No prohibition here, Garland, so how shall we toast your safe arrival?'

Instantly at her ease, Garland ordered a Daiquiri. Blumenfeld asked for a White Lady and then they started on small talk. Both agreed that Jack Shea had performed brilliantly, taking two gold medals for America, and wasn't it great that Roosevelt was running for the Presidency? Blumenfeld wondered if she knew about the poor soul whose accident had created their chance meeting?

'Why would I follow her?' asked Garland. 'She knocked me flat.'

Blumenfeld laughed, his agile eyes flashing. 'OK, let's forget her for the time being. What shall we eat?'

Editors of national newspapers ran to tight schedules. Garland looked over the lavish menu and settled for prawn cocktail and grilled sea bass. Blumenfeld toyed with the thought of oysters, then ordered the same as Garland. Over a bottle of chilled Chablis, he told her about his own arrival in England.

'I came off the ship in Liverpool to discover the British were very friendly folk. They understood most of what I said. In mainland Europe, it can be hard to fathom the locals, half recovering from war and half intent on more of it. Doesn't suggest a rosy future, does it?'

Garland said that despite all that, she was hoping to tour Europe. 'Paris, Rome, Venice, they all sound gorgeous but I can't do any of that yet. Earning a living is my priority.'

'So this career of your's, what's the end game?'

Garland told him that she had covered many topics as a Reuters hack. Now fashion and sport appealed, along with travel, business and social topics. Perhaps by reporting on the British lifestyle through American eyes, she might even syndicate stories for the American press.

'Fashion, sport, travel and business? You're not too fussy then.'

Was this a criticism of her career plan or just an observation? Garland smiled and studied her hands. She wore no rings. Her nails were clean and trimmed. Her Mickey Mouse wristwatch was a cult item. She had bought it at Macy's for three bucks, one of eleven thousand sold on the first day of issue. 'No, I'm not fussy. Still chasing good stories. Like when we met.'

'And I'm wondering what's really ticking in Garland's world?'

'Sorry, I don't follow.'

'No husband? No young man? No poor devil back in Manhattan crying his eyes out?'

Surely the editor wasn't making a pass, or was he? 'No, sir. No damage in my wake, I assure you.'

'So you're still looking.'

'You're being very inquisitive, Mr. Blumenfeld.'

Blumenfeld leaned towards her with a chuckle. 'Hell no. I'm just trying to establish if you're here for the social whirl or for the tireless labors of a dedicated journalist? It will help me point you in the right direction.'

Garland lifted her chin. 'Just the latter. But I do like some fun and I need an income. It's a case of Have Pen Will Travel.'

Further discussions about her plans were interrupted by the arrival of the delicious sea bass. Afterwards while enjoying a rich blend of coffee, Blumenfeld mused about his youth in Watertown, Wisconsin, where everyone spoke German. Now he'd love to write a book at his country home in Essex, pen in one hand, a glass of wine in the other. 'But there's never enough time as editor, so that ambition remains on hold.'

Blumenfeld could expand no further. A man in a speckled grey suit with wide-lapels had stopped beside Blumenfeld and leaned down to murmur in the editor's ear. Her host sat up and looked across the restaurant, raising his hand in acknowledgement.

'Excuse me, Garland. A friend wants a word. I won't be long.'

Garland saw Blumenfeld rise and thread his way to a corner table where an elderly woman was locked in conversation with two men. Blumenfeld took the chair vacated by the young man now hovering in front of her.

'Oh, please sit down,' suggested Garland. 'You want a drink?'

'No, thanks.' The man shook her hand and sat down. His grip was strong and the skin was rough. She noted wavy brown hair and a weatherbeaten face, features that looked out of place in this sophisticated London restaurant.

'Donal Ryan,' he said. The inflection and his eyes were warm and kind.

'And now you're having lunch on the *Daily Express*. Hope you enjoyed it.'

'I'm Garland Ross,' she said. 'Fresh off the liner from Quebec. I loved my sea bass. What about you?'

'For me, I had the coquilles St.Jacques. Always my favorite.'

Garland was wondering what this was about? Ryan, she had noted, was shy, almost self-conscious. She looked once more across the busy tables. Blumenfeld was heads down with the elderly lady but Garland couldn't hear what she was saying. 'Maybe you'd like coffee with some Jamesons? Mr. Blumenfeld recommends it.'

'No thanks,' said Ryan. 'My clients are getting ready to leave.'

'Your clients?' Garland had a lead now.

'Bloodstock,' said Ryan. 'They're racing folk and I take care of their horses.'

'I don't know anything about horses. So you all come to the Savoy to talk about racing?'

'Personally I prefer Mulligans in Dublin. You can say what you like in that pub.'

'My family came from Dublin. From Monkstown, I believe.'

'Oh, yes. I know it. Just south of the city.' Ryan nodded.

Now Blumenfeld was on his feet and shaking hands with the three diners who all looked briefly in their direction. Then the editor returned and Ryan stood to surrender his chair.

'Thanks,' said Blumenfeld. 'Any hot tips for Epsom this week?'

Ryan shook his head. 'No ideas, Mr. Blumenfeld. Your tipster at the *Express* is a far better prophet than me.' Ryan smiled. 'Nice meeting you.'

'Likewise,' said Garland. 'Maybe at Mulligans next time?'

Blumenfeld offered no explanation for the brief interlude. Garland knew that editors received solicitations from all quarters. After signing the bill to his newspaper's account, Blumenfeld walked with Garland to the Savoy forecourt. 'I'll be in touch shortly,' he said. Then he climbed into a cab and disappeared into the traffic on the Strand.

She'd heard that line before. In the newspaper industry it passed as code for a brush-off. There had been no job offer. Not even the hint of one. Having crossed the Atlantic apparently in vain, Garland felt all of three thousand miles from home.

She wandered down the Strand to Trafalgar Square where she spent an hour in the National Gallery, enjoying the art but otherwise feeling sorry

23

for herself. She was making no headway in her career. Most female writers were professional socialites who kept the right company and had no concerns about salaries. How could she compete? She took a bus back to her hotel where the switchboard operator had taken a message from Mr. Blumenfeld. Would Miss Ross please return his call?

Garland raced to the phone booth and was soon talking to Blumenfeld who now sounded more brisk and business-like. He had an idea, a way of kick-starting her future in British journalism. Would she care to cover an event at the Home for Tired Nurses? Before she could reply, he explained it was an annual open day when the trustees hoped their benefactors, among them a certain Lady Lucy Houston, would make further donations to the Home. The *Daily Express* would use Garland's piece, especially if she could get an interview with this particular lady. Garland agreed to do her best.

The assignment made no sense until Garland asked the switchboard operator about this Home for Tired Nurses. Apparently it was an institution in Hampstead for the women whose exposure to the horror of field hospitals had been one experience too many. Lady Houston, she learned, was among the most famous women in Britain, but not always for the best reasons.

Unable to gather further details, Garland went up to her room and wrote a letter to her mother, explaining she would do this story and then maybe head for Paris. London might have been a mistake. After reading it over, she tore it up and climbed into bed.

Next day Garland went down early for a boiled egg and toast before showering and putting on a jacket and pleated skirt. Armed with pad and pencil, she took a red bus to Hampstead where she was directed to the Home for Tired Nurses. Once inside the gloomy building with its contrasting scents of disinfectant and fresh flowers, she introduced herself to the staff and tried chatting with the inmates. A sad desolation appeared to haunt the premises. Many of its frail residents had lost both soul and sense in the downpour of high explosive at the front line.

The pace picked up around noon with an influx of prestigious visitors. A staff member nudged Garland and pointed to a short and rather stout woman in a long coat who was toting an oversize handbag. 'You wanted Lady Houston? That's her.'

The woman, Garland decided, had been dining at the Savoy with Donal Ryan. The one who had summoned Blumenfeld from their table. Garland hovered until she found an opportunity to introduce herself.

'Who did you say you are?' The question came in a curious cockney la-di-da with a sharp look from simmering brown eyes.

'Garland Ross. Here for the *Daily Express*.'

Lady Houston's suspicion vanished and out poured a lengthy soliloquy, praising the dedication of women who had come to aid soldiers in their darkest hours. The nurses were a blessing to humanity, an entire flock of nightingales. Lady Houston placed a gloved hand on Garland's shoulder.

'Good heavens, my dear, they're so, so brave these women. No one needs a nurse more than a warrior on his deathbed, when she may be the only soul to help him to the inevitable destiny. And yet, so often, far too often, we overlook the welfare of those who gave their care, day after day, month after month and year after year. It must have been the most unbearable of all hells.'

The homily ended when staff members captured Lady Houston for their own agenda. The heiress dismissed Garland as easily as one might drop a soiled dressing.

However the quotations were good. Garland returned to her hotel where she wrote a piece praising the matchless style and imagination of Lucy Houston, Dame of the British Empire. She typed it on her Remington portable, edited it and re-typed it. Then she left the hotel and took the subway train to Blackfriars. Here she handed her work to the front desk of the *Daily Express*, requesting it should be delivered immediately to Mr. Blumenfeld. She thought no more about it. She'd been doing stories like that for years.

The article appeared in the *Daily Express* next morning, prompting Garland to suspend any plans for Paris. Something, she hoped, might yet come of it and at midday a call from Blumenfeld was relayed to the hotel's telephone booth.

'Bad news first, Garland. Having checked with my team here, the view is that our unions won't appreciate having you on the staff since you'd be taking work from British nationals.'

'That's not what I wanted to hear,' said Garland.

'I can't comment on the unions, but Lady Houston was very impressed with your story. In fact she's made you an offer. The role of her private secretary is available as her previous aide has retired for medical reasons. If you're interested, the job would include a generous salary with all living costs paid and free travel.'

'Heck, I'm not that fond of old women. I have no nursing skills and I don't have the temperament for plumping cushions and serving tea all day.'

'She has other staff for that, and your temperament, Garland, is nothing compared with Lucy Houston's. Beside she's a bigger story than anything you'll find in business, travel and fashion. You would have to sign a gagging clause. I figure you'd enjoy working for Lucy but I'll say no more. If you want it, she's not one who waits for answers.'

'But I can't write about her, is that it?'

'That's the deal.'

Garland Ross took a deep breath. 'OK. Please tell Her Ladyship I'm very happy to accept her kind offer.'

'Good move' said Blumenfeld. 'So you'll need to get to Southampton Ocean Terminal on Monday next. Lady Houston's chauffeur, John, will be waiting at noon outside the terminal.'

'And where will I be going?'

'I've no idea, but you'll learn more about life than you'll ever find in Bloomsbury. Just keep in touch.'

The line went dead. Garland stared at the hotel carpet. Even in Manhattan such major decisions took more time. She walked to a local store and bought two bottles of Muscadet. She would share these with any hotel guests or staff willing to reveal more about Lucy Houston, a tough little woman who took nightingales to her heart, and to whom Garland's future was now committed.

5. Bristol Aeroplane Company – June 1932

COLONEL BLACKER TIPTOED FROM HIS bed leaving his wife Doris asleep under the quilt. He shaved, trimmed his mustache and put on a clean shirt, a regimental tie and a blue serge suit. After making sure his two young sons were also asleep, he closed the door on his Chichester home, got into his Crossley tourer and started the engine.

The dawn was rising behind him as Blacker drove to the west, admiring the fullness of June in southern England. Blooming hedgerows and rolling fields of lush wheat contrasted with the scrawny soil of the Khorasan highlands where he had served. How the people there survived on the lean offerings from their land had surprised him more than their sporadic ambushes. In Hampshire, though, Nature was exploding with the promise of a fine summer and a massive harvest. It was the very best of seasons.

Since returning from India, Blacker had made time for family duties. Military fathers, when on leave, had to compensate for their long absences. Shopping trips, the London Zoo and a day's sailing had been fun for all, but Blacker had lost no time in furthering his objective. With the patronage of his father-in-law Lord Peel had brought John Buchan into the fray and now the four men with Etherton comprised a loose committee. Four sound hearts in joined commitment. Everything was tickety-boo.

Blacker drove on across the plains of Wiltshire and Somerset. He was delayed by steam tractors near Devizes where horse-drawn milk-carts twice blocked his road. Children with leather satchels and grey socks drooping around their ankles further slowed the traffic as they boarded buses. Shopkeepers were cranking down their frontage awnings. Noticing the faded canvas he recalled Buchan's concerns. In a dormant economy, how would their venture secure the necessary backing?

Blacker had considered many options but he knew his colleagues were better suited to luring funds from lean pockets. He would concentrate on practical factors starting at Bristol.

His destination lay within a wide area of fenced grassland owned and operated by the Bristol Aeroplane Company. Alongside their sign at the entrance was another reading *Beware! Random Aircraft Movements*. Blacker followed the perimeter road to a cluster of brick buildings and a car park.

He climbed from the Crossley to stretch his limbs. He had been driving for five hours.

The smell of mown grass below the cascading songs of skylarks high above the runway reminded Blacker of a very similar day back in 1911 when he was just twenty-three. It was at this very spot he had first seen a real flying machine. It consisted of needle-thin struts poking through sheets of frail vellum. How such a device could defy gravity and waltz among the clouds had puzzled him. When the pilot took off to demonstrate its airborne agility, young Blacker was bewitched. He wanted that experience and decided at that moment to become a pilot.

Blacker's family contributed towards the cost of a flying course at Bristol Aviation. Flight in those days was the surest route to premature death for most youngsters, but the Blackers did not consider their lad might suffer such a fate. Fearless, he enrolled for tuition in the new Box Kite.

The course had been rudimentary. For three days an instructor chalked the theories of flight on a blackboard before introducing the class to the Kite itself. Since the machine could only carry one occupant, students had no on-board instruction and had to figure things out on their own. To reduce risk, early flights were confined to elongated hops over the grass, hopefully in a straight line. Students were then permitted to rise higher, to waggle the wings and turn the machine, learning to adjust the throttle so they could make a controlled, but rarely graceful, return to earth. And always into the wind! The instructors drummed that advice home. Downwind landings in a Kite generally led to a coffin party.

Young pilots were taught to evaluate the prevalent strength and angle of the wind. Smoke, flags, windmills, washing lines and plant motion all provided clues to the direction of invisible air mass. When basic navigation, meteorology and survival had been learned, students were released to make a full circuit, a large rectangular route around the field at 500 feet above the ground.

The instructor chose a hot sunny day for Blacker's first solo. After clamping on his leather coat, helmet and goggles, Blacker had settled in the tiny cradle seat, ignoring any apprehension. An engineer spun the wooden propeller behind his back and the Rhone rotary engine fired. Blacker's feet reached out ahead as the Kite's pram wheels began to roll, turning ever faster between their skids until he was up and climbing.

Over the airfield boundary he went, across the road and then over a farmyard where carthorses bounced in alarm. After two minutes, Blacker completed his turn onto the crosswind leg, now passing over fields where laborers were stacking hay. The men in shirts and waistcoats paused to wave their caps as he flew over them. Blacker did not return the gesture while gripping the control stick. Turning downwind, he now flew parallel to the airfield. A spinney of poplar trees was approaching so he applied more throttle to climb above their branches.

On a broad haystack below his flightpath, he could see a naked couple. Abandoned clothing lay on the bulky mattress. Blacker caught sight of buttocks in the sunlight and felt obliged to wave an apology to the startled couple. He turned the swaying Kite towards the home field, reducing the revs until he succeeded in making a passable landing. He had achieved the first objective.

This morning he chuckled at those memories as he limped towards the main building. In a rudimentary Reception area he was met by the company secretary. Blacker had not seen Jenny for some years, but she was much the same, a bit grayer and broader, but still the warm soul at the heart of the company.

'Colonel Blacker! What a treat to see you.' With a soft west country burr she came from her desk. 'Sir Stanley is expecting you, Colonel, but he's still in a meeting.'

Blacker couldn't help noticing Jenny's smile above a very ample bosom. He looked away, not wishing to stare. 'I'm happy to wait.'

'In that case, tea, coffee or something stronger?'

'Tea please,' said Blacker. She was looking at his right eye. His monocle had that effect on some people.

From the electric urn on the filing cabinets Jenny filled a teapot. 'It's ever such a long time since you won your wings here, Colonel.'

Blacker smiled. 'One of my best times in the good old Box kite.'

'And you're one of the few that survived the war.'

As Jenny made the tea, Blacker glanced at photographs on the walls featuring the factory's history. 'Oh, those were the times,' she said. 'Weren't they just? We had Box kites cartwheeling down the grass, kites sticking out of trees and hedges. One even landed on a church burial.'

'And on my first flight I came across a courting couple on a haystack, in flagrante as it were. I almost lost control.'

Jenny sat down leaning on her elbows with a cup between her hands. 'And I hear you're a married man these days?'

'Oh yes. Tied the knot five years ago. Doris and I have two boys.'

'How lovely, but it must be difficult for your wife, having you overseas so often.'

'I've nearly done with foreign duties. After this next operation, I'll be at home on a more permanent basis. I want to see my sons grow up.'

Jenny lowered her voice. 'Since it was me who typed the correspondence, I do admit to having inside knowledge.'

'Quite so, Jenny, but this flight is no military secret. We're merely keeping it quiet till it's all set up.'

'Very sensible, Colonel, but everyone here is so excited. Our company on top of the world! Sir Stanley will be introducing you to the entire Pegasus design team.'

'I look forward to meeting them.'

'And are you hoping to fly over Everest yourself?'

'Most definitely – as observer and photographer.'

'It must be very hazardous. Rather a worry for your wife?'

Blacker had stock answers for such questions. Lord Peel, Doris, John Buchan and Percy had all been quick to mention safety concerns. 'The RAF, as you know, have been successfully operating a squadron of Wapitis in the eastern Himalaya for years. Many are fitted with your Bristol Jupiter engines, but the Jupiter can't handle Everest. For that we need a Pegasus.'

'It must be dangerous whatever engine you use.'

Blacker's mustache twitched. 'Risk is something we can't avoid. It never stopped our lads going over the top in the Great War, did it?'

'Indeed, Colonel, 'Jenny stared at her cup. 'That's how I lost my husband in France.'

'I'm so very sorry.' Blacker's tone softened. 'I never knew that.'

'Still, I have a good job and a nice home. Plenty to be thankful for.'

The Bakelite phone on the desk rang. Jenny swiftly hoisted the receiver, listened and replaced it with a firm clunk. 'Sir Stanley will join you in the Engineering department, Colonel.'

Jenny stood up, escorting Blacker to the door. 'It's the first block on the left. You'll find Sir Stanley with Mr. Fedden, the Chief Designer, and the team of engineers led by Cyril Pitt.'

'Pitt? We'll need your best expertise out there. Would this man Pitt appreciate a trip to India?'

'You'll have to ask him. He's one of our best engineers – even though his humor might need fine tuning.'

'We'll need humor too. Happy units rely on it.'

Jenny stood in the doorway and began giggling. She poked his arm and her voice fell to a whisper. 'That day when a certain young pilot was making his first flight?'

'Yes?'

'That was our haystack.'

'Our?' The monocle fell from Blacker's eye. He felt a sensation he hadn't often known.. He was blushing down to his collar.

'Me and my dear husband.' Jenny giggled, as she gave him a gentle shove. 'Down here in the West Country, we've had a good laugh about that.'

'Yes, I can imagine.'

'No need to be embarrassed, Colonel. Just watch where you go in your aeroplanes and take good care of our Pegasus.'

Blacker hardly knew what to think as he left to meet the engineers.

6. Southampton Water – June 1932

ON THE TRAIN TO SOUTHAMPTON Garland almost changed her mind. Only a week before, she had alighted at the same port from her Atlantic passage. She had barely tested the market for her skills, and yet here she was, off on an adventure based on the briefest of interviews with a woman she hardly knew. Had her instinct for a good story overplayed its hand?

As she stepped off the train, she told herself that she had coped with tougher assignments in Harlem and New Jersey. She felt good in a cornflower blue dress with white piping. Her hair was tied in a braid. Clutching her shoulder bag, she hired a porter and trolley who took her suitcases through the art deco terminal. At the main entrance a white Rolls Royce was waiting. The chauffeur was in a tailored charcoal uniform but wore no cap. Garland noticed his frizz of grey hair and bluish grey eyes. 'Miss Ross?'

'That's me.'

'I'm John, Lady Houston's chauffeur. I'll deal with the porter, Miss.' He opened the rear door to the Rolls. Garland stepped into a capacious interior of polished hide. As they drove away from the terminal she noticed the porter studying her with blatant curiosity, one foot on his barrow as he rolled a cigarette.

Soon away from the busy dockland, the Rolls cruised through green pastures flanking Southampton Water. In the hushed interior, Garland saw the chauffeur checking her in his rear-view mirror.

The Rolls finally rumbled softly over a cobbled slipway onto a jetty in the Hamble River where John turned off the engine. Garland looked out towards a magnificent schooner anchored offshore. Now this represented serious money! A trail of smoke drifted from its single yellow funnel. A light onboard began signaling in bright flashes of Morse code. John toggled his headlight switch to return the message. Another burst of morse came from the yacht. Only then did John get out to open Garland's door.

'I'm sorry, Miss Ross...' he began.

Garland stepped out. 'There's a delay with the boat?'

The chauffeur looked surprised. 'So you read Morse?'

'Yessir. My pa taught me when I was ten years old.'

'I learned morse in the Royal Navy, Miss. Before Fritz shot me in the

Battle of Jutland. Got hit in my shoulder. I felt like Nelson at Trafalgar until the surgeon saved me.'

Garland took a closer look at the chauffeur. He was about forty, fit and battle hardened, she supposed. The type of man an heiress might prefer to have at hand. John was willing to chat. The delay might be useful.

'Well, this is my first day. How long have you been with Lady Houston?'

'It's been five years now, Miss. Where she goes, I go. The Rolls or the Packard must always be nearby. As must all her assets and staff. Instant access at all times or you need a foolproof excuse.'

'Millionaires are the same in New York, believe me.'

'Oh, so you've met a few, Miss?'

'Sure. We breed them in America.'

The morning breeze was tickling the waters of the Hamble River but there was no movement on the yacht. Garland sauntered to the front of the Rolls as the chauffeur unloaded her bags.

'If you forgive me for enquiring, Miss, how did you come by this job? You're a long way from America.'

'I met Lady Houston last week in London. At the Home for Tired Nurses I wrote a piece for the *Daily Express* and then I was offered this position. I admit to knowing little about secretarial work, but I'm red hot in shorthand and typing.' Garland saw a blue anchor tattoo on John's wrist as he handled her bags. 'She seemed such a sweet lady... So that's why I'm here today.'

'Sweet? Not unless she wants to be. But if you can write and type, run errands, organize sudden and random requirements, entertain her guests, pour drinks, listen to her stories and keep your smile throughout, that's all she'll want. And looking after her dog, Mungo.'

'A dog?' Garland pulled a face. 'Nobody mentioned a dog.'

'The mutt rules her life, Miss. She's got no children, you see. So if you worship Mungo, you'll have the time of your life.'

Garland had never owned a dog. The way they messed city streets was repulsive. She saw a launch leaving the yacht and heading towards the jetty.

'So Mungo rules. I get it. Thanks for the advice.'

'Any time, Miss Ross.'

They walked down to meet the launch. Garland hopped over the gunwale to a seat beside the helmsman while John passed her bags to a deckhand.

With reverse thrust, the launch cast off, turning back to the yacht. Garland waved to the chauffeur who raised a thumb.

On the water, the wind was pushing up a good chop against a retreating tide. The launch began bucking as bursts of spray flew past the cockpit. Looking north towards Southampton, Garland could see the funnels of ocean liners rising in bright colors between gantry cranes.

Garland watched more keenly as her new home grew closer. She had read that Lady Houston's schooner *Liberty* was one of the largest private vessels on Lloyds Register, over 300 feet on the waterline. As the graceful hull of the vessel turned on the tide, an enormous sign of glowing neon tubes became visible. It was strung aloft between the masts.

'What's with the sign?' Garland asked.

The helmsman shrugged. 'Means what it says, Miss. *Down with Macdonald The Traitor.*'

According to her sources at her Kensington hotel, Lucy Houston had offered financial help to the British government only to be rejected.

'She hates the Prime Minister,' added the helmsman steering to the lee of the yacht. 'If Lady Houston had her way, she'd fill MacDonald's pockets with rocks and drop him in deep water. And this summer she plans to sail the coastline with that sign blazing all the way.'

Garland tried to imagine how much press coverage this bizarre exercise might generate, but the launch was nosing towards the Jacob's ladder. She climbed the steps to the main deck where a staff member in a white uniform stood waiting.

'I'm Torrance, Chief Steward. Welcome aboard *Liberty*, Miss Ross.'

'Thank you.' Garland said. 'Should I remove my shoes here?'

'No, Miss Ross, that won't be necessary. Heels can be worn if you stick to the coconut matting.'

Garland could hear the crackling in the fluorescent sign as Torrance escorted her through mahogany doors with brass handles into the main accommodation area. A thick blue Wilton carpet lay between a gallery of photographs on both sides of the corridor. Each picture revealed a moment in Lady Houston's life. A dimmed sepia print showed a line of chorus girls in frilled knickers throwing their legs high in a cancan. Garland stopped for a closer look.

Torrance pointed to a dancer in a tight bodice. 'Her Ladyship likes this one. Shows how she started in the dance halls of London and Paris.'

Her homework had been useful. Garland had discovered that her new employer, a carpenter's daughter from Camberwell, had started life in vaudeville when she was just sixteen. Over subsequent years, Lucy's charm had attracted three husbands, the last of these being the famous Sir Robert Houston, a shipping magnate whose massive fortune came from supplying the British Army in the Boer War. London gossip said Sir Robert had collapsed when his new wife had shredded his will which would have given her a mere twenty percent of his fortune. The will had been redrafted and months later the tycoon went the way of all mortals, leaving Lucy with every penny.

A second photograph caught Garland's attention. It showed pilots lifting the Schneider Trophy after winning the famous Air Race in 1931. Lucy Houston had confused her critics, and particularly those in the upper classes, by sponsoring the race, demonstrating how wealth could be put to imaginative use.

'That's how she got into this row with the Prime Minister,' observed the steward. 'The government refused to pay for the Supermarine engines, so her Ladyship stumped up the cash. She won the trophy and also the right to say whatever she likes about the government.'

'So there's freedom of speech on the *Liberty*?'

'In a manner of speaking. However, on board any ship, Miss Ross, we must do what we're told, whatever we may think.'

Garland understood and moved on, guided by Torrance to a door leading off the corridor. Her bags were already waiting.

'And these are your quarters. I hope this suits you, Miss Ross. Laundry and bed linen are supplied every three days. All food and drink come from the Chef's staff in the galley. For anything else, feel free to ask me. Meanwhile, I know Her Ladyship will see you, when she's ready.'

Torrance left Garland to settle. She noticed the bed had enormous puffed pillows, a folded red spare blanket and sideboards for rough weather. The soft carpet extended to a tiny bathroom covered by a mosaic of black and white tiles. Soaps, lotions and flannels filled a chrome rack above the basin. Fluffy towels with a bathrobe hung on the towel rail.

Peering through a brass porthole Garland could see sailing dinghies and cattle grazing on the shoreline. She had barely arrived and already she had so much to tell them back home.

She kicked off her shoes. The gentle bass vibration from the engine room was comforting. She felt a long way from London and New York. Had Mr. Blumenfeld landed her straight in the middle of a fantastic story?

'Oh yeah, Mr. Torrance.' Garland whispered as she flung herself down on the bed. 'This will definitely suit Miss Ross.'

7. The Royal Geographic Society – June 1932

BLACKER AND ETHERTON HAD ARRIVED at the Royal Geographic Society in Kensington Gore to find John Buchan and Lord Peel waiting in the hallway. There were handshakes all round, then the doorman ushered them upstairs to the office of the Secretary. Here Arthur Hinks greeted them and they took places at the boardroom table. Across its broad and polished surface many expeditions to hidden corners of the planet had been debated and sanctioned.

Arthur Hinks put on his reading glasses, cleared his throat and began thumbing through the type-written proposal compiled by Etherton and delivered by messenger a week previously. The four supplicants waited in silence.

After a final ruffle through the pages, Hinks leaned back in his chair to study his prestigious guests. 'I do find it intriguing. But are you sure it can be done?'

'Entirely feasible, Mr. Hinks,' said Colonel Blacker. 'I visited Bristol Aviation last week to ask that very question. Their designers are confident that controlled supercharging will compensate for reduced atmospheric pressure, meaning that their new Pegasus engine has sufficient power to clear the highest peaks. In fact, they estimate a performance capability up to 35,000 feet.'

'But field tests have not yet proved it?'

'The Pegasus has evolved from the Jupiter engine which has performed impressively for ten years. As I say, the Pegasus team envisage no problems with their ongoing test program. I saw the engine running on the test rig. A mighty machine.'

Hinks tipped his head. 'I know precious little about mechanical things, so I'll take your word on it.'

'It's my word and my skin, Mr. Hinks. I shall be riding the Pegasus as the observer.'

Hinks then turned to Lord Peel. 'I understand, My Lord, that you intend to base the aeroplanes in northern India, to the south of the Himalaya?'

'In the state of Bihar,' said Lord Peel. 'At Purnea to be precise, where both the Maharaja of Dharbanga and the Raja Banaili have volunteered to help.'

'I haven't a clue who they are, but their titles are imposing. I note you have yet to obtain permission to over-fly Nepal?'

'Arthur, I'm dealing with our Delegation in Kathmandu on this point,' said Percy Etherton who had become a Fellow of the Society after his epic hike across Asia. 'Currently we believe the Nepalese authorities will allow us access to their skies.'

'You may be cosy with the Nepalis, Percy, but I'm surprised if their authorities are overwhelmed with enthusiasm for your project.'

'They're coming round to it. Just a question of time.'

'You're all aware the Royal Geographic is dispatching an expedition to Everest next year. Our climbers will be based in Tibet – to the north, because the Nepalis do not permit us to approach Everest from the south. So if men on foot cannot enter via Nepal, why would they permit aviators to fly over the Kingdom?'

John Buchan fielded this question. 'Because the aeroplanes will be flying so high that no one on the ground will notice their passage through the heavens.'

'But if somebody should happen to see them?' Hinks asked. 'What happens then?'

'They'll have a moment to remember,' said Buchan.

Hinks ignored the author's attempt to lighten the tone. 'Sneaking in over the border is not the Royal Geographic's way. You must secure permission and since hardly a soul in Nepal has ever seen an aircraft, it may take a year or two to get it.'

'They regard aeroplanes as mechanized chickens,' said Blacker. 'And we all know chickens are harmless creatures.'

'Mechanical chickens!' Hinks gazed at him. 'I suppose you're planning to send an entire flock over Everest?'

'No, no. Just two Westlands. They'll use cameras to record the approach routes through the foothills to the Himalayas, something that's never been done from the air. And there'll be close-ups of all the peaks as well. Imagine what your Society members will then have to study.'

'Surely a survey of so much uncharted territory must be of value for the Royal Geographic?' added Lord Peel.

Hinks shifted in his chair, thumbing the document. 'Yes, a survey might be useful. I'm a cartographer myself, so I welcome the benefits of aerial photography, but I see you plan to produce a film as well. Now what's that all about?'

John Buchan came in swiftly, 'Gaumont-British are currently producing the film of my Thirty-Nine Steps. If the flight goes ahead, they'll buy its film rights and will assign their director Geoffrey Barkas to the project.'

'Never heard of him. And why should the Royal Geographic assist with the production of a commercial film? Our purpose is strictly scientific. We're not here to glamorize epic adventures.'

Before any of the visitors could comment, Hinks raised yet another concern. 'Your proposal implies that you'll need corporate support to achieve much of the flight. If you are to link the Royal Geographic to British companies to sell their merchandise, we may have another problem. I'm afraid to say that paying for your expedition remains completely out of the question.'

Lord Peel's fingers drummed with impatience on the table's edge. All were aware that few had mourned Hink's departure from his lectureship at Cambridge, where his temper had caused one ruckus too many. Yet, with RGS patronage, they'd have a greater chance of raising the funds.

Buchan looked at Hinks. 'Let's agree that aerial surveys will provide vital reference in the Himalayan region. Climbers need all their strength as they go higher where mis-planned routing can be so very costly.'

'Yes, yes,' Hinks said. 'So what's your point?'

'We're not here for your money. We understand the Society's funds are limited and earmarked for terrestrial expeditions. With your support, together with funding from Gaumont-British and other sponsors from industry, we can mount our expedition on its own merits.'

'And the best of luck to you, especially in today's economic mayhem. I imagine that with all your connections you'll have the means of bettering your chances.'

'What we seek from your Society, Arthur, is a token of support,' said Buchan. 'An official approval for the scientific nature of the exercise.'

'Only that?' Hinks looked more interested.

Buchan leaned forwards. 'It's no secret the ultimate prize, the first conquest of Everest, will be contested by the French, Italians and Swiss. Surely our photographs should be in your archive, so that the first conquest, by air or by foot, can belong to you at the Royal Geographic?'

Hinks pulled off his spectacles with a smile of surrender. 'Very well, gentlemen. In principle, I do agree. I'll talk to our Committee next week and, I may add, they very rarely veto my recommendations.'

8. On board Liberty – June 1932

GARLAND SENSED THE DIFFERENCE WHEN she woke that morning. A heavier beat rumbled through the yacht's hull. Flickering reflections and swaying motions proved that *Liberty* was on the move. She got out of bed and walked barefoot to the bathroom. Closing the etched glass door, she peeled her nightdress over her head, looped it on the towel rail and stepped under the shower to turn on the taps.

As the warm water cascaded onto her body Garland appreciated all this luxury that Blumenfeld had sent her way. Even though she was disappointed that no job in London seemed imminent, this adventure on the *Liberty* might prove to be even more fun. She hoped as much, as the soap suds fell down her stomach and thighs to the tray where the water rolled this way and that across her toes to the yacht's motion.

After toweling dry, Garland lifted the porthole curtain to see a welcoming but breezy summer day. She had no idea where the yacht was headed so she put on her underwear and a casual trouser suit. She brushed her hair, found her deck-shoes and strapped on her wristwatch. Then leaving the cabin she headed down the carpeted corridor to the galley where Torrance was supervising breakfast.

'Good morning, Miss Ross. I hope you slept well?'

'Just great. Such a comfy bed.'

'So will Brazilian coffee from my new dripolator suit you, Miss? Or do you prefer tea? The chef will provide breakfast.'

'The coffee smells great but I usually don't eat breakfast.'

'Come with me, Miss. I'll bring the coffee to your office, just next door. In fact, Mr. Graham is waiting for you there.'

'Mr. Graham?'

'Her Ladyship's lawyer. He has your contract, Miss.'

Garland followed Torrance to a cabin near the galley. It had been converted to accommodate the administration of Lady Houston's life. Behind a mahogany desk and two leather-backed chairs were rows of Eastlight files consuming a wall of shelves. Through the porthole, Garland could see the distant coastline. Mr. Graham sat in one of the chairs, reading a paper and holding a cup of tea.

'Ah, good morning, Miss Ross.' The lawyer stood up. 'I hope you had a good rest? I'm Willy Graham, Lady Houston's legal advisor.'

'It's all very comfy,' said Garland. 'And I see they've changed the view. Do you know where are we going?'

'Heading west along the Hampshire coast towards Bournemouth so Torrance says. A lovely day to be at sea.'

'So it seems. And this is my office?' Garland took her coffee and sat down. Torrance left, closing the door behind him.

'You'll soon get the hang of it,' said Mr. Graham. 'Mostly it holds the mail, philanthropical records and news clippings that fascinate Her Ladyship. The important stuff is in her head, if not in mine.'

Garland could tell by his accent that Mr. Graham was Scottish. She wondered when he had joined the ship. 'I believe you have my contract?'

'Just a formality we need to cover – particularly since you'll now be working for an individual who exercises a considerable influence in the British way of life.'

'So I understand,' said Garland as the lawyer pushed the contract across the desk. 'For starters, she's obviously no friend to the Prime Minister.'

Mr. Graham frowned. 'That sign, frankly speaking, is not something I would recommend. But she regards the PM as traitorous and wants to share her view with the public. The press is making a field day out of it.'

Garland scanned the contract. The term was for a year with sub-clauses governing dismissal and renewal. A generous annual salary at £1500 was stipulated with free lodging and living costs. Any medical fees would be paid by her employer along with three weeks of paid holiday. Not too bad, Garland thought, as she turned to the second page and read for a few moments. 'But, this is what we Americans call a gagging clause.'

'I believe so.' The lawyer nodded. 'When working for Lady Houston, we all have to sign non-disclosure agreements, as we call them here.'

'Mr. Blumenfeld mentioned it, but I'm primarily a journalist, you understand.'

'I do. But Lucy Houston invites many leaders of society into her life. You'll be party to intimate details and conversations, hence this clause is necessary and mandatory.'

'So, no scoops for me then?'

'Not if you want to work here.' Mr Graham said. 'I had a feeling you might not appreciate that clause.'

'I prefer freedom of speech, liberty as you call it. But in this case I'll make an exception.' Garland took a pen from the desk and signed the document and its copy. 'There, Mr. Graham. Silence assured.'

The lawyer counter-signed each page and then stood up, putting one copy in his brief case. 'That's your copy, Miss Ross.'

'You can call me Garland.'

The lawyer hesitated as he reached the door. 'Thank you, Garland.'

Garland sat at her new desk, staring at the parade of files. She'd find administration easy enough, particularly the gleaning of magazines and newspapers. A list of favorite topics had been provided by the previous assistant along with sharp scissors. The daily pruning would help her to understand the British way of life.

With nothing to do, Garland returned to the galley where Torrance was having coffee. He topped up Garland's cup and pointed to the seat opposite. Garland sat down.

'Mr. Graham will be leaving us in Torquay. He comes and goes according to the situation.'

'Which appears to be distinctly provocative at present.'

Torrance chuckled. 'That's Fanny's style.'

'Fanny?'

'Her Ladyship. She was born as Fanny Radmall in South London, not far from my patch. Then she changed her name to Lucy which she felt was more refined. Her surname became Brinkman, then Byron and finally Houston. Four identities in one lifetime.'

'And four lifetimes, it seems.'

'I suppose so, Miss.'

Garland felt close to Torrance and he probably knew more about the heiress than anyone else on board. She decided to change the conversation. 'Tell me about this lovely yacht, *Liberty*.'

'She was built in 1907 for one of your compatriots, Joseph Pulitzer – also a newspaper man as I recall. Then Lord Tredagar purchased her and lent her to the Royal Navy as a wartime hospital ship. After he got her back, he sailed her twice around the world, visiting every country of the British Empire. Then Sir Robert Houston bought her and now *Liberty* cruises mainly in British and Mediterranean waters.'

'Such a history.' Garland was already feeling constricted by that gagging clause. 'And somebody told me he died on board?'

'That's right. And so did Joseph Pulitzer. I don't know how many souls died aboard during the war, but if you believe in ghosts, Miss, you'll find plenty here.'

'Luckily I don't,' said Garland, finishing her coffee. 'But maybe I'll take a stroll around the deck. I might spot a few.'

Torrance laughed. 'Watch out for the lads, Miss. There are fifty-five men on board and you're the only young woman among them.'

'I feel safe enough.' Garland smiled at Torrance as she went to the main door and out into the breeze that sped across the deck.

Liberty was cruising through the Solent with the green fields of Hampshire on the starboard side. Garland lifted her face to the sun, feeling its heat. Nobody was visible except for a bow lookout. The crew were presumably still at breakfast. She strolled past the life boats and various stanchions and marine equipment.

Garland was turning back when a growing roar stopped her in her tracks. Looking up, past the *Liberty*'s yellow funnel and the huge sign above, she saw a silvered flash of wings as a biplane thundered past. It climbed with a tremulous blast from its exhaust and the pilot waved as he banked across *Liberty*'s bows.

Now she heard voices on the bridge-above. She could see Lady Houston standing with the Captain at the wheelhouse door. Lady Houston leaned over the railing.

'It may be a lovely day, Garland, to hang about waving at seagulls and noisy pilots but you and I have work to do. I'll see you in thirty minutes. In the stateroom.'

Garland nodded. 'I'll be there.'

Exactly half an hour later, Garland stood somewhat nervously at the door to the stateroom. She gave it a hard knock and, clutching her notepad, went inside.

Lady Houston had returned to her bed and was now wearing a turban of bright blue silk with a woolen shawl. Her dog, Mungo, looked up and stared at Garland.

'Come on in, my dear. He's harmless. Now pull up that chair and we'll get to know each other.'

Garland looked around the stateroom, imagining events that must have occurred there. It was a handsome space with whirled walnut panelling and Persian rugs.

'Wasn't that a marvelous sight?' Lady Houston's voice had a mellow note. The accent today was London cockney blended with French gaiety and topped off with grandee English. 'I said. Wasn't that a marvelous sight?'

'Yeah, it's a gorgeous morning.'

'I mean the aeroplane, Garland. And a little less of *yeah*, if you don't mind.'

'Oh yes. He came in so close.'

'For a good look at my sign,' said Lady Houston. 'Those pilots recognize what *Liberty* stands for, which is more than MacDonald does.'

Garland was listening, notepad and pencil poised. The coast of England continued passing beyond the state room windows as *Liberty* prowled on to the constant murmur from her engine.

'With money one can achieve almost anything, and that explains just why I'm so, so infuriated with that ridiculous, ghastly man! Prime minister, my ass! For Chrissake, when I offer him the money for a fighter squadron to protect our capital from that little shit Hitler, guess what? MacDonald shoves my money right back in my face!'

'But why?' asked Garland. 'It was such a generous offer.'

Lady Houston's cheeks, though sallow, hinted at her previous beguiling beauty. Though she wore little or no makeup. Garland sensed her mind, behind the watchful eyes, was sharp as neat gin.

'I'll tell you why. If he had accepted my offer, MacDonald fears his Government would be obliged to heed all my opinions on their management. And believe me, Garland, Number 10 wouldn't wish to know what I think! I hate, loathe and abominate MacDonald's policies towards our fading global influence. Most of all, his willingness to offer London up as a naked virgin to the risk of imminent Nazi rape.'

'This risk?' Garland said. 'Can you elaborate?'

'Well, it's obvious, isn't it? Germany's spending money like dog piss. Soon enough the Hun will have his modern army, a superior navy and an overwhelming air force. And we Britons will still be struggling to find our knickers in the morning.' Lady Houston banged a jeweled fist on the bedside table.

Since letter dictation was no pressing issue, Garland kept her notebook shut. 'Surely we must beat him at his own game? Your sign on the deck is one way but perhaps you could shame him, upstage him somehow?'

Lady Houston fixed Garland with a fierce glare. 'I can't think of anything more dramatic than a squadron of fighters fitted with Supermarine engines! For god's sake, girl, what's this rubbish you're talking?'

'I can't imagine.' Garland stared at the woman who had once ripped up a million pound legacy because it wasn't enough. Perhaps Lucy Houston, a commoner at heart, was striving for recognition by the British Establishment? Due to her huge inheritance, she had conspicuously bypassed the middle classes and most aristocrats, thereby achieving notoriety instead of recognition. 'I was trying to think of a constructive solution because nobody appreciates rejection.'

'And what do you know about rejection?' Lady Houston asked. 'Have you ever been shown the door? By some baboon in trousers?'

'Sure. It goes with being a journalist.'

Lady Houston leaned forward, her eyes glowing with new luster. 'I was referring to your love life? You've not told me about it.'

Garland fidgeted. 'What do you mean?'

'For God's sake, girl! A man! Some love! A sexual ballyhoo!'

Garland took a moment to respond. 'There is no man. In that respect, I have no love life.'

Lady Houston wagged her head. 'I thought as much. Mind you, a girl like you, with such a pretty face and figure, will easily attract some lucky fellow. Believe me, Garland. Look at me! I've managed to haul a few men into my bed over the years. More than a few, I can tell you.'

Turning her head towards a vase of scented lilies, Garland hoped to hide her embarrassment. 'You must tell me the secret sometime.'

Lady Houston began toying with a massive ring on her third finger as a tremor resounded through the hull. The *Liberty*'s bows had just smashed into the swell from a passing vessel.

'Well, my dear, I once had great physical charms. I was pretty, rather than beautiful, but I could be naughty in the finest clothes when necessary. Now my attractions are mainly financial.'

Garland opened her notepad on a fresh page to make a hint. 'Have you any letters to send?'

Lady Houston rifled through a pile of correspondence on a tray lying on the bed. 'I have letters from everybody, most of them asking for money. Here's one from Oswald Mosley seeking funds for his Fascists. That's outrageous! And here's another from a fisheries manager who knows that I adore herrings. And this one is from some colonel who wants me to send his aeroplane over the Himalayas. Whatever next? Tell them all NO, and I don't care what you write, Garland, so long as it's not offensive. When you've typed them up, using the red paper I like, bring them back for my signature. Then you can take Mungo out for a stroll on the deck. He must get to know you.'

Garland scooped up the letters while Lady Houston rummaged in the drawer of her bedside table until she found a book. 'You call yourself a writer, Garland?'

'I'd like to think so.'

'Well, here's something you must read. It may give you inspiration.'

Garland took the offered book in its brown paper cover. 'What is it?'

'Forbidden literature. Provided by a friend of mine.'

'You mean prohibited? Like alcohol in the USA?' said Garland.

'That's exactly what I mean. Nobody in Britain is allowed to buy this book. So much for liberty! Just don't leave it lying around.'

Garland peeked at the front page. 'D.H. Lawrence?'

'A wonderful author, you'll see.' Lady Houston began laughing mischievously. 'And be sure to tell me how you like the heroine. She's a woman who does not suffer rejection lightly.'

'Of course, m'lady,' said Garland as she went to type the letters.

9. The Palace of Westminster – July 1932

AFTER ENJOYING RELATIVE SUCCESS AT the Royal Geographic Society, John Buchan was feeling very much in tune with his invented character, the wily Richard Hannay, who had driven the action in The Thirty-Nine Steps. The excitement of the hunt pulsed through his creative veins, making him realize, not for the first time, that adrenalin was the stuff of life.

Outwardly though, Buchan showed no sign of this. In his customary understated manner, he entered the Palace of Westminster, signed in with the clerks and made his way to the Members' smoking room. He had unearthed useful information at the entrance. The clerk confirmed that the Member for Renfrewshire had signed in and was still within the Palace.

As a Member for the Scottish Universities, Buchan regularly visited Westminster where he preferred to do business in the smoking room. Here Members were spared the turmoil of parliamentary business. In the relative peace of the smoking room, the main agenda might be shaped by non-confrontational and less theatrical posturing. Here members could make judicious use of compromise to fuse the future of nation and empire. Buchan hoped that some of Britain's dynamic energy might help his cause that afternoon.

He sat down beside a carved stone window overlooking the River Thames and opened the evening newspaper. Morale in the Civil Service had hit new lows, Hitler's Nazi movement was gaining power, and the price of mailing a letter in the United States had risen from two to three cents. There was not much to divert readers from their miseries.

Buchan continued reading until he saw the young Member for East Renfrewshire arrive in the smoking room. Outside the House, he was known as the Marquess of Douglas and Clydesdale, or as Clydesdale to his friends. As firstborn son to the Duke of Hamilton, a senior family in Scotland's ducal hierarchy, he would inherit the Duchy with all its perks and responsibilities. Until then, he would serve at Westminster while enjoying a bachelor's life in the great cities of Europe.

Buchan closed his paper and stood up. 'Clydesdale. Good to see you.'

The Marquess wore a grey chalk-striped suit with the tie of the Royal Air Force Reserve. Quick eyes in a firm face flashed a welcome. 'Hello John.'

Clydesdale's strong handshake reminded Buchan that he had won a boxing blue at Oxford University. Below the relaxed, courteous surface of the man was a highly driven and combative spirit.

Buchan returned to his seat in the bay window. 'I'm glad you're here. I'm onto something that might interest you. I'd be grateful for your opinion.'

Clydesdale took a seat, looking curious. 'You must be planning some wonderful new fiction? Or it something with a political hue?'

'Neither.' Buchan sat forward. Through the windows the Thames reflected the afternoon sun. 'Do you remember when Alan Cobham landed his seaplane out there? Between Westminster and Lambeth bridges?'

Clydesdale did remember. 'I was at Eton. We boys were thrilled by his audacity. Why do you ask?'

Buchan the storyteller sensed he had set his bait. Clydesdale was a good friend to Winston Churchill and many influential Whitehall characters. His support would add value to the proposal.

'Can you recall why Cobham was in such a daring state of mind that day?'

'Not a clue. But if Cobham could land there, so could enemy pilots. Was he trying to prove a military weakness in our defense strategy?'

'An interesting thought,' said Buchan. 'But no. And he wasn't short of fuel either. He was returning from a long airborne journey that had taken him almost to the very top of the world. Landing on the Thames was his signing-off statement. After confronting the Himalayas, he claimed it was easy to dodge tugs and barges.'

'That's debatable.' Clydesdale watched a steam tug guiding two heavily loaded lighters below Westminster Bridge. 'So where's all this leading?'

'Back to the top of the world.' Buchan smiled. 'Everest. I'm helping to assemble an expedition to be the first in history to fly over the summit.'

Clydesdale's fingers were laced together. 'Please go on.'

'You're a Squadron Leader of the RAF Reserve. You're also a highly experienced pilot who understands mountain flying, in those deadly unseen airs that battle with the highest bluffs. We're looking for a Chief Pilot. We thought this unique role in our planet's history might appeal to you?'

Clydesdale was a serious man with meaningful objectives, and never an emotional type. 'Putting that offer aside for a moment, John, who are *we*? And what type of aircraft do you intend to use?'

'You've heard no doubt of Colonel Blacker?'

Clydesdale nodded. 'So have most pilots. His machines took more bullets during the war than any other in the service. Amazing that he survived at all.'

'Blacker and the engineers at Bristol Aviation believe a Westland Wallace with the new Pegasus engine can do the job.'

'The Westland is a military machine,' said Clydesdale.

'Yes. But with its armaments stripped out, and with oxygen tanks, heated suits and special boosting for the engine, it should make the altitude. The designers reckon it will fly to 35,000 feet.'

Clydesdale thought for a moment. 'They may be right. However, you can't buy military machines on the open market.'

'We don't intend to. A strategic partnership with the Royal Air Force would make more sense?'

Clydesdale glanced around the smoking room. 'A partnership with the Royal Air Force?'

'Yes, preferably. In short, we'd like you to join us on the Flight Committee with Lord Peel, Colonel Blacker, Percy Etherton, Arthur Hinks of the RGS and Stanley White for Bristol Aviation. We were hoping you might persuade the Aviation Ministry to supply us with two Westlands.'

'Two, you say?'

'To double the chances of success.'

Clydesdale's cautious stance never flickered. But surely an opportunity to fly the first machine in history over the world's most famous mountain was hard to resist?

'I can make enquiries,' Clydesdale said finally. 'No harm in that, but you appreciate how these Ministries stand at present. All strapped for cash.'

'Yes. And meanwhile aviation is expanding across the world. The Americans, Germans, French and Italians are all building larger, faster and more versatile machines. We cannot sit back while our competitors forge ahead. Hopefully your friends at the Ministry might see that our endeavor can provide valuable research and development opportunities.'

'So I imagine. Oxygen, heating and life support...' Clydesdale nodded. 'I'm happy to ask them.'

'We'll also require the services of the Royal Photographic College and technical input from the scientists at Farnborough. High-altitude photography and medical considerations are vitally important sciences.'

'I'll think it over,' said Clydesdale.

'You have my telephone number in Oxford?'

'Yes.' Clydesdale rose to his feet. 'Give me a week or two. I'll call you when I have some answers.'

10. Office of the Secretary – July 1932

AS THE MOMENTUM TOWARDS THE Himalayan objective increased, so did the need for improved headquarters. To help things along, the College of Aeronautical Engineering allocated two spare rooms in their Chelsea establishment. Here the Everest Flight Committee made its first base.

In his role as Honorary Secretary to the enlarging operation, Percy Etherton supervised all correspondence and research material now accumulating in files and folders perched on the shelves. A world map on the wall provided clues to the geographical scale of the enterprise. On the highest ridge of the Himalayas, a red pin showed the precise location of their principal target.

Even if progress was steady, Etherton knew that the time for achieving their objective in 1933 was shrinking proportionately. As he tossed yesterday's page from the desk calendar into the wastebasket, the college clerk arrived.

'Today's post, sir.' The clerk's strained voice sounded to Etherton like a damaged accordion. 'There's a letter came by messenger from the Foreign Office.'

'Thank you. And how are you today?'

'Still groaning like a stuck and very sorry goat, sir.' The clerk's eyes were bloodshot and weary. 'It's the pollen.'

'You have my sympathies.' Etherton disliked people who discussed ailments too willingly. 'I know how you feel. I'm allergic to cats.'

'But you wasn't gassed by Fritz, was you sir? I could never climb Everest.'

'Nor would I recommend it. Anyway the pollen will go soon enough.'

The clerk departed with a long wheeze as Etherton slit open the first letter. It was from Gieves & Hawkes, the Mayfair outfitters. It would be a pleasure, wrote their manager, to donate silk inner lining for gloves to be worn by aircrew. A fair start, warm mitts for the men.

The second letter held an offer from Siebe Gorman, to manufacture special waterproofed and kapok-lined flying suits. Power from the biplane's dynamo would warm a grid of electric wiring sewn into each suit. After a glance at the notes and diagrams, Etherton put this in tray marked Colonel Blacker. The aircrew were doing well this morning.

The Director of Medical Facilities at Farnborough's Royal Aircraft Establishment had also written. His atmospheric pressure capsule, along with trained personnel, was available for altitude simulation and survival training for the airmen. The Establishment hoped that useful medical data would emerge from the exercise. Official boffins were joining the cause!

On the financial front, things were equally promising. Castrol would offer free and plentiful supplies of oil and lubricants for all aircraft. The company would alert overseas agents and additional notes provided the viscosity of engine oil at various temperatures.

All this goodwill was giving the Honorary Secretary a most uplifting start to his day. Etherton now reached for an envelope he'd been saving. It was addressed in scrolled violet ink and the letter inside was on a rather hideous shade of red paper. The correspondent, Lucy Houston, explained that she had received his letter, given it much consideration but was unable to offer support for reasons of poor health. The P.S. suggested that Percy Etherton should advise Mr. Blumenfeld at the *Daily Express* of developments.

Now this was a shame!

Like all the committee, Etherton had hoped that Lucy's sponsorship of the Schneider team might be repeated for an Everest flight. Yet now the heiress was apparently too sick to grasp the opportunity. Etherton re-read the rejection and filed the letter, making a note on his Actions sheet.

Etherton had learned to accept bad news with buoyancy and now he stabbed his paper knife into the letter from the Foreign Office. This, thank God, held better news. In the adroit diplomatic language he knew so well, the Indian Office had granted general approval for the flight, subject to the Nepalese Government also giving it the go-ahead.

Nepal sided with India in most matters, so this particular hurdle was now less challenging. Even so, silk gloves, spheroid pressure capsules, oil changes, hot suits and fresh oxygen would amount to nothing if nobody was going to pay for it!

Etherton passed an hour writing notes, listing priorities and revised tactics. Management had been his skill during much of his life. Piloting aeroplanes had never caught his imagination. Hadn't he seen enough airmen stagger like flaming haystacks from their crashed machines in Normandy? Recovering their bodies, with the stench of burned flesh... those were his worst memories. Aerial operations were for Blacker and Clydesdale to decide. Etherton would be happy enough to stay grounded.

By late morning Etherton had finished with paperwork. He would head for the Grosvenor House. At noon the hotel bar was often busy with well-heeled individuals from international society. There he might perhaps stumble across another potential sponsor?

11. Torquay, Devon – July 1932

LADY HOUSTON CLEARLY ENJOYED TRAVELING as fast as conditions allowed and while the launch sped from the *Liberty*, now anchored off the Devon coast, Garland was studying her boss beside her in the launch cockpit.

Lucy Houston was wearing a voluminous purple shawl over a grey satin dress that reached to her low-heeled shoes. A fluttering ribbon, also in purple, tied a sun hat to a chin held against the wind. The diamonds on ungloved fingers reflected the sunlight and despite a hint of hardness in the eyes, there was an undeniable charisma. A cheeky, come-and-get-me allure reinforced the resolute manner with which the heiress faced the approaching resort of Torquay. The woman, thought Garland personified the aura of Britannia and her rule across the waves.

Feeling all the better after days of seafaring, Lady Houston had decreed shore leave for the crew and a stroll onshore for Mungo. The terrier stood with his front paws on the gunwale, his black nostrils sniffing at the scents of land. Holding his lead was Torrance, not in whites today but in blazer and flannel trousers. His tourist kit, as he told Garland, was ideal for the Devon-shire resort of Torquay which broadly shared *Liberty*'s advertised views about the treacherous fool in No 10.

The launch came sweeping up to a timbered pontoon. Torrance stepped ashore first to help the terrier and Lady Houston transfer. As Garland skipped onto the landing stage she noticed John the chauffeur in cap and uniform hurrying to assist the landing party. He had been shadowing the *Liberty* on her passage along the south coast.

'Well done John.' Lady Houston patted her chauffeur on the shoulder.

'And where are we heading today, milady?'

'Let's see... Mungo will go to the beach with Torrance. You, John, will take me to the Imperial. Then you can drive over to the chandlers for some gin. A few dozen bottles of Beefeater, if they have it, otherwise Gordons will do. Get some Pimms as well.'

'Two dozen of each?'

'We'll need more if we go to the Cowes Regatta. Make it five dozen if they give us a good discount.' Lady Houston wagged her finger at her steward.

'Remember, Torrance, do not let Mungo off the lead. He takes to liberty far too easily. Don't lose the little sod.'

Then she turned to Garland. 'So that leaves you, my dear. You can have time to yourself while I'm having my barnet done.'

Garland realized the plan had been there all along. The heiress enjoyed pretending that life was guided by eccentric impulse, when in reality Lucy Houston planned impulse with guileful exactitude.

'Now I think of it, you could do with a new frock. Torquay has some lovely shops. Get something saucy. And you could also do with a new twist to your barnet – something with pizazz! So when you have bought what you need, come and join me at the Imperial.'

Garland did not understand. 'A twist to my barnet? With some pizzazz?'

'Barnet Fair means hair to us Londoners. I'll pay for your new hairdo at the Imperial hair salon.'

'Her Ladyship has never offered to pay for my hairdo.' Torrance said quietly.

'Not surprising' said John. 'You're as bald as an egg.'

Lucy Houston gave a fishwife's cackle as she ran a hand over Torrance's scalp. 'I'll get you a syrup if you want one.'

'Syrup?' asked Garland.

'Syrup of figs,' said Lady Houston. 'Wig!'

The steward set off towards the beach with Mungo. John escorted Her Ladyship to the waiting Rolls. After closing the door, he took some letters from the glove box.

'Your mail, Miss Ross. Forwarded to the lawyer when *Liberty* is at sea.' He lowered his voice. 'All sweet and dandy on board?'

'Still learning.' Garland returned John's smile as she transferred the mail to her shoulder bag. She leaned down to her employer through the open window of the car. 'Lady Houston, are you saying I'm not wearing the right outfits for the job?'

Lady Houston turned her sweetest eye on Garland to answer with a sly purr. 'I've seen my lads on *Liberty* drooling after you with their tongues hanging out. It seems that you have it, my dear, so you may as well learn to flaunt it!'

She put her hand into the great handbag that rarely left her side. It came out with a new £50 note as John started the engine. 'Get something you like and be at the Imperial hair salon at noon.'

'I can't take this, Lady Houston. Really I can't.'

'For pity's sake, Garland! Get yourself a new dress or give the money to a worthy cause. See you later.'

Garland stood as the Rolls shot off into the streets of Torquay. The launch was returning to *Liberty* to ferry other crew members ashore, and down on the beach Mungo was hauling Torrance along like a husky.

Garland took a deep breath. She was free for the moment at least. Before she went shopping she would stop at a cafe where the tables below new parasols looked so inviting. She gathered her thoughts over some coffee. Two letters had come from the USA. Her mother and sister were OK but missing her. She would write to them later. Meanwhile a generous gift and a visit to the hair salon were her's for the taking.

Garland tasted her coffee thoughtfully.

So, if she had it, she should flaunt it? The advice was puzzling, as was the loan of *Lady Chatterley's Lover* which Garland had felt obliged to begin reading. What exactly was Lady Houston's game?

12. Aerial Photography – July 1932

WHILE GARLAND WENT SHOPPING FOR pizzazz, Colonel Blacker was in Putney addressing a meeting of seven skilled professionals. All were struck by his tone, crisp as a breach-bolt, as he thanked them for coming to discuss their mutual objectives.

'We've made a start on oxygen supply, heated clothing and anti-freeze inhibitors for the fuel. Today we're here to consider the photographic elements. Before I ask Colonel McCleod of the Geographic Section of the War Office to provide the details, I shall make other introductions.'

Blacker used a handkerchief to polish his monocle. With a flick of his fingers, he returned the eyepiece to its place and surveyed his audience with the confidence of a seasoned campaigner.

'Let's start with Mr. Cyril Pitt, chief engineer to Bristol Aviation.' Blacker pointed at a slightly built middle-aged man seated in the second row. 'Mr. Pitt is the engineering wizard who comes with Bristol's new Pegasus engine, isn't that so?'

Pitt had no objection. 'I don't do wizardry, Colonel, but if you can't see without polishing that monocle, you'll have a terrible time trying to find Everest.'

There was a ripple of laughter. In his army days, nobody would have dared to address a Colonel like that. However he rather admired Pitt on whose skills the aircrew would totally rely.

'My optician assures me that my sight is fit for purpose. So assuming we find our way with the aid of your engine, and assuming I can identify the mountain, I'll be operating the cameras. It will be for Mr. Burnard from Westland Aviation to advise us how to link the cameras, heating jackets and automatic film advance to the dynamo driven by your Pegasus.' Blacker raised a finger towards a taller, lugubrious individual. 'Mr Burnard will oversee the engineering and maintenance of the Westlands after adapting them for our requirements.'

Silly remarks were not Burnard's style. Lifting his eyebrows, he gave the assembly a brief nod as Blacker moved on. 'Now to introduce our Chief Pilot, Squadron Leader Clydesdale.'

The Marquess of Clydesdale had recently agreed to join the Flight

Committee and was now in charge of planning aviation operations. 'Pleased to meet you all, gentlemen.'

Blacker proceeded. 'I'm sure you've all heard of Mr. Sydney Bonnett. He has recently completed a tour of Africa with Alan Cobham and, besides being the most resilient of travelers, Mr. Bonnett is a professional and highly acclaimed cinematographer.'

The cameraman gave a self-effacing shake of his head as Blacker pressed on. 'I must add that the motion picture contract, like that of the Westland biplanes, remains under negotiation. But until we agree terms – as I know we will – all motion picture filming will be directed by Mr. Geoffrey Barkas here. You may have seen some of his previous films, such as *The Somme* and *Q-Ships*, both favorites of mine,' added Blacker.

Geoffrey Barkas, an energetic individual in blazer and slacks, made a theatrical bow. 'Thank you, Colonel. *The Infamous Lady* is actually my favorite but I think any film about the famous lady, the mountain they call the *Goddess of the World*, will be far more challenging.'

Blacker saw Pitt and Burnard exchange thoughtful glances. Even Clydesdale's brow seemed to pucker. Barkas came from the creative world which explained perhaps why they viewed him cautiously.

'Whatever it takes,' Blacker said. 'We'll do our part to assist your production.'

'Very good of you, Colonel. I'll be counting on your thespian talents throughout. I foresee roles for you in many scenes.'

Blacker proceeded hastily. The idea of being filmed was most unwelcome. Action, in his experience, did not occur in front of movie cameras.

'We'll see about that. Now to introduce Airman Fraser from the RAF who will explain the proposed camera systems. I understand that Fraser may be seconded to the expedition, to supervise camera storage, maintenance and dark room facilities.'

Airman Fraser, the youngest among them, was wearing the drab blue uniform of the RAF. 'I'll do my best, sir.'

'Well said, Fraser.' It was so much easier dealing with service men than with filmmakers. 'So now that we all understand our roles, I shall ask Colonel McCleod of the War Office Geographic Section to take over.'

McCleod, a ginger haired man in wire-framed spectacles, stood up and walked to the front as Blacker took a seat. He had a thick Scottish accent.

'G'd day, gentlemen. If you're wondering why the War Office and the geographical arm of the RAF has any interest in this Himalayan flight, I shall enlighten you. Everest is most unlikely to feature in any military conflict and at her altitude death is easy to find, so I'm here simply to tell you about the photography. '

On a table of green baize lay a selection of cameras, assorted lens, plate-holders and film spools. 'The RAF regards high-altitude photography to be of vital importance in the modern world, and as Colonel Blacker intends to survey the terrain from high-altitude, we're offering to help. Let me explain how.

'Presently, only an eighth of Earth's surface has been mapped with any degree of accuracy. Aerial photography is a valuable and economical way to capture detailed records of any terrain. Foremost in the new technology is this Williamson Eagle Camera.'

McCleod hoisted a bulky instrument, some fifteen inches long, from the table. From its gray metallic body sprouted a bug-eye lens which he pointed towards his audience.

'This is the Mark 3. With four hundred and fifty working parts, it can deliver over one hundred exposures at speeds determined by the observer or pilot. A single exposure at 35,000 feet generally captures ten square miles of territory directly below. On average, each exposure shares a sixty percent overlap with neighboring exposures. After processing, the assembled prints reduce distortion. It's a well tested system but never yet deployed over the Himalayas. As I understand it, you will have two Eagle cameras so this doubles the chances of obtaining excellent surveys of the target areas.'

McCleod gently returned the Eagle III camera to the table before selecting a smaller hand-held camera for his next topic.

'Now I must point out that the photography of land with vertical shots can be strangely deluding. For example, a steep cliff photographed from above will show up like a knife blade on its edge, thus entirely masking its real and daunting topography. To counter this, we recommend observers to take oblique shots with this smaller Williamson P14. Its exposures are particularly sharp, so by matching the survey strips to the oblique shots the cartographers can provide reasonably accurate mapping. This camera provides the best overall images of mountains.'

He aimed the camera at his audience and they heard the sharp click of its shutter. Putting down the P14, McCleod now drew their attention to the largest item on display. It was three feet long and resembled no more than a rectangular plywood box with a hole in one end.

'To complete the test schedule, your team will test this infrared camera courtesy of Ilford's Research department. The device has the unique ability to peer through cloud cover and the Air Force is very anxious to learn how this new invention performs at altitude.'

Blacker was in two minds about this infrared camera. It's new technology had excited the defense industry, but the aircrew in their Himalayan program would have a busy schedule without being obliged to carry bulky cameras into clouds, especially clouds where brutally solid mountains lurked. Clydesdale had lobbied successfully to include the equipment in the plan, believing it would bring more support from the Air Ministry. Blacker had to admit that the Chief Pilot's policy seemed to be working favorably. He could hear muttering in the seats behind him and turned to see Pitt head-to-head with Burnard, the Westland engineer.

'Mr. Pitt! If there's something you need to say...' Blacker raised his voice. 'Can we wait until Colonel McCleod has finished speaking? We have a lot to discuss today.'

Pitt's cherubic face was deadpan. 'I'm sorry sir. I do apologize.'

'Never mind, Mr. Pitt. Your views are most welcome. Please feel free to air them.'

Pitt waved away the offer.

'Surely,' Barkas called out, 'if it's sufficiently important to reveal to Mr. Burnard, we should all be entitled to hear?' Clearly the film director had an ear for potential conflict.

Pitt shot a suspicious glance at him. 'It was nothing of significance Mr. Barkas.'

'Then why say it?' the film director asked. 'If it concerns these infrared cameras I'd like to know.'

Blacker said nothing, waiting to see which combatant in this sudden drama would take the prize. A few seconds passed.

'Since you insist, Mr. Barkas, I'll tell you, said Pitt finally. I couldn't help noticing the size of these infrared boxes. They're large enough. So I was telling Mr. Burnard that the aircrew seem to be taking their coffins with them.'

'That's enough, Pitt.' Blacker barked. 'Perhaps you can offer such ideas to

Mr. Barkas for his screenplay? Neither the Chief Pilot nor myself are remotely nervous about flying with such cameras. Do you hear me?'

'I do indeed, sir,' said Pitt, visibly startled. 'I do indeed.'

13. On board Liberty – July 1932

LADY HOUSTON, GARLAND AND THE dog Mungo returned to *Liberty* early in the afternoon, leaving Torrance onshore to visit his relatives in Torquay. Lady Houston had asked John to ferry Torrance in the Rolls while she took a nap in her cabin. Garland would stand in for Torrance and with the weather set fair, *Liberty* was riding at anchor, steam in her boiler and a skeleton crew on watch.

Garland stayed near the galley, waiting for the customary telephone summons from Lady Houston for tea and chocolate biscuits. Garland was in her new dress, of crisp, yellow rayon with a new Gucci belt ensuring a tight fit around her waist. At the Imperial Hotel, Lady Houston had approved of both purchases before sending her to the hairdresser for pizzazz, a fashionable phrase coined by *Harper's Bazaar*. Garland's hair fell onto her shoulders while she leaned on the ship's rail watching pleasure craft and admiring the coastline of Devon extending into the haze.

The call for tea was among Lucy's most predictable requirements and, sure enough, at five p.m. the galley telephone rang. Garland hurried inside to take the call. 'Yes, milady?'

'Brandy and ginger, if you please. And Scottish oaties with Marmite.'

'Oaties? Marmite?' Garland wavered. 'What are they?'

'Oaties are Scottish biscuits, Garland. Marmite is in a black pot with a yellow lid. You'll find them.'

The line went dead. Lady Houston no longer sounded cheerful. The request for a strong drink seemed odd.

Garland set aside the kettle and soon found the Hennessy brandy and splits of Schweppes ginger ale. Tumbler and ice bucket were at hand. She located the oaties in a painted tin, but where was the Marmite?

On the highest rack, beyond her reach, Garland saw a potbellied jar with a yellow lid. Taking a chair, Garland hopped up to reach for the Marmite. Stretching higher on her toes, her fingers found the jar as she heard a voice behind her.

'Signorina. Allow me help you.'

Garland grabbed the marmite and spun around. A slim sun-tanned man had entered the galley. He was wearing the pressed white suit of an officer, but she was sure she hadn't seen him since she'd joined the *Liberty*.

'Who are you, may I ask?'

'Marco, the yacht's radio officer.'

Garland stepped off the chair, noticing that his braid epaulettes featured a tiny radio mast. His smile was so dazzling and his dark-brown eyes found her wavelength in an instant. Garland felt weak at the knees.

'So where have you been for the last month?'

'In Rome. My grandfather passed away so Lady Houston sent me home. And now I'm back. And who, signorina, are you?'

'Her Ladyship's new secretary. Garland Ross.' She looked away, down at the box of oaties. Were her hands trembling? Garland wasn't so sure as she hastily assembled the order. 'You must excuse me. Torrance is ashore, so I'm doing tea for Her Ladyship. You gave me a shock.'

Marco shrugged an apology. 'No. You must excuse me, Miss Garland. I'm so very sorry. I had no choice.'

'No choice?'

'I see your beauty in that lovely dress. I had to meet you.'

Another whooshing surge of adrenalin shot through her. She glanced through the galley windows across the sweeping teak decks of the *Liberty*. The gangways were deserted and the launch was returning from Torquay with rowdy crew aboard. Lady Houston would be waiting.

'For god's sake, I must hurry!' Garland spluttered as she lifted the tray and left the galley, stepping past the Italian. He stood aside, his arms folded and wearing a look of profound pleasure. Garland resisted throwing a backward glance as she sped along the corridor.

Lady Houston was at her desk when Garland set the tray down. Lady Houston was watching closely. The Schweppes hissed as Garland opened the bottle for the waiting brandy. 'There you are, my Lady.'

'Thank you, Garland. Goodness. You're glowing like a red light in the Rue Saint-Denis.' Lady Houston spoke in a French accent.

'It's the heat.'

Lady Houston picked an oatie from the plate. 'Maybe you've been canoodling with one of my crew?'

'Of course not.'

'Oh but one should canoodle when one gets the chance. How else would

I have become the owner of this yacht?' Her Ladyship took an oatie. 'Nicely done, Garland. Not too much Marmite.'

'And you eat it?'

'It builds strength and stamina, Garland, just as brandy with ginger fires the mind.' Lady Houston pointed to the letters that had arrived with the chauffeur earlier that day. 'Speaking of health, I want you to send this message to my doctor in Harley Street. I want him to know the pills are working wonders.'

'I'll see to it.' Garland took the handwritten message.

'And tell him I'm feeling so well that, after Cowes, I will sail for Scotland as planned.'

Garland stood at the door. 'Shall I look in later, Lady Houston? Is that it for the moment?'

'That's all, my dear. Torrance will be back soon, You can forget about me. Just ensure you send this as a cable from the Radio Room.'

Garland's knees quivered. 'Perhaps I can send it from Torquay – when the launch goes to fetch Torrance?'

Lady Houston dunked an oatie into her brandy angrily. 'I keep a radio room and an officer for the purpose of sending cables, Garland. Just give it to Marco. I want my doctor to have my news now.'

Garland left Lady Houston with her strange meal, and headed back along the yacht's carpeted corridors. Back in her own office, she sat down to write the message. *All in fine order, thanks to your wonderful pills. Will be going to Scotland after Cowes just as you recommended. My sincere thanks. Bless you. Lucy Houston.*

Since she'd been ordered to take it to Marco, there was no way out. She took a mirror from her handbag, snapped it open and took a look. Then she left her office and made her way to the radio room astern of the bridge.

Marco was there, sitting before a panel of dials, cables and meters. On the desk was the Morse key for transmissions to the outside world. His tie was loosened and he seemed surprised by Garland's arrival.

'Signorina Garlandia?'

'Please send this cable to Lady Houston's doctor. It's urgent.'

Marco took the typed draft and read it. 'Why so urgent? The lady is well and going to Scotland.'

'I think you should send it now.'

65

Marco sat up and his fingers stroking the Morse key. 'You remind me of a beautiful ripe peach in a summer orchard...'

'A peach! Hurry up for god's sake and send it,' whispered Garland.

Marco gazed at her. Never took his eyes off her as he tapped out the message. Then so casually he rose to his feet and placed his hands on Garland's bare shoulders.

'That's not necessary,' said Garland with little conviction.

'But what should one do with a ripe peach? Relax, Signorina. We are shipmates and we are the only foreigners onboard. So that means we must get to know each other much, much better.'

14. Lord Peel's Home, Belgravia – August 1932

TEN DAYS HAD PASSED SINCE the photographic conference in Putney and an August heatwave held firm, sending London's residents to park and pub for their summer refreshments.

Life was no different that evening at Lord Peel's Belgravia home. In the Georgian townhouse just off Eaton Square, His Lordship was hosting the core members of the Everest Flight Committee. Over dinner his guests had a good laugh when Blacker reported how the West Country engineers had clashed with the film director. In Blacker's opinion, humor for the ground crew would be essential, particularly when wrestling with the gizzards of propulsion units in insect-ridden heat. If the coffin analogy was too flippant for Barkas, what would happen when they reached India? Film directors, to Blacker's mind, were pushy individuals of arguable talent, best confined to studios and not released upon the parade grounds of reality. Lord Peel agreed with his son-in-law. Life in India was never the same as in Britain.

The conversation rumbled along, helped by a generous torrent of whisky supplied by their host from a cut glass decanter. The fluid gold was the treasured product of Glenlossie, the Scottish estate where Lord Peel shot grouse every year.

As host, Lord Peel sat at the head of the table. On his right were the two Scots, Buchan and Clydesdale. Blacker and Etherton sat to his left near an electric fan luring fresh air through the open windows. For dinner, they had enjoyed lamb cutlets with fresh vegetables. The cook, who also acted as housekeeper, had retired for the night, saying she would tidy up next morning. With Glenlossie to hand the committee now focused on the underlying problems of their venture.

'Shortly, my friends,' Lord Peel began, 'this summer heat will roll into autumn. If we're to launch the expedition as planned, our best chance will be next spring, before the ferocious Indian summer. Do we agree on that?'

'We'll have about six weeks in April and May,' Blacker estimated. 'So we must be on station in March. For that, we must leave London by the end of January, mid-February at the latest.'

'Five months from today.' Clydesdale considered the dates. 'Realistically, how can we get everything in place by then?'

Detecting some doubt in the air, Buchan felt it should be stifled. 'But we have so much in place already. A host of willing companies, reduced fares from P&O and Imperial Airways, free fuel from Shell Oil. Even Lloyds are proving constructive with their insurance quotes. The Air Ministry, Westland and Bristol, the Royal Geographic, all on our side. And some substantial deals with *The Times* and Gaumont-British. We can find the equipment and crews, so all components are in place – bar one.'

'And that's the money.' Lord Peel spoke for them all as he swilled his whisky. 'We've approached our sources, our chums in Whitehall, not to mention scores of organizations and private individuals. And we remain woefully short of funds.'

A snort from Blacker revealed what he thought of his father-in-law's brutally accurate summary. It held a whiff of defeat, which Blacker would never consider. He would speak first.

'So we must find a way. For example, the Vickers Aircraft Company in Ireland are offering two Vespa aeroplanes which, though fitted with Jaguar engines, might also make it over the Himalayas.'

'But with their own crews aboard,' Clydesdale said. 'And how would it serve British and RAF interests if Vespa was the first to claim Everest?'

'Point taken, so we haven't yet accepted their offer.' Blacker tugged his mustache. 'So how to break this impasse? Regardless of funding, we still need government approval for the Westland biplanes. As you've said, Clydesdale, these belong to the RAF and are not for civilian operation.'

'That's true, but I've been bending ears at the Air Ministry. Their photographic and scientific advice may be useful, but their official approval for the expedition hinges on another matter which, dare I say it, might be awkward in respect of present company.'

Lord Peel looked up. 'So what's the problem?'

Clydesdale shifted uneasily in his chair. 'The Air Ministry fully acknowledges the unparalleled skills and knowledge of our team, but there's a reluctance at Staff level to assign the unique hazards of the expedition solely to our command. The weather, the machines, the crews and support systems all require, in their view, a command structure that can only be delivered by a senior and experienced RAF officer.'

Blacker's colleagues waited for his response. This statement from the Chief Pilot clearly cast concerns on his leadership role.

'But they'll provide full support so long as we accept a leader of their choice?' Blacker asked.

'I imagine so,' said Clydesdale.

Buchan agreed. 'A reasonable trade to get two Westlands.'

Clydesdale pushed on, looking relieved. 'A suitable candidate for Expedition leader would tip the balance, especially if approved by the Chief of the Air Staff who believes that national defense interests will benefit from high-altitude operations.' Clydesdale lifted his tumbler, sniffing the whisky. 'I'm sure you all know of Air Commodore Peregrine Fellowes?'

'Peregrine, the fastest of birds, and the best name for any pilot,' said Blacker. 'Yes, I've met Fellowes on several occasions. He was decorated after the Zeebrugge raid when he volunteered to bomb the dam.'

'Though he was shot down and captured in the process. To my mind,' said Etherton, 'Fellowes is an excellent choice but has anyone asked him how he feels about a jaunt to the Himalayas?'

'Not yet,' said Clydesdale. 'I wanted your approval first.'

'Then do we approve?' Lord Peel noted a universal endorsement. 'So that's settled. Perhaps you should contact Fellowes tomorrow morning?'

'I'll certainly do that,' said Clydesdale. 'And since we're on the subject, you might approve my choice of Second pilot. Flight Lieutenant McIntyre is an officer in my squadron, a top notch navigator and a superb pilot. I know Fellowes would approve.'

'Two for the price of one,' said John Buchan. 'So is that also agreed?'

Again the diners gave their consent. These men had survived the Great War by adapting to circumstance, so if the RAF would only provide Westlands on their terms, these realists could compromise.

'With the RAF our costs will be substantially reduced,' Clydesdale went on. 'And if Fellowes accepts the invitation, there's another bonus. He knows most of airfields in the Middle East because he helped to build them.'

'Excellent' said Lord Peel tapped his knuckles on the table. 'But may I remind you, funding remains our main problem. Given all our sponsors, donations and payments for rights, we still face a hefty shortfall. One way or another, we'll have to meet ongoing costs. At least £100,000 is required.'

Around the table, the view persisted that all available routes had been tried. Where in these dismal, penny-pinching times could they locate so much money?

On an impulse, Buchan leaned towards Clydesdale. 'Your mother the Duchess, doesn't she know Lady Houston?'

'Yes, they're quite friendly.'

'But we've already been kicked out by Fanny Houston,' Blacker pointed out.

Buchan ignored the interruption. 'If your mother tells Lady Houston that the RAF will be taking a major role, surely that would help? She sponsored the Schneider teams. She might yet be tempted, especially if she was to hear it from a Duchess?'

'For heaven's sake, John,' Clydesdale said. 'Lucy Houston could buy the entire Hamilton clan many times over. Why would a title make any difference to her?'

'I'm willing to bet Lucy will listen to a Duchess.' Buchan grinned. 'With you as Chief Pilot, we could yet persuade her.'

'I read today that *Liberty* is leaving Cowes Regatta for Scotland,' said Etherton. 'Lady Houston intends to stay at her estate in the Cairngorms for what's left of the summer.'

'Is there anything you don't know, Percy?' Blacker asked.

'I'm heading for the Highlands myself,' said Buchan. 'I'd be happy to approach her – if it helps.'

But Etherton had done his homework. 'No offense, John, but you may not be the ideal suitor for Lady Houston.'

'Why so?'

'You're too close to *The Times* who are refusing to publish her high-minded opinions about the PM. Lucy always takes a shine to handsome young men, and preferably those with a title.'

The diners laughed as Clydesdale shook his head disbelievingly. 'You leave me no option, blast you! I'll go north this weekend and discuss it with my mother.'

'Worth a try and we'll cover your expenses.' Lord Peel set down his glass with an approving thump. Reaching for the Glenlossie, he thrust the decanter towards the Chief Pilot. 'Help yourself. We can leave it to the ladies to take things forward from here.'

15. Dover Strait – August 1932

THE *LIBERTY* SAILED FROM COWES at midnight. Heading east into the moonlit Solent and English Channel, the yacht made Dover Strait by noon next day. The sight of undulating chalk cliffs on the vessel's port side gave Lady Houston good reason to stop dictating letters to Garland. She called Torrance to bring her tipple and asked Garland to fix a lead to Mungo.

'I know of a terrier who leaped from a ship once. The dog dived in to chase dolphins,' the heiress explained. 'I'm going out for fresh air, and you Garland, can take a breather. I don't suppose you're getting enough sleep at present.'

Ignoring the sudden innuendo Garland helped Lucy Houston into her heavy coat. Had the ship's gossip mongers discovered Garland's dalliance with Marco? She clipped Mungo to the lead.

Initially Garland had been wary of the terrier, hearing rumors of its snappiness from other crew members. She then learned it was not Mungo, but his owner, who was likely to snap. Garland liked the terrier. His scruffiness was endearing and the way in which he oscillated his head with those pleading amber eyes was impossible to ignore. Mungo could predict human behavior and was smart enough to avoid chasing dolphins. Garland passed the lead to Lady Houston who took her drink from Torrance before he threw open the stateroom door. A mild swell was pulsing across the sea's surface as *Liberty* pushed ahead at twelve knots. Into this breeze across the deck, the owner walked towards the bows.

'A nice soft day, Miss Ross,' Torrance remarked. 'But there will be tears in her eyes when she comes back.'

Had Torrance also developed psychic skills? Garland stood with the steward, watching Mungo anoint a polished deck cleat while Lady Houston remained staring at the French shoreline on the starboard side.

'Another job for the deckhands,' muttered Torrance.

'I should thank you, Torrance – for helping me out.'

'Helping you, Miss?'

'You know durned well. When I asked you to take that message to the radio room on my behalf.'

'It was nothing, Miss.'

'I just didn't feel like... seeing Marco,' she explained.

'That Italian knows how to push his luck, if you ask me, 'specially since he's a married man.'

Garland's heart jumped at the revelation. Marco wore no wedding ring and had mentioned nothing of his life in Italy. To her muddled mind, matters had been getting out of hand. She felt it might be wiser to see less of Marco, not wanting to add emotion to the situation. Her visits to the Radio Room had been thrillingly outrageous but an extended love affair on the *Liberty*? Out of the question, she decided.

'Her Ladyship just told me I've not been getting enough sleep.'

'We're her family, so she likes us all to get a good night's rest, preferably in our own cabins.'

Torrance set his stare on the horizon with a knowing smile. Garland's nod indicated she understood.

'Just as well I took the message,' said Torrance. 'I found the Italian gentleman was halfway through another bottle of my gin.'

'Gin? From your bar stock?'

'Must have helped himself. I checked the inventory and several bottles are missing.'

'So what happens next?'

Torrance folded his arms. 'Not a lot, Miss. In the old days, the quartermaster would strip him naked and flog him out there over the windlass. Nowadays radio operators are prized staff for this newfangled equipment, so I can't see him being punished for a misdemeanor. He's promised to replace the gin at Inverness.'

These were issues for officers and stewards to sort out but Garland feared that her clandestine visits to the radio room were now public knowledge. 'Less said, soonest mended?'

'Yes, Miss. Always the best way.'

Standing in the doorway Garland and Torrance watched as Lady Houston wandered around the deck with Mungo. On the port bow, a ferry was leaving Dover harbor for its run to Calais. As it passed across the bows of the *Liberty*, blasts came from both ships' whistles. Then with the white cliffs abeam, Lady Houston paced back but she was weeping openly. Wiping her cheeks with the back of her hand she passed Mungo's lead to Garland.

Garland took a handkerchief from her sleeve. 'I hate seeing you so sad.'

'Of course, I'm bloody sad!' Lady Houston grabbed the hanky. 'Look at those chalk cliffs! You may not understand, but beyond them lies the land the British have always defended. This was the last view of their homeland as seen by a million British soldiers when they sailed over these waters to die in France.'

'It's a dreadful thought.'

'Yes, Garland, it is.' Another choking sob blurred Lady Houston's words. 'The thought of all those final farewells for those brave men and women. I'm sorry, but it just breaks my heart.'

Garland took her employer's arm while the steward closed the stateroom door.

16. Yeovil, Somerset – August 1932

THE SPECK IN THE SKY was just visible from the Yeovil airfield. Flirting with the low shred of cloud, the pulse of its engine grew louder as the speck transformed into a silhouette of wings, fin and undercarriage and finally into that of a powerful biplane.

The Westland descended for a classic three-point landing, a kiss from the two main wheels with the grazing bite of the tail skid. The engine's note faded as the biplane slowed and then returned to a steady pulse while it taxied to the apron where Blacker and Pitt were waiting.

Pitt wore green overalls, an oil rag drooping from his thigh pocket. He shouted above the gargling thunder of the Pegasus radial engine while it burnt off residual carburetor vapors before shutdown. 'There's your Westland, Colonel. See the wide undercarriage? That's for a torpedo.'

Colonel Blacker's hands remained stuck in his trouser pockets as he assessed the two sets of broad wings sprouting from the twin cockpits. 'We won't need torpedoes on Everest.'

'So stripped down to remove the weight of weaponry and munitions, she's perfect for the task, sir.'

'I expect you're right, Mr. Pitt.'

At first sight the Westland was exactly what Blacker had in mind. After some cajoling from Clydesdale, the Air Ministry had authorized the Westland company to evaluate the new Pegasus engine. For several days, Pitt and his fitters had worked tirelessly so the test pilot could rate the combination.

'I like what I see,' said Blacker. 'And you're confident the Pegasus will take her up to 33,000 feet with cameras and oxygen on board?'

'Very hopeful, sir.' Pitt nodded. 'But high-altitude tests will prove it. I reckon you'll have four thousand feet of clearance over the summit.'

Clydesdale had determined this was the minimal safety margin in ideal conditions, though everybody knew these rarely existed in the Himalayas. Wild chilling gales galloped through these altitudes, catching on precipitous slopes and flaying the shoulders of the terrain. Enormous piston thrusts of invisible air could hurl an aeroplane in any direction. The safety margin of air above such a merciless landscape was crucial in the evaluation process.

'And will these flights test anti-freeze inhibitors in the fuel?' Blacker asked. The thought of cruising over any landmass with frozen fuel pipes was not much to his liking.

'Of course, sir. 35,000 feet over Dorset or India feels much the same to the inlet manifold of a carburetor. Though, I dare say the view is very different.'

The Westland men wheeled a stepladder to the cockpit where the test pilot, Harald Penrose, was hoisting himself free. Moments later, he skipped onto the grass to remove his helmet and deliver his immediate analysis.

'Good. Very good! She's a fairy with a rocket in her skirts. I took her to 20,000 feet in fourteen minutes with muscle galore in reserve.'

Blacker now saw a taxi arriving. The passenger was his other reason for this visit to Yeovil. Leaving the engineers to their reviews, Blacker limped over to greet him.

Air Commodore Peregrine Fellowes was in a herringbone sports jacket, grey flannel trousers and brogue shoes, standard mufti daywear. A few years older than Blacker, his high forehead hosted reticent grey eyes. He carried a brief case under his elbow.

'Good to see you, Air Commodore, sir.' Blacker shook his hand. 'I'm sorry to report you've just missed the landing.'

'And good day to you, Colonel. You can blame my delay on cows blocking the railway near Salisbury.'

'Bovine blockage, eh?' Blacker chuckled. 'A routine hazard in India. And I understand Clydesdale has briefed you on our little jaunt?'

'Some jaunt,' Fellowes said, as they ambled over towards the activity around the biplane. 'It's a major undertaking, but worth a try, that's for sure. You'll be pleased to hear that the Chief of Air Staff thinks so too.'

Blacker glanced at the Air Commodore. He knew that respectful caution was the best approach to officers of higher rank. 'I understand from my colleagues you may be tempted to accept the role of expedition leader?'

'Yes, it was mentioned,' said Fellowes affably.

'I certainly share their hopes in that respect.'

Fellowes stopped walking and turned to Blacker. 'Kind of you to say so, Colonel, but I would never want to supplant a professional like yourself, especially after all you've done for the project.'

'Good heavens! That's no problem.' Blacker's monocle came out for routine polish as he quickly thought this over. Why on earth would he feel supplanted? With an Air Commodore in the mix, they would have two

Westlands, RAF ground crews, access to well-equipped bases with mess facilities and a score of intangible benefits besides. Transfer of the leadership role seemed a small price to pay.

'As I see it,' Blacker continued, 'the operation will be semi-military, semi-civilian, so we'll easily collaborate. If you keep the flight crews under your command, I'll deal with the camera units, the Indians and so on. I'll have plenty to do, believe me.'

Fellowes looked relieved. 'That's fine with me, but I haven't agreed yet. I wanted to meet you first and examine the aeroplane.' Then he hesitated. 'However there's one more hitch to confront.'

Blacker's eyebrow clamped on the monocle.

'A personal matter,' explained Fellowes, 'but not insurmountable. My wife Eleanor likes to think I've finished with overseas postings. We've spent so many years in Turkey, Persia and Palestine that a peaceful life in the Chilterns has claimed her body and soul. I imagine you'll know what I mean, Colonel, since you too are a family man.'

'My memsahib took that line initially.' Blacker agreed. 'But Doris accepted it would be wiser for her to stay in England with our boys. She knows I won't be traveling for ever.'

'But Eleanor is not prepared to remain here. She would prefer to come out to India with us.'

'I see...' Neither Blacker nor Etherton had contemplated taking ladies to India. 'It will be no luxurious affair in Purnea. It's a backwater with malaria, leprosy, beggary and worse. I imagine Mrs Fellowes understands all that?'

'Yes, Eleanor knows that. And there'd be no need to worry about her cost to the expedition as that would be covered privately.'

'Wish we were all so lucky... You've heard we're having the very devil of a time with the funding?'

The Air Commodore radiated optimism. 'Let's assume someone, somewhere will make it happen,' he said. 'I could borrow an aeroplane, flying out with Eleanor, alongside Clydesdale and McIntyre in their Moths.'

'We haven't planned the outbound flight yet, but if you're bringing your own wings and RAF goodwill, how can we fail? Yes, I'm sure Mrs. Fellowes can make it to India.'

Fellowes smiled, looking at Blacker's good eye. 'So pleased you agree. Now let's see what Mr. Penrose says about his Westland. It's the machine that will dictate most events in this enterprise, don't you agree?'

'Very true. We must fly even higher than Everest.'

And with the Air Commodore now apparently on board, the two leaders went to meet the test pilot and examine the equipment.

17. Kinrara, Scotland – September 1932

LIBERTY REMAINED AT SEA FOR three nights on its passage from the Solent. After calm seas in Thames and Humber, less friendly waters prevailed in Dogger, Forties and Cromarty, all regions known for grumpiness. *Liberty* had sailed on many wild seas during her circumnavigations, lifting her hull over the swells with contemptuous ease to dismiss those that rose against her.

Preferring to ignore these thumps, Lady Houston took to her bunk with magazines. Though she could have transferred to travel by car, she chose to stay with the ship, explaining to Garland that rough and smooth are what happens in life, both on land and sea.

Garland had been confined to her quarters. While *Liberty* traversed the diagonal swells she was enduring seasickness. Staying near the WC, spasms rocked her to the core. Torrance told her to stay in bed until the seas or the nausea abated. With his usual cheeriness, Torrance advised her to drink gallons of water. He'd cover for her while she 'fed the fishes'. The description made her dash to the WC and then back to her bunk where she finally managed to sleep.

She woke to the trill of her bedside phone with Torrance saying that *Liberty* would be docking within the hour. Garland climbed unsteadily from the bed and showered. Today she chose a tweed skirt and a cardigan, assuming this to be correct Highland attire. The sea was calmer now and to the steady note of the engine she prepared her suitcases.

Apart from the last few days, she had enjoyed her time on board. Life on a luxurious yacht was at its best in coastal waters. At sea, and especially at night when *Liberty* churned into an invisible space, she had felt threatened by the void of the unknown. On the trans-atlantic crossing from Montreal, she had experienced a similar anxiety, but on *Liberty* the fear seemed more menacing.

With daylight sickness and fears were forgotten. Garland went to take coffee in her office. Here she checked all relevant correspondence was ready in boxes for transfer to *Kinrara*. Then she walked onto the deck for a look at Inverness.

Under a bright sky, the granite city stood firm behind a flotilla of moored fishing vessels. As the *Liberty*'s bows nudged towards the harbor wall, Garland could smell the crisp Highland air. It felt like pure oxygen. Bit there could be no more visits to the Radio Room now, she thought.

The arrival of a vessel as impressive as *Liberty* attracted numerous officials and onlookers. Soon the crew were hurling monkey-fists and mooring lines towards the dock while *Liberty*'s propellers thrashed the water at her stern. Garland could see a a delivery van parked beside a black Packard. This American import was considered more suitable for the Highlands and she could see John chatting with the van's driver as the Harbormaster boarded to check papers and mooring arrangements.

The crew began transferring baggage to the dock and then to the van while Lady Houston sailed from her quarters, wrapped in her plum coat with an oversized cashmere scarf trailing near to the dock. Behind came Torrance with Mungo on his lead.

Garland had typed the orders for the next phase in Lady Houston's peripatetic life. Torrance was to take annual leave, as were many of the crew. Garland, John and Mrs. Munro, the housekeeper at *Kinrara*, would stand in for the Steward.

The Captain and officers lined up in uniform at the gangway. Garland waited with Torrance while Lady Houston thanked them all and with a wave to her crew walked without aid down the gangway.

'She would have made it in Hollywood.' Torrance whispered to Garland. 'A proper Garbo.'

As Torrance followed the owner to the dock with Mungo, Garland exchanged a glance with Marco. Standing in line with the officers he pursed his lips and blew her a silent kiss. Garland raised her eyebrows and waved a finger. Seasickness had kept them apart for days and even if they had met what was the point? The man was married and a philanderer. It was clear to her now. Garland walked down to the Packard where Lady Houston stood ready to go.

The Packard and the van set off, out through the dock gates, along the grey streets of Inverness and up into the hills. In the Packard, Lady Houston took the back seat of the car with Mungo curled beside her. Garland sat beside John in the front. The baggage and the food hampers prepared by *Liberty*'s chef were all in the van.

The convoy sped along in the stupendous grandeur of Perthshire's glens and forests. Rumbling past crofts and lonely villages, then speeding over high moorland below a clear sky, the two vehicles reached *Kinrara* in time for a lunch of smoked salmon sandwiches.

Lady Houston then retired to her bedroom on the upper floor of the lodge advising Garland to get acquainted with the housekeeper, Mrs. Munro. This ruddy-faced woman who looked strong enough to strangle a sheep, told Garland that Lady Houston would read the newspapers, then doze for a wee hour in her own sweet time. The mattresses in Her Ladyship's beds, along with all bedside furniture, were identical in all of her homes, to help her to feel instantly settled. It was another of Her Ladyship's wee foibles, said the housekeeper in a strangulated accent.

Mrs. Munro was now on call if needed, so Garland was free until her shift began. Making a brief visit to her room, a stark and sterile place in the garret, she ensured all her bags had arrived. From the window, she could see the River Spey glistening in the valley between rough meadows and moorland.

Leaving by the back door, Garland set about exploring the estate. Heading for the river, she took a path through unfenced land where birch saplings rose as silver stalks between the dark trunks of juniper and pine. These gave way to clumps of golden bracken and thickets of gorse and always the glitter of the Spey was somewhere just beyond. Soon she could hear the water as it raced over boulders and then she was at the river's bank, near a long pool of resting water. She sat down on a slab of rock.

She was considering the strange foibles of her own life when suddenly she felt a push against her elbow. Mungo was looking up at her, wet-nosed and bursting with terrier pleasure. He was enjoying this wilderness after the confines of the yacht. She rubbed the dog's spine, knowing how it always pleased him. When she returned to the lodge with Mungo her employer was sitting in a wicker chair on the lawn.

'This is really the most gorgeous place, Lady Houston. I never knew Scotland was so beautiful.'

'Glad you like it,' Lady Houston said. 'Nothing's changed in this glen since the ice age. It's my idea of heaven. Generally the business of man fits so poorly with the business of Nature.' Lady Houston pointed to a chair. 'Sit down, my dear. I want to talk to you.'

Garland could hear bees humming in the roses over the conservatory doors. Was this to be a conversation or a monologue? She gave Mungo another stroking as she took a seat.

'I see you've made your mark with him.' Lady Houston laughed. 'My last secretary hated dogs so we had to dismiss her, didn't we Mungo?'

Lady Houston began fiddling with her rings as she gazed at the dark blue shadows along the Cairngorms.

'To me this glen is a theater for the four seasons of Nature. That's all that happens here. I've always loved it. From my very first visit with Robert.' Lady Houston sighed at the memory of her husband. 'I do so adore the mastery of Nature.'

They sat in silence as the evening sunlight flamed across the purple slopes of heather. Grouse were calling in odd staccato squawks. Much further out, where the hills folded, a small herd of red hinds and their calves had stepped from the shadows to graze.

'So Garland, I've been meaning to ask about your love life.'

'There's not much to say is there? I guess I live in hope.'

'You can't afford to dream forever, Garland. Before you know it, you'll be my age and what good will that have done you? Without issue, without teeth and lonely as hell.'

'I appreciate your concern.'

Lady Houston fixed her stare on Garland. 'I was barely into puberty when I began dancing on the London stage. Every night of the week, except Sundays, I'd take a bus to the West End to change into tight corsets and bright garters. Linking arms with the other girls we lifted our feet and showed our thighs to the audience. One night after the show an older man, my Fred, invited me to a hotel off Piccadilly. We drank two bottles of wine and then hopped upstairs. He very carefully removed every stitch of my clothing and there, lying naked and ready on the bed, I gave Fred the very best of my attention.'

Garland made no comment as Lady Houston continued. 'We became ravenous for each other so we eloped to Paris. What a city it was! Such class! Such decadence! For a young girl like me, Paris was a huge and beautiful playground.'

'I've never seen Paris. It must be wonderful.'

'Go with someone you love, Garland. Anyway, I soon discovered that Fred was having it off with other women and so I too began my own affairs. We fought like ferrets and then drowned in remorseless sex to settle our differences. When Fred died, I was no older than you are now.'

'That must have been difficult.'

'No, not really.' Lucy Houston giggled. 'He left me £6000 a year for life, even though we never married.'

Garland could see the deer moving into the shade of the hill. If only this was an interview, she'd be celebrating a scoop by now, and she'd barely asked one question.

'So I had my independence and I returned to London and met Theodore. Also a handsome man, well placed in society and when I married him I became a Lady. But, don't let the title fool you, Garland. Ladies are only women when all is said and done. Theo was after my money, and I had to leave him. Eventually we got a divorce.'

'And then you married Sir Robert?'

'No, no. There was another before he came along. I fell for a baron, the enormously lovable but helplessly chaotic George Byron. He became bankrupt and our affair just fell to pieces. Even so I loved him from the bottom of my heart. He cost me a ton of money when we parted and that's when I spent some time with the Suffragettes. A good cause, but not for recovering lost fortunes, so I had to take up with Sir Robert. He was never so charming as George. Tough as a steel brick was Robert. We were only married for two years before he died.'

Garland had heard the rumors about Sir Robert's death. As a reporter, she might have pressed ahead, but as a private secretary she thought better of it. 'Such a short time.'

'My detractors believe I hastened his demise in one way or another. Robert died on the *Liberty* but there was nothing mysterious about it. He merely lost his final battle and I inherited his fortune. That's why I can afford to live here. In all my life, I've only done what was best for me and for my country.'

Lady Houston pushed aside the tartan blanket and got to her feet. 'Let's go in. Tell Mrs. Munro we'll have a quiet day tomorrow, but on Saturday, assuming I'm fit, we've been invited to the Oban Games by a Duchess. You've not met one of those yet, have you Garland?'

Mungo stood to yawn and stretch before trailing after the two women into the lodge.

18. Oban Games – September 1932

THE SKIRL OF FIFTY PIPES surged into the arena with the power of a musical tsunami. Plumes, kilts, capes and sporrans moved as one, all keeping time to the beat of bass drums. The annual Argyllshire Gathering in Oban on the Atlantic coast was under way.

Standing close to the arena ropes where the bandsmen turned to reverse through their ranks, John Buchan was mesmerized by the bloated cheeks and rippling fingers of the pipers. Small wonder, he thought, that such formidable and disciplined men had often led British troops into conflict.

In the faces among the crowd, Buchan identified the resilient self-sufficiency for which Highlanders were famous. Many men wore kilts though others, like himself, were in tweed suits. Grannies, mothers and daughters in starched pinafores and tartan hair ribbons. He could see all were in good humor.

Since the dinner at Lord Peel's London home, Buchan had been in touch almost daily with his colleagues. Clydesdale's mother had been persuaded to telephone Lady Houston. The Hamiltons would love Lucy to join them at the Oban games. Sensing some resistance to the lengthy journey, the Duchess had applied pressure. The weather forecast was excellent, the company would be entertaining and the sandwiches and teacakes would be exceptional. Lucy and her staff would also be welcome to overnight at Inverary Castle, home to the Duke of Argyll.

On hearing that Lady Houston had finally accepted the invitation, Buchan had travelled north on the LMS railway. At Glasgow he took the branch line to Inverary where he spent the night in the George Hotel beside Loch Fyne. Using the hotel's sole telephone Buchan called Clydesdale to learn that Fellowes had approved the Westland test reports and had agreed the command structure. Clydesdale added that he would be at Oban with McIntyre, the designated Second Pilot. All of this was positive news. Buchan had gone to sleep listening to the lap of wavelets along the shore. Next morning he had taken the first train to Oban.

Now he was looking for any sign of Lady Houston, aware that her capricious nature might easily have detained her elsewhere. He was sure that MacDonald the Prime Minister was the one Scotsman unlikely to be present, especially if alerted to Lady Houston's possible attendance.

Buchan strolled from the arena towards the car park. Here he soon caught sight of the Duchess of Hamilton standing with Lady Houston. Excellent, he thought. The bait had served its purpose. He would not intrude while the Duchess and her guest were enjoying a lively gossip between their vehicles. Further behind, he saw two chauffeurs chatting to an attractive young woman supervising a black mongrel. Of course he could delay for a few minutes.

In the arena the band began playing a slow march as Buchan spotted an Alvis car approaching across the grass. He stepped out and raised his hand as it pulled up. The driver was Clydesdale and another young man sat in the passenger seat.

'Flight-Lieutenant McIntyre?' said Buchan after greeting Clydesdale.

'The man himself,' said Clydesdale. 'Mac, this is John Buchan the architect of our enterprise.'

Buchan shook McIntyre's hand seeing a youthful, masculine character with flyaway eyes, vibrant mustache and a charged smile. He was the quintessential pilot. 'So you're the Second Pilot?'

'Aye, the job calls for a Glaswegian, someone mad enough to take Clydesdale's word for it. He says it will be like a Sunday school outing.'

'Please describe it just like that to Lady Houston,' Buchan said, noting that both women had also seen the arriving car. 'The less said about risk, the better.'

McIntyre jumped from the Alvis. 'Negotiations are for the Chief Pilot. I'll be in the beer tent if you need me.'

McIntyre left for the refreshment marquees, leaving Clydesdale and Buchan to join the Duchess. She made the introductions with gushing informality.

'Lucy, this is my son, Douglas. And I believe you know John Buchan?'

'Never had the pleasure.' Lady Houston shoved her stick into the soil and offered her hand first to Clydesdale, then to Buchan. 'But I have read some of your books.'

'And I've been reading your work, Lady Houston,' said Buchan. 'That piece in the *Saturday Review* was great stuff. I thoroughly applaud your views of the government.'

'Thank you.' Lady Houston retrieved her stick. 'You know how to flatter, don't you just? But I won't stay silent while MacDonald abandons us to the Nazis. Surely it's his duty to protect the people from mortal danger?'

'I do so agree.' An energetic soul in her late sixties, the Duchess tried to humor her wealthy guest. 'My son is a Reserve RAF officer with a bomber squadron. He'll be doing whatever is needed to protect the nation.'

Lady Houston turned to Clydesdale. 'But how can you protect London if you're in the Himalayas? Your mother has been telling me about some flight you're planning over Everest?'

Clydesdale had not taken a drink and the topic was already turned to their key objective. Buchan's eyes flickered a warning.

'Yes, we're setting up an expedition with the RAF. But it won't proceed if war breaks out. Fortunately the War Office see no likelihood of that in the immediate future.'

'I hope they're right,' said Lady Houston. 'I don't trust that nasty Adolph Hitler. Not one bit!'

Buchan stepped in. 'Clydesdale intends to make a photographic survey of the mountains, Lady Houston. With detailed photos our climbing teams can identify the best routes to the summit, so that British climbers can be first on Everest! To fly the Union Jack on top of the world.'

'Good heavens!' Lady Houston looked inspired. 'That would be wonderful but this expedition sounds like a most expensive undertaking?'

'These things generally are,' Clydesdale said. 'However, by developing high-altitude capabilities for future bombers, we can justify most of the costs.'

Lady Houston nodded. 'Come to think of it, I do believe someone wrote to me about this expedition but I had to turn him down. I was reading about Everest the other night as I sailed to Inverness. The *Daily Express* keeps on about those climbers who disappeared up there.'

'That's the endless mystery of Irvine and Mallory,' Buchan said. 'It intrigues us all.'

Lady Houston stepped closer, shining with energy. 'I was reading of an artist in Shetland who has psychic powers. He's been in touch through the spirit medium and he's convinced that Irvine and Mallory communicated their success in reaching the summit.'

'How very odd!' The Duchess said.

Lucy Houston responded immediately. 'I don't find it odd. Not at all. I'm certain that spirits exist on the mountain. It's just a question of making contact. I take it you know Everest is called Goddess Mother of the World?'

'Makes sense to me,' said Clydesdale.

'And you'll agree that a Goddess has the power to give and to take?'

'Maybe so?' Buchan smiled.

Lady Houston glared. 'Why is there any doubt? It's simple. Irvine and Mallory got to the summit where the Goddess swept them to her soul!'

In the awkward silence that followed, Buchan saw Lady Houston glance towards the Packard, where the staff were setting up the picnic. Her features froze when she saw her dog Mungo had stopped beside the picnic. His back leg was raised high in the air.

'For Chrissake, Garland!' she yelled. 'You stupid girl! You cannot allow Mungo to piss all over our lunch!'

19. London – September 1932

AS DISCUSSIONS IN OBAN CAME to halt with embarrassed apologies, Percy Etherton was making better progress five hundred miles to the south in Mayfair.

He had been busy relocating headquarters to the Grosvenor House on Park Lane. Having spent years commanding operations from rat-infested redoubts, dank caves and porous tents, a base in a prestigious West End hotel was a lot better. With gratitude he accepted a complimentary suite from the management who was happy to sponsor this element of the expedition. Bar drinks, room service and restaurant food would be billed monthly with a 20% discount.

Etherton had arranged to meet Air Commodore Fellowes and his wife Eleanor for an informal meal. Since RAF support was tied to Fellowes acting as operational commander, it was essential to improve civilian and military interests with a show of hospitality. In addition Blacker has asked Etherton to assess Mrs. Fellowes. Would the presence of an English lady on the expedition be a hindrance or a blessing?

Over lunch, Etherton quickly formed a positive opinion of the Air Commodore. The man was tailor-made for the job and knew more about aviation than the entire Committee. Initially he was uncertain about Eleanor Fellowes. In her mid-forties she was possibly used to getting her own way, as were many conservative women in the Shires, but how, he wondered, might Eleanor react to the desperate grasp of a leper?

This became a conceptual test that Etherton privately applied to all those proposing to visit India. The sub-continent was full of horrendous surprises which had to be confronted realistically, even with benign ruthlessness. But by the end of the meal, Etherton understood that the couple had served in many insalubrious locations and India was no different. With their respective duties broadly agreed, the Fellowes departed.

His first use of the hotel's sponsorship had returned a fair dividend. Hoping for similar results from his afternoon schedule, Etherton took a taxi in the hotel forecourt to his next assignment.

Ten minutes later, as the cab drove around Trafalgar Square, his attention was drawn to hordes of pigeons pecking on seeds sold by vendors. He was reminded of the mobile military lofts whose pigeons flew to and fro with coded messages taped to their legs. Their homing abilities and courage in the incessant gunfire had always impressed him. He paid off the cab at the Admiralty Building in Whitehall and paused to admire the two black chargers of the Blues and Royals on duty at Horse Guards Parade. Such horses too had faithfully served their masters in the war.

As he passed Downing Street, Etherton wondered how the Prime Minister rated Lady Houston's vendetta against his government? Perhaps MacDonald might be forgiven for rejecting proposals from an eccentric heiress who paraded her opinions in bright neon around the nation's shores? Squadrons of new fighter aircraft were not vote-winning policies for a demoralized population who believed that the Great War had been the one to end all wars.

Bullies and extremists would always exist in human society, so a realistic defense strategy remained a duty for all leaders. For failing in this respect, he decided MacDonald deserved Lady Houston's scorn.

Walking down Whitehall, Etherton understood why key ministries, along with the Palaces of Buckingham, Lambeth and Westminster, the War Office, the Treasury and the Admiralty were located here. All lay near his destination, the Foreign Office, surely the taproot of the British Empire.

He signed in at the front desk. An usher then escorted him up the broad marble stairway where oil paintings depicted famous Britons in noble pose. The building spelled power and influence and every footfall made an echo.

At a door marked Middle East Desk, the usher introduced him to the duty Officer, Neil Jacobs. Whilst his colleagues were in touch with many senior civil servants, Etherton preferred dealing with those who maintained daily contact with embassy staff around the world. Their opinions often reflected more accurate assessments than those of their politically driven masters.

Etherton took a chair and Jacobs began. 'You'll be pleased to learn, we're very happy to assist you with all the diplomatic elements of your mission.'

'A much valued support, believe me,' said Etherton.

Jacobs pointed to a folder on his desk. 'In the blueprint for your enterprise, we understand the Chief of Air Staff has authorized access to RAF bases on the flight to India. That makes it much easier. When your team reach their destination, we'll hand you over to the India Office who will liaise with local representatives in Bihar and Nepal. You probably know most of them.'

Jacobs opened a map where a red line traced the proposed route. 'Your airmen should have no difficulties from London to Paris, then Nice and south to Rome. However, on leaving Sicily they'll be into Arabian skies. Our people will see they don't fall into the wrong hands for the fuel, supplies, carnets, visas and so on.'

'That will be immensely helpful.' Etherton was delighted.

'All part of the service,' said Jacobs. 'Assuming your pilots reach India in one piece, they must remain mindful about dissidents. In some places, the activists are getting out of hand.'

'Mainly hot air in my opinion.'

Jacobs paused for a moment. 'I appreciate you know India better than most. These blisters of agitation are erupting because they want us out.'

Etherton had noted this and privately felt that Gandhi's agitators might eventually prevail but sponsors of the expedition might take fright if the flight created risk of civilian unrest. 'Maybe these protestors will win independence one day but until then, you're right. They're just blisters.'

'Hopefully they won't burst on your pilots.' Jacobs quipped as he rose to take Etherton to the door. 'I hear you're going to the Coronation in Nepal.'

'You're well informed, Mr. Jacobs. Invited by the King himself.'

'So there should be difficulty in obtaining the flight permits?'

'Unlikely. But you can never tell with Asian potentates.'

'It's been a pleasure meeting you. Your exploits are something of a legend here. Do keep in touch, won't you, sir?'

Back outside, where the afternoon sun still shone on the soul of the Empire, Etherton felt he had won the support of the Foreign Office but if Buchan and Clydesdale failed with Lady Houston, all these gains in London might be irrelevant.

He looked up at Big Ben. The clock showed 4.30 p.m. He had time to visit Shell if he took another taxi.

Five minutes later he walked into the International Aviation department of the Shell Oil Company's head office on the Strand. Etherton was hoping to consolidate Shell's generosity with fuel requirements. The offer resulted from a visit made by Clydesdale some days earlier. The Chief pilot had turned up unannounced and left thirty minutes later with an offer of free fuel all the way. If all life could be so easy! Etherton still had to check the facts.

Though the sponsorship manager was unavailable, his secretary would record Etherton's needs. Would Shell kindly forward details of Asian fuel depots to his office in Grosvenor House? Could Shell indicate levels and grades of aviation fuel held by these depots? What period of time would be required to establish supplies of inhibiting anti-freeze for the fuel? Finally did Shell's kind offer extend to the return journey for the smaller aeroplanes?

The secretary scribbled away. She would pass it all to her boss. 'Good luck,' she said. 'And stay in touch, won't you?'

It struck Etherton as odd that both officials had used exactly the same phrase. 'Keeping in touch' was evidently an obsession. Hadn't he travelled for months on his long trek across Asia with no communication whatsoever? While he could endure long periods of solitude, it occurred to him that the modern world could not.

To finish his duties for the day, Etherton headed for Fleet Street where newsmen could be found snouting for scraps of tittle-tattle or juicy scoops. Still these newspaper types could be useful. This evening he planned to join Blacker for an evening drink with the film director Barkas and *The Times* correspondent Mr. Shepherd. John Buchan had initiated these bits of the jigsaw, but Etherton felt he should double-check the situation.

Etherton now found himself among busy home-going commuters. He recalled similar huge crowds within the great bazaar in Ordam Padshah, the pilgrimage center in Asia's interior. Reportedly he was one of only five white men to have entered the shrine. He had always made a point of visiting religious centers on his travels attempting to understand the spiritual values of others. Confucius had put it another way, saying that ignorance was the night of the mind, but a night without moon and star. It was one of Etherton's favorite epigrams.

The rendezvous was at the pub where many famous luminaries had created great quotations. Dr. Johnson, Boswell, Thackeray, Dickens and Voltaire had all been patrons of Ye Olde Cheshire Cheese in Fleet Street.

'Over here, Percy!' Blacker's rigid tones ripped through the hum of conversation. He was at the bar chatting with the two front-runners for the media jobs. Etherton deduced the individual in an embroidered casual jacket had to be a film director, so the beaky fellow with the gaze of a startled mongoose was Mr. Shepherd. His guesswork proved correct and Blacker ordered a beer for Etherton before returning to his theme. 'I was explaining, Percy, that we must prepare the facilities in India. Mr. Shepherd says he will need to send and receive cables.'

'Cable facilities are a priority,' said Etherton. 'We'll never be far from a post-office, Mr. Shepherd. Mostly they provide a good service – but not always, I should warn you.'

'I'll manage,' said Shepherd. 'India is India.'

Blacker agreed. 'Mr. Shepherd is a realist, Percy, but Mr. Barkas here is traveling on a more ambitious scale. He's bringing a six-man crew and several tons of equipment. I've suggested his crew should operate as a self-sufficient unit, in respect of travel, food and lodging. In any event, their expenses and production costs will be down to Gaumont-British.'

'That's fine by us, Mr. Barkas,' Etherton said. 'Obviously we want to help with your production. I'm going to India to prepare the base in Purnea, so with a list of your needs I can start the ball rolling.'

The film director was pleased. 'I'll send a comprehensive schedule. Photos of the main locations would be massively helpful. I'll get my AD to send you a list.'

'AD?' asked Blacker.

'Assistant Director. Mine is a veritable wizard. Tom Connochie can turn string into wire or sand into gold. He fixes everything, thus allowing the crew to function without interruption. It's a most important job.'

'So this man Connochie will be liaising with me?' Etherton enquired.

'Yes, that's what assistants are for. I'll have enough on my hands directing the camera action.'

Etherton wondered how the film director might react to Indian poverty. Deciding not to comment he turned to the correspondent.

'The Air Commodore is taking his wife. Clydesdale has his chum McIntyre as Second Pilot. Mr. Barkas has his AD. So do you too have an assistant, Mr. Shepherd?'

The journalist shook his head. 'Correspondents are solitary folk.'

Etherton warmed to the journalist's modesty. 'I understand you may fly east with the aircrew?'

'It's the best way to cover the story from start to finish,' said Shepherd. 'I've never been to India so it will be an experience.'

'You'll enjoy sandstorms, bedbugs, not to mention camel's bollocks and goat's eyes, if you're lucky.' Blacker's warning came with a chuckle.

'Now, Mr. Barkas,' said Etherton. 'I don't believe we've seen a script yet?'

'Because there is no script,' said the film director. 'I write as we shoot, to capture freshness and spontaneity. And the production we have in mind, will be spectacular!'

Etherton was nonplussed. 'I see.'

'To be frank I'm not hooked on survey photography. Rows of static images say nothing to my soul! I'll cover the human sides of the story, reshooting key scenes with adjusted dialogue. A dramatized documentary.'

Blacker peered at Barkas through his monocle. 'So what exactly do you mean by *spectacular*?'

'The dramatic locations of Makalu, Chomolungma and Kanchenjunga with monks, rajahs, biplanes and elephants. All in Movietone!'

Blacker stared at Barkas, searching for words. 'That sounds most invigorating and artistic no doubt, but our task is to fly over Everest. I do hope we understand each other?'

Fearing a clash of personalities, Etherton interceded quickly. 'I'm sure we all respect our differing objectives. It's simple. Mr. Shepherd will record the facts and Mr. Barkas will accentuate the drama.'

20. Kinrara Sunday – September 1932

LIFE IN THE PURPLE HILLS of Kinrara was so different to *Liberty*'s world on the ocean wave. Gone was the comforting hum of the ship's engine with the ever shifting motion. No longer could she hear the odd shout from a crewman and the purr of wind in the rigging. In the isolated glen of the Perthshire highlands the silence came with a melancholic note. Garland began to miss the urban buzz of New York and London, and inevitably those warm memories of the yacht's Radio Room!

The austere bedroom in the gables, where the plumbing rattled and the bed springs pinged within a lumpy mattress, made her pine for the daily banter with Torrance and the crewmen. At Kinrara the staff were polite, but they had the weirdest of accents and customs. Never mind caber tossing and shot putting, Scots insisted on strange eating habits, such as 'high tea' in the middle of the afternoon.

Garland was eating a fresh scone at the kitchen table while reading a news report that 25% of Americans were now unemployed. She should count her blessings, she decided, as Mrs. Munro returned after taking high tea to Lady Houston.

'Her Ladyship is not herself. The poor soul's in a terrible state.'

Garland looked up. 'She seemed OK yesterday.'

Mrs. Munro placed her hands on her hips to stare at Garland. 'OK? Whatever that means I dinna ken, but Lady Houston is swearing, uttering words we should never hear, and especially on a Sunday.'

'I guess she's tired. It was a long trip to the games yesterday. And since the visit to the Duke of Argyll was abandoned, we had a long drive home.'

Mrs. Munro sniffed. She removed her apron and hung it over a chair. 'Lady Houston can only sleep on her special mattress from Harrods and His Grace hadn't thought to get one for her.'

'Dukes can be so thoughtless.' Garland's attempt at humor was lost on the housekeeper. 'It's a shame we couldn't stay longer. I was hoping to talk to John Buchan and the Marquis.'

Mrs. Munro brightened. 'Och, he's a great man is Buchan. When you've finished your scone, Miss Ross, Her Ladyship wants to see you in the drawing room.'

Garland had exchanged few words with her employer since the humiliation caused by Mungo's misdeed. They had lingered at the games for an hour, watching cabers being hoisted by grunting giants and tippy-toe dancing over swords and Targe shields. Garland had then had been summoned to the Packard for the run home. During the drive, Garland had sat up front with John. Lady Houston sat with her sinful dog in the rear seat and then went straight to bed on their return.

By Sunday afternoon, Garland feared she'd been banished for failing to police Mungo's behavior. She did her own correspondence and then she walked to the river, following sheep tracks through the heather. Beside the lively Spey, she had looked back at Kinrara. Smoke drifted from two chimneys but nothing moved in any doorway or curtained window. It was the home of the richest woman in Britain, but today it looked like a battered tombstone. Still feeling sorry for herself, Garland returned to the lodge.

Garland finished eating and licked strawberry jam from her fingers. Then she went to the drawing room. Lady Houston was by her desk and speaking on the telephone. The glowing peat in the fireplace was reassuring.

'Sit down, Garland. This won't take long,' said Lady Houston before resuming her conversation on the phone. 'I know they don't want Clydesdale to fly over Everest. I read it in the paper, but it's pure tosh. Clydesdale is Member of Parliament to advance British fortunes. His electorate is being bloody ridiculous! We need plucky leaders, Willie, to accomplish great things, or I don't know my head from my ass! Are we to be ground underfoot by this wretched government?'

Mungo, stretched before the fire, pricked up his ears when Lady Houston's tirade at her lawyer lifted to a higher pitch. 'No, all is not right, Willie. About that I'm quite certain. I'll think on it overnight and we'll talk in the morning.'

Lady Houston rammed the telephone back on its cradle and wandered angrily around the sitting room, stopping beside a model of the Supermarine winner of the Schneider Trophy. Its propeller was driven by a tiny electric motor. It made a soft whirring sound as Lady Houston turned it on.

'Lawyers, Garland! Do you know what they actually do? Nobody would ever achieve anything if they all followed legal advice.'

'You might be right about that.'

'Of course I'm bloody right!' Lady Houston picked up a sheaf of papers. 'Now, Garland, what are we going to do with all this stuff the Marquis foisted on me? I had no choice but to accept it. How could I do otherwise when the Duchess, John Buchan and those young pilots were all standing around like helpless penguins? How could I?'

'They were so hopeful you might help their expedition.'

'I don't know about that, but I tell you this much. At least we're dealing with real men!' Lady Houston put on her reading spectacles, 'This man Percy Etherton, the so-called Expedition Secretary, served with the Royal Garhwal Rifles. He then travelled to Mongolia and Siberia with horses, camels, mules and yaks before becoming our Consul-General in Turkestan. I've never heard of the place. Where is it?'

'I haven't a clue,' said Garland, 'but I can find out.'

'It won't be part of the Empire with a name like that. But I like this man Etherton. He speaks Hindustani, which is more than I do. And what are we to make of this Colonel Blacker?'

'He's the man behind it all. A famous soldier I believe.'

'Yes, but this is very odd.' Lady Houston bent to scrutinize the page. 'His grandfather died – would you believe it – in a duel. How stupid is that, I ask? But it gets worse. Colonel Blacker once designed a machine gun that blew the propeller off his aeroplane while testing the device. Does the man have a death wish?'

'I think the Colonel has lucky angels.'

'Why do you say that?'

'Because if not, he'd most certainly be dead by now.'

'It seems these pilots are intent on crashing their machines though Air Commodore Fellowes, was shot down in battle.'

'He would have assessed such risks. That's war for you.'

'Far too many crashes! That's what I see here.'

Lady Houston subsided in a chair. She reached for a Kleenex tissue from a box on the table, waving it at Garland. 'A white flag, my dear. I must apologize.'

'For what?'

'I was wrong to shout at you as I did.'

'I'm your secretary, Lady Houston. Shout at me as much as you like. It happens all the time in the newspaper business.'

'But you were not to blame for the dog pissing like that. It was rude and thoughtless of me to shout at you.'

Garland had never before heard Lucy Houston apologize. 'No need to worry, Lady Houston. But thanks all the same.'

'You're such a sensible girl. So we'll leave it at that.' Lady Houston gave Garland an affectionate smile. 'Now I recall some weeks ago on *Liberty*, you said something I thought was very wise.'

'What was that?'

'You said I could beat MacDonald by upstaging him. You suggested some dramatic gesture?'

'I was probably speaking out of turn.'

'Not so my dear. We fight on the same side – as do most women of principle. Perhaps this Everest flight is the answer.'

'So they still want you to sponsor their expedition.'

'Of course. All that money for the Schneider Trophy makes me an obvious target for anyone with a hole in his budget. Mind you, Garland, I don't care much about the money. In truth there's little else to do with money but to dispose of it wisely, especially as I already own everything worth having.'

'Your philanthropy, Lady Houston, is legendary.'

'I hope so because I cannot tolerate wealthy people who grow mean and avaricious. Pleonexia is a terrible by-product of the capitalist system. And what's the point of cash when facing the inevitability of death?'

Garland tapped her finger nails on her notepad. 'Then, why not sponsor the expedition? It would make a fantastic story, something to give Fleet Street and Britain a big smile.'

'Yes, Garland, you'd be right about that. But what they propose is to conduct a most dangerous flight in the full glare of the world's press. It would be a very public disaster if something went wrong.'

Garland nodded. 'The pilots are not letting that worry them. So why let that put you off?'

Lady Houston plucked another paper from the folder. 'How do you rate the Squadron Leader?'

Garland looked at a photograph of Clydesdale in RAF uniform. 'I spoke to him briefly as he only wanted to speak to you. I thought him very shy for someone in the public eye.'

'I rather like shyness in men. It can be so charming but don't be fooled by British aristocrats! They may be mousey as choirboys and as ruthless as killer ants. The Marquis seems reliable. I don't think he's lost any aeroplanes yet.'

'I talked to his friend, McIntyre. Call him Mac. Mungo, he said, was a 'fine hoond'.'

'So this Mac of yours. Is he dishier than Clydesdale?'

'Dishier? Well, since you're asking, I suppose he is.'

Lady Houston's demeanor softened. 'What I want is your advice, as a friend. If you were in my place, with my checkbook in hand, what would you do about this expedition?'

'First off, I'd meet the two pilots again, to see if I'd missed something. Give female intuition a chance. After all, they're putting their hides on the line. There's something romantic and bold about it! The message is Britain is strong. Britain can do it! It would be one in the eye for Ramsey MacDonald! Not to mention Hitler.'

Lady Houston appeared to like that. 'Your opinion is so helpful, Garland.'

A block of smoking peat fell onto the grate. Garland quickly took the tongs and returned it to the fire.

'Do you know, Garland, I think I'll take your advice. Ask the Marquis of Clydesdale and this man Mac to come here to discuss it all. And you and I can make up our minds up about which of the two is the most dishy.'

Garland managed not to laugh. 'Will tomorrow be suitable?'

'That depends on how urgently they want my money. We're not going anywhere, are we?'

21. Farnborough – September 1932

THE FELLOWES WERE DRIVING TO the Royal Aircraft Establishment at Farnborough. The complex was home to the scientific side of air travel and today the Air Commodore would be reviewing all the technical factors. He was considering these as he guided his Riley through the lanes of Surrey and he was not a slow driver. He had purchased the two-seater Gamecock from the widow of a fellow pilot who had died for no technical reason whatsoever. The poor devil had hit an oak tree on his final landing. That's all it took. In contest with a light aeroplane a stout tree was usually the winner.

Eleanor was in a particularly cheerful frame of mind. Her Hermes silk scarf flailed in the wind and she wore the Raybans he'd given her for her birthday. He glanced across at his wife.

'You're the cat who got the cream.' Fellowes shouted above the hum of the car's engine. 'Free chocolates all the way to Everest!'

Earlier that day they had taken a tour of the Fry Chocolate Company organized by Eleanor's father, a Conservative MP. They had seen legions of nuts, raisins and marzipan crumbs rattling along belts into hot vats for chocolate coating, then onwards for drying and wrapping. The staff had suggested which items would survive the heat and humidity of prolonged travel. Guesses were offered about what sweets Indian children might appreciate. All agreed the Viceroy Governor of India would appreciate Fry's Special Assortment in a presentation box.

In the Chairman's office they were advised that the board had approved the loan of the company's Puss Moth, a three-seater biplane. It could make the roundtrip to India bearing Fry's name with a selection of their products which Eleanor would dispense at her discretion.

'And they'll taste much better from our own aeroplane,' Eleanor laughed as the car slowed at a crossroad. 'You say it will take a month to get to India?'

'Allow a month each way. It depends on the weather.' The Air Commodore had often flown the route in RAF aircraft. 'We'll be in loose formation so a problem with one machine might affect our progress. Anything can happen and usually does.'

'These other aeroplanes? What do they amount to?'

The Riley was speeding along and closing on a charabanc. Fellowes tapped the brakes, poised behind the cumbersome vehicle until the road was clear. Then surging past, he changed to fourth gear.

'Clydesdale will bring his Gypsy Moth Mark Three to be flown by McIntyre. Clydesdale will command a larger Fox Moth with two passengers. One will be Hughes, Clydesdale's private mechanic who knows De Havilland machines down to the last rivet. The other will be *The Times* writer, Shepherd.'

Eleanor rolled her eyes. 'All the way to Karachi with a reporter?'

'That's the idea. All that assuming we secure the backing.'

'Which can only happen if they snare Lucy Houston.'

Fellowes tut-tutted. 'You can't trap a clever old vixen like Lucy Houston. She's far too smart. One offers suitable incentives instead.'

'I find it odd that a woman with her wealth needs any incentive. I'm told she carries several thousand pounds in her handbag.'

'Fry's believe the expedition is good for British chocolate. So if we boost other British products maybe Lady Houston will go for it.'

Eleanor turned to face him. 'You do know that Lucy Houston is completely batty?'

Fellowes briefly diverted his attention from the road. Eleanor was going a bit far, considering what Lady Houston had done for the RAF. 'If you mean her argument with MacDonald, I totally agree with her.'

'Well yes, but I do question her values, her love of the limelight. It's not the done thing really is it? She's little more than a jumped-up show girl.'

Fellowes' foot hit the brake and a pheasant flew from the hedgerow. 'Dancer or heiress, it makes no difference. It takes guts to write out a huge check. Lady Houston has immense courage.'

Eleanor said nothing as the car picked up speed. She placed a hand on his knee. 'Let's drop it, shall we?'

'Yes, let's do that,' Fellowes snapped.

They drove in silence, until Eleanor spoke again. 'But I have one request, one privilege you might say, if I'm to accompany you.'

'Only one?'

'Yes, just the one. I want absolutely nothing to do with the press.'

'Hard to avoid. But you'll keep your personal views about Lady Houston under wraps.' Fellowes pulled up at the gates of the Establishment where a guard waved them through. 'However as expedition leader, I shall be highly involved with the press.'

'You've always put duty first.'

'That's what Air Commodores do.'

'And wives have duties too. Receptions and so on. I'll need to be properly equipped,' said Eleanor.

'That sounds like shopping.'

'I'm just wondering what the Army and Navy Stores recommend for Puss Moth travelers?'

Fellowes ignored the question as he parked beside the establishment offices. He applied the hand brake, allowing the engine to idle. 'You take the car and visit your friends. I'm sure they'll have plenty of advice. I'll be finished by six.'

Eleanor moved over to the driver's seat as Fellowes got out. Having adjusted her Raybans and rearview mirror she waved as she set off. Fellowes watched the Riley pass out of sight before heading to the Officer's Mess to meet the Station Commander.

By six Fellowes had finished his business and walked out to find Eleanor waiting for him. He reclaimed the driver's seat. 'Enjoyed yourself? Plenty of ideas?'

'A list as long as your arm,' said Eleanor. 'So how did it go, Perry? Assuming it's not a military secret.'

'All very useful. We discussed pressure chambers, lightweight oxygen cylinders and various options for microphone and tube connectors in masks and helmets.' Fellowes started the car's engine and flashed a smile at Eleanor. 'It's much more fun to talk about chocolates.'

22. Oxford – September 1932

AFTER TRAVELING SOUTH ON THE Royal Scot overnight train, Buchan was at home in Elsfield, the honey-colored stone hamlet three miles from Oxford. This proximity to the University and the famous Bodleian Library made the village an ideal base for authors and academics.

For some months, Buchan had been developing a novel tentatively titled *The Three Fishers*. It reminded him of the effort made by the Everest Flight Committee in locating funds. Their lack of success was bloody irritating and why were eminent financiers ignoring this great opportunity? He decided not to work on the novel today.

Instead he would complete an article of gory non-fiction about the Massacre of Glencoe. This ghastly event had occurred in 1692 when the King's troops butchered every man, woman and child they could find for refusing to swear allegiance to King Billy. His power relied on homage paid by important families and dissent could not be tolerated.

During his research, Buchan learned the clansmen who perished in the bloodbath were primarily the Donalds. Was it possible that the incumbent Prime Minister might be a descendant of the few survivors? If so, it suggested that in two hundred years, the decimated clan had recovered to take power at Westminster. Major comebacks, he decided, were therefore possible. Perhaps the flight committee might also recover its luck? Buchan put down his note pad and was tuning the radio for the BBC news when the telephone rang on the hall table.

The call was from Mr. Shepherd who began by saying how he had enjoyed meeting Colonel Blacker, Etherton and the film director. Then Shepherd asked of news from the Chief Pilot? Buchan said that he'd heard nothing from Clydesdale. Nor would he leak any hint to the newshound how the Duchess of Hamilton had earwigged Lady Houston on the question of sponsorship.

Shepherd then wondered about Clydesdale's electorate. Why had the citizens of Renfrewshire decided that their MP should stay at home caring for their domestic affairs? Did Buchan have any views on that?

'It's all conjecture,' Buchan said. 'They'll reach an understanding. In any case, we won't find a better qualified man at this stage.'

'Perhaps McIntyre could become Chief Pilot?' Shepherd suggested. 'Or even the Air Commodore?'

'Since you plan on flying to India, you'll be the best judge of their abilities by the time you arrive.'

'I'm not questioning anyone's flight skills. I was wondering if perhaps McIntyre might fare better with sponsors?'

'Mr. Shepherd,' said Buchan wearily. 'It might suit the electorate of Renfrewshire to keep Clydesdale here, but the honor of making the first flight might then go to McIntyre. Or it could yet be a pilot from America, France or Germany. Frankly, I can't comment on any of your suppositions. I must go, Mr. Shepherd. I have deadlines to keep. Let's meet when I'm next in London.'

Shepherd left it at that, fearing perhaps that, if aggravated, Buchan might question his suitability as the official reporter.

Nevertheless Fleet Street might soon focus on the expedition's desperate need for funds. The Committee had forged ahead with planning and recruitment, but without the lifeblood of money. Only they knew that the entire project was hanging on a thread.

At his desk, Buchan switched off the radio. He returned to a paragraph in his article, describing how the blood of slaughtered clansmen had turned the river pools to scarlet while leaping salmon fled upstream. It must have been a terrible scene.

Then the telephone rang again. Buchan let it ring, hoping that his housekeeper might take it, but it continued trilling and he had to obey the damned thing. He pushed back his chair and returned to the hall.

'Buchan here.'

'John. So glad I found you.' It was a rather breathless Lord Peel. 'You'll never guess who just called me.'

'Do tell.'

'She's Garland Ross, the American girl who is the assistant to Lady Houston. She tried to get a message to Clydesdale via the Duchess, but had no luck, so she called me instead. Lady Houston wants to meet Clydesdale and McIntyre at Kinrara to talk about the flight.'

'Well now... that is promising,'

'I thought so too. I told Miss Ross I'd find Clydesdale and naturally I thought to try you first.'

'Glad you did. I believe he's been shooting pheasants over the weekend. If I do find him, I'll let you know.'

Buchan put down the phone. This was very good news. Why would Lady Houston bother to see the pilots otherwise?

Through the open study window the sound of bells drifted from the city. Oxford campanologists were at practice. It sounded to Buchan like a celebration as he picked up the telephone to set about finding Clydesdale.

23. Perthshire – September 1932

FOR YEARS THE PERTHSHIRE HIGHWAY authorities had paid scant attention to the single-lane road. Those who dared to take it through the Cairngorms were treated to forests bursting with pine, moody moorlands and rock gantries rising between lochans of rippling water. A strip of wild grass ran down the middle of the road, wide enough for Clydesdale's Alvis. Chips of flying stone spattered the flanks of the tourer as it sped along.

'We should have taken the main road.' Clydesdale said. 'This is a very debatable short-cut.'

Flight Lieutenant McIntyre sat in the passenger seat. With an ordinance survey map on his lap, he had been identifying landmarks in the glens along the way.

'Och man, for God's sake! Speed isn't the only joy in life. Where else can you see such a grand sight?'

'From over Everest, perhaps?'

The two men laughed. They were on their way to an encounter that would, in one way or another, seal any hopes of realizing that objective. As airmen, they could easily confront the aerial challenge but negotiating for the entire project with Lucy Houston might be a rare adventure.

'She asked us there for midday.' McIntyre checked his watch. 'We have an hour in hand. Time enough for a dram before we meet her?'

'No, Mac. We need clear heads for this. Later we can drown our sorrows or celebrate.'

McIntyre slid the map into the door pocket having memorized all significant features of the local topography. He estimated arrival at Kinrara in forty minutes. Like Clydesdale, his eyes frequently scanned the dashboard gauges with the ingrained habit of men who relied on machinery. 'Surely she wouldn't ask us to come all this way, just to say No?'

'She might. Lady Mercurial is quite capable of that.'

'Nevertheless the old trout is smart enough to know you're an MP, a future Duke, good with your fists and a Squadron-Leader. You also go to parties with her friend Churchill and, if we're to believe the press, you're the tenth most eligible bachelor in the nation.'

Clydesdale stared ahead, steering past the deeper holes.

'I think she might ask for your hand in marriage,' Mac added.

With a loud crunch a front wheel crashed into a pothole. The car lurched as Clydesdale braked and switched off the engine.

McIntyre pushed open his door. 'No need to over react. Maybe she'd like to be a Duchess, that's what I was thinking.'

Clydesdale got out to stare with extreme irritation at the punctured tyre. 'Just as well we have time in hand. You deal with the jack. I'll find the spare.'

For the two Reserve pilots from Glasgow's 602 Bomber Squadron a wheel change was simple. With a rawhide mallet, McIntyre soon tapped home the winged nut while Clydesdale hoisted the spent tyre to its housing. Then they cleaned their hands on roadside moss.

'Lucky there's no traffic.' Clydesdale regarded the track where sheep and highland cattle wandered at liberty. 'Not a soul here.'

'But take a peep up there.' McIntyre pointed to the dark silhouette of a falcon coursing through the sky above them. 'That's a peregrine! It says it all. Your man's spirit is up there watching out for us.'

'Peregrine Fellowes has many attributes but reincarnation is not among them,' Clydesdale said drily.

'Please yourself.' McIntyre watched the bird. 'I'd be quite happy to be a falcon. Look at it!'

The falcon closed its wings to slice down onto a covey of grouse fleeing for their lives above the heather. The raptor descended like a blue bullet and seized one grouse in an explosion of feathers. While survivors scattered, the peregrine looped up to land on a rock.

'That's how to hit a target.' McIntyre winked at his friend. 'Just remember I'm as keen as you are to fly over Everest. We must both get lucky and we'll be over the summit within the year.'

Clydesdale managed a smile. 'The lady awaits.'

With a growl from the Alvis that echoed through the glen, the two pilots resumed their journey to Kinrara.

105

24. Kinrara – September 1932

IN HER ROOM, GARLAND PUT on her tweed jacket and skirt. Her cream silk blouse, open at the neck, showed a hint of cleavage when she glanced in the mirror. Seamed stockings, purchased in Torquay, added pizzazz to her legs. She was putting on her shoes, when through the garret window, she saw the Packard arriving. She hurried down to meet Willie Graham who had just been collected from Glengarrig railway halt.

'Hello-o, Miss Ross.' The lawyer beamed as she opened the door. 'And how's life in the Highlands for Garland?'

'It's a change from Manhattan. Great when the sun comes out.'

'Such are the vagaries of mountain weather,' Mr. Graham stepped into the hall. 'And how's my client? Is Her Ladyship feeling any better?'

'Sadly not. In fact, she hasn't come down.' Garland closed the door behind Mr. Graham. 'She's feeling chesty and disgruntled. Affairs at Westminster are making her fret. She asks you to go to her bedroom, if you don't mind.'

'I serve my clients in boardrooms or bedrooms. It's all the same to me.' Willie Graham had gold-rimmed glasses, bright eyes and a stoop. Having advised Lady Houston for some years he was rarely surprised by her volatility. He left his hat and coat on a chair, following Garland up to the landing. A stag's head with Imperial antlers stared moodily from a wall mount. Close by, under a glass dome on a table, stood a stuffed wildcat held in a permanent snarl. The lawyer took a look. 'Pride and fury. Just like their owner.'

'Got it in one.' Garland laughed as she stopped at Lady Houston's door. 'I'll take the dog out for a stroll.'

After opening the kitchen door, the terrier vanished on rocket-fired legs into shrubs around a grassy circle. Here, according to Mrs. Munro, Lady Houston would place her bed in hot weather. Closer in spirit to the deer and wildcats, thought Garland. Mungo was hunting rabbits and red squirrels, so she sauntered to the yard with the game larder, garage and stables. John was cleaning the Packard. He stood up, wringing out the shammy. 'Lovely day, Miss Ross.'

Garland returned his smile. 'Out here it is.'

John flipped the leather around the headlamps. 'So she's in bed today. That's a shame when she's expecting company.'

'But you never know. They might get lucky. I reckon the flight would be a wonderful tonic. To divert her from other problems.'

'That may come in handy. I heard there's some trouble on the *Liberty*.'

'Trouble? That's the first I knew of it,' said Garland.

'A steam valve. But the engineers will attempt repairs.' Despite the isolation, John always knew more about Lady Houston's world than most. 'Any chance I can go to Aviemore? I've errands to run.'

'I imagine so. As long as I know how to find you.'

'Just snap your fingers. I'm there whenever you want me.'

Was that a teasing provocation in John's eyes? His body as he leaned across the car was fit and muscular. 'I never snap my fingers, John, not at you or anyone.'

John raised a finger and listened. 'But hear that, Miss? That's the sound of an Alvis. If Her Ladyship wants pilots, she clicks her fingers and here they come.'

The Alvis was coming up the drive and the terrier was leaping, snapping and barking at its wheels. If Mungo were to dive below them it would end all Everest plans. She hurried to intervene. 'John, I reckon you're free till 2.30. After that Mr. Graham may want a ride to the station.'

'Whatever you say, Miss.'

Garland succeeded in lifting Mungo from the ground as the pilots got out. Both wore tweed suits, polished shoes and Air Force ties. They looked the very picture of young hopefuls.

'Good morning, Lord Clydesdale.' Garland attempted to hold the wriggling dog in her arms. 'Sorry about that. I didn't want him to spoil your car.'

'Ah, and it's the same fellow who soaked our lunch-basket,' Clydesdale laughed. 'I think you've met Mac?'

Garland smiled. 'I hope you had a good journey?'

'Only one burst tyre, but that's to be expected.' McIntyre patted Mungo's head. 'Och, ever the wild beastie.'

Garland took the pilots to the study while the lawyer and Lady Houston remained busy. Garland felt enlivened by the breath of adventure with wide horizons that had arrived with the two visitors. 'May I offer you a drink? A dram perhaps?'

'Aye,' McIntyre glanced at Clydesdale. 'I can never refuse a lady. Thank you. A dram will do wonders for my nerves.'

25. Farnborough – September 1932

WITH A GRAND FLOURISH, THE technician cast open the doors to a spacious laboratory. The overhead neon lighting added a clinical austerity to the scene as the technician pointed to the only prominent feature in the room.

'And that, gentlemen, is the pressure chamber. Inside that steel bubble you can fly to forty thousand feet without leaving the lab.'

Fellowes was back once again at Farnborough. This time the cameraman Bonnett had joined him and together they studied the steel spheroid before them. It was over eight feet in diameter with portholes of thick glass around its polished circumference. A hatch provided an entrance to its interior.

'You'll find there's nothing to it,' the technician was saying. 'We shut you inside and count to thirty-five thousand.'

'Thirty-five thousand?' Bonnett's eyes grew as round as the sphere itself.

'We accelerate the process so there's no need to worry, Mr. Bonnett. Half an hour will be quite sufficient.'

This did little to convince the cameraman who had flown all over Africa and was now preparing for the Himalayas. 'I don't have a choice, do I?'

'It simulates the highest flight ceiling attainable by the Westlands,' Fellowes explained. 'We must all pass this little test, before they let us near the real thing.'

'It looks highly claustrophobic,' Bonnett said. 'Is it really necessary?'

'Only if you're planning on survival over Everest.'

The technician was eager to proceed. 'Once you're in the flying suit, we'll hook up the electrical and oxygen feeds and today we'll be testing the new lightweight Vibrac tanks.'

'New Vibracs?' grumbled Bonnett who remained far from happy.

'Again, no need to worry. The oxygen tastes just the same.'

'Thanks but no thanks. I'm a cameraman, not a guinea pig.'

'Claustrophobia is not my idea of fun,' Fellowes tried to agree. 'That's why I prefer open-cockpit machines.'

Tempted to make a wise-crack, the technician remembered he was dealing with a senior officer. 'Closed-cockpits are the future, sir. As will be the use of oxygen. So shall we don our flight suits?'

Bonnett whispered to the Air Commodore. 'I heard if the oxygen fails it only takes half a minute to lose consciousness? Is that true?'

'Just a guideline,' Fellowes replied. 'Some people can last for four minutes before passing out.'

'So we could end up as brainless guinea pigs!' concluded Bonnett. But his objections were only delaying the inevitable. Better to get it over. 'All right then, where's my bubble suit?'

The technician led them to a rack of flying suits. Sizing each man, he passed over a suit. 'Hop into this and then into the sphere. You can talk until the pressure falls off, then speech will be harder. If you drop a piece of paper, it will fall like a stone. And don't cut yourself by accident. Your blood will fly like crazy paint.'

Fellowes and Bonnett had heard enough. They hauled on their suits, adjusting zips and fasteners with help from assistants. Then bending low the two men slid through the sphere's hatch onto rudimentary seats. The technician leaned in to arrange linkages to the masks, meters and gauges.

'So off you go. I'll be watching through a porthole. If you get into trouble, tell me through the voice tube. After reaching the altitude, we'll pause for five minutes before bringing you down. That will at a gentle pace, mind you, to ensure you don't get the bends.'

The hatch closed and the bolts went home. All external sound suddenly vanished as the test flight to Everest got under way.

Bonnett familiarized himself with the tubes and dials connected to the world outside. Then he recalled how the Air Commodore had once dived into the barrage of gun fire protecting Zeebrugge's dam. 'The things one does for King and Country...'

'Very true,' agreed Fellowes. 'For King and Country, Mr. Bonnett. How right you are.'

26. Kinrara – September 1932

Lucy Houston shifted against the stacked pillows on her bed, becoming increasingly irritated as every minute passed. Her dark mood was focused upon the lawyer who sat beside the bed.

'Willie, you're a trusted friend. I've listened to your counsel and hear what you say. Indeed there may be others willing to help Clydesdale get over Everest, but do we want to hand that honor to the Irish, and to the Vickers aeroplane company? Do we Willie? No, we do not!'

Willie Graham had gone on at length about his obligation to provide his client with honest appraisals. Her support would involve a great sum of her money, with risk of possible ridicule in the world's media but his caution was giving her a headache.

'We can agree on that much,' the lawyer conceded.

'So that's that. Now be a dear, Willie, go and ask Garland to bring up Mungo and Lord Clydesdale. The Flight Lieutenant can stay with you in the study. You can mentions your concerns to him. Ask Mrs. Munro for anything you need. We'll talk later.'

Lucy Houston watched the lawyer depart, leaving the door ajar. Now she plucked a Hacibekir Turkish delight from a box on her bedside table. She popped the delicacy into her mouth as she listened to distant voices and movements. Once, when in Tangier with *Liberty*, she had seen traders sucking on sweetmeats while they considered their affairs. Subsequently she had adopted the habit and was reaching for a second delight when the Marquis of Clydesdale tapped on her door.

'In you come!' Lady Houston popped the cube into her mouth. 'Pull up that chair. I hope you don't mind if I stay in bed.'

'Absolutely not, Lady Houston.' Following Mungo into the room, Clydesdale advanced with nervous respect. He sat down shaking his head when she offered him the box of Hacibekir. 'I'd rather not, Lady Houston.'

'It's the rose and lemon variety.' Lady Houston licked the sugary dust from her fingers. 'A drink then? Something in your hand while we chat?'

'No, thank you. Your secretary just gave me some tea.'

'Very well.' Lady Houston chewed for a moment, absorbed in her thoughts.

'Garland's such a sweet girl. Did she tell you that I apologized for shouting at her when we were at the games?'

Clydesdale clasped his fingers together. He shook his head, indicating it was of no consequence.

'Some days I feel tired so my doctor says I should pace myself.'

'I'm sure you'll be fine.' Clydesdale stared at the terrier. He had heard that Mungo was the most treasured of all her belongings.

'Talking of doctors, will you be taking one with you?'

'On the expedition?' Clydesdale brightened. 'Oh that's a priority. Someone experienced in high-altitude medicine, tropical disease and so on. At this stage, we've settled on Dr. Bennett from the RAF.'

Lady Houston studied the young man. He was certainly good-looking and came with the endorsement of their mutual friend Winston Churchill. Nevertheless she was deeply concerned. 'I understand your team has been testing all the equipment?'

Clydesdale warmed to his task. 'Exhaustively. We've run tests on everything. Air Commodore Fellowes and our chief cameraman have done their high-altitude tests. Everything has been thoroughly developed by the best scientists in Britain.'

'It all sounds very wise but what about the aeroplanes? I know they're not the same as we used for the Schneider Trophy.'

'No. The Schneider machines were built for speed. Our Westlands are designed for robust operation at extreme altitude with large wings and broad propellers to catch the thin air.'

'And yet no parachutes?'

Clydesdale shook his head. 'We must reduce the payload in each Westland to an absolute minimum meaning parachutes will be discarded. One would be extraordinarily fortunate to land safely by parachute in the Himalayas.'

'I imagine so. All those crevasses and ice cliffs... And with no survival equipment and miles from human settlements. It all seems very dangerous, even to an old bedridden trollop like me.'

Clydesdale blinked and cleared his throat. 'In the unlikely event of engine failure, we can glide to emergency landings in the Terai grassland.'

'Assuming you have the right conditions.' Lady Houston said. 'I read that Westland's test pilot has already proved the glide ability. How many miles did he glide?'

'You are well informed, I must say. Penrose covered seventy miles with no power, justifying our decision to discard parachutes.'

'But it was the oil pump that failed. A broken shaft, wasn't it?'

'It happens, as do burst tires. We'll be using sturdier pumps.'

Lady Houston shifted her position, peering deep into the eyes of the young Marquis. 'What you tell me thrills me through and through. But I'm not going to help you commit suicide.'

'There's very little chance of that, Lady Houston. We've worked it all out most thoroughly.'

'Yes, so you say, but tell me. Isn't it all frightfully dangerous?'

'No more than walking over Hampstead Heath on a foggy night. Seriously, Lady Houston, Everest remains the highest mountain in the world. Surely it must be a risk worth taking?'

For seconds, a silence hung in the room. The windows were open wide allowing the Cairngorms breeze to enter at will. Lady Houston had to make up her mind, his last words ringing in her ears.

'It requires a lot of careful consideration, but it is the adventure which appeals to me.' She felt a sudden empathy with the anxious young man. 'Yes, I will help with your expedition.'

Clydesdale's face erupted in happiness. 'I'm so pleased to hear that.'

'How much is it you're after? Remind me.'

'We seek a sum of £100,000, Lady Houston. For that we can deliver success for all concerned.'

'£100,000?'

'Yes, Lady Houston.' Clydesdale confirmed. 'For the world's most famous mountain.'

'Very well then, I'll instruct Mr. Graham to make the necessary arrangements. I'll ask my friend Mr. Blumenfeld of the *Daily Express* to represent me on the Committee, assuming that suits you?'

'An excellent idea. No problem. I can't thank you enough, Lady Houston,' Clydesdale looked as though he could hardly believe the sponsorship had finally been granted.

'My friends call me Lucy,' said Lady Houston. 'Anyway, don't thank me. You can thank Garland for persuading me to upstage the idiot in Westminster. MacDonald's loss shall be your gain.'

Lady Houston tugged a shawl over her shoulders and reached for the telephone beside her bed. 'Yes, Garland. I've decided to help the Marquis with his flying expedition. See if we have a bottle of Mumm Cordon Rouge and bring five glasses. Ask Willie and the Flight Lieutenant to join us. And bring my check book with you.'

27. Mayfair Hotel – September 1932

THE SAXOPHONES AND TRUMPETS OF the Bert Ambrose Orchestra were blazing in the background when the expedition leader and his wife entered the lobby of the Mayfair Hotel. Fellowes wore a black tie and dinner suit while Eleanor swished along in a gown of olive silk, her hair scooped high and held by a tortoiseshell comb. Soon the ballroom rhythms were lost in the hubbub of the launch party.

Armed with dry martinis, the Fellowes mingled. They began with Sir John Salmond, Chief of the Air Staff, who was chatting with Sir Philip Sassoon and the Master of Sempill. Then they had a few words with Colonel Blacker and his wife Doris who had engaged with John Longley of Shell Aviation. In one corner they spied John Buchan with Percy Etherton and His Highness the Maharaja Jam Sahib of Nawanagar, resplendent in embroidered shirt and jacket. The Lords Lytton and Burnham, also Committee members, were exchanging welcomes with Ralph Blumenfeld, the latest to join their ranks.

Blumenfeld's presence surprised no one. His skill as a newsman would be beneficial, but his principal duty would involve stewardship over Lucy Houston's interests. No objection had been raised to his appointment.

Strolling among the guests, sampling canapés, chinking glasses and shaking hands, the Fellowes dallied with accountants from Deloittes who were trading City gossip with underwriters from Lloyds. Everything was going to plan they said, so the Fellowes moved on, briefly interrupting Colonel McCleod, locked in debate with the director Barkas about zoom lenses on Rolleiflex cameras. They managed a quick word with Arthur Hinks of the Royal Geographic Society as he pondered the origins of the Himalayas with Mr. Shepherd.

Finally the Fellowes met up with the two younger pilots. Clydesdale and McIntyre had attracted the avid attention of three young women whom Eleanor recognized as debutantes. In 1907 she herself had done the season, the expensive introduction of teenage girls to society and the Royal Court. Things hadn't changed so much in twenty-five years. Two bachelors, both pilots heading for Everest, were bound to appeal.

'Mrs. Fellowes is traveling out with us,' explained Clydesdale to his captivated audience.

McIntyre stepped forward. In his mess jacket, with his striking looks, he was a star. 'Good to meet you, Mrs. Fellowes. If you're in charge of chocolates, I'll be on my best behavior.'

Clydesdale brushed aside Mac's humor. 'Allow me to introduce Miss Kirkpatrick, Miss Astor and Miss Bourke-Taylor.'

'This is so-o exciting,' sighed one of the debutantes. 'Are you going all the way to India? With chocolates?'

'That's the idea,' Eleanor smiled. 'If they survive the heat.'

'We'll have to eat them first.' McIntyre gazed at the freckled shoulders of Miss Kirkpatrick. 'I adore chocolates.'

A blonde girl, a stunning vision in black chiffon, burst into life. 'I'd simply love to be coming. In fact, daddy's one of your sponsors.'

'And who might that be?' Eleanor asked.

'*The Times*,' said Clydesdale. 'The Astors have taken the exclusive story rights.'

Eleanor understood. 'It will be a great story.'

Percy Etherton had stepped onto a dais and was calling for attention. The conversation faltered and faded as the assembly turned to face him. He raised his voice.

'My Lords, Ladies and Gentlemen. On behalf of the Mount Everest Flight Committee, may I thank you all for coming tonight. We are honored by your support for the great venture ahead. But before I introduce our expedition leader, Air Commodore Peregrine Fellowes, I must first ask you to raise your glasses to our magnificent patron who, for reasons of ill health, is unable to attend tonight. Allow me to propose a toast to a great lady whose bold and formidable vision has made our endeavor possible. I give you the toast! To Lady Houston. To Lucy!'

A hundred glasses lifted with a chorus. 'Lucy.'

'Without Lucy Houston,' Etherton added. 'We would not be here preparing for the expedition which begins here in Mayfair and ends at the top of the world. Now for details, let's hear from Air Commodore Fellowes.'

To continuing applause, Fellowes took over. Eleanor stayed with the two pilots and their admirers, pride stirring inside her as her husband began with some personal comments.

'I've enjoyed all measures of fortune during my career but the opportunity to lead this unique expedition to the Himalayas is the most unusual of all.

'Percy Etherton has rightly paid tribute to our patron, but he too has performed considerable feats of organization. And none of this would have transpired without the inspiration of Colonel Blacker, so it is to him, a toast is in order. I give you, 'Colonel Blacker.'

Up went the glasses again. 'Colonel Blacker.'

Fellowes was by nature softly-spoken so he raised his voice for the attentive audience. 'The timing of the flight depends entirely on the weather. We must reach India before the summer monsoon in May next year. If we miss that deadline, there can be no attempts until later in the year. During the monsoon all flight in the Himalayas is impossible.

'You will have read that Chief Pilot, Squadron-leader the Marquis of Clydesdale and Second pilot, Flight Lieutenant McIntyre will command the two Westlands. Both are experienced pilots from the Royal Air Force Reserve. So a toast to the Royal Air Force, if you please.'

Those guests holding drinks were unable to clap but glasses were raised again. 'Hear, hear!'

'And much of our progress can be attributed to the talents of John Buchan whose renowned imagination has given The Royal Geographic Society, *The Times* and Gaumont-British an opportunity to relay our story to the world at large. A toast to them all!'

'Hear, hear!' The audience loved all these big names.

Fellowes continued with more tributes. 'We have benefited from the advice of many engineers in aviation, medical and meteorological areas but also the photographic experts and others in the technical and diplomatic fields have been very generous with their help. Not least, I must mention our many Indian friends who have most gallantly offered to host our band of brothers.'

Glasses were raised. 'Hear, Hear!'

Eleanor noticed the applause for their Indian hosts was led by Colonel Blacker who stood like a steel pillar in his mess jacket. She had also caught Miss Astor's delight at the mention of her father's newspaper. Few of the audience noticed that no mention of Nepal was made in this context. To many, Nepal and India were indistinguishable and only core Committee members knew that the Nepalese had yet to issue the crucial permits. Silence returned allowing Fellowes to continue.

'Our objectives are varied. New systems of life support, stronger engines and better aircraft will add to mankind's tireless energies in the sky. Our photographic results will help climbers towards the most daunting peaks. They may even provide some clues to the mystery of Irvine and Mallory for whom Everest proved to be a fatal attraction.'

The mention of the climbing mystery brought a murmur from the assembly. All had often wondered about the climbers' final moments.

'During this winter, the Westlands will undergo final testing. Then, armed with Lady Houston's bounteous generosity, the Houston-Mount Everest Flight Expedition will set out to pay our respects to the greatest mountain in the world! Now if you please, charge your glasses and make your way to the Ballroom where dinner will be served to the magic of Bert Ambrose and his Orchestra.'

The distant music seemed to swell as the audience excitedly gathered themselves and prepared for dinner.

28. Kinrara, Perthshire – September 1932

WHILE THE MAYFAIR HOTEL REVERBERATED to the dynamic hopes of British society, Garland Ross sat alone in a wicker chair on the lawn at Kinrara.

The approach of evening on the Cairgorms made her wonder if she was so lucky to be admiring the beauty of the Highlands? She hankered for some of Mayfair's fun tonight.

Was it a blessing to work night and day as secretary to a national icon? Sure, the job had its moments. She was in daily contact with notable individuals, but to them she was little more than a telephone operator, a part-time maid, dog-walker and note taker to Her Ladyship.

Garland twiddled with the ends of her hair, gazing at the dark silhouette of the mountain crests. She was only four months into the job and already she was missing the buzz of Manhattan with its endless car horns amid the cries of street-hawkers and newsmen.

It was, she decided, her Cinderella moment..

Lady Houston had retired to bed, advising her staff she could manage without them. Mrs. Munro the housekeeper had gone to the village with John, leaving Garland to cover unscheduled requirements. Meanwhile, far to the south, at the Mayfair Hotel, Lucy's latest enterprise was being launched on the world's stage.

Garland felt that the Flight Expedition was proceeding thanks in part to her input. She had made the suggestion on how to belittle MacDonald, to fly the flag for Britain, and Clydesdale had made his pitch, pushing on a door unlocked by her.

Only three days previously, the pilots had drunk champagne before disappearing in their Alvis to London. Now within months they'd be heading for India. She would have enjoyed that part too.

Fairness, Garland knew, was no automatic part of life. Her experience in reporting human drama had taught her that much and since there seemed no way out, she had to get on with it. Her contract curtailed her natural desire to write and record the adventure. One day, she felt, Lady Houston might be persuaded to relent and allow her to write a biography.

Garland checked her watch. It was time to feed Mungo before his final run. After that he would go to his basket in the corner of Lady Houston's bedroom, inured to the sounds of Her Ladyship's grumbling and swearing in her sleep.

Garland rose and sauntered to the lodge kitchen. Here she prepared a bowl of Milk-bone biscuits. These came from Harrods where Lady Houston's orders had priority status and were despatched by train to the Highlands. Garland was surprised to see no sign of the terrier. Normally he'd be on the floor by now, fixing her with a concentrated stare.

But tonight there was no dog and as she set the bowl on the scullery floor, the electric bell rang. Garland went upstairs, passing the imperious stag and the stuffed wildcat, to the bedroom.

'You called, Lady Houston?'

'Where's Mungo?' Lady Houston was reading a magazine and wearing a thunderous glare. 'Mungo should be here by now.'

Garland produced a comforting smile. 'He must be outside, chasing coneys. I'll go find him.'

Garland returned downstairs. She hadn't actually seen the dog for a while. She must locate the little devil, the commander of Lady Houston's soul.

Taking the biscuit bowl whose rattle generally brought the terrier from the thickest cover, Garland was startled to meet John standing in the yard. At his feet stood Mungo, eyes bright and tail twitching as usual. 'Oh John! You gave me a shock! I never heard you come back.'

'When I got to the village I found Mungo in the back of the car. So I had a quick drink and brought him straight home.'

Garland put her hands on John's firm shoulders and kissed his cheek. 'Thank you, John! For a moment, I thought we'd lost him.'

She looked at Mungo. 'You're a rascal. You cause all sorts of problems. No more rides in the car without telling me first!'

Garland also saw John's startled look. She could feel her body touching his. 'Please excuse me, John, I don't know what came over me.'

'Gratitude perhaps?"

'Yep. I was real worried.'

'Never you mind, Miss.' John's eyes flickered. 'I quite like a kiss.'

She noticed his shirt, open at the throat, as she bent down to pick up the dog. Then for a moment she thought of Lady Chatterley and the gamekeeper Mellors as she hurried upstairs with Mungo.

29. Somerset – October 1932

DURING THE AUTUMN, BOTH WESTLAND and Bristol aviation companies pursued vigorous programs to prepare the two RAF biplanes for their venture. After trials, approval and certification, it was then time to dismantle them for a long sea voyage to Karachi.

To minimize any risk of hitches, the fitters and engineers had carefully assigned components to respective containers. The Westland (G-ACAZ), was known informally as *Lucy* to her engineers. Another wag, possibly McIntyre, provided the moniker of *Akbar* for his biplane, the Westland Wallace (G-ACBR).

Chief engineer Cyril Pitt now stood with his workmates beside these dismembered machines. The huge single-blade propellers lay on the workshop floor. Fuel tanks had been rinsed to neutralize petroleum vapors. The nine cylinder stacks were wadded with waxed paper. Magnetos and electrical units had been fastidiously wrapped in sealant to counter salt corrosion. As far as Pitt was concerned, the lads had completed the task. 'All this palaver,' he said. 'It would have been so much easier to fly them to India.'

Burnard's team of Westland fitters, mostly Yeovil men, had unbolted the wings, fins and stabilizers to partner the fuselage in each wooden crate. Later, carpenters would secure the containers and painters would spray 'WESTLAND AIRCRAFT' in bold lettering on each load. The machines lay like swaddled mummies. It was hard to imagine all this would soon be in hostile skies over Nepal, but the job was finished so they headed to the canteen.

Throughout these activities, three officers from HM Customs and Excise had been on hand to verify items on the manifest. These officers were installed at a table, while the engineers joined a line for the tea counter.

'Strange how they stick together,' Burnard observed in a tone steeped in cheddar and cider, slow and easy.

Pitt glanced at the Customs men. 'They remind me of vultures. Always searching for something to feed on.'

Burnard took his tea from the tea lady who knew just how he liked it, milk and three sugars. 'What makes you an expert on vultures, Mr. Clever Dick, especially since you've never been to India?'

Pitt knew he was being provoked for the amusement of the workforce. 'I have, in fact, studied a variety of vultures. I went to the Bristol Zoo to learn about the wildlife of India. I saw a leopard, a pregnant elephant and a few snakes.' Pitt took his tea, no sugar no milk, and followed Burnard to a table.

'So you went to the zoo?' Burnard winked at his workmates. 'They should have kept him in as an exhibit, shouldn't they lads? You learn anything about tigers?'

'That they are known to eat people.'

'I don't see why you're so interested.' Burnard said. 'We're not going to India to hunt big cats. We're there to keep our kit airworthy. No time to tease tigers.'

Pitt rolled his eyes. 'I know that! But if we're surrounded by jungle beasts, I need to understand them. And there's another reason,' he added quietly as he sipped his tea.

'Such as?'

'I'm not free to say.'

Pitt could goad workmates with a rainbow of words but also with a wall of silence. Other workmates had joined them, eight in all, sat around the scrubbed wooden table.

'Go on, Mr. Pitt. Tell us,' urged one apprentice. 'Are you training to be a snake-charmer?'

'Not bloody likely, son! I wouldn't sit cross-legged showing my flute to a cobra even if he was nailed in his basket. They can spit in your eye before you play a single note.'

'Who told you that?'

'Mr. Barkas, the film chappie. He's been to India.'

'This other reason?' Burnard persisted. 'We're still waiting.'

'I'm not at liberty to say.'

'What's that supposed to mean? I bet Customs officers wouldn't take that for an answer.'

Pitt looked around, pretending he hadn't heard. The men were eating sandwiches and biscuits from their lunch packs. The Customs officers were chatting, oblivious to the resident workforce.

'That's because they're not asking silly questions.' Pitt opened his lunch box and took out a Mars bar. He peeled the wrapping with finesse as Burnard and his men watched suspiciously.

'What's that you're stuffing in your face?' Burnard asked.

'This time I do have an answer, since you asked so nicely.' Pitt bit off a chunk and held up a cross section of the bar for all to see. 'I don't know where you've been all year, but in Bristol we like to keep up with the times. This is one of the first Mars bars to reach my local shop. I'm in the business of innovation and development, so I had to try.'

Pitt took out his penknife. Unwrapping the bar, he chopped it into equal pieces. 'Since we're destined to be shipmates, Burnard, I'm willing to share this source of eternal energy with you.'

Pitt ceremoniously offered a portion to each man who took a piece and chewed reflectively. Burnard however waved his finger at Pitt. 'Not till I know about this secret. This other reason you went to the zoo?'

Pitt smiled. 'I'll tell you when we reach India.'

'I like this Mars,' reported one of the fitters. 'Got anymore?'

Pitt tossed another morsel of Mars over the table. He assessed the final chunk and carefully bit off a piece. 'There's a bit left for you, Burnard. You won't mind if it has my teeth marks on it?'

30. Stamford Lincs – November 1932

REPAIRS TO *LIBERTY* HAD REQUIRED the expertise of Clyde shipbuilders at Greenock. Lady Houston had therefore not sailed south as intended. Nor was she too pleased about the cost of the overhaul. With amber tints spreading across the Spey valley she knew that winter would be cozier at her home in Hampstead.

Lady Houston and Garland left Kinrara on a misty November morning. John drove with the terrier beside him. Lady Houston and Garland sat in the rear of the Packard as it followed the A1 south with occasional stops for fuel and refreshments along the way.

It would be a long journey, but Packard's de luxe Eight had been designed for that purpose and Garland was happy to be on the move. She saw how the wilder country and farmland gave way to areas of denser population across the border and the industrial spine of the nation. To Garland the land seemed threatened by winter, and she was keen to see fresh sights and return to a city. Meanwhile Lady Houston was burrowing through the newspapers, sharing opinions with Garland when she found a topic of interest.

In *The Times*, Lady Houston read that Mr. Shepherd would be traveling to India as official correspondent for the expedition. 'That's all very well, I suppose,' she said. 'But they should have asked me first.'

Garland leaned over to scan the piece. The soft fur of Lady Houston's sable coat brushed her cheek and the favored scent, Chanel 5, competed with traces of naphthalene. Maybe because of this distinct aroma, Mungo preferred to ride up front.

'They did try to reach you,' Garland said. 'But you were unwell.'

'Blimey!' barked Lady Houston. 'At my age, feeling unwell is a regular event. You'll find out when it's your turn, Garland. All I'm saying is they should have asked me first.'

'Well. The expedition will be leaving soon and that will make you feel so much younger.'

'Bad manners, I call it.'

Garland looked ahead at the straight lengths of road linking Scotland to London. John was not wearing his cap and she could see his face reflected in the windscreen mirror. As their glances crossed, he gave her a wink.

'What's so funny?' Lady Houston asked, seeing Garland's smile. 'I pay for an expedition and *The Times* gets all the glory. I'd have much preferred the *Daily Express* to have taken the rights, with my good friend Ralph.'

'Sure, that would have been better.'

'But as you know, Garland, those wretched Astors refuse to publish my opinions, despite all I've done for the Air Force! It's no laughing matter.'

'No, I realize that too,' said Garland quickly.

'And so you should.' The papers rustled as Lady Houston moved on to another piece. 'Look here. It says that an Indian has just made the first flight between Karachi and Bombay. Jehangir Ratanji Dadabhoy Tata. What a name! Now he's starting an airline. See how he makes the headlines without having to sell his rights to any paper.'

'When your crews fly over Everest, *The Times* will give you column inches by the yard. Bound to.'

'My point is that India is slowly prizing itself from the governance of our King and Parliament and it's all down to that little gnome Gandhi, stirring up the Indian people after all we've done for them. I'm not happy.'

'I'm sorry about that,' said Garland.

'Sorry you should be! Being American, you may not appreciate how much the British Empire has contributed to the world. It's a shame the Indians don't.'

Lady Houston lowered the newspaper. She pressed her finger on a button in the armrest, lowering the dividing pane of glass between front and rear compartments in the car. 'Where are we now, John?'

'Five miles from Stamford, milady.'

'And you did make reservations, Garland?'

'Of course. As you requested.'

'So John, we'll overnight at The George. I've had enough of this bloody road for one day.'

'Very good, milady.'

The glass divider stayed down and the Packard pushed on over the flat landscape of Lincolnshire. Lady Houston seemed happier, knowing she'd soon be inside her favorite coaching inn. Having abandoned the newspapers, she turned to Garland with a sly look.

'Now tell me, my dear. That book I lent you? Lady Chatterley's Lover. I keep meaning to ask how you enjoyed it?'

Garland had been expecting this. She had read the book several times. One evening, alone in her upstairs garret, she had lain in bed, devouring every word, relishing with vicarious energy every thrill that Lady Chatterley had experienced in the game-keeper's shed. On subsequent nights, Garland had often gone to sleep with the image in her mind of a brown blanket and two naked lovers.

Lady Houston prodded Garland's elbow. 'I hoped you might find it stimulating.'

'I haven't finished it yet.'

Lady Houston's eyes narrowed. 'I lend you a book, and this is how you thank me? You're as ungrateful as *The Times* when I hand them an expedition.'

'It's not that simple, Lady Houston. You know I've been busy.'

The heiress ignored her and shouted. 'John, do you remember that book I lent you back in the spring?'

'The one about the gamekeeper?' John called over his shoulder. 'course I do. Hotter than Coleman's mustard. I liked it.'

'So you agree that Garland should also like it?'

'Who doesn't like a cracking love story?' John called back.

Lady Houston giggled girlishly. She placed her finger on a privacy button, holding it until the dividing glass had risen. 'You see, Garland. John says it's a cracking story.'

'Why, My Lady, is it important to you that I read this book?'

'Why? That's obvious. You call yourself a writer. You should appreciate a finely crafted story.'

'If it's so wonderful, why is it banned?'

'They've censored it, Garland, because of its explicit nature, as you must have noted. MacDonald's government fear that a wide distribution would influence the public. If Lady Chatterley can be emancipated, with all her sexy pranks under a pheasant-keeper, how might that influence the women of Britain? It could release a flood of wanton hussies, turning loyal housewives to all manner of sexual abandonment. All searching for self-fulfillment and then it might destroy the current situation, in which men behave exactly how they like.'

'Wanton hussies?' Garland raised an eyebrow. 'I don't know about that.'

'For a young woman in the prime of life, it would be very odd not to feel lustful, wouldn't it? I was a shameless and very wanton girl in my time. Men

125

always fell for that, I learned. Far more fun to be sinful than sinless, and all because the female of the species is more deadly than the male.'

From roadside signposts, Garland could see Stamford was approaching. She thought of telling Lady Houston that she had never wanted to be a writer of saucy fiction.

'Well, I'll try to finish the book, since it's so important to you,' she said. 'But what I'd really love to do is to write the story of your life, Lady Houston, your biography.'

Lady Houston stared over John's shoulder. She took some time and then smiled. 'You're a remarkable young woman, Garland. You're sharp, reliable and attractive. You're bold, funny and enlightened. If I'd ever given birth to a daughter, I'd have wished for one like you.'

Garland felt as if the air had been knocked out of her. She turned to look Lady Houston in the eye. 'That's real kind of you.'

Lady Houston gave an endearing smile. 'But if I was your mother, Garland, I'd be concerned how, having reached thirty with all your qualities, you have yet to find a decent mate. Believe me, Garland, a woman of your age needs a man to fulfil her needs.'

Garland turned to the outside view again as the Packard cruised into the outskirts of Stamford. It was a pretty town with stone houses on empty streets. There was hardly a soul in sight.

'I'll bear all that in mind, milady. Thank you.'

'And we'll be in London all winter, my dear. There'll be another opportunity for us to discuss that idea of your's. It needs some consideration.'

'I understand. But I have one more question, Lady Houston.'

'Yes?'

'Where did you get the book from?'

'I got it from an Italian, from where the book was published.' Lady Houston giggled. 'In fact, you know him quite well. He's Marco, my radio officer. Such a wonderful young man.'

The Packard had come to a halt outside The George where John hopped out to help them, Garland tried to hide her embarrassment but Lady Houston continued laughing as she stepped out.

'Now, Garland. Take Mungo for a stroll. He hates long distance driving as much as I do. I'm going to dine in my room, so you two can make your own arrangements. Perhaps you should compare notes on D.H. Lawrence?'

31. Lincoln Sands – November 1932

THE WORK OF D.H. LAWRENCE was never discussed over dinner, which was just fine with Garland. By the time she returned from the darkened streets of Grantham, John had taken the Packard for re-fueling. When she returned Mungo to Lady Houston, new orders were issued. Garland was to be ready at 7 a.m. next morning when they would be leaving for Skegness.

Garland had no idea where this was. The name sounded dubious and the departure hour was most unusual. After having a cottage pie in the hotel's bar, Garland went to bed, wondering what Lucy knew about Marco and how long had she been savoring any secret of their activities. Garland went to sleep before finding an answer and was woken at 6 a.m. by one of the staff knocking on her door.

As ordered, the Packard was ready at 7 a.m. and ten minutes later, after Mungo's first stroll of the day, they set off, heading east towards the dawning skies over Lincolnshire. Skegness according to John was nothing to get excited about. Just a long swathe of sand with a few houses perched on the shore.

Garland sat with Lady Houston who was again busy scanning the newspapers. Not a word passed as the Packard maintained a fair speed over the fen panoramas near the Wash. The newspapers rustled. John drove and Mungo went back to sleep. Just another day in Lucy's fast lane, thought Garland, as she too nodded off.

She woke to feel Lady Houston pushing at her shoulder. 'You can't sleep now, my dear. I want to show you something I really love.'

Garland sat up. The Packard slowed to turn onto a long beach of sand glistening beneath the ripples of a retreating tide. A string of eight horses were gathered on the beach, all fretting and tossing their heads as their nostrils hooked the breeze coming off the North Sea. A man sat on a motorcycle nearby. They had been waiting for Lady Houston's arrival and the man waved as the Packard stopped beside him.

'Now you see why I had to leave early,' Lady Houston said to Garland. 'These are my darlings and I adore to see them at work.'

Garland had seen photographs on *Liberty* and at *Kinrara* of race horses in the winner's enclosure, but she had never met them face to face. She saw the motorcyclist dismount. He placed a short plank of wood below the stand to prevent it sinking and then turned. It was Donal Ryan the trainer. He was coming to meet them.

Lady Houston was out of the car before John reached her door. Garland quickly followed onto the damp sand.

'Leave Mungo inside,' said Lady Houston. 'He cannot beat race horses, and believe me, Garland, these young fillies and colts can really gallop.'

Ryan kissed Lucy Houston on her cheeks, shook hands with John, and then turned to Garland. Below a flat cap, his blonde hair curled into the collar of his leather jacket. His eyes smiled as he took her hand. 'So we meet again.'

He held her hand as Garland returned the smile. Handsome men she now realized were never far from Lady Houston. 'Seems a long time since the Savoy,' she said.

'Well yes, I suppose. Anyway, you're here for the morning run.'

Lady Houston wanted a report on each horse. Garland noticed the jockeys wore water-proofed jackets over breeches and boots. They lifted whip hands in salute as Ryan and Lady Houston came to each horse.

'This is Silver Belle,' said Ryan. 'She'll be going well for Goodwood next year. A lovely filly, she is.'

Garland reached out and felt the warm breath from the flaring nostrils. She sensed the energy in the filly's chest, the limbs straining to unfold. At that moment, she felt just like that herself.

The inspection was brief because race horses did not stand easily when a mile of firm sand lay before them. Ryan pulled down his cap and went to his motorcycle.

'Now you'll see what thrills me.' Lady Houston took some binoculars from John. 'These darlings can do forty miles an hour in just a few seconds.'

Garland had once ridden on a Harley Davidson in Chicago. 'Any chance I can ride with him? I love motor bikes.'

Lady Houston was surprised. 'Have you got room for Garland on the bike, Ryan?'

The trainer seemed uncertain, but then nodded. 'Why not? But you'll get wet and you'll have to hang on tight.'

Garland swung her leg over the pillion, tucking down behind Ryan as he kicked the engine into life. With a deep grumble from its single cylinder, the Enfield surged forward as she wrapped her arms around Ryan. The horses began with a controlled canter and then, with a signal from Ryan, burst into a full gallop. In a blur of action, Garland saw hooves and haunches pulsing and pushing at the sand. The engine roared as Garland glanced behind. Beside the Packard she saw Lady Houston and John and wondered just what they would be saying.

The horses held in a loose group, maintaining a gallop for over a minute. Then Garland saw Ryan raise his hand and point forward. Whips rose to fall on shining flanks as each mount accelerated for a final push, racing against each other. Silver Belle took the lead, her grey legs slashing through the Skegness strand. Garland gripped Ryan's jacket until with a beep from his horn, he signaled his jockeys to pull up and regroup. However he did not stop as Garland anticipated, but increased the revs for a higher speed. The waves flashed by and flocks of seagulls and sand-pipers rose ahead of them. Finally Ryan slowed and halted.

'Enjoyed that?' he called over his shoulder. 'We made sixty five.'

'You bet,' Garland was breathless.

'You must try riding a race horse some time. You'll find that's even better.'

Garland was still holding on tightly. She was about to lift her arms from his chest.

'No,' said Ryan, turning the bike around. 'We're not finished. Now they go back through the waves. Lady Houston calls it their bubble-bath. She says salt is good for their health.'

'Then it must be. She's always right.'

Ryan did not reply. The Enfield was now back alongside the horses who skipped through the ripples of the receding tide. Then the return run began. Each horse created arches of spray with seawater soaking their flanks. Then with another blast from Ryan's horn the stringed pull up to regroup near the Packard.

Ryan stopped the bike and Garland dismounted. He settled the bike on its stand and reported to Lady Houston. 'A good run that was.'

'Very impressive.' Lady Houston was satisfied. 'So when I need to have a filly trained I know where to come, don't I just? You need dry slacks, Garland. You'll have to change in the car.'

'It was such fun,' said Garland. 'I'm sorry.'

'No need to apologize, Garland. I'm just jealous. I can't ride bikes or fly to India. I've no choice but to settle for my *Liberty*, my two cars and of course, my Silver Belle. You've done well, Donal. Thank you so much. I'll be in touch.'

Lady Houston would not stand in the chilling breeze any longer. She waved to all the jockeys as John opened the car door.

Garland turned to Ryan before she too hurried to the Packard. 'She must get down to London. I loved that ride. And I still hope we meet at Mulligans one day.'

'Mulligans?' Ryan looked puzzled. 'Oh yes, I remember now.'

32. Heston Aerodrome – 16th February 1933

IN FEBRUARY 1933 THE HARDY residents of London were taking winter on the chin. A dismal cloud cover hung over the city where stark hedgerows and naked trees stood in bleak disarray while smoke from thousands of chimneys loitered in the sky.

Eleanor Fellowes observed this grey mantle from a car on the Great West Road and understood why birds migrated south. She felt much better knowing she was about to follow them.

Half an hour earlier the driver of a staff car had picked them up at the RAF club where they had spent the night. Despite intentions to get to sleep early, the couple had talked till midnight. Eleanor appreciated that her husband's first task as commander was to safely deliver three small aircraft and seven travelers to India.

It would involve a journey of 6000 miles, much of it over inhospitable terrain where anything might happen. Routine RAF operations had never daunted Perry, she thought, but now both of them would be in the media spotlight. Any development, success or failure would be reported and the expedition leader would take the trophy or carry the can.

Eleanor was prepared for both eventualities. Contemplating the layered smog above the suburbs, she wondered if she was being selfish to abandon friends and family. For them it would be coal scuttles and hot water bottles while she headed to the sun. Surely she was the only woman alive poised for adventures all the way to the Himalayas? No, not selfish, she decided, but incredibly lucky. She had rolled up her hair ready for her fur-lined helmet. She wore a no-nonsense trouser suit and her canvas flight suit was in the boot of the car.

Perry had been studying the wasteland on either side of the road. In fact, he was making notes. 'We're only ten miles from Piccadilly so I suppose it makes sense.'

'What makes sense?' she asked.

'The government is considering this area for London's new airport. I think it's to be called Heathrow.'

'So they'll cover all this with concrete,' she said. 'I prefer to be flying off a grass field. Much nicer.' She felt for his hand and squeezed it. 'We're going to have a wonderful time.'

'So shall we drop in to Paris for starters?' he asked. 'We'll find a good restaurant. Will it be moules or oysters for you?'

'Not fussy. It will be 'magnifique' either way.'

The RAF car arrived at Heston's strip of heathland where, near some hangars, many spectators were crowding around three biplanes parked side by side on the grass.

The smallest of these, a De Havilland Gypsy Moth III, had been flown down by Clydesdale from Scotland after Christmas. As it could only carry one pilot, its mechanic Hughes had come by train. This machine was assigned to McIntyre for the flight.

Alongside stood the larger Fox Moth to be flown by Clydesdale. Inside its cramped fuselage, Hughes and Shepherd would travel with baggage, spares and assorted paraphernalia tucked between their legs. Clydesdale's seat was positioned unusually above and behind his passengers. The Fox, said Clydesdale, was like pushing a barrow on flat tires.

The third aircraft, Fry's Puss Moth, was distinctive in creamy paint with a chocolate livery stripe. Its configuration put the pilot in front of the passenger and the cabin had protection against the elements due to plexiglass windows. With lockers stuffed to capacity there was only enough space for the overnight bags.

Eleanor carried only her large handbag, her home from home. It was awash with travel accessories. As they thanked their driver, Mr. Shepherd came from the crowd, very keen to see them.

'Good morning, Air Commodore and Mrs. Fellowes. At last we're all here.' The correspondent did not look ready for a major journey. He wore a black overcoat, polished shoes, dark suit and tie.

'Your kit, Mr. Shepherd?' Fellowes enquired cautiously. 'You can't go all the way to India wearing a city suit, can you?'

'Good lord no. I'll change into flight gear before take-off but I'm on business now. To report the send-off.'

'And today it will be chilly up there,' added Fellowes. 'Just warning you.'

'Thank you, sir,' Mr. Shepherd gestured towards McIntyre who was posing for photographers by the Gypsy Moth. 'At least Mac looks the part, all togged up in his snappy gear and thick boots. The photographers love it. And you, Mrs. Fellowes, are you still determined to avoid the cameras?'

Eleanor had a special weapon for such folk, a disarming stare to reinforce her resolution. She deployed it now. 'I've told you, I'm a supernumerary. What can you write about somebody like that?'

Shepherd thought for a moment. 'Very well. I capitulate.'

'Mr. Shepherd, we must get airborne,' Fellowes decided. 'Cloud's thicker than gravy and we don't have all day to find the thin bits up there.'

He guided the correspondent away leaving Eleanor to merge into the crowd, broadly unnoticed, just as she intended. She was surprised that so many people had come to wave them off on this gruesome winter morning. Beyond she could see Hughes, the mechanic, poking around each Moth checking hinges, flanges, flaps, cowlings, wires and braces with fastidious attention. Furthermore she knew the poor man had great fear of flying. She had to admire his dedication this morning.

Shepherd was now presenting the pilots to the photographers. While Eleanor stood in the crowd, watching Perry pose alongside McIntyre and Clydesdale she heard a voice at her shoulder. 'Excuse me, but you are Mrs. Fellowes?'

'Do we know each other?' Eleanor did not recognize the elderly lady with a tartan shawl over her shoulders.

'I'm Douglas Clydesdale's mother,' came the whisper.

'Your Grace!' Eleanor's gloved hand leaped from beneath her shawl as she inclined her head to the Duchess of Hamilton. 'You found me in the nick of time. We're about to leave for Paris.'

'Lucky you! I'd adore to be flying today. I saw you with the Air Commodore, so I put two and two together.'

'I'm so pleased,' said Eleanor, 'that he persuaded his constituents to let him go.'

'Just puff and nonsense,' whispered the Duchess. 'Mind you, Lucy Houston told me she'd have withdrawn her support, if the people of Renfrewshire had bayed any louder.'

'And if your son had not persuaded Lady Houston... well, nobody would be here today.'

The Duchess looked heartened. 'Now I wonder if you could help me. I'm also here for another duty. Douglas left this behind. It's his little mascot.' The Duchess opened a brown paper bag in her hand. 'Yes, that's his Saint Christopher. He's had it since he was six. Would you give it to him, Mrs Fellowes?

We've said our goodbyes, but I forgot to hand it over and I can't bother him now.'

Eleanor took the packet and put it in her bag. 'Don't worry, Your Grace. I'll make sure he gets it.'

Yet another spectator came to join them. Extending his hand, he lifted his fedora. 'Good morning, Your Grace. Good morning, Mrs. Fellowes.'

'Do I know you?' said the Duchess politely.

'Ralph Blumenfeld, Your Grace. I represent Lady Houston on the Committee. I'm here as her witness for the great departure.'

'So pleased you came,' beamed the Duchess. 'I recall Lucy saying you might come. Such a pity she isn't here.'

'Cold mornings in February don't suit Lucy. She'll have to read about it in tomorrow's *Express*.'

Eleanor remembered meeting the editor at the Mayfair Hotel. 'I thought it was only *The Times* who were covering the story?'

Blumenfeld shrugged. 'Yes, but they can't have it all to themselves, Mrs. Fellowes. Besides Lady Houston holds rather strong views about the Astors, so feel free to tell me how things are going, anytime you are inspired.'

Eleanor had never once submitted reports to any newspaper. 'I'll try to remember that, Mr. Blumenfeld.'

Now her husband was at a public address microphone. The crowd's chatter faded as his address cut through the morning air.

'My lords, ladies and gentlemen, on behalf of the flying party, we are delighted to see you here today. We'll be flying out to India in these sprightly Moths, having sent the two Everest machines out on the P&O *Dalgoma* to Karachi. Meanwhile others in our crew will head for India independently. I ask for three cheers for all our sponsors and supporters and most of all, to the inspired generosity of Lady Houston. Without her undying love of all things British, none of this is possible. For Lucy Houston, Hip. Hip!'

'Hooraay!' yelled every soul in sight.

'Hip, hip!' shouted Clydesdale.

'Hooraaay!'

The sound of each cheer had the effect of clearing the sky. A finger of sunlight now poked through the mist as the British roared. Eleanor knew this was the moment to get airborne. After reiterating her promise to keep an eye on the Chief Pilot and all his men, Eleanor left the Duchess with Mr.

Blumenfeld and went to put on her flying suit and boots. The three pilots were agreeing final plans, because none of the Moths carried radios. At the Puss Moth she climbed into the rear seat. Shoving her handbag down between her boots, she hoisted the webbing harness over her shoulders and clipped home the catches. She was ready.

Five minutes later, the pilots, along with all passengers, were poised for start-up. Heston's manager stood before the biplanes on the grass, his thumbs upright to confirm 'all clear'. Three propellors were swung and the engines caught, sending wild waves across the grass.

For two minutes the engines held a constant note, warming the oil to ease piston rings while information flowed to the instrument panels. Then each Moth shook and moved to face the prevailing wind, pausing for several seconds like high divers balanced on their toes. With their engine notes rising to full throttle, all three biplanes accelerated across the field.

Each Moth rose from Heston, each carrying the goodwill of the nation, to climb towards a blue hole in the grey overcast, the smallest of doorways to the world beyond.

33. Imperial to Sharjah – February 1933

BLACKER HAD BEEN SNOOZING WHILE the airliner, a Handley Page Hannibal Type 42, droned across the Persian Gulf. Now his instinct suggested that something was about to happen. He opened his eyes and sized up his fellow passengers who had boarded in Kuwait for the leg to Sharjah. Two Indian traders, three managers from Shell Petroleum, three elderly Arabs in white djellabas and two merchants from the Levant. All had been offered refreshments by Imperial Airways. Even if Blacker chose to speak to anybody, it would mean a shouting match against the constant thunder from four Jupiter engines on the massive wings. The Hannibal nevertheless was a splendid piece of equipment.

The cockpit door opened and one of the pilots was squeezing through to survey the passengers. The young man, in white shirt and black tie, looked at ease in this new world of air transportation. He came down the narrow gangway to Blacker's seat.

'Colonel Blacker, sir. The Captain wonders if you'd care to join him?'

Blacker had not expected this. 'A grand idea. Thank you.'

'I'll warm your seat while you're up there,' said the co-pilot.

Blacker stood up, attracting a measure of interest from other passengers. Carefully he made his way to the cockpit where the Captain sat in the left seat, keeping watch through ribbed windscreen panels. The skipper pointed to the empty seat where the dual controls moved in parallel.

'Take a seat, Colonel,' he shouted. 'I'm Patrick O'Brien, chief jockey today. We're halfway to Sharjah. Ground speed is around 75 mph at five thousand feet. Down on the starboard side, you can see some oil wells.'

Blacker took the seat and juggled his monocle to study the sepia-colored expanse below. A web of tracks scarred the desert floor, all leading to flaring wells, glowing orange like tongues of fire rising from a dirty carpet. Further beyond was the coastline with the shimmering reefs and turquoise seas of the Gulf. Blacker appraised the cockpit panel, counting four sets of dials, one for each 550 hp engine. Otherwise the display was very similar to the Westland's fascia; altimeter, magnetic compass, roll and pitch, airspeed indicator and fuel gauges.

'A fine piece of kit,' he said. 'The largest aeroplane I've ever flown in.'

136

Captain O'Brien cocked his head. 'But you're the one heading for Everest, Colonel. First over the top! Sounds fun to me.'

'Hopefully, yes. I'm going ahead to prepare the base, so fun isn't my immediate consideration. But, you have a point.'

'If you need a spare pilot, count me in,' shouted O'Brien. 'Flogging this bus from Cairo to Karachi gets very tedious.'

'I'll put your name on the list, Captain, but I warn you these RAF chaps have it all tied up. They're an exclusive lot. Only agreed to have me along because I was once a military pilot.'

Captain O'Brien adjusted a lever and tapped a gauge where a needle oscillated. 'I hear you'll be using Bristol engines, like us.' The Captain's voice rose above the engine noise. 'That new Pegasus is a piece of kit.'

'It better be.' Blacker glanced at the altimeter. 'We'll need to climb six times higher than this.'

'Six times colder too. Chap could freeze his bollocks off.'

'Electric suits,' Blacker said. 'I mean to get home with my extremities intact.'

'But what if your Pegasus stumbles?' The Captain waved at his stack of dials. 'If we lose an engine, we can generally make it home on three. If your Peggy quits, you'll be kissing the devil's ass.'

'I've kissed it before, and survived.'

'Make sure you keep it running.' Captain O'Brien made an adjustment to the course. 'I read your team made it to the Riviera in one piece. India's a fair distance in a Moth.'

'They've got the experience. McIntyre is a class A navigator, a human homing pigeon. Fellowes and Clydesdale will use the flight to hone their skills. Personally, I prefer to ride with you in comfort.'

'How do you fancy honing your own skills, Colonel?' said Captain O'Brien 'You fly the Hannibal, now you're here.'

Blacker grasped the wheel as Captain O'Brien lifted his hands from its twin. This was the first time he'd taken control of a four engine airliner. He could sense the ponderous weight and purpose of the Hannibal as it bumbled along the Gulf coastline. Down below, the lateen sails of dhows bristled like white fins in the azure sea. Fishermen were at work under flocks of seabirds. He teased the control to the left. The airliner rolled to port with lugubrious grace. Then back to the right and onto the given course. It did indeed feel like driving a bus.

Colonel Blacker remained in the cockpit for the rest of the journey, even when Captain O'Brien resumed control to skim the Hannibal down for a perfect landing on the beaten desert. Blacker appreciated the company of a like-minded airman. Good craic was rare enough in any part of the world. They were still talking when Captain O'Brien shut down the engines.

34. Fleet Street – March 1933

LORD PEEL AND JOHN BUCHAN had not attended the Heston farewell. Both had been tied up with business elsewhere. However they would be the first to hear of any progress from reports filed en route by the aircrew.

To date, the three Moth biplanes had reached Marseilles and then to Sarzana in Italy with no difficulties. The latest news caused Blumenfeld to convene a meeting at the *Daily Express*.

Lord Peel came direct from the House of Lords. Buchan had been at Gaumont-British with Hitchcock's producers. Once inside the black Vitrolite building on Fleet Street, they claimed the sweeping oval staircase to the executive floor. Here Blumenfeld's assistant knew how to greet high-profile visitors. She provided two tumblers of whisky and then a cardboard folder.

'The editor thinks you must see this, My Lord,' said the assistant, passing a printed sheet to Lord Peel. 'The pilots have sparked a diplomatic incident. They've been held by the Italians.'

Lord Peel's good humor faded as he read the report before handing it to John Buchan. 'Arrested at Naples Airport? What's this about?'

Buchan had a brief look at the report. 'It amounts to confiscation of their cameras. So not total arrest.'

'Apparently they flew down into the crater of Vesuvius and photographed it,' said the assistant. 'But why is that a crime?'

'Vesuvius may be a phenomenon of Nature for most people,' replied Buchan. 'And Italian authorities regard the volcano as a military zone and therefore a secret.'

'A military zone?' said Lord Peel. 'And the ruins of Pompeii?'

'Italy under Mussolini doesn't operate in a rational manner. Photography is forbidden in many areas, especially aerial photography.' Buchan pushed aside the folder. 'Black shirts thrive on suspicion. Any excuse will do.'

Blumenfeld now came to join them. He took a drink from his assistant, who then retired.

'My apologies,' said the editor. 'I've been on the line to my opposite number at *The Times*. Off the record, they have received a torrent of correspondence from Lucy. The problem lies in mixed objectives. Fleet Street thinks she has financed the expedition for the noble cause of aviation. The reality is that

Lucy's jingoism contrasts with moderate political thinking. India, she thinks, should dismiss any hope of leaving the Empire because it's not in their best interests.'

Lord Peel knew as much. 'Never mind India. This Italian business could become a fair old row if we're not careful.'

Blumenfeld agreed. 'Without doubt. But it makes a good story in the meantime. And since *The Times* won't publish Lucy's exhortations, she's now lobbying other newspapers, including us here. If we don't publish her letters verbatim, she'll publish them in her own *Saturday Review*. That's why she bought the paper.'

Lord Peel nodded. 'It must be embarrassing. She's paid for an expedition whose rights are held by *The Times* and they're not going to play ball with her.'

Buchan shrugged. '*The Times* can only release stories relevant to the operation, not the whimsical notions of a sponsor.'

'She's not far off the mark about India.' Lord Peel observed. 'Mahatma Gandhi is increasingly taking the public with him and may soon be in a position to drive us out.'

'The way of the world, gentlemen,' said Blumenfeld. 'But any nation leaving the Empire would infuriate Lucy. In any event, I've agreed with *The Times* that we'll stick to a restrained policy on Lucy's political views. Mind you, Shepherd is writing exclusively for them but in India, other reporters are bound to get involved. It will be harder to control the news then.'

'We'll cross that bridge another day,' Lord Peel said. 'Meanwhile I hear that Lucy has been in bed for much of the winter?'

'It never stopped her complaining,' observed Blumenfeld. 'I visited her in Hampstead the other day. Her secretary Garland is a good friend of mine.' He glanced at his watch. 'Sorry to be brief, but we're setting up tomorrow's first edition. Help yourselves to the whisky. My people will keep you informed of any developments and Garland will monitor the situation in Hampstead.'

After the Editor had left them, Buchan and Lord Peel sat listening to the noise of journalists, editors and photographic staff preparing for shifts that would run through the night until the newspapers fell from the chutes.

'I love the busy racket of a newsroom,' said Buchan. 'To me it's the greatest marketplace where all life happens.'

'So true,' agreed Lord Peel. 'By the way, I've spoken with John Astor. He has set *The Times* on course for an Everest conquest and intends to sponsor a summit attempt.'

'But not this year's expedition with Ruttledge?'

'Ruttledge is going in from the north.' Lord Peel was no mountaineer but he understood Himalayan topography. 'The north face might take years to conquer. No, John Astor believes, like you, the best route to the summit is via Nepal to the south.'

'And that all depends on how the Government of Nepal reacts to our enterprise.' Buchan paused. 'It's a cliffhanger now, just waiting for official approval. When Etherton gets to Kathmandu to meet the King, we'll have our answer. If successful, it could open routes for climbers galore. On the other hand, if our pilots cock things up, all routes may be out of the question.'

'Our crew haven't even left Europe, and already they're under arrest! Just for violating Vesuvius!'

'You have a way with words,' Buchan laughed. 'You should try writing a novel one day. But you're right, we're in a very odd situation, taking funds from a lady who is determined to defend London by flying the Union Jack at the top of the world.'

'Win some. Lose some.' Lord Peel got to his feet and prepared to leave. 'Well, that's it for today. I'm taking Mrs. Blacker out to dinner, now that the Colonel's gone off on his travels. We'll see what tomorrow brings.'

Buchan stood up. 'Give my regards to Doris. I'll tell you if I hear anything.'

They thanked the secretary and left the office. Down in the hallway, below the splendid flutes of a pendant light, they each went on their way.

35. Gwadar, Baluchistan – 7th March 1933

IN A SERIES OF HOPS averaging 300 miles daily, the de Havilland Moths steadily covered 5000 miles of their journey from London to Karachi.

Those little problems in Naples had been overcome. Their cameras were returned, minus exposed film of Vesuvius, after a financial 'settlement' with Italian customs officers. Soon the Moths were bypassing thunderous clouds to Sicily where they dropped down at Catania airfield near Mount Etna. Unchastened by their experience in Naples, the pilots had a good look down the volcano's smoking throat before they flew on to Tunis. Here they turned east to cruise along the African coastline overnighting in Libya and Egypt. For two days in frantic Cairo, the crew rested while Hughes applied his artistry to ensure each Moth was ready for the challenging sectors ahead.

Leaving Cairo, the pilots indulged in grand aerial tourism, admiring the Pyramids, the Nile and the Suez Canal at low altitude before venturing across the Sinai Desert to the Holy Land. From their swaying seats in the heavens, they surveyed the birthplace of Jesus Christ and flew on over Jerusalem, eventually reaching Amman, Baghdad and Basra.

With Iraq's southern marshes behind the tail, the longest leg of 850 miles provided plenty of visual drama. They cruised along the Persian shoreline where dark mountains slid as jagged razors into crystal seas. At Bandar Abbas they landed to refuel but here Customs officers delayed them, demanding to know how many rats were traveling undeclared on their manifest?

After unloading each aeroplane to prove the absence of rodents, the Moths took off with full tanks, humming along in the afternoon heat, until they alighted minutes before dusk on the haunting emptiness of Gwadar, India's most westerly airstrip.

The deserted strip lay at the throat of a peninsula of rare and beautiful symmetry, its paired bays of sand curving into a broad mushroom in a turquoise ocean rimmed by flying surf. When each engine died, the seven travelers stepped down to stretch cramped limbs on the dusty grit of India.

Not a human was in sight. No hint of anything that could pass for normal amenities. No pushy traders, no passport inspectors, no zealous officers. Instead a pack of surly bush dogs slunk around a mud-walled hut hosting piles of empty fuel drums. The light was failing and they could not fly at night. The aviators had to make camp beside their Moths and face the greater problem of ravenous hunger. Onboard rations were running low.

McIntyre sought a solution. Walking with Highland bravado towards the dogs, he forged a path between the snarling creatures into the hut's dim interior. There he found a telephone that amazingly connected to an operator who spoke English. Their food requirements were relayed to enterprising victualers somewhere in the void and half an hour later, fruit, milk, bread and bottled water were delivered by rickshaw. Dinner was attempted as darkness fell and soon they all settled down in cockpits or below the wings. Comfort was a distant hope. The dogs were never silent, sleep was intermittent and desert sounds intruded throughout a long night while the three Moths rested, their wings catching at the light of the Moon and Milky Way.

In the early hours, a heavy dew came on silent breath from the ocean. Carrying with it a damp chill, the travelers waited until the eastern skies brightened when Hughes fired up the Monitor paraffin stove, a much-loved item provided by sponsors. The kettle was boiling when Shepherd and Fellowes materialized from the darkness to join him over the hissing ring of heat.

'By God, this is cold.' Shepherd thrust his hands into the pockets of his flying coat and yawned, failing to shield his mouth. 'I didn't have a wink's worth.'

Fellowes also stifled a yawn. 'But at least we've reached India.'

'Will that mean decent food at last?' Hughes asked as he lined up six mugs for the brewing kettle. 'I'm wasting away.'

'You'll be fine in Karachi,' said Fellowes. 'The RAF has a good mess there. You'll eat like a king.'

'Forget royalty, sir. I'd be happy to eat like an engineer. That grub last night wasn't fit for those effing dogs.'

Fellowes wasn't going to admit to sharing Hughes' opinion. The bread had been solid, the fruit musty with mould. Lifting morale was a commander's duty especially at the start of a day that would guarantee hot and dusty travel over empty territory, all of 300 miles to Karachi. It was essential to leave early but there was no sign of his fellow pilots.

Taking his pocket torch, Fellowes walked over to the Gypsy Moth. Clydesdale and McIntyre were asleep below its wings on sand awash with dew. Nudging each pilot with his boot, he returned them to life before heading for the Puss Moth where Eleanor was still snoozing in the cabin. Although Eleanor had sat cramped for ten hours on the previous day, she had remained in the seat overnight, away from surface hazards of dogs, scorpions and spiders. He gave her a gentle push. 'I'll get some tea, my love. And then we're off to Karachi.'

Back at the stove, all the men were assembled and Fellowes took a mug of tea from Hughes. It warmed his chilled fingers. 'Thanks, Hughes. You'll feel better soon. In India people love to supply whatever you want.'

Shepherd was nursing his tea. 'Those buggers last night certainly tried.'

'Like a bleedin' bible tale,' said Hughes. 'Bearing gifts of dysentery, they were. I reckon the milk was siphoned from a dead camel. I'll stick to black tea with sugar.'

They were all accustomed to Hughes odd remarks. The engineer had suffered from stomach gripes for much of the journey, and his comments were invariably caustic.

Shepherd tried his tea and promptly threw it down. 'You're right, Hughes. It's even worse than your eloquent description.'

Fellowes continued drinking. 'It must be water from a semi-saline well. If you boil it, it's safe enough.'

'You have iron guts, sir,' said Clydesdale adding his tea to the sand.

'Tastes like cat's piss,' Shepherd decided.

McIntyre took a hip flask came from his flight suit and poured in a fair wallop. He tried it and smiled. 'Aye, cat piss with brandy.'

The men stamped their feet to revive circulation as the glistening starlight faded. When the biplanes had refueled, every drop of petroleum had been strained through Clydesdale's handkerchief. Dirt in the carburetor was a constant threat in the desert, making filtering essential. A breeze rocked the Moths' wingtips as if they now wanted to get airborne.

Fellowes took a mug of tea to his machine. Opening the cabin door he again nudged his wife's shoulder. 'Your tea, darling.'

Eleanor yawned and sat up. 'I need to spend a penny first.'

Fellowes put the mug down and helped Eleanor climb from the Moth. She stared at the wasteland. 'Perry, where do I go?'

'Take your pick of a million acres. I'll ensure you get privacy.'

Fellowes returned to his men, raising his hand. 'May I ask you, gentlemen, to admire the sunrise? Eleanor needs a moment, if you understand me..'

The men turned to the east while Eleanor went into the desert.

'A good idea,' said Clydesdale, unzipping his flight suit.

Soon all the men were watering the dust of Beluchistan. Fellowes grinned at Shepherd. 'All part of the travel experience.'

Shepherd adjusted his flies. 'But what fun! I love the shenanigans with the authorities whenever we touch down, sandstorms cutting out the light of day with nothing but chocolates to keep us alive. Wouldn't have missed it for anything.'

'You missed the best bit,' said Hughes. 'Sharing the cabin with me.'

'Do y'hear that, Shepherd?' asked McIntyre. 'Will you put that in your next report?'

Shepherd protested. 'Our readers don't need to read about Hughes and his tummy troubles however I will report that dive you made on the camel train. I thought you were going to crash in the dunes.'

'Aye, and so did I,' McIntyre could make a joke at any time. 'Those Bedouin robes were the only things catching the breeze and I needed a close look to estimate wind direction.'

'Lucky they didn't shoot you,' said Hughes. 'If I was jogging along on a camel and a biplane suddenly came up my djellaba, I'd open fire with all I had to offer.'

'I think that's enough, Hughes,' Fellowes warned. 'Eleanor has finished so we can all about turn and get on with it. The sooner we make Karachi the better.'

In twenty minutes the camp was clear and stores were loaded. Each Moth rid itself of dew as its engine started, dispersing clouds of whipped sand and spray. Taxiing to the end of the strip they turned with engines revving to accelerate and rise, climbing so their occupants could again admire the beauty of the Indian Ocean as they set course. In three hours, they'd be back in a world of chef-prepared food, proper beds and tiled toilets at the RAF base in Karachi.

36. P&O. SS Mooltan – March 1933

AS THE THREE MOTHS SET course from the bleakest corner of India, other expedition members were nearing their destinations. For those riding in comfort over the lustrous blue ocean, life on P&O's *Mooltan*, had been far more comfortable.

During the voyage to Bombay most of the 600 passengers and 400 crewmen had heard snippets of intriguing information about the Everest flight. Ship's gossip in 2nd Class came mainly from the engineers, Pitt and Burnard who were now regarded by many as a 'Laurel and Hardy' act. Generally to be found in the stern bar, neither engineer took offense at being likened to Hollywood's famous comedians.

On the upper decks of the 20,000 ton steamer, the First Class passengers had met, albeit en passant, the sprightly gentleman known to all as Percy. His role as Secretary had created an aura not much relished by Etherton himself. At the Captain's table, in the saloon bar or while dodging quoits on the games deck, passengers were forever attempting to waylay him in lengthy inquisition. Often they wanted to know about the aristocracy. Was the Marquis of Clydesdale really the most eligible bachelor in Britain? Had John Buchan ever been to Everest? Was *The Times* planning to publish all the photos of the Himalayas and was Lady Houston a grand old bird who had lost her marbles or was she an astute visionary?

Etherton struggled to provide entertaining and polite replies. In the confinement of a liner such intrusions were inevitable and it explained why he had spent so much time in his cabin.

This lay on *Mooltan*'s port side, supporting the belief that 'Portside Out, Starboard Home' was definitely for posh people. Etherton had lived in alternating luxury and deprivation all his life so he gave no serious thought to such acronyms. He hadn't selected the cabin, a spacious veneer paneled suite and bathroom, but it was one of the best available. Each day his bunk was freshly made up.   Clean towels and bath mats bearing the P&O logo appeared by magic with a steward. All of had been provided by P&O's sponsorship. Such perks on the way to the Himalaya were very welcome. Things would change in the charged heat of India.

Sitting at the leather-topped desk in his floating office, Etherton reflected this was how Lady Houston conducted business on the *Liberty*. What might have happened without Lucy's change of heart? For sure, he'd not be sailing to India now.

Hearing a knock, Etherton looked up to see a cablegram sliding under the door. He scooped it up to learn that the pilots had reached Karachi. Now ahead of schedule, they would relax after their journey.

For Etherton this was news to be shared with his fellow expeditionaries. Whereas passengers in Second were barred from entering First Class, it was easy for him to pass in the opposite direction to contact the engineers and the film unit known to all as 'The Barking Filmies.'

Everyone was aware of the equipment familiarization programs conducted by Barkas. When the passengers learned these men would be filming the great flight, they became ever more inquisitive and soon believed the director would be creating a visual epic.

Etherton's route followed the promenade decks. He had to duck past the flailing energies of a keep-fit class and then step over the pawns on a deck-chess tournament, until he reached the stern bar. Here the two engineers were at their table, shirt sleeves rolled up, pints of beer at the ready.

Pitt was shuffling a pack of cards. 'You're just in time for a hand, sir. Three card brag with a minimum stake of five pennies.'

'I have to disappoint you, Pitt. We're docking tonight and I've got too much to do.'

Pitt lamented. 'A pint of IPA instead?'

Etherton drew up a chair. 'I can settle for that.'

Burnard went for the drinks, leaving Pitt to stash the cards. 'So, you're off to Kathmandu while we transfer from this old steamer to another floating bucket of rust for Karachi.'

'That's the idea. I'll be at the Governor's residence. Then I take trains to Patna and Nepal for the flight permits.'

'A bit late for that now, don't you think, sir?'

'Merely a formality.' Etherton hoped this was true as his attention was drawn to the film crew on the weather deck. The unit was grouped around a large camera on a tripod. Astern, the ship's wake rustled on an indigo sea. 'What's Barkas doing down there?'

'Testing focus on the long lens. It keeps them busy. As for the sound men, they fiddle with their machines as if life itself depended on it.'

Burnard came back with three pints of beer. Etherton enquired no further about the filmies. If Barkas had to train his unit while on the high seas, at least it kept them out of trouble. 'Now I have some news. The Westlands are in Karachi, ready for assembly with RAF fitters working to your instructions.'

'I'd prefer to be there, when they bolt the wings on,' said Burnard.

'So if we lose them over Everest, we'll know who to blame,' said Pitt. 'And the pilots, are they still wandering at large in desert skies?'

'No, no,' said Etherton. 'They're all in Karachi, currently regrouping at the Sind Club. You'll soon be there to approve the Westlands. Then they'll fly to Delhi to meet the Viceroy while you take trains from Karachi to Purnea along with Dr. Bennett and all his kit. And you'll be traveling of course with your favorite film director and his crew.'

'That will be enormous fun,' said Burnard.

'A testing journey,' suggested Etherton. 'But in Purnea you'll have a good base in the jungle at Lalbalu while you get ready for the real action.'

'Sounds like we're declaring war, sir,' said Pitt. 'How long do we have to stay at this jungle resort?'

Sensing a lack of enthusiasm, Etherton tried to improve the case. 'Personally, I love it up there, near the Terai. Wonderful wildlife in the foothills, friendly people in the villages and lots to amuse you. You'll enjoy it, so long as you follow the basic rules.'

'Rules?' asked Burnard and Pitt simultaneously.

'Don't drink water unless you see it boiled. Ensure your mosquito nets have no holes and don't eat rotten curry.' Etherton gave this advice with confidence. It had always worked for him. 'And don't go wandering around at night. That's best left to wild dogs, cobras and big cats.'

'Big cats?' Burnard asked. 'What kind of cats?'

'Burnard has a fat tabby cat in Yeovil,' Pitt whispered. 'He's hoping it's that kind.'

Etherton laughed. 'There's the odd tiger perhaps, leopards aplenty and maybe a few bears. All of them quite numerous in the hills.'

'I've been telling him that, sir,' Pitt explained. 'Now maybe he'll listen to you.'

Etherton drank some beer. 'In any case, your camp at Lalbalu will be well defended. We'll be issuing rifles and ammunition, courtesy of Mannlicher firearms.'

'How very kind of them,' said Burnard, 'but we've come to service Westlands, not to shoot cats.'

Etherton finished his beer, casting his look over the hazy horizons of the Indian Ocean. *Mooltan* was sailing easily and he had much to accomplish before she docked at Bombay. 'The Mannlicher is the finest of weapons, Mr. Burnard. I advise you to keep one in your tent – just in case you go out for a leak during the night.'

37. Indian skies – March 22nd 1933

FELLOWES WAS FIGHTING THE ONSET of drowsiness in the cockpit of his Puss Moth. A catnap was out of the question while skimming through an ochre-tinted haze at 4000 feet above the plains of Rajasthan. This meteorological condition often loitered in Indian skies, making navigation onerous. Dead reckoning skills, the balance of careful guesswork with known facts, had to be perfected by all pilots.

To keep awake, Fellowes ate an apple and recorded his notes of track and crosswind components on a clipboard, detailing the time flown on each heading. From these pencilled jottings, he could construct an educated guess of the way points in the so-called flight plan.

Staring ahead through the windshield, Fellowes thought about his fellow airmen. Top of the list was the Chief Pilot. The young man had been a fantastic credit to the entire operation. Having charmed the old stoat Lucy, he had used his same magic during their stopover in Baghdad to secure an audience with King Feisal. After this they had been afforded preferential treatment from the authorities through Iraq to Persia. Clydesdale's charisma, he decided, would be particularly helpful with the elite of India.

Fellowes checked his heading and lifted the starboard wings as the Moth cruised on, drawn by valiant pistons towards Jodhpur. His mind turned to McIntyre, a phenomenal navigator and certainly not one for reticence. Armed with wolfish grin and slick repartee, Mac eschewed rules, preferring spontaneity and experiment. He flies as he lives, thought Fellowes, and that's close to the line! Small wonder women fell to his charm like grass to a scythe.

While at Karachi, Fellowes had enrolled a third RAF officer Ellison to act as reserve pilot. With five aircraft now in operation, it made sense. RAF personnel were easy to command. They loved machines, boundless skies and common purpose. Politicians and government contractors were harder work, generally mired in the conflict of self-serving interests.

Fellowes had also selected his ground crew from RAF servicemen at the base. Aircraftsman Clark would supervise the airscrews, the single-blade propellers. These might require balancing to prevent cavitation and the brass trimming on tips and leading edges could need attention.

Another danger for the airscrews was during take-off when the pilot had to handle the Westland very carefully. When its tail lifted the propeller thrashed only six inches from the ground. A single bounce or over-reaction could drive the spinning prop into the turf, tipping the entire assembly into a lethal somersault. Clark's skills would not be needed if this should occur.

Far ahead, through the spinning arc of his own airscrew, Fellowes suddenly detected a dark object. His fingers tightened on the stick. He was closing on a hazard at 110 mph. He had warned his fellow pilots to watch out for vultures and collision with a bird as big as a turkey was a mortal possibility up here. With a flick, Fellowes swung the Moth away allowing the vulture to pass astern, out of harm's way.

If a bird struck a biplane, it would be for Aircraftsman Hensley to repair any damaged fabric, rigging and control wires that had to expand or contract with the temperature. Hensley would ensure the spring linkages were tensioned correctly.

A third recruit was Aircraftsman Young, a quiet man whose task was to supervise the oxygen equipment and associated reports which would be sent for analysis at Farnborough. Each Westland carried four oxygen tanks, each holding 165 gallons, in a rack within the rear fuselage.

Sergeant Greenwood was to command the ground crew. The sergeant, a solid, reliable fellow, would act as overall inspector of maintenance with help from Pitt and Burnard. Fraser alone would remain in Purnea where his cameras and film stock were not left to the mercy of the jungle.

And so Peregrine Fellowes in his Puss Moth mulled all of this while occasionally spotting features in the land underneath. It was a question of staying confident and alert. His gauges indicated he had fuel available for course adjustments if needed.

In a moment of good visibility he noticed a blur of action below. He then identified the registration markings on the Westland Wallace as it burrowed through the haze several hundred feet below. Now he was sharing the sky with a steel ostrich. Though Mac was overtaking him a risk of collision still remained.

Fellowes decided to alert his two passengers in the rear compartment. Shepherd had squeezed into a third seat for the flight and was dozing with his head against a folded sweater. Eleanor was staring absent-mindedly at the passing scenery, or the lack of it. Her resilience had surprised him and her courtesy to all strangers had been laudable throughout.

'There's a Westland down there,' Fellowes pointed. 'Keep a lookout. And watch out for any vultures.'

Eleanor nodded but Shepherd remained deep in dreams.

Fellowes checked the console. Every instrument spelled normality and his memory spooled back fifteen years, to the day when he had aimed his bomber at the lock gates. From Zeebrugge harbor on the Belgian coast submarines slithered out to destroy British shipping and when he attacked, it felt as if every gun in Germany was blazing at him. Holding his course, he dropped enough explosive to shatter the dam to the U-boat lair before ground fire brought him down. Trailing smoke and debris he met with a rough landing and an even rougher capture by thoroughly angry Huns. They had dragged him from the wreck and treated him to the heavy end of their rifle butts before he passed out.

Well, he had dealt with that task and this Everest assault was no different. His team was strong and if all the human and mechanical ingredients worked perfectly, they would achieve the objective.

Nevertheless there were weak links. While the airmen faced the hazards of flight, the surface travelers also confronted many difficulties. They were down there now, below the haze, finding their way through the exotic confusion that was India.

Fellowes flew on to his rendezvous with the Himalayas. In the rear seat Mr. Shepherd continued to doze while Eleanor quartered another apple and passed the pieces through to him.

38. Kathmandu, Nepal – March 1933

HIS HIGHNESS THE MAHARAJA SIR Joodha Shum Shere Jung Bahadur Rana, Knight Grand Commander of The Order of the Indian Empire also acted as Prime Minister and Supreme Commander of the Nepalese Armed Forces.

The sum of these titles created a charter for their owner to act however he desired. His was the final word in a governance that extended from the grasslands of Nepal's southern Terai, across the forested foothills riven with deep chasms and terraced pastures, all the way and ever upwards to the massive glaciers and snow peaks to the north. Here his territory of total power ceased on the frontier marked by the Himalayan skyline.

The Maharaja's duties for his 500,000 subjects included maintenance of public order, provision of means to grow subsistence food and protection against unwelcome influence from the outside world. Taken together, Etherton pondered, this was an onerous responsibility for any head on mortal shoulders.

Etherton was being driven through Kathmandu, the grubby but endearing capital of the isolated nation. Throughout his life he had broadly supported the concept of democracy, but there were drawbacks to the system. When he thought about it, even the likes of Mussolini, Stalin and Hitler exercised less power than the Maharaja who had inherited his role as head of the Rana dynasty without a single vote. The concept of democracy had not penetrated Nepal and yet most of the inhabitants seemed to be forever smiling. The status quo under one man's rule had its merits. All that any nation needed a wise, firm and broadly respected leader on the helm. That was the key to it, however the leader got there.

Etherton had met Maharaja Sir Joodha on the previous day to discuss the flight plan. Today he would hear what had been decided. The entire future of the expedition currently assembling in India depended on the outcome.

Without approval, the operation was doomed. But if the Maharaja granted just one flight permit, then Fellowes could launch his Westlands at Everest. This was a major issue to resolve.

The Maharaja accepted that most of his people had never seen an aeroplane. Though he was intrigued by the future of flight, his regressive advisors feared that exposure to such machines might distress the population and prove counter-productive in the long term. From their viewpoint, the flight was as an unwelcome foreign influence. What was the point of progress, they argued? Modern inventions could threaten the amiable but feudal lifestyle that had prevailed in Nepal for centuries.

Etherton had explained that few people might notice the biplanes as they flew over the nation at high altitude. They'd be just two tiny specks, like vultures, far beyond the clouds. Had this assurance been accepted? In gambling jargon, this was the end game. To console himself, the Secretary to the Expedition considered he'd done all that was humanly possible.

For ten days since leaving the *Mooltan*, he'd been on the move. At Bombay he had taken a train to Patna where the Governor instructed his officials to assist by all means possible. Suitably grateful, Etherton boarded another train for Purnea, knowing for sure that his travels would become more arduous from now on.

All trains bound to the north-east were forced to halt on the banks of India's greatest river. To cross the Ganges, passengers had to alight from their train into a mob of porters and vendors, all howling for attention. After this came another scrummage at the jetty where a veteran paddle steamer took on passengers until it was nearly sinking. The steamer then meandered across the turgid river currents like an overloaded tub of vegetable curry. It was not a pleasure cruise to the far shore, where the process reversed itself until passengers finally boarded the onward train for Purnea.

The township was in a region famous for growing indigo for the world's denim trade. Aside from this important contribution, Purnea had a few notable facilities. The bank, telegraph office and general stores were checked by Etherton personally. Though primitive, each was fit for purpose and he had continued on to Lalbalu, twelve miles beyond the township. Blacker had drawn up the site plan for the flying base and Etherton had checked on its progress.

In the clearing which comprised the Lalbalu base, he counted a dozen pup tents for the ground crew. Three large canvas hangars and a variety of awnings were also ready to protect the big biplanes from sun and dust. He was advised the herdsmen would drive their goats and sheep off the grass whenever a trumpet signaled an approaching aircraft. Other watchmen would be hired and facilities for water, fuel storage and the latrines were almost complete.

Satisfied by the site visit, Etherton returned to Purnea to spend the night at Raja Banaili's palace.

Next morning came the forty-eight hour ordeal of the narrow gauge train to Raxaul on the Nepalese border. Transferring to the Nepal Government Railway the track through the grassy swamps of the Terai, a region harboring malaria, fugitives, rhinos, wild elephants and predators of many descriptions. Etherton saw none of these from the train as it clicked along at an average speed of 7 mph towards the foothills. He remembered the day at Tiger Hill when Blacker had revealed his grand plan. So much had happened in a year, he thought.

When the track ran out at Amlekganj, Etherton was transported by a lorry for thirty jolting miles to Bhimpedi. This hamlet crouched in hills protecting the route to Kathmandu via the formidable pass of Chisapani. Fortunately the Maharaja had sent servants and ponies to help Etherton through this arduous sector. In his sturdiest boots, he trekked with guides along slender tracks, past brutal drops and over nightmare bridges swaying far above torrents.

While clambering between the boulders and ravines, Etherton heard from guides how teams of eighty porters had heaved entire motor vehicles over the pass to the isolated roads of the capital. So much for evading influence of the wider world! One female porter had even carried a piano on her back across the pass. Etherton had struggled to imagine the sight.

After descending from Chisapani, the modern world returned without subtlety. Some vehicle under the spasmodic control of a demented daredevil rushed Etherton to Kathmandu at speeds that would have won applause on the Brooklands circuit. But this was no contoured racetrack and the road was choked with farmers and merchants moving loads by ox and elephant.

Etherton had mentioned none of these experiences when first meeting the Maharaja. Instead he had thanked His Highness for the assistance so generously provided and for granting him audience, the standard overtures of diplomatic lickspittle.

The Maharaja had an introspective demeanor. He was much the same age as Etherton and speaking through the drapes of his mustache gave a vivid description of King George V's visit in 1911. Six hundred elephants and thousands of laborers had constructed the road to a hunting lodge where rose-beds had been installed to remind the British monarch of his London home. The King, who was also the Emperor of India, took a position on the lead shikari elephant and with one shot, managed to kill a charging tiger.

'You may find roses, but you don't find tigers in London's Green Park,' the Maharaja had chortled. 'I've read your letters and I understand you now require two flights over the mountains for reasons of photographic importance? I can understand the reason to make one flight, but two? That may present difficulties, so I must think about it.'

Etherton had waited overnight at the British Legation with Colonel Daukes. The resident diplomat and his squeaky wife had treated him to a tour of temples. Tinkling prayer wheels and the murmuration of monks preceded the gory sacrifice of goats and chickens. They went on to admire a statue of Ganesh, the elephant god, who was accredited for an ability to remove obstacles. Etherton felt it was a very fitting finish to the tour.

In the staff car, Etherton and Daukes were now passing through a suburb of mud-brick shacks. Rotting garbage lay between stalls where craftsmen worked on brass, leather and woolen items. Young women in saris, some carrying dark-eyed infants, moved gracefully aside. The car with a fluttering flag on its bonnet sailed through and finally accelerated out of Kathmandu.

They had been summoned by the Maharaja to the Gurkha training base for the second meeting. Under a gilded sign with crossed kukri knives stood the Gurkha Sergeant detailed to escort them through the dignitaries, officers and consular officials assembling at the parade ground. Fresh paintwork shone on the barrack bungalows where Gurkha flags swung to the breeze. The base would have passed for Aldershot, had there not been vultures circling overhead.

The Sergeant led them towards a pavilion over a saluting rostrum. A cordon of armed Gurkhas stood around the enclosure where officers of the General Staff were conferring with the Maharaja. Then, snapping boot heels together, the Gurkha Sergeant saluted. 'His Highness will receive now you, sirs.'

Maharaja Sir Joodha wore full military dress today. His black brocaded frock coat, festooned with epaulettes, gold buttons and leafed medals, was further garnished by a scarlet sash matching his trouser stripes. A high-peaked cap, a size too small, greying hair and gold-framed spectacles provided Sir Joodha with an aura of wisdom rather than military power. The visitors stepped forward to shake hands.

'So pleased you're here.' The Maharaja waved towards the parade ground. 'You'll enjoy the march past.'

'We are honored, your Highness.' Etherton began. 'I'm told you have thirty thousand men on parade today?'

A gold tooth glinted in the Maharaja's cascade of whiskers. 'One soldier for every foot of height, from sea-level to the top of my Kingdom.'

Etherton had to hurry things along before the parade began. 'Indeed so, but I failed to mention something of importance, when we met yesterday.'

'And what might that be?' asked Sir Joodha.

'A consensus exists in London that a Nepali should be first to set foot on the peak of Sagarmatha. With thirty thousand men, you have plenty of choice. Furthermore my colleague, John Buchan, is convinced that aerial photographs will assist any Sherpas brave enough to climb the mountain.'

Sir Joodha Shum lowered his head, seemingly to examine the reflection of his face on his polished boots. 'John Buchan may be right. Our Sherpas are the best of climbers. But you must be aware of the rumors circulating about the fate of Irvine and Mallory?'

'Yes, Your Majesty,' Etherton replied. 'Are you alluding to the belief they were thrown off the summit by angered gods, for disturbing the sanctity of the mountain?'

'It's a popular view held by many. I don't share it myself.'

'It explains why we have also advised the Dalai Lama in Tibet about the integrity of our intentions.' Etherton hoped this mention of religious sensitivities would be reassuring. 'And please remember our machines will fly so high as to be unseen from the ground.'

'But not unseen by the Gods.' The gold tooth twinkled.

'I doubt if the Gods will object, Your Highness. Why should they? A strictly scientific survey with cameras is the sole intention. We have no wish to offend religious sentiments.'

The thumping discharge from a 12 pound artillery field gun interrupted the negotiation and staff officers checked their watches. The parade was imminent. Thirty-thousand men, two regimental bands and a squadron of light artillery were waiting. The Maharaja had to make a decision.

'Very well, you have permission to fly two sorties over our highest mountains. We will require prior notification by cable, followed by written reports on each flight and copies of all terrain photographs.'

157

'Understood and agreed,' said Etherton. 'With my deepest appreciation, Your Highness.'

The Maharaja put out his hand. 'No practice flights over Nepal can be permitted and there must be absolutely no crash landings.'

'We can comply with all those conditions.' Etherton took the monach's hand and inclined his head with diplomatic gratitude. Try telling that to British pilots, he thought.

The Maharaja fitted his cap, patted his tunic and then stepped up to the podium to take the salute and the Sergeant escorted Daukes and Etherton to their reserved seats. They sat down as the Gurkhas began marching to the skirl of bagpipes. Heads turned as one to face the eyes of the ruler. Passing by, in ranks sharper than a kukri blade, all boots fell in unison to the drumbeat.

'That went well,' Daukes whispered. 'For a moment, I was worried that the Gods might get the last word.'

'So was I. But Ganesh gave us what we needed!' Etherton felt jubilant. His long journey had been successful. 'And now it's back to the Chisapani and to Purnea where I will reveal the good news.'

39. Hampstead Heath – March 1933

'ALL IS NICE AND DANDY here,' said Garland, speaking from Hampstead, Lady Houston's London home. She was on the line to Ralph Blumenfeld. 'We're still waiting for news and Lucy is chomping at the bit.'

'Well, this might pump fresh blood into Her Ladyship,' said Blumenfeld. 'We've just heard from Fellowes. Everyone has made it safely to Purnea and they're now preparing for action.'

'Now, that's great!' said Garland. 'Maybe you'd like to tell her yourself? She's waiting for the Duchess of Hamilton who's coming to lunch.'

'Don't let Mungo spoil it,' Blumenfeld warned. 'She told me all about that Oban incident. Meanwhile, Garland, be patient. This may not be the job you fully desire, but in the long run, believe me, you won't regret it.'

'Thanks, Mr. B. I'll remember that. Putting you through.' Garland flipped a switch to Lady Houston's extension. It was best that such news went direct. Through the winter months Garland's life had become boringly repetitive. Day after day there was routine paperwork and audiences with her employer who had remained, effectively housebound where everything seemed dead in winter's chill. Life's great circle weighed on Lady Houston's mind. Her thoughts of morbidity worsened with the season.

Thank God for some good news, Garland decided. Hopefully it might change the mood. John had gone to collect the Duchess from Belgravia and the Rolls was arriving in the driveway.

Byron Cottage was a sizable detached home, purchased in 1908 by Lucy's husband of the day, Lord Byron. Set in two acres, the exclusive property consisted of shrubbery, flowerbeds, garage yard and guest lodge. The cottage, clad in pebble-dash, sat in a cul-de-sac where birds sang to welcome the spring.

Garland met the Duchess at the door. After taking a stole and hat from her, Garland led Her Grace to the living room where Lady Houston was waiting. The table was laid in a bay window and sandwiches lay ready. Lady Houston asked Garland to find some sherry for her guest.

'After that message from Mr. Blumenfeld, I'll dispense with tea,' said Lady Houston as she settled in a chair. 'Brandy and ginger for me, if you please Garland. Then you can take Mungo out for a stroll.'

In the kitchen, Garland prepared both drinks and took them back to find Lady Houston in full flow about the new American President. She'd been thinking of little else since Franklin Roosevelt's inauguration on March 4th.

'Roosevelt makes a fine stand for liberty. He's a man who speaks for the people and I believe he'll sympathize with my concerns that our government know nothing of the world beyond Westminster.'

The Duchess looked unsettled by this outburst of political energy. She sat looking with bemusement at the heiress. 'You and the new President may share many views in common. Not that I've ever met him.'

'And he loves our Winston, which is why I'm so hopeful. With Roosevelt in the White House, the government will now be forced to acknowledge the dangers being spawned in Berlin.'

'I'm sure they will.' The Duchess said politely. 'Sure of it.'

Lady Houston dropped the subject and picked up her notebook by the telephone. 'So, the Air Commodore says they tested the Westlands at high-altitude over Karachi and both machines have now reached Lalbalu. Isn't that exciting?'

'Simply wonderful!' The Duchess agreed. 'I'm so relieved they're all in one piece after all that trouble along the way. I was terribly upset when I heard the Fox Moth had been destroyed.'

Garland saw Lady Houston's confidence vanish in an instant. For several seconds a taut silence filled the living room.

Then Lucy Houston flared. 'What's this news? Tell me what happened? Nobody bloody told me!'

'My son's biplane was torn apart by a windstorm while on the ground at Allahabad.'

'Torn apart?'

'I'm told it's beyond repair. Douglas is very upset.'

Lady Houston swung to face Garland. 'Why wasn't I told?'

'Because nobody told me, your Ladyship. I suppose they didn't regard it as important.'

'I consider that to be very important news.'

The Duchess attempted to comfort her hostess. 'There were no casualties, Lucy. They salvaged most of it and, luckily a kind Indian gentleman has loaned them another Puss Moth.'

'An Indian lent them an aeroplane?' Lucy quickly took some brandy.

'What's wrong with the RAF out there? Don't they have spare aircraft?'

'Mr. Chawla is the first Indian to have flown from England to India and he's very happy to help. Even *The Times* knew nothing of the Moth's destruction since Shepherd was elsewhere when the storm occurred.'

Lady Houston was mollified. 'That makes it a little better. But remember it's me who's the sponsor. I must know what's going on.'

'Quite so Lucy.' The Duchess raised her sherry glass and smiled. 'My son says it's all going to plan.'

Lady Houston's fingers gripped her brandy glass. 'Garland, didn't I ask you to take Mungo out?'

Garland made a grab for the dog, who had retreated below the table. With the squirming terrier in her arms, Garland left the sitting room and closed the door, leaving the older ladies to chat about exciting events, none of which were happening for her.

In the kitchen, John was drinking tea. He was ready to return the Duchess to Mayfair when requested.

'Hi, John. I hear the pilots are raring to go. Isn't that great?'

'For them, maybe.'

'What's up with you?' She paused at the door with Mungo. 'You're not so happy?.'

John stared at his mug. 'I'd rather be India, Miss. I'd like an adventure. '

Garland sighed. 'I know the feeling. When I've dealt with Mungo, and after you've taken the Duchess back home, it's my guess that Lady Houston will retire for the rest of the day. The housekeeper will be back at six and we'll be free.'

'So?' John's eyebrow lifted.

'We could go completely crazy,' Garland suggested. 'We could go to the Old Bull and Bush for a drink. Now how's that for an adventure?'

40. Purnea, India – March 1933

IN FRESH KHAKI SHIRT AND knee length shorts, Colonel Blacker walked from the bungalow that had become their headquarters. The building had been loaned to the expedition by the Maharaja of Darbhanga, a local landlord for whom Blacker held the greatest respect. He took a silk handkerchief to polish his monocle before having a good look at the dawning day.

At 5.45 a.m. the air was syrupy and sullen, but at 80 degrees Fahrenheit, it felt relatively bearable. Shortly, under the shameless sun, the mercury would leap to 100 degrees. He wondered how the newcomers would react to the daily rocket ride of heat and humidity? Who would be the first to crack?

Blacker strolled further into the open land, the maidan that bordered the bungalow. The entire team and all its equipment, with the exception of the wrecked Fox Moth, had now assembled. This was a fair achievement in itself. But now at last, the real business of the enterprise was about to begin.

Foreseeing no change in the weather Blacker turned back to the bungalow where his colleagues were still sleeping. Now he could hear the soft thud of hooves in a slow canter. Then Tom Smith, a lean sunburned man in his forties, came through the trees. The estate manager was riding a bay horse which he pulled up alongside Blacker. 'G'day to you, Colonel. No need to wake you then.'

'Hello Tom. No, I rarely need dawn calls,' said Blacker. ' A fine mount you have there.'

Smith leaned down to pat the gelding's neck. 'I got him from Raja Banaili last year. A reject from the polo stables, but he's perfect for hoofing around the estate.'

'No better way,' agreed Blacker. 'You joining us for breakfast?'

'That's why I'm here. To make sure the houseboys are ready.'

The planter and his wife had volunteered to supervise the domestic facilities for the visitors. Clearly Tom was leaving nothing to chance. My kind of man, thought Blacker, as he walked beside the horse back towards the bungalow. On the wide verandah, he could see the houseboys, Framjee and Golwalla, preparing breakfast at a large table.

'How's the Memsahib?' Blacker asked. He had met the planter's intriguing wife a few weeks previously. 'I didn't see Mrs. Smith when we came in last night.'

Smith dismounted and tied the reins to a tree. 'Sally's fine, thanks Colonel. She was in town chasing supplies when you got here. It's a fair sized crowd you've brought along.'

'Thirty-five all told. I hope we don't drive you all mad.'

'It's too late for that, Colonel.' Smith grinned. 'The entire population has been buzzing like a hornet swarm for days. And I heard that crowds at Lalbalu caused some pilots to abort their landings.'

Blacker nodded. 'The strip was chockablock with welcome. The pilots had to make several passes to scare them off.'

Smith laughed. 'Raja Banaili has ordered the Police Superintendent to send a detachment to prevent that happening again.'

The two men reached the breakfast area as Fellowes came from the bungalow. Like most pilots, the Air Commodore preferred a clear runway on the approach and was pleased to hear Tom's news.

'And while I remember,' Tom added. 'Sally has arranged an outing for Mrs. Fellowes this morning. A ride around town to see the sights and to meet the Ranee.'

'That's very kind of her,' said Fellowes. 'Eleanor will enjoy some female company.'

The houseboy arranged the rattan chairs and the Air Commodore sat down next to Blacker. Within minutes the reserve pilot Ellison, Shepherd and Dr. Bennett emerged from the bungalow, all rather wash-eyed and sweat-soaked. Minutes later they were followed by Eleanor, and then by Clydesdale and McIntyre who stopped in his tracks.

'Heaven's alive, it's hotter than porridge. So I wasn't dreaming.' Mac stared at the horse. 'I thought I smelt manure in my sleep.'

Clydesdale took a glass of papaya juice. 'I didn't get any sleep thanks to the mosquitoes.'

'Och man, they know blue blood tastes better.' McIntyre dropped into a chair. 'There must be a hole in your mosquito net.'

Sitting down beside Clydesdale, Eleanor patted his shoulder. 'I'll find a needle and thread after breakfast. Take no notice of him.'

Blacker observed the newcomers as he sipped his tea. He could sense an underlying excitement, like the first day of a school term. They had endured weeks of relentless travel, jousting with bureaucracy, weather, food and hygiene in conditions rarely experienced back home. Despite all that, a warm collective humor prevailed, the essential for any venture.

They were attacking scrambled eggs on toast when they were interrupted by the arrival of a motorcycle. Its rider was a young Indian in a white shirt, long black shorts and striped socks. He approached rather nervously holding a wad of papers as Blacker waved him over.'

'Must be a tax collector?' suggested McIntyre. 'He has enough documents.'

'Those are the guides to the Himalayas,' said Blacker. 'This is our meteorologist, Mr. Gupta.'

After general introductions, the young man took a seat beside Eleanor who passed him a cup of tea. 'So, you're a weatherman?'

'Indeed, I am, Madam,' said Gupta.

Eleanor offered him a bowl of sugar cubes. 'Then maybe you can explain, Mr. Gupta, how you can predict the weather over Everest when we're a hundred miles to the south?'

The question had the unfortunate effect of overwhelming Gupta with embarrassment. Blacker felt obliged to intervene and rescue the young man.

'Gupta is in touch with the met office in Calcutta where records are collated daily from the regional weather stations. He evaluates the pressure gradients and wind patterns before launching hydrogen balloons here in Purnea to fine-tune his predictions. Isn't that how it works, Mr. Gupta?'

'Indeed so, Colonel, sir. I send my balloons up to 30,000 feet, above the height of your mountain. Tracking them with a theodolite telescope, I measure the drift every ten minutes to establish average wind speeds at specific heights. It's a mathematical procedure.'

Eleanor remained curious. 'But that can only apply to the wind above Purnea? It cannot relate directly to Everest, surely?'

The Air Commodore had to enlighten his wife. 'Fair point, Eleanor,' he said. 'That's why I'll go up at dawn each day in one of the Moths. I'll climb as high as I can above the haze. If I can see the Himalayas, then we have a second appraisal of the situation. Mr. Gupta's records will be matched with my visual assessment. Right, Mr. Gupta?'

'Yes, very nicely said, sir.'

Eleanor buttered her toast and then asked. 'But what happens when the

164

haze is too thick to track your balloons as they rise? Yesterday when we flew in from Gaya it was like soup.'

'A very dirty pea soup,' added McIntyre. 'If we can't see the balloons, Eleanor, we just stay on the ground.'

Eleanor pushed a plate of sliced mangos towards the meteorologist. 'Please help yourself, Mr. Gupta.'

Blacker reached for toast and marmalade, his head buzzing with all this chatter. Like Fellowes he felt that breakfast conversation should be kept to Trappist levels. Taking ladies on the expedition had never been his preferred option, but that didn't matter now.

41. Lalbalu Aerodrome – March 1933

TWELVE MILES AWAY, THE GROUND crew were stirring after their first night in the camp at Lalbalu. During the night, and with only a strip of canvas between himself and the Indian jungle, Pitt had not slept well. He had been kept awake by a hubbub of shrieking owls and nighthawks. The weird yowling of jackals and feral dogs had included a snuffling, coughing grunt that he attributed to leopard, hogs or worse. He had just two hours of sleep and now had to get on with the job.

On the groundsheet under his camp bed Pitt could feel a Rigby Mannlicher rifle with a pack of .350 mm ammunition. 'Strictly for defensive purposes,' Colonel Blacker had advised when issuing the firearms. But rifles made Pitt anxious. Blasting off into the darkness might be commonplace for Blacker and his military chums, but Pitt and his mates were not so keen.

Nevertheless, this would be good material for the reports he would now begin writing for the *Bristol Evening Post*. Readers in the West Country would love knowing how he confronted nocturnal dangers as he stood armed and ready to defend the camp from marauding beasts. In their armchairs, or at the formica tables in their local pubs, they would appreciate all the checks he made for snakes and spiders before crawling into his tent.

Pitt pulled on his overalls over cotton underpants and vest. Leaving the Mannlicher under the bed, he poked his head outside the tent. Hughes and the RAF men were contemplating the stove and kettle. He went to join them.

The camp lay beside the grassland of the flying base. The cackle of crows and trilling songbirds echoed from the trees around this wide clearing. Not far from the stove, a troop of langur monkeys had taken balcony seats in a giant banyan tree. A dominant male had even climbed onto the ridge of the hangars where the Westlands were parked. How long would it be until these local pirates began raiding the cockpits? Should he describe all this to his readers as a comical anecdote or a horror story?

The camp had been designed by Colonel Blacker. He had positioned the crew quarters near the hangars to improve security and ease of maintenance during operations. Latrine tents had been erected in a downwind corner of the encampment. Much further out, isolated on the field perimeter, another marquee covered their precious fuel supplies.

This was the domain of Mr. Gallimore, Shell's fuel expert. His job was to supervise the anti-freeze additives. Highly volatile and dangerous, the fuel was stored in steel drums, ready for hand-pumping into the Westlands' copious tanks. Pitt heard Sergeant Greenwood mention an imminent refueling to Mr. Gallimore.

'I'd forget that if I were you, Sergeant.' Pitt interrupted. 'First I need to clean and replace the filters. After all that shit in the sky from Karachi, they'll need love and affection before you juice up.'

'So they won't be flying today?' suggested Gallimore.

'Not a chance. I have to double-check all fuel feeds and carb intakes.'

'Very well. Filters first,' said Greenwood. 'Then we refuel.'

As custodian of the two 'peggy' engines, Pitt's role effectively gave him the last word on their welfare. The conversation changed to comments about the pleasures of Lalbalu. Everyone shared Pitt's opinion of their first night in camp. 'As quiet as a drunken football mob.'

'I've often slept outside,' Sergeant Greenwood admitted. 'But never was I woken by an elephant rubbing its ass on my tent.'

'Sure it was an elephant?' asked Hensley, the chief rigger. 'Could have been one of those monkeys wanting a cuddle.'

Sergeant Greenwood shook his head, his brow drooling with sweat. 'Believe me, I can evaluate a buttock, son. When I looked up, this huge bulge was rubbing the pole of my tent. If that elephant had made one step back, I wouldn't be here now.'

'What a shame,' said Corporal Bradley, supervisor of electrical components and heated flying suits.

'And another thing,' said Greenwood. 'Those monkeys are sneaky bastards. If we don't watch out, they'll be off with our spares, tools and all. More police are coming to guard us and with luck that includes keeping the monkeys at bay.'

This was all magnificent stuff for Pitt's Bristol readership, but his literary thoughts faded at the sight of an exotic car rolling towards them. He wondered if it was the police arriving, but no, this was a shooting brake with a single occupant. The vehicle came charging and lurching over the track as Pitt stared disbelievingly. 'We can fit him with wings if he wants to get airborne.'

The shooting brake stopped with a balloon of dust, through which the

167

driver emerged like some prophet. He was middle-aged and definitely not one of the local tribesmen, who were all as thin as pipe cleaners. This gentleman was a portly Indian wearing a tailored hunting jacket, winged jodhpurs and leather boots.

'Good morning! Good morning! So you are the boys of Lalbalu preparing for the Himalaya?'

'Who's this, then?' Bradley mumbled.

This was no place for the inappropriate thoughts of a dozy electrician. Pitt now identified the shooting brake was a customized Rolls Royce. He stepped towards the newcomer, hand outstretched. 'I'm Cyril Pitt, Chief Engineer.'

The visitor pulled off his buckskin gloves. 'May I introduce myself. I am your host, Raja Banaili. I offer you all a heartfelt welcome and will ensure you have all your desires while you stay with us.'

'That sounds enticing, sir. We thank you for that. You're up early, if I may say.'

'Indeed I am.' The Raja radiated bonhomie. 'This is the best time of day in this season, I tell you. However on this particular occasion, I've been on duty all night.'

'Celebrating with the officers?' suggested Bradley.

The Raja brushed aside this suggestion. 'No, no, they all retired early. I have a problem with a tiger near here. Unfortunately our stripy friend has taken no fewer than fifteen souls from local villages to date, so I cannot permit it to continue with the habit. I spent the night in a tree with my rifle, keeping watch over a goat we pegged out for the tiger's pleasure.'

Around the stove the men looked at one another. Maybe Mannlichers were very necessary?

'And did you get him?' asked Pitt. 'The tiger?'

'No, I'm sorry to say I did not. The most juicy of goats and the most dangerous of predators were not destined to meet below my tree. But there's no need for concern. The police will post sentries to keep you safe.'

So they had passed a night like slabs of fresh meat in a butcher's yard. Pitt felt the energy for his news report building by the minute. He reached for the teapot.

'I believe tigers don't like the smell of engine oil, so we should have no problems. Seeing as you're offering sentries, the least we can do is to offer you some tea, sir?'

The Raja rubbed his hands together and accepted immediately. 'A cup of char? Please! But what I really want is to see your aeroplanes.'

Pitt caught the excitement in the Raja's eyes. The man who could confront man-eaters also enjoyed aviation. 'That's easily arranged, sir. Let's go to the hangars where all your questions can be answered.'

'That, Mr. Pitt, will be the most wonderful start to my day.'

Taking their teacups, the men followed Pitt and Raja Banaili to the hangars. Nobody noticed the langur monkey that descended from the banyan tree to scamper over and seize their teapot.

42. Purnea – March 1933

BY MIDDAY EVERYONE UNDERSTOOD EXACTLY why they had risen so early. The soupy dawn soon became a roasting crucible measuring 98 Fahrenheit in the shade. Perspiration flowed from brow and armpit and copious supplies of chilled lemonade were called for.

Despite such discomfort, the tasks allocated to each crew member were vigorously pursued. Fellowes ordered that all checks and inspections should be completed as soon as possible, readiness being the priority. Only then could they relax to enjoy the more leisurely lifestyle suited to the steam oven of Purnea.

While engineers fielded spanners and tweaked calibrators at Lalbalu, the pilots sat on their verandah revising maps and flight plans. When they next took to the sky, there might be neither time nor opportunity to correct mistakes. All airborne activities began by thinking on the ground.

Eleanor Fellowes made her contribution by sewing up Clydesdale's mosquito net with a needle. She then went to help Fraser who was preparing a darkroom to process exposed film. After laying out developing trays, rinsing sinks and overhead clip lines, Fraser had wired a red lamp over the trays where chemicals would create images of historic value. From the stores, Eleanor found blackout material for the window and on a card, she wrote *Do Not Enter!* ready to attach to the darkroom door. Finally she prepared folders to store the photographs.

Eleanor admired the youngest member of the team. When she enquired about his work, Fraser explained each procedure with a nervous stammer demonstrating how differences in grain and tone were adjusted. Fraser offered to process the films in her Kodak camera but she had declined the offer. Her films could wait, she said, as she left to tell the houseboys that under no circumstances should they to enter the darkroom. She had just delivered this essential instruction when a Dodge pickup truck arrived with Sally Smith at the wheel.

Eleanor scooped up her bag, her sun-hat, dark glasses and the latest copy of *Tatler*. This she would give Sally as a token of goodwill, hand delivered from Mayfair. The heat was scalding under the metal roof of the pickup. 'Hello Sally. So kind of you to come over.'

'My pleasure entirely.' Sally was obviously accustomed to the heat. Not a bead of sweat showed below her thick brown hair fastened by silver combs above each ear. 'The flight is the most exciting thing ever. And to think that it's all happening in Purnea. I'm so pleased to meet you, Mrs. Fellowes.'

'Just Eleanor, please. I much prefer that.'

Sally Smith had the glow of a thoroughly capable and unpretentious woman in her late thirties, thought Eleanor. But was there a touch of Bohemia in the mix? Sally's rings looked similar to those worn by the local Indian women, her shirt was made from sari material and her loose overalls were blue denim. Not the standard home county attire she thought, as she got into the pickup. It certainly didn't matter.

'So then, where first? The Ranee is dying to meet you. And so is the Country Club secretary. He's offering honorary membership to you all. At the golf club there's a similar offer. So that makes three possibilities. It's all very basic here.'

'Up to you, Sally. Whatever you decide.'

Just as Sally engaged gear, Shepherd came running from the bungalow, brandishing an envelope. 'Any chance of a lift to the cable office?'

'Jump in the back,' shouted Sally. 'We'll go there first.'

Shepherd settled in the truck's bed with his latest bulletin. Sitting under his topee with his hands gripping his bare knees, Eleanor thought of taking a photograph, but this was India and, as she had found out, unusual sights were two-a-penny.

The Dodge followed the track around the golf course. Here the resourceful Blacker had obtained permission to use the longest fairway as a landing strip for the Moth biplanes. These were anchored to stakes driven into rough near the 8th hole and the unusual sight had attracted scores of people. Raja Banaili had ordered his militiamen to maintain security. Armed with lahti sticks, these guards waved to the Dodge to indicate all was well.

They turned onto the road to Purnea. Weaving through the traffic, Sally pointed out fields of sugar cane, indigo and jute scattered in the landscape. The sugar cane, she said, was the most profitable and, while the fiery breeze blasted through the Dodge window, she pointed to a wide acreage of indigo.'That's one of our best crops. Tom calls it Purple Smoke and prefers it to the Wild Blue variety.'

Sally swerved to avoid a cyclist, an elderly man wobbling dangerously while he changed the hand grasping an umbrella above his head. Next a line of pack camels came into view and the Dodge had to veer around them. Eleanor was soon thinking that air travel was a far safer option.

'The Raja really enjoyed his visit to Lalbalu this morning,' said Sally. Your men showed him the Westlands, the flight suits and even gave him a dose of pure oxygen. He was transported.'

'I'm glad to hear that.' Eleanor had just seen a group of lepers squatting sadly below a tree. 'Must keep the Raja happy.'

The Dodge stopped in Purnea's main street at the cable office. Shepherd clambered out and came to Sally's window. 'Thanks so much. Don't wait. I owe you a drink.'

'This evening at the club will do nicely,' smiled Sally, before she pulled out into the traffic.

'You'll be lucky,' Eleanor warned. 'He's so tight with his expenses that we think he's a skinflint.'

The Dodge soon reached the spacious compound of the Banaili palace. Here the servants explained the Ranee was not receiving guests, because she was not at home.

'Logic at its finest. We'll meet her soon enough.' Sally drove back to the main road and pumped the accelerator to overtake more camels. These were hauling wagons stacked high with sacks of produce. 'That's jute going to market. Everything is heading for market in India.'

Sally was full of local information, but was far more interested to hear about the expedition and its sponsor. 'This Lady Houston? Have you ever met her?'

'No, I never had the pleasure.' Eleanor recalled Perry's advice not to divulge her personal thoughts about the sponsor. 'She's something of a maverick in British society. Took a shine to our Chief Pilot though. That's the real reason we're all here.'

'So nothing to do with MacDonald then? All that traitor business?'

'That played a part, but basically Lady Houston just wants to put the British over Everest before any other nation does so.'

'Sounds reasonable to me.' Sally was arriving at the country club. 'We all have reasons for what we do. I came here at the beginning of the war. I came to find a husband in the Raj.'

'So you're one of the Fishing Fleet girls?'

Sally laugh was more than hearty. 'Yes, I suppose I was. But we British don't really belong here, you know. One day, Tom and I will go back to England. Probably we'll buy a farm in the Midlands to grow whatever makes sense. No indigo, that's for sure.'

Eleanor tipped up her sunglasses. She had seen enough for one morning. The heat was ridiculous and she was drowning in perspiration. 'Empires come and empires go, Sally. So let's enjoy it while it lasts. In the meantime I could do with a really long cold drink.'

43. Byron Cottage, Hampstead – March 1933

THE NEWS CLIPPINGS ARRIVED WITH the morning's mail delivery. Garland's job was to filter those which reflected Lady Houston's wide interests in world affairs. News from Paris was always welcome and Garland had heard all about marvelous restaurants such as Tortoni and Maison Dorée where deviled whitebait and souche flounder were served with a heady froth of champagne *au couleur rose*, pink being Lucy's favorite color. Paris, claimed Lady Houston, was then a fountain of lascivious energy.

Garland had a suspicion that her employer rarely revealed the full story. Conversely the public always hankered to learn more about their wealthiest Dame. Another group of clippings recorded any comments or tittle-tattle about Lady Houston, her yacht and her ongoing row with the Government. And now of course Garland noted the flight expedition was very much in the news.

Garland leaned her elbows on the desk and glanced at her watch. It was late morning. She had walked the dog, paid the gardener, and then passed the time with this routine paperwork.

The L-shaped room lay across the corridor from the kitchen. The paint on the walls was fading. The carpet on the floor was threadbare because Lady Houston would not waste money on refurbishing her secretary's office. Garland had become accustomed to this lack of style in the workplace. Perhaps, she wondered, too accustomed?

From the window, she looked down the drive past the gates that led to the city. Garland felt like a caged bird. Se was trapped in an ivory cage with a very dominant parrot for company. The thought of another season niggled.

She heard John's footsteps in the corridor. Then he was at her door. 'I was told to be ready at ten thirty. Two hours later and she's still not here. Is she all right?'

Garland shrugged. 'Did I tell you to be ready?'

John dismissed her query. 'No, Miss. But Her Ladyship did. She had to be in Mayfair by midday.'

Garland swung her chair towards the chauffeur. 'She was ready at eleven,' said Garland. 'But then she took a call from Winston Churchill.'

'The beloved Winnie?' John perked up. 'That explains it.'

'Yes. He's rapturous about her actions on behalf of the nation. I spoke to him briefly before I transferred him. He wanted to know if Lucy was feeling better and I told him I thought so. Then they talked for ages. After that, she told me to get hold of the editor of the *Bristol Evening Post*. I can't imagine why, but that involved another lengthy call.'

An electric bell sounded, ringing again and again. The length of the summons often reflected Her Ladyship's mood. Three long rings implied it was urgent.

Garland hurried to the dayroom to find Lady Houston radiating fury. 'You called, Lady Houston?'

'Yes, Garland. That's why I use the bloody bell. I'm cancelling appointments for the day. I shall stay here.'

'Whatever you prefer.'

'But I've decided we'll go to Jersey this summer. That means I have new jobs for you, Garland.'

'Good.' Garland smiled. Jersey sounded OK. 'My notebook's ready.'

'Good?' Lady Houston was suspicious. 'It's not good. I get tired with all this moving around. It's not worth having homes all over the place when it takes so much effort and money to enjoy them. First you must alert the housekeeper, Mrs. Tippet, in Jersey. Then you can ask the Captain to position *Liberty* at Hamble.'

'I'll do all that.' Garland turned.

'Not so fast, Garland. There's more.' Lady Houston pushed a hankie up her jumper sleeve and picked up a copy of *The Times*. 'Mr. Churchill told me to read this piece about Germany's expanding power. Both Churchill and I have warned MacDonald. But what has he done about countering the Luftwaffe? Sweet fanny zero I tell you!'

From Mrs. Munro in Kinrara, Garland had learned how, years earlier when acting as Chancellor of the Exchequer, Churchill had assisted Lady Houston with her inheritance taxes. A check to the Treasury for £1.5 million had been signed by Lucy while Churchill personally checked the zeros. Also it was Churchill's friendship with Clydesdale that had persuaded the Air Ministry to support her Everest flight.

Garland tried offering some cheer. 'At least Mr. Churchill is constructive. Surely he thinks the expedition offers many benefits?'

'So what? We may as well give Hitler a key to the skies over England.'

175

'I'm sure it won't come to that.' Garland said. 'I can't believe the British people will let the Germans to walk in.'

'You mean fly in, Garland, you silly girl! Wars, from now on, will be decided in the sky. Land invasions can best succeed after capturing the skies. That's why I support aviators. But I can't stop the Germans on my own!'

'But you're doing all you can. And it will be your crews that reach the top of the world.'

'Yes, but only if they survive the attempt! They're not running errands in downtown Manhattan. They're trying to survive in a jungle teeming with reptiles and man-eating tigers, and that's before they even take to the air.'

'Sure. But those must be the facts of life in Bihar.'

Lady Houston glanced angrily at Garland and grabbed a newspaper. It was the *Bristol Evening Post*, a new addition to the list of periodicals provided by Romeike & Curtis, the clipping agency. The paper buckled as Lucy Houston stabbed it with her finger.

'Bristol aviation's chief engineer, Cyril Pitt, is filing reports from Bihar. He writes about having to sleep with a rifle to defend his camp against large wild cats and marauding dogs. Meanwhile the heat is sapping their strength as mosquitos hover nearby. It's very worrying, Garland, if the chief engineer has to suffer so much.'

Garland stepped over to glance at the article. 'Put that down to colorful reporting. As a journalist, I can tell you that sometimes we have to brighten up a story. We stretch the truth a tad.'

'Which explains why I have yet to give you my life story. But the Marquis assured me it was safer than walking round Hampstead Heath. Reading this, I don't see how Pitt's life is remotely safe.'

Garland struggled to stay calm. She had just heard one reason why the idea of a biography unsettled the heiress. Then it was Hitler, then the Marquis and now the engineer. 'So what did Pitt expect to find in India?'

But Lady Houston was reading again. 'Pitt says thousands of Indians crowded onto the runway when they came in to land. It was like trying to land in Oxford Street. How do you do that without killing hundreds of people?'

Garland read the report. 'I guess they'll seal the airfield now that the aircraft have arrived.'

'You don't understand. This gift of mine to Clydesdale was not meant to lead to possible death for Indians, Britons or anyone for that matter.'

'Your crews are volunteers. They accept the risks. And as for Indians, they're good at dodging trouble.'

Lucy Houston refused to be comforted. 'Pitt makes these perils very clear. Furthermore Ralph Blumenfeld says his reports are annoying *The Times*. Their sponsorship was exclusively reserved for their man Shepherd.'

'I believe that was the understanding.'

'So that might create a legal problem as well. Call Willie Graham and warn him. We don't want any arguments with *The Times* or *Bristol Evening Post* during the expedition.'

Garland made notes on her pad. 'Sure, I'll call him.'

'And you can ask Ralph to inform the Committee about my feelings on all this.'

'I'll do that too.' Garland hoped the dark mood would fade from the agitated woman before her. 'Pitt's reports may be over-dramatic but they obviously appeal to his readers. To me, it suggests you're achieving your objectives, Lady Houston. The British people are inspired.'

This summary appeased Lady Houston. She pushed herself from the chair. 'You're quite right, my dear. That is the plan, but things can go wrong. Just look what happened to Monsieur Faure and his mistress the Red Widow.'

'The Red Widow?'

'Her real name was Marguerite Steinheil.' Lucy said. 'A fine looking woman. They found her naked with Monsieur Faure.'

'Oh!'

'You may be surprised, Garland, but Monsieur Faure was then the President of France. They found them locked together like mating dogs, but the President was dead.'

'Dead?' Garland gasped. 'At least he went out with a bang.'

'The best way to go, I say, but Marguerite had to leave without her hair. The servants had no choice but to cut it from his fist which was locked around her beautiful titian tresses. She vanished without even picking up her corset.'

Garland's jaw fell.

'And it all went unreported.' Lady Houston clapped her hands together as though the storytelling had improved her mood. 'I've changed my mind. Tell John to be ready in ten minutes. I'll go to my hairdresser in Mayfair as planned.'

'John's ready, but I'll let him know.'

'And you can tell them this, Garland. All the Lords, ladies, pilots, engineers, film men, editors, Governors and Maharajas... I am ultimately responsible for the expedition's welfare and I shall tolerate no trouble.'

44. The Club, Purnea – March 1933

THE PURNEA GOLF CLUB CONSISTED of a single storey building beside the course where the occasional presence of a Moth biplane might now be expected to interrupt play.

Not a single club member had the least intention of complaining. Even the stuffiest among them regarded Moth movements as a welcome inconvenience. At least there was something new to discuss other than the growth rate of plants. Together with a handful of local dignitaries, many of the club members turned up for a special event to welcome Fellowes and his men. Staff in turbans and braided uniforms served drinks while on the lawns outside, the crowd chattered like finches as the sky slipped from orange to pink to crimson in tribute to another day gone.

Etherton had just returned from Kathmandu carrying the official permits from the Nepalese Authorities for two flight sorties. Standing at the bar, he was catching up on developments with Clydesdale, McIntyre and Blacker. Chances of success had doubled at a stroke, Etherton explained, as Fellowes came to join them.

'But permission comes with provisos,' Etherton continued. 'We must notify them of the flight plans and you're not permitted to make forced landings in Nepal. All in all, we got what we wanted.'

'No forced landings?' Fellowes found this very funny. 'So, if a Peggy should quit, we must only land by intent. Which means sod all. In any case, well done Percy. A master stroke.'

Etherton smiled. 'I explained to His Majesty that his people would be unlikely to see the Westlands, so he finally agreed. I might add it will be easier to fly to Kathmandu than to walk there, if they ever decide to join the twentieth century.'

Blacker wasn't about to debate the value of Nepal's isolation. 'Well, Percy, we've been busy in your absence. The Westlands are now ready for action whenever conditions are right.'

'Which won't be tomorrow according to Gupta.' Fellowes said. 'High altitude winds will prevail, I'm sorry to say.'

Clydesdale glanced at the sky. Little had altered and the sapping temperature and humidity seemed likely to persist. 'That means we'll have to endure another day with the blasted film crew.'

McIntyre chortled. 'You might get a job in Hollywood when all this is over.'

Clydesdale was drinking gin and tonic. His mother had told him to do so to keep malaria at bay. 'It's ridiculous,' he said. 'We've been posing for Barkas and his crew all day. They're at it tirelessly. A shot of Blacker rubbing his monocle, then a sequence when I study a weather report, and another showing us talking to a monk. But then we have to do it all over again because the wretched sound recorder doesn't like the humidity.'

'That's India.' Blacker snorted. 'Grin and bear it.'

McIntyre was enjoying a beer. 'Why suffer when we have alternatives?'

'Such as?' Blacker enquired.

'This afternoon, I visited some open water near Lalbulu. I saw it from the air. It's a reservoir close to the airstrip and it would make a perfect lido.'

Fellowes nodded. 'I also had a look-see. It's an ideal location to keep everyone cool and happy. I've asked the Indians to erect a diving platform so Mac can show off his fancy swim suit for the camera.' Fellowes poked a finger at the Chief Pilot. 'You may not be lured by the big screen, Clydesdale, but Mac's got the bug.'

'I'd strip to bare bollocks if Barkas asks me,' said Mac. 'Anything for a swim in cool water.'

Etherton tapped a new cigarette on the bar, eyeing Mac as he lit it. 'This pool you found? Safe is it?'

'Och aye. The local clerk of works dived in and swam around like an otter. Said there was nothing to worry about.'

Etherton was unconvinced. 'They all say that in India. In the meantime, I must tell Mr. Shepherd about the permits. The poor fellow needs something to write about.'

Etherton went to seek out the correspondent but was soon captured by Sally Smith who introduced him as 'the man behind it all' to the planters and their wives. Fellowes and McIntyre fell into conversation with the Raja of Banaili and his wife. The Ranee beamed politely, a golden sari around her bountiful midriff, while her husband eulogized about his visit to the air base and his own desire to fly.

Meanwhile Clydesdale remained at the bar in a blissful period of solitude until Barkas came to join him. The film director was sporting a blue cotton suit and white paneled shoes. 'You did so well today, Lord Clydesdale.'

'Thank you Mr. Barkas,' Clydesdale said with no emotion.

'I'd say you have a natural talent, but I suppose most politicians are actors in one way or another. Most importantly, you look wonderful on camera.'

'Kind of you to say so.' Clydesdale had to acknowledge the director's total self-belief and attention to detail, but the man would never get a dinner invitation to Lennoxlove, home to the Duchy of Hamilton near Edinburgh.

'I need to float some ideas past you. Some exciting film concepts, assuming you have a moment?'

On the long flight out, Clydesdale had learned from Shepherd that the director was known for his zealous, possibly manic, approach to the film craft. 'No time like the present.'

Barkas came closer, rather too close. 'We must have footage of take-offs and landings. Can we shoot these before your actual departure? What do you think?'

'We'll be flying local sorties for test and evaluation. You're welcome to film those.'

'Brilliant. Having those shots in the can is good sense. In case we fail to film the real departure, you understand?'

'Of course.' Clydesdale was gazing out beyond the bar room to the lawn where several hundred guests were hobnobbing beneath the silhouetted palm trees. Fruit bats were leaving their roosts, flapping around like prehistoric creatures on the hunt.

'...and I'd like to run flight tests with the smoke, if we may? My A.D. Connochie has set it all up. We have red, white and blue.'

Clydesdale frowned. 'What was that about smoke?'

'It's called stannic acid,' Barkas continued. 'We have pots of the stuff. It comes in crystal form and when your observer releases it into the slipstream it creates clouds of puff in red, white and blue.'

'And what exactly is the point of these smoke puffs?'

'It will be a masterful shot, signifying the moment of triumph over the world's highest mountain! Poof! Poof! Just like that!'

Clydesdale's concerns grew. 'I doubt if we can countenance such manouvres. We're meant to be photographing the mountains, not painting them with poofs in the colors of the Empire.'

The film director adjusted his silk cravat as he weaned a cigarette from a black enamel Dunhill case. 'Perhaps you'd like to think on it, Lord Clydesdale? We can shoot these stannic sequences at low level at Lalbalu. That would make it easier and the footage could be spliced into the summit sequences.'

'Mr. Barkas, this is primarily a scientific operation, not a cinema spectacular. I'll give it consideration, but I fear you may be disappointed. Excuse me, please.'

Clydesdale made a courteous nod to the director and adroitly joined Sally Smith who in no time was introducing him to her friends. They all seemed to him decent, straight-talking folk with their feet on the ground.

The party continued long after sunset when flares were lit around the lawn. Dr. Bennett had brought a selection of 78 rpm records, having guessed that expats always loved new music. The doctor put the gramophone beside the dance floor and, to everyone's delight, persuaded Eleanor to join him in a foxtrot. McIntyre offered Sally his arm while Ellison, Shepherd and Connochie also found willing partners from among the planters' wives. Finally Gupta stunned the entire assembly by arriving on the dance floor with his wife, an eye-popping beauty in a shimmering emerald sari. Her swaying body, long sensuous arms and cascading black hair created such a stir that everyone had to watch.

'Oh for the old days,' mused Etherton, now back at the bar.

'That sight makes my monocle go misty,' agreed Blacker. 'Gupta's a lucky boy.'

The two men watched the dancers flow and glide to the music. Both the Raja and the Ranee were delighted by the latest hits from London.

'Our host is quite a player,' Blacker remarked as the Raja romped past. 'Tiger shooting one night, fox trotting the next. I wish I had his energy. I'm ready for some shut-eye.'

'Me too,' Etherton agreed. 'I've had three nights on slow trains.'

Beyond the main gates, they found one of the Vauxhalls lent to them by Raja Banaili. The driver was awake and they were soon on their way.

Crossing the golf course the car's headlights caught and lingered on the three Moths. Blacker was pleased to note the watchmen were also on the job and within minutes they were at the bungalow. As the car disappeared, they heard cries of alarm coming from the bungalow. Both men rushed towards the dim lights of the porch where the houseboy Framjee was windmilling his arms in dismay.

Etherton raised a finger. 'What's going on? What's all this noise about?'

Framjee stammered. 'Naja in the bedroom, sah.'

Etherton turned to Blacker. 'You like cobras. You can charm the blighter out of there.'

'Which bedroom, Framjee?' Blacker needed no prompting. 'Where is it?'

'The one for the Doctor Bennett, sah.'

Other residents would soon be returning to collapse in their beds. Blacker saw a ceremonial shield displaying a fan display of swords and knives. It was fixed to the hallway wall. Reaching up, he prized a khanda from the shield and ran his thumb over the weapon's edge. It was sharp enough for a sideways swipe. Gripping it firmly, Blacker scurried down the corridor. 'Bring a torch, Percy.'

In the dim light of the corridor, the houseboy, Golwalla, was standing outside the room shared by Dr. Bennett and Ellison. 'In there, Colonel, sah. On the mat.'

The door creaked as Blacker opened it. 'By god, he's a big fellow. A king I'd say. Hold the lamp, Percy, and I'll show him the khanda.'

Etherton focused the light on the dark coils of a cobra as it stirred. Looped on the floor mat between the beds, the snake's head fanned and hovered. In a flash, it sensed danger and struck forward, but so did Blacker. The khanda blade sliced through the air, severing the snake's head in one blow. Its body began coiling and flicking aimlessly on the mat.

As he stamped on the severed head, Blacker looked around for other dangers. Then he flicked the twitching body up and through the open window. 'Bye bye Mr. Naja.'

'Fine swordplay, Blacker!' Etherton said. 'Your grandfather would be proud of you. Now, Framjee, please clean the floor and watch out. We don't want any more cobras sleeping here at night, do you hear me?'

'Yes, sah,' said Framjee as Blacker lifted his foot from the hooded head. 'No more naja, sah. I promise!'

45. Lilos at Lalbalu – March 1933

THE GROUND CREW RETURNED TO their camp in Lalbalu around midnight. Regardless of any hangovers, the demands of military routine meant that the ground crew were back on duty at 6 a.m. Various jobs in the hangars kept them busy until 9 a.m. when the temperature in the shade reached 96 Fahrenheit.

On the hour, Sergeant Greenwood ordered all men back to the shaded canteen tent. Here they settled in canvas chairs for a break and soon learned of the cobra's demise from one of the drivers assigned to the ferry service between the two bases.

'Imagine getting out of bed in the dark and stepping on the damned thing!' Burnard squirmed in his chair. 'I'll be glad to get home once this little jaunt is over. I can't sleep here.'

'Anyone else fancy waking up with a cobra for a necklace?' asked Pitt.

Burnard slammed down his teacup. 'Pitt, keep that idea for Bristol's thrill seekers. Don't frighten the wits out of us.'

Clark's mind was elsewhere. 'I had dreams of gorgeous girls sliding their sweet little tongues down my throat.'

'Watch yourself, Clark,' said Pitt. 'That's how Eve seduced Adam.'

'And look what happened.' Burnard pointed to the crowd of Indians on the far side of the aerodrome. 'Two became four, four became eight, eight became sixteen and, before you know it, you've got the population of India and the entire world.'

Pitt sipped his tea. 'Tongues don't make babies, Burnard. Maybe you didn't know that?'

Burnard ignored the question. He was watching preparations for a game cricket on the airfield. The pitch was measured and wickets installed while the camera crew set up in the outfield. Meanwhile Barkas was selecting boys from the crowd and shortly these extras were bowling googlies and batting like demons before the Movietone camera. Regrettably Barkas had to abort several takes. Finally Connochie and Bonnett abandoned the camera and walked over to join the ground crew.

Connochie was tousle-haired and sweaty. 'Who wants to be in the movie?' he asked wearily.

The sergeant spoke for all. 'We're not here to play cricket.'

'We only need two batsmen. 'Barkas wants to show us batting against the locals. Is nobody up for a bit of sport?'

Hangovers and heat gave the offer no appeal. Undeterred, Connochie seized a glass of water, swallowed it in one and shook his mop of hair. 'A chance to act with India's youngest sportsmen and you can't be bothered! Sergeant Greenwood, you're the senior officer here, please detail two men to represent Britain. Can't let the side down, can we?'

'Listen, mate,' said the Sergeant. 'We've been up all night. It's topping a hundred in the shade and I need them fit for their jobs. But fifteen minutes can do no harm. Helmsley and Bradley, you both stayed in last night. Get over there for Mr. Barkas and bat for the nation!'

With loud sighs of exasperation, the two RAF men finished their drinks and stood up to muted applause.

'Give me football any day,' said Bradley.

'Too bad. Cricket's the religion here,' said Connochie. He downed a second glass of water before leading his recruits back to the pitch.

'And you, Mr. Bonnett?' Pitt watched as the cameraman subside into Bradley's vacated chair. 'Aren't you going to film them?'

Bonnett hoisted his sandaled feet onto an empty box and lay back. 'The other cameraman, Fisher, enjoys cricket. I'm for a nap. I'll be ready when Barkas needs footage on the flight action.'

Sergeant Greenwood tut-tutted. 'No chance of that, Mr. Bonnett. Fellowes wants the kites kept in their hangars today.'

Bonnett thrust his hands behind his head and lay back further. 'I know that, but Barkas hasn't yet found out.' He wore the smile of a seasoned campaigner as he shut both eyes.

The cricket continued while the temperature swelled. The more they drank, the more they sweated. The glare and heat became unnervingly aggressive.

'Mad dogs and Englishmen,' Burnard yawned. 'How about a visit the new swimming pool?'

The Sergeant looked at his watch. 'That's a good idea.'

Grabbing bottles of water and lemonade, the men left Bonnett to enjoy his snooze and headed to their store. Here they found canvas chairs, lilo inflatables and a canopy complete with poles and stakes. These were carried to a cart drawn by two oxen.

This means of transport had materialized thanks to an enterprising tribesman named Aziz. Armed with chipped teeth and a permanent smile, he had procured the contract to move diverse loads around the airfield. Now he agreed to take their load to the reservoir as the engineers set off for their destination, ten minutes walk from the aerodrome.

They emerged from the scrub onto a sandy beach. In the shallows of the reservoir stood an elephant firing jets of water along its flanks. Its mahout, sat astride the neck below an umbrella, staring as the men stripped to their underpants and rushed headlong into the tepid but refreshing water. Soon they were all splashing around like mad children.

When Aziz and his oxcart lumbered into view, the men abandoned the water and set to work. The canopy was pitched, chairs were erected, lemonade and water bottles were passed around. In his wet pants, Pitt sat down to open his notebook. Cobras, cricket, awesome temperatures and a daft film director were wonderful topics for his tales from Bihar. While his companions dried out, he began to scribble.

'Think you're Rudyard bloody Kipling?' said Burnard. 'What are you saying about that elephant? He likes the water, doesn't he?'

'The largest pump on four legs.' Pitt did not look up as he wrote. 'And if you used your eyes, Burnard, you'll see the elephant is, in fact, a female, a cow. The bulls have big mzoomahs down below and when they're in musk, like our friend Clark here, their cheeks go red. They can even attack their handlers.'

'So you're an expert on elephants too... From Pegasus to Pachyderm in one step.'

'I've said before, Burnard. I just deal with the facts.'

It was too hot to argue. They sat under their canopy while others hauled lilos onto the water. Soon the elephant and its mahout backed away with ponderous grace to follow Aziz and the oxen into the scrub.

Everything was delightfully peaceful until Burnard sat up. 'My God! Pitt! What's that little bird sitting on? Look there! And that is not a floating elephant turd.'

Pitt looked up. 'What little bird? Where?'

'Out there! In front of Fraser, on his lilo!' Burnard jumped up.

Pitt saw the pipit bird flutter up to seize an insect. Then it returned to its island perch, a long dark shadow in the water just beyond Fraser. A snout and two eyes showed above the surface.

186

Pitt dropped his notes and yelled. 'Fraser! Wake up you blind little sod! That's a crocodile! Get back here double lively!'

46. Lalbalu – March 1933

LATER THAT AFTERNOON, WHEN EVERYONE had assembled in the shaded hangar, Fellowes called for silence.

'First I'll begin with the news that Calcutta Met believe the pressure patterns are set. Mr. Gupta will release hydrogen balloons and I'll go up at dawn to assess conditions over the Himalayas. Until these high altitude winds abate, I fear we have no hope of flying to Everest.'

From the assembly there was a collective groan.

'In any event, the essentials are now in place. Today I approved an emergency landing strip at Forbesganj, a hundred miles to the north. We left several drums of fuel there in case it's needed. The strip was cleared by elephants and labor supplied by our hosts, the Banailis and Darbanghas who have done so much to help us.'

There was some laughter and yes, their Indian hosts had delivered all types of surprises. Fellowes waited for silence.

'So while we wait for improved conditions, we must keep busy and focused. Mr. Barkas has devised an ingenious schedule for his film showing our preparations and pre-flight action. He has great hopes for the film, so this is our chance to assist him.'

The prospect of working for Barkas was not too popular but there were no wisecracks. The director himself was listening as Fellowes continued. 'These scenes may involve sports and social events at the Country Club.'

The men preferred the sound of that.

'Finally, and most importantly, take care of your health and security. We cannot afford to lose anyone to cobras or crocodiles. These creatures are exceedingly dangerous because you rarely see them until it's too late. And due to such risks, I must, most reluctantly, ban any further visits to the reservoir pool.'

His directive met with a general moan. The heat was their greatest common enemy.

'But sir?' McIntyre's brawny accent cut through the carping. 'Permission to speak, sir?'

All eyes spun towards Mac. Fellowes would listen to the Scotsman. 'Of course, Mac. What is it?'

'Rifles, sir,' said Mac. 'We have half a dozen Mannlichers and surely some of us can shoot straight?'

'Doubtless you can, Mac, but I can't have marksmen sitting around when they should be on other duties. We're not on safari.'

'But, sir, when not airborne, I could do some reptile culling?'

Applause met the suggestion. Mac could shoot the crocodile that had given young Fraser the ability to run on water. The lad had been lucky to escape with his life. Kill the croc and they could swim again.

'I will lend you my Mannlicher,' Pitt said. 'So long as I get it back at night. There are lots of scary felines here.'

Fellowes saw the nod of approval from Blacker. If the slayer of serpents approved, then Mac's offer was also worth accepting. 'Very well, Mac. Borrow Pitt's rifle and do your best. But until you succeed, no more swimming. That's clear.'

Fellowes saw Shepherd scribbling notes on a pad. He called out to the correspondent. 'Will that do for tomorrow's news? It's the best we can do till the weather improves.'

'Splendid copy.' Shepherd smiled. 'They'll love reading about the crocodile hunter who flies to the top of Everest.'

47. London – March 1933

WITH A COPY OF *THE Times* under his arm, John Buchan stood on the platform at Oxford Station. Around him, businessmen in bowler hats were waiting for the fast train to London. Briefly Buchan looked to the east, out over the spires and towers of the University. The rising sun, he realized, would now be shining on Purnea, though it would be mid afternoon out there.

The express pulled in and Buchan took a seat in First Class where several passengers were reading *The Times*. It gave him cause to reflect on his role in delivering the Everest story to the public. The editor had revealed that circulation was rising as readers followed the epic story of man, machine and mountain and he opened his paper to search for the latest news from India.

The train raced through Didcot, along the Thames Valley passing Reading and Maidenhead to reach Paddington on time. By then Buchan had read Shepherd's report, learning of hellish temperatures where the aircrew twiddled pencils and mustaches while they acted for filmmakers or stalked crocodiles. When would the Himalayas graciously deliver a change in the weather? Nature, reported Shepherd, remained very much in charge.

Once in London, Buchan headed for the book department at Harrods where he had agreed to sign his work. Though this means of promotion was in its infancy and somewhat tiresome, it was to his benefit so he would try to radiate goodwill. On arrival the department manager took him to a leather-topped desk where his books were stacked and fresh coffee was waiting.

Most customers were easy to please. Some would get a personal message before he added his signature with a Parker pen.

For Dorothy. John Buchan... This was for Harrods cleaner.

Such a pleasure to meet you. John Buchan... For Mrs. Vandegroot from Holland.

Follow McNab. John Buchan... For a young lad from Dorset.

For a glorious young lady who bought two copies, he wrote *For Susie Anstrutt-Caruthers by an admirer. John Buchan.*

This routine continued until Buchan looked up to find Arthur Hinks standing before the desk. He stood up. 'Arthur! A nice surprise. What are you doing here?'

190

'Lord Peel told me you were here, almost next door to the Royal Geographic, so I took the opportunity to come by.'

'Glad you did.' Buchan would take a break with Hinks. 'Such bad luck about the weather. For two weeks now, nothing but haze, invisible mountains and strong winds.'

Hinks did not find it too depressing. 'It's always a tricky time of year when the young monsoon starts to flex its muscles.'

'So our chaps better get up there quick.'

'Sooner the better,' said Hinks. 'I had a cable from Richardson, one of our climbing team in India. He found time to visit Purnea and meet the airmen. He had a very jolly time. Fellowes took him up in the Fry's biplane.'

'Did they see the mountains?'

'No, but Richardson revealed that his team have established a radio transmitter at Darjeeling to communicate with climbers and maybe they can relay relevant weather reports straight to Purnea.'

'The Westlands don't carry radios, but it may help this forecasting business,' agreed Buchan. 'Just remember their aerial photographs will be priceless, a perfect map for climbers.'

The two men paced together over the Harrods carpet. 'I was thinking the RGS could launch a dozen climbing expeditions for what Lady Houston has given Clydesdale and Co.'

'So it better pay off,' said Buchan firmly. 'And I'm sure it will, especially now that Etherton managed to get a brace of permits.'

'Etherton could charm the whiskers off a cat,' said Hinks. 'But Blumenfeld did mention that Lucy Houston is turning fretful. She finds the waiting very boring and stories of jungle beasts are giving her sleepless nights.'

'Tricky. But we need to keep the sponsor sweet.'

'If Lucy had ever travelled further than the Cote D'Azur,' said Hinks, 'she would understand that real expeditions are hazardous. Falling from mountains, meeting hippos or catching a poisoned arrow up the ass. Anywhere one goes, there may be danger.'

Buchan could see other customers gathering. 'Forgive me Arthur, I must return to my post. The weather will break soon enough. Then they'll be on their way and Lucy can sleep like a lamb again.'

'That sounds rather optimistic,' said Hinks as they reached the sales desk. 'Now that I'm here, I must buy one of your books.'

'Not a chance.' Buchan stooped to pick up a copy of the *Thirty Nine Steps*. He opened the book to pen another inscription.

To Arthur from John. The Royal Geographic will soon have its photographs of the highest peak and your climbers won't be far behind.

48. Purnea – 3rd April 1933

BELOW THE RAFTERS OF THE Dharbanga bungalow, Colonel Blacker was experiencing some apprehension. This was very unusual for him. Lying prone in his bed, he listened to the crickets outside and a rhythmic purring from Clydesdale in the neighboring bed. Then he wondered if any cobras had arrived below his bed during the night. He hated the blasted things, despite his skill at dealing with them. Next he thought of his home in Sussex where Doris was looking after his two sons. They didn't understand exactly what he was doing in India, but was it possible that, by the time they woke up, he might have accomplished his goal? His family's welfare depended on him and if he failed to return, how would they cope?

Blacker knew how to go over the top, rushing headlong into a barrage of bullets and exploding shells. As a pilot over German lines, he had often heard the sharp crack of lead ripping through his biplane's fuselage. But going over the greatest mountain on Earth was something else altogether. Up there in Nature's domain, there would be no rifles aiming at him, but also no parachutes, no landing fields and no chance of survival should a wing suffer fatigue or if the Pegasus was throttled by ice. He and Clydesdale, with all their equipment might then nosedive into a cavernous glacier, to remain there frozen for a millennium or longer. But that wasn't going to happen!

Besides, it was far too late for any change of plan.

Today the weather forecast was promising. The venture was stirring to the spin of God's coin and he could hear Fellowes footsteps going out to the verandah to fly his Moth. In ten minutes he'd be climbing into the sky for the weather check. If things looked promising from above the haze, he would land at Lalbalu and set in action a whole train of events.

'Time to get going.' Blacker broke the silence with a prod to Clydesdale's ribs.

'What's up?' Clydesdale lifted his head and blinked. 'What time is it?'

'Five-thirty. We have a date with the Goddess, if we're lucky.'

Thirty minutes later, Blacker and Clydesdale had washed, shaved and breakfasted. Then, with others of the crew, they took the road to Lalbalu, passing the meteorological station where Gupta was sending a silver balloon into the haze.

At the airfield the stage was set. Even at seven in the morning, hundreds of local Beharis stood on the field perimeter. They were mesmerized by the sight of Barkas supervizing his cameras and when the Westlands were pulled from the hangars they had even more to admire.

Even as the aircrew stepped from their cars, a trumpet sounded to warn of an incoming aircraft. It was Fellowes in the Puss Moth who came slipping in for an easy landing. Minutes later, Gupta arrived with his balloon reports indicating a wind speed of 60 mph at 30,000 feet. This lay within the limits of McIntyre's navigational plan which allowed for a brief visit to the summit area of no more than fifteen minutes. Any longer would increase the risk of fuel shortage on the way home.

'So, gentlemen!' Fellowes announced. 'All things considered, it's finally time. Off you go!'

With a sense of relief, together with the adrenalin of impending action, each man went to his assigned task. Cameras were loaded. Heated jackets for the cameras were checked. Oxygen tanks, valves, fuel and oil levels were all given the final once-over. So well practiced was this procedure that when the aircrew came out in their heavy flying suits, both Westlands were waiting with their inertia starting handles already installed.

'All pricked up and ready to go,' said Blacker as he walked with Clydesdale to the Westland *Lucy*.

Pitt stood by the handle, supervising start-up. As the engine caught, the joyful sound of cylinders bursting into life shattered the febrile atmosphere. Billowing smoke rolled into the hangars as the ground trembled. Then the Pegasus engines were allowed to tick over, warming their steel limbs for action while the aircrew climbed to the cockpits.

It had taken so many months to reach this moment, so many meetings and so much money that Blacker wondered for a second if he was actually still asleep in the bungalow? But no, this was for real, as was the swamp of sweat inside his flying suit. The sooner they left for cooler air, the better.

He clambered up the steps and squeezed into the observer's cockpit. All cameras and film magazines were in their allotted positions. The oxygen flow levers beside his seat were primed and electrical leads were in place. With forty-six items on his checklist, he had plenty to do. Meanwhile for Clydesdale in the forward cockpit, there were another sixty-five items to confirm.

Blacker saw Mrs. Fellowes climb the ladder to pass a small brown envelope to Clydesdale. She was speaking to him through the flaps of his helmet. On the ground, a monk was blessing the biplanes for the benefit of Barkas and his camera crew, and around the airfield perimeter he saw many hundreds of spectators. Etherton brought a second package and climbed up the ladder to his cockpit. Blacker leaned out to take the package.

'The Royal Mail!' Etherton shouted. 'Letters for the King, the Viceroy and Lady Houston. To be delivered via the summit of Everest!'

'I'll see to it, Percy.' Blacker grinned. 'My pleasure.'

He stuffed the mail package down between the oxygen bottles in the rear section. Then he ran a camera cloth over his monocle, refitting it firmly before pulling down his flying goggles with their fur trim. Up front, Clydesdale was raising a hand to signal release of the chocks that retained their Goodyear tires.

Now the Pegasus roared louder as he felt a surging pressure against his spine. The Westland was rolling, lifting and thundering forward. Seconds later they were airborne with its partner *Akbar* alongside.

The flying base disappeared below into the haze but McIntyre would remain in visual contact, holding position slightly astern. For minutes the two Westlands appeared to hang in a void. No trace of land. No sight of blue sky, just an all-encompassing mass of dust through which they maintained a steady and controlled climb.

The first leg followed a bearing to Komaltar, a tiny settlement in the forested fingers of the foothills. The haze was so thick that Blacker was unable to locate the village. When he tried to report this to Clydesdale his intercom began buzzing incessantly. Damn it! So now they'd have to rely on written messages passed between the cockpits. Pad and pencils lay to hand.

At 10,000 feet McIntyre flew the Wallace closer as agreed. Clydesdale raised a thumb to indicate everything was in order. The climb then continued to 20,000 feet when both pilots applied more power to their engines, hauling both machines up through the dust haze and into the sharpest and most brilliant blue sky.

The Himalayas stood on the northern horizon. Beyond the sturdy wings, through the struts and humming tension wires, was a jagged wall of startling beauty. Far to the east, the Kanchenjunga Massif dripped like white icing sugar. To the west Annapurna and the Karakorum showed as tiny thimbles above the horizon. And there ahead, over Clydesdale's shoulder and through

195

the spinning prop, was their objective, the incredible Goddess Mother with her spume of spindrift cloud flying like a scarf.

Having discovered a fault in the heating jacket of the cine camera, Blacker pulled off his gloves. Using his thumbnails he pressed together the copper contacts in the power lead. He needed a full charge before he could begin filming. Now he checked his altimeter. The needle quivered and was moving up to 25,000 feet, but more slowly. It would need to edge a lot higher than that.

The original surveyors had fixed the summit of Everest at 29,028 feet so they needed to win at least another 4029 feet from the atmosphere, if not a bloody sight more! They could impact the mountain due to lack of altitude and they should be much higher by now!

As he ducked back into his cockpit, out of the ripping blast of the slip-stream, Blacker became aware of a sluggishness. This was not the best of times to be feeling drowsy. He ran a check. He had a cramping sensation in his feet and also a lightheaded emptiness. That meant reduced oxygen. Hadn't they given him a foretaste in the bubble at Farnborough? And this felt alarmingly similar.

He passed a message to Clydesdale about the problem as the Westland fell into a sweeping downdraft. *Lucy* bucked up, then down, then up again, like a feather in a gale. Blacker grabbed the cockpit coaming while the biplane floundered insanely. However it soon recovered and Clydesdale activated the spare oxygen supply. In seconds, Blacker felt the revitalizing rush of oxygen but then another fist of wind came barreling down from the mountains. This punched the Westland, pushing her down several hundred feet in a second, leaving his stomach far above. Blacker looked towards the front cockpit where Clydesdale sat, calm as ever, looking over the trembling wingtips as he surfed *Lucy* through each wave of the jet stream.

While its turbo lashed all 650 horse power, the Pegasus fired on stub-bornly, shoveling air over the Westland's wings and still heading for their target, now ten miles ahead. But was it ten miles or five? It might have been one or two. It was so hard to estimate since the terrain was so huge and domi-nant, so unexpectedly different at close quarters. He scanned the sky for the Wallace and saw the flash of wings in the distance. Up here it looked like a fly lost in a West End theater.

Blacker seized the Williamson P14 plate camera, and began taking shots of

Makalu. The mountain was hewn like a switchblade knife thrust into glacier arteries. He exposed a plate at Everest while the Westland rolled and pitched. He checked his belt and the line that kept him hooked in the cockpit. Bloody hell! Blacker grinned inside his mask. This was some ride!

Passing over the monstrous haft of Makalu, Blacker's heart missed several beats. The altimeter was still at 28,000 feet. The summit remained above them and they were closing in on the most unforgiving surface imaginable at a groundspeed of around 50 miles an hour.

Blacker heaved open the flaps to a trap door in the cabin floor, allowing more scything air to charge up to his mask and goggles. Now he looked straight down onto the silvered shoulders and buttresses of the great mountain, all moving this way and that as *Lucy* danced in the wind above.

Then as suddenly as the downdraft began, a reverse action set in. The up-draft helped Clydesdale to coax *Lucy*'s nose up, pushing her towards the final gradient. Slamming the trapdoor shut, Blacker repositioned his camera as Clydesdale closed in towards the snow-capped crest.

A minute later, with the engine still thrusting against the elements, *Lucy* the Westland passed above the snowy peak with just a few hundred feet to spare. Clydesdale turned and raised his hand. Blacker waved back in unspoken triumph. They had done it!

49. Hampstead – April 3rd 1933

GARLAND COULD HEAR THE OFFICE telephone ringing. The bell kept up its strident summons as she checked her bedside clock. It was 7.30 in the morning. Wearing her black satin nightdress, Garland hurried barefoot downstairs to her office. She sat down on her chair, stifled a yawn and picked up the receiver.

'Can I help you?' Garland never gave out number or name as this line was ex-directory. 'Who's speaking, please?'

'That you, Garland?'

'Oh hi, Ralph! Yeah. What's up?'

'Apologies for getting you up so early. I just heard from Lord Peel. They've done it, Garland! They've just flown over Everest!'

Garland brushed the hair from her face. 'Oh my God, that's the best news. So they finally got there.'

'Yeah, Clydesdale and Blacker made it over the summit.'

'Lady Houston will be ecstatic.'

'And rightly so,' said Blumenfeld. 'It's the triumph she wanted. The *Express* will run the story tomorrow as we only have bare details.'

'Lady Houston will want to know everything. I'll tell her Ladyship as soon as she's up.'

'However McIntyre and Bonnett did not succeed,' said Blumenfeld. "They had a problem, but are safely back at base.'

'What happened?'

'Oxygen failure. McIntyre turned back so the Doctor could check on Bonnett. He effectively passed out. Apparently no harm done.'

'Anything else?'

'That's it. Clydesdale skimmed the summit by a whisker. A triumph for Lucy! If she gives the *Express* some quotes later, I'm sure we'll try to use them.'

'I hear you.' Garland smiled. The editor was hunting for the sponsor's scoop. 'I'll do what I can.'

'And I'll keep you posted. Lord Peel is acting as liaison. A final thought, Garland. I'm holding a weekend bash at my home in Great Dunmow on Easter Sunday. You're very welcome if you can get away.'

Garland thought quickly. 'A neat idea, thanks. I'll have to ask, but I'm due time off and other staff might cover for me.'

'Please come as I may have a surprise for you.' He rang off.

Garland replaced the receiver. A surprise? She turned to find John standing in the passage outside.

'You must excuse me,' said Garland. 'I'm not dressed yet.'

'I had noticed, Miss. I heard the bell ringing on and on,' John explained, 'I thought it must be urgent.' For several seconds, he held her gaze in silence. 'So was it?'

'Clydesdale and Blacker flew over Everest. I must tell Lady Houston.'

'That's the stuff to get her going.' John laughed. 'Another feather in her cap. Did, I hear you saying you're due time off?'

'I might have done' Garland wanted to step past John but he wouldn't move. 'John! I must get dressed and ready. Lots to do.'

John gave a slow nod and then stepped unhurriedly aside.

Garland skipped past him, up the stairs and back to her room. She could do without discussing her plans at this time of day.

By 8 o'clock, she was dressed and told the housemaid that she would take breakfast to Lady Houston. Taking the tray she went upstairs to find Lady Houston was already awake and sitting against her pillows.

'Good morning, Lady Houston. I've got some news for you.'

But Her Ladyship did not want to hear. 'Before you say a word, Garland, first let me tell you about my dream.'

'Of course.' Garland stopped in mid flow, holding the tray.

'Panic, Garland. I felt a panic. It was deep in my throat.'

'How very unpleasant.'

'More than unpleasant, Garland.' Lucy Houston looked pale, rather drained. 'I had a drowning sensation, of losing my breath in dire anxiety.'

'That's really odd, Lady Houston. Were you by any chance, dreaming of McIntyre and the cameraman Bonnett?'

'Why would I do that?'

'Because they just failed to fly over Everest due to oxygen problems. Imagine if you were experiencing their sensations? The cameraman passed out for a while.'

Lady Houston was spooked by this piece of news but Garland had her full attention. 'Yes, and they made it safely back to base but this is the best news. Clydesdale and Blacker went over Everest, in your biplane *Lucy*!'

199

Lady Houston absorbed this revelation with no reaction for five, maybe ten seconds. Then came her broadest of smiles and she grabbed Garland's hand. 'What a lovely start to the day!'

'Isn't it just?'

'I feel like the champion of the skies! We'll have champagne with breakfast. We can toast Clydesdale and the glass-eyed Colonel. Then I'll get dressed to be ready for phone calls. And mark my words, Garland, there'll be plenty of those today.'

50. Bungalow in Purnea – April 3rd 1933

THE WESTLANDS HAD RETURNED TO base before noon. Mac's machine was first home and both crewmen went directly to Dr. Bennett before debriefing on their failure to reach the peak. Thirty minutes later, Clydesdale touched down and once again Dr. Bennett ran checks before releasing the jubilant aviators.

Etherton departed as soon as Clydesdale had described his success. From the Post Office in Purnea he sent the first cable to Lord Peel who would advise the London network. Only then could Shepherd be given the full story. Scrambled versions of the truth were to be avoided and, according to Shepherd, other reporters had arrived in Purnea. How they would handle the emerging story was anyone's guess.

Etherton returned to the bungalow where the houseboys had laid out lemonade and iced beer for the inevitable inquest. Observing Blacker and Clydesdale as they relaxed, he found it hard to imagine that only a few hours previously they'd been soaring through the highest skies over the Himalaya.

'So, as I see it,' Etherton summarized, 'you have bagged the main objective. That's a wonderful achievement, but you say there are technical problems to be resolved?'

'That's correct, Percy,' agreed Fellowes. 'Oxygen delivery, survey camera systems, goggle fitting and heating controls. All need refining.'

'The oxygen?' said Blacker. 'Until Bonnett stood on his bloody tube and snapped it, his system was working perfectly. If he hadn't used his wits to wrap a hanky round the leak, he'd have been a goner. We must carry handkerchiefs and tape bandages in future. As for me, I failed to turn on the tap correctly.'

The analysis had hardly commenced when Fraser came running from the bungalow. The young man was dripping with sweat, his youthful features clouded with misery.

'Sir.' Fraser addressed Fellowes. 'I'm sorry to tell you that the Eagle cameras recorded no survey shots of any value. From the smaller cameras I've extracted a few good pictures, but there are no photographs of the type you need.'

'Are you saying we have no survey photographs?'

'I believe that's the case, sir.'

There was a heavy silence and Fellowes suppressed an urge to swear. 'So Fraser, can you fix this problem?'

'I'll try, sir.'

'Assuming you do so, then we must test them as soon as possible. Perhaps a sortie to Kanchenjunga might do the trick?'

'That would make sense,' said Etherton.

Fellowes looked at his colleagues. 'The weather's finally on our side. What do you think?'

Blacker instantly agreed. 'If the monsoon arrives early we may not get another chance.'

Putting down his iced drink, Fellowes opened the regional map that lay with their log books and reference material on the table. 'Ellison and Bonnett can take *Akbar*. I'll fly *Lucy* with Fisher as my cameraman. That gives you a day off after all the excitement.'

'Maybe Bonnett would like a day off?' suggested Clydesdale.

'On the contrary,' said Blacker. 'As soon as the Doc gave him the 'all clear', he was raring to go up again. He said it is the most exciting location he's ever filmed and I'm not surprised. I've never seen such grandeur, height or scale in all my travels. The size of the mountains is unbelievable.'

Etherton turned to Fellowes. 'Your plan seems reasonable but if you fly to Kanchenjunga, I remind you not to overfly the highest peaks. They remain particularly sensitive, indeed holy, in the local sentiment. And don't go too near Nepal as that will breach our agreement with the Maharajah.'

'Easy to comply with on both counts.' Fellowes said. 'We'll be in Indian airspace all the way, testing our cameras while Bonnett shoots his footage for Barkas.'

'Barkas...' Clydesdale shut his eyes and left the name hanging. 'So assuming the operation fits within fuel and oxygen reserves, it presents a good opportunity. Should we advise the lads at Lalbalu for early action?'

Fellowes nodded as he looked up from the map. 'Permission to fly, as we've learned, is given by the mountains. Not by us.'

Blacker beckoned to the houseboy. 'Framjee. Find a driver please to take this message to Lalbalu.'

Framjee inclined his head. Having witnessed the Colonel's swordplay with the cobra, he highly respected Blacker. 'Yes, sah.'

The pilots continued with their plans until they were interrupted by a Post Office messenger whose motorcycle had no silencer. He left the engine running as he delivered three cablegrams. When the intrusive machine had departed, Fellowes sliced open an envelope to read the contents aloud.

'*His Majesty The King offers you his best congratulations on a great success.*' Each man lifted his glass.

'How very kind of His Majesty,' said Fellowes, while Clydesdale opened and read another cablegram.

'*Delighted to hear the glad news of your great victory over Everest. I send you my warmest congratulations and appreciation of your great achievement and of the pluck and courage you have shown. God bless you. Lucy Houston.*'

Clydesdale passed the cablegram to Blacker. 'At least we got something right. Lucy has what she wanted.'

'And may God bless Fanny!' Blacker raised his beer. 'The only woman on Earth to pick up the gauntlet! My grandfather would have adored her.'

'A dangerous man was your grandfather,' Clydesdale said quietly as he opened the third cablegram. 'And how's this for the ultimate paradox? *My most hearty congratulations to you and your colleagues on your glorious achievement.*'

'And who's that from?' asked Etherton who was enjoying the accolades.

'You'll never guess.' Clydesdale laughed aloud. 'Do we dare tell Lucy? It's from the Prime Minister, Ramsay Macdonald.'

51. Kanchenjunga – April 4th 1933

IT WAS MID MORNING IN Lalbulu where Air Commodore Fellowes was growing ever more restless in the hangar. His take-off was an hour behind schedule and his flight suit had been designed for minus 70 Fahrenheit. Buckets of sweat were filling his boots.

The delay was due to his insistence that the Eagle cameras should not malfunction again. The equipment was of such importance to the RAF that the fitters had to double-check all mechanisms. Everyone was trying to be patient including the engineers who had completed their tasks and were standing by ready to launch the flight.

As Fellowes paced around the hangar he stopped beside them. 'This heat is...' He left the sentence hanging.

'...driving us all mad?' suggested Pitt.

'Yes, you could put it that way.' He did not deny the truth. 'I'm just keen to be off.'

'I gather this is your first flight in *Lucy*, sir?' Burnard asked.

'I've flown Westland Wapitis often enough. They're much the same, I'd say.'

'In some respects,' Pitt agreed. 'But this is no Wapiti, sir. This is *Lucy* with her own mind. Like Lady Houston she needs careful handling.'

'Useful advice, but an unknown machine gives me no concern, I assure you. I'm conversant with all procedures.'

'I'm very relieved to hear that, sir,' Burnard could see the camera fitters had finished and were beckoning the crews forward. 'Enjoy your flight, sir and bring her back in one piece.'

Minutes later, Fellowes followed the cameraman Fisher into the glaring sunshine. Ellison and Bonnett had climbed into *Akbar* and now he used the steps to board the Westland. Once in the cockpit, his impatience began to fade as he ran the check list. When the pilots were ready, both Pegasus engines were ignited.

The flight plan was similar to the Everest sortie in terms of distances and wind forecasts, but obviously the bearings were different. While the Westland climbed up through the haze, Fellowes adapted to the biplane. It felt more punchy than his Gypsy Moth, more lively than a Wapiti. Soon he was up through the haze to see Kanchenjunga shining on the horizon. The massif had a hammered, dimpled look, and astonishingly bright. He now had a visual line to the summit zone which, according to cartographers, topped out at 28,169 feet. His altimeter told him he had to climb another 10,000 feet.

Though navigation was easy, Fellowes now discovered that his oxygen mask kept slipping from his face. Only by clamping the contraption to his cheeks could he suck in oxygen, but fortunately the internal microphone and intercom were still functioning. 'All well back there, Fisher?'

'No problems, sir.' Fisher's voice crackled in his headphones. 'Cameras appear to be working perfectly.'

'We'll press on then.'

Fellowes kept one hand on the stick, the other against his mask. All the while he was checking oil temperature, fuel status, oxygen pressure, super-charger booster, goggle rheostat, airspeed, engine revs, compass and altimeter. The camera intervalometer by his left knee confirmed the Eagle was recording the wilderness below. So far so good.

But then, ten minutes later, as the Westlands converged with the mystical mountain on the border of Tibet and Sikkim, Fellowes could see clouds building on its various summits. Bubbles of giant shaving foam were forming visibly as he used the intercom.

'Fisher, we won't argue with those clouds, but we'll go as close as we can. Are you all set for filming?'

'Ready, sir. I'll open my cockpit now.'

'Go ahead, Fisher. Shoot what you will.'

Fellowes felt a wobble in the biplane's headlong rush when Fisher opened his cockpit lid, but the machine settled, racing forward with an airspeed of 150 mph towards the crenellated scars and ravines on the vast snow fields below. Turning near the clouds he caught a glimpse of the other Westland on his flank. Ellison was also steering clear and hopefully Bonnett would not be stamping on his oxygen pipe today.

A huge jolt hit the Westland as it piled into an invisible wall of turbulence. *Lucy* began losing altitude and shaking so violently that Fellowes feared he might spin out of control. Then the shaking stopped abruptly but the 'Peggy' continued to grind on, as if nothing had happened. Fellowes noticed his fingers were shaking faster than his heartbeat. It was one of the most violent bumps he'd ever experienced. 'Everything all right, Fisher?'

'Nearly left my teeth in the camera, sir. Otherwise all in order.'

'That cloud is a monster.' Fellowes turned onto a southerly heading. 'Seen the Wallace recently?'

'Can't say I did, sir.'

'Very well, we'll go home on our own.'

Fellowes was not about to reveal a fresh discovery. While jousting with the cloud banks he had not recorded all his headings. With spasmodic oxygen supply, his mind had become a flurry of shaken thoughts. And so had his dead reckoning. His compass provided a rough idea of Lalbalu's position, but the cloud below was unrolling like a broad fluffy carpet, denying all visual reference to the ground. Far to the south he could see the familiar ochre haze.

After flying for thirty minutes at an altitude above any mountains that could be hidden in clouds or haze, Fellowes felt sufficiently confident to throttle back and sink slowly under the pull of gravity. He would maintain a powered glide while trying to fix his position.

'Fisher,' he said. 'Keep your eyes peeled. I'm not one hundred percent sure of our whereabouts.'

'Yes, sir. Does that mean we're lost, sir?'

'It means we'll need some luck.'

'I'll cross my fingers.'

'Try crossing your bollocks too.' Fellowes was watching his fuel gauge. He had no hope of reaching Lalbalu on the fast dwindling fuel in the tanks. He would keep this news to himself for the moment.

Descending through the haze, he disconnected the oxygen supply as he caught intermittent glimpses of the ground. Plantations, settlements and patches of jungle showed below until he saw a train steaming along a railway line. But where was it going? Grasping the throttle, Fellowes leveled the Westland several hundred feet above the train, hoping to get a compass bearing. Passengers on the train's roof were pointing up while every moment his fuel was draining away!

'Fisher. We'll make a brief stop to find out where we are.'

'Very good sir.'

'Are you strapped in?'

'Certainly am, sir.'

A passable area lay ahead, a field stripped of its harvest. Fellowes reduced power to set up a landing speed of 65 m.p.h. With touches to rudder and ailerons, he steered the great biplane down for several lively bounces. It ran for a hundred yards and then halted. The train with its surprised passengers passed by, puffing dismissively into the distance.

'Well done sir.' Fisher said on the intercom. 'But the locals don't look so happy.'

Fellowes was studying his map, trying to locate the railway line but he couldn't find answers. He was still lost and what was Fisher talking about? He looked up to see hundreds of Indians rushing from fields nearby. By the look of them, none had ever seen an aeroplane.

'What's that railway line? Can you get out, Fisher, and make enquiries?'

'Outside with that lot?'

Scores of Indians had surrounded them. Some were fingering the fragile surfaces of the tailplane. He gave the throttle a shove, hoping the racing slip-stream might deter them.

'We must hurry! Just ask them!'

Fisher took off his helmet and clambered down where he had to shout over the constant swish of the airscrew. 'Which way to Purnea? Where is this place? Where's that train going?'

Standing up, Fellowes made dramatic gestures to the crowd, trying to discourage them from the lethal danger of the propeller. With no starting handle he could not restart the Pegasus. He had to keep it running. But every minute meant less juice but Fisher had learned something from the Indians.

'This is Shampur!' Fisher shouted. 'Purnea's that way.'

'Get in, Fisher.'

With Fisher was back in his cockpit, Fellowes put spurs to the Pegasus. The engine's blast made the crowd withdraw and turning around, Fellowes thrust in the throttle to fire the biplane forward. With minimal fuel onboard, it soon left the ground. Fellowes put on his helmet and used the intercom. 'Well done, Fisher. At least we're no longer lost.'

'That's good to know.'

'But I warn you we cannot make it back to base. Not enough juice. We'll fly towards Dinajpur and see what happens when the engine stops.'

'Another unscheduled landing, sir?'

'Quite likely, Fisher. But it's flat down there. I should find somewhere to put down safely.'

He had not told Fisher they had only ten minutes of fuel in the tank.

He leveled out at 500 feet, keeping the railway in sight, while searching for suitable landing places. Ten gallons might take them fifty miles in the right direction, a gamble worth taking.

Through the rigging cross-wires, Fellowes saw how the landscape featured wide belts of jungle between strips of agriculture. After ten minutes came the first cough of fuel starvation. The Pegasus was giving notice and the interruptions became louder and more ominous.

'Fuel out, sir?' Fisher sounded remarkably calm.

''fraid so. Belt on?'

'Believe me sir, I'm glued to it.'

'Here we go then.'

Lucy's nose dipped towards the fields of Dinajpur. Fellowes was aiming for a pasture where some buffalos were grazing. It looked smooth enough as the Pegasus popped like a slow machine gun.

At a hundred feet above ground, Fellowes wondered if he would reach his chosen patch, but he resisted an urge to stretch the glide. Instead he lowered the nose, gaining more speed to shoot along, fifty feet above ground. A building appeared in the flight-path and he clamped his fingers on the control stick.

'Sir!' Fisher was shouting in his earphones. 'Sir!!!'

'For God's sake, man. What is it?'

'That's a school! Full of kids in the yard!'

'Shut up Fisher!' yelled Fellowes as he swept towards scores of upturned faces. *Lucy* was responding to the law of gravity and he had no choice but to obey.

52. Lalbalu – April 4th 1933

AFTER THE STAMPEDING TAKEOFF OF the two biplanes and even before the drumming of their exhausts had faded, the ground crew were back in the shade for refreshments. In theory, they were contemplating three and half hours of peace, the duration of a full tank of fuel.

Under her watchful eyes Sally's staff had laid out refreshments but other spectators around this impromptu picnic were chatting so loudly that she had to shout above their noise.

'Before you demolish all the food, Raja Banaili has issued an open invitation for Sunday. You are all welcome to attend his Easter races.'

'Is that races for people or cars?' Barkas called out.

'Most people don't race in this heat, Mr. Barkas. Cars and petrol are too valuable to risk, so we're talking about horses.'

'I'll be there with my cameras.'

'You might even enjoy a quick gallop?' suggested Sally. 'The Raja has plenty of mounts available and Tom can lend you some breeches.'

'I hate wearing breeches,' snapped Barkas. 'I'll stay with the camera.'

After a laugh at the director's expense, everyone reverted to previous conversations. Etherton yarned with Clydesdale, Sally and Eleanor while Barkas, booming like a bittern, shared his views about horses with Shepherd and Dr. Bennett. The ground crew took their drinks outside to some peace below their canopy.

It was here that Aziz, the ox driver, came to inform Pitt that he'd just seen the crocodile. 'It is there now, sahib. It is there!'

Pitt raised a finger. 'Sssh, Aziz! No need to tell everybody. Wait a moment, we'll come and look.'

For several days since Fraser's narrow encounter, various individuals had tried to shoot the scaly brute. McIntyre and Shepherd had been out at dawn, lying on groundsheets in the bushes, rifles loaded and ready. After a volley of shots one morning the target had vanished in a fountain of churning bubbles and had not been seen since.

Pitt had a proposition for Sergeant Greenwood. 'Bring a rifle. We may get a shot. Aziz says the croc's there, lying in the sun.'

'Let's go,' Greenwood said eagerly. 'While Fellowes is admiring Kanchenjunga, we'll sort out the enemy.'

Both men left the base unnoticed, retrieved their weapons and ammunition before joining Aziz behind the hangar. Sauntering at ox pace did not appeal so they walked ahead while Pitt considered how this adventure might inspire his readers. Stopping short of the reservoir, they loaded the rifles, then approached the shoreline cautiously. And there was the crocodile! It was out in the sun, but floating on the surface upside down. Four clawed feet thrust skywards into swarms of feeding flies.

Briefly Pitt was disappointed, thwarted by the diminished value of his story. Sergeant Greenwood on the other hand was elated. 'Now we can go swimming again. Even better, it's just what I need for my wife.'

Pitt had to question this. 'Not fussy about what she eats?'

'No, Pitt. She has always wanted a crocodile handbag.'

The oxen came into sight. Aziz grinned happily as the Sergeant pointed to the corpse. 'We'll take it back on your cart, Aziz. Then you can help me to skin it.'

'Very good, sergeant sahib. Ten rupees.'

'Better to skin it here, don't you think?' Pitt could smell putrefaction. 'We don't want that near our tents.'

Greenwood's nose wrinkled. 'Then we'll skin it here, Aziz. Five rupees. How's that?'

Aziz lifted his shoulders and agreed. Then wading into the water, he grabbed the croc by the tail to drag it ashore. With deft knife strokes along the soft belly, Aziz and Greenwood peeled away the skin. They deposited the gory corpse in a clearing where a squadron of vultures were already waiting.

With a cloud of flies flying escort, Pitt accompanied the cortège back to camp where Greenwood paid the five rupees and displayed the pungent skin to anyone who was interested. Curiosity turned to incredulity when Greenwood revealed he would cure the skin and offer offcuts for sale. Some day his wife would own a genuine Lalbalu handbag.

'Any orders?' asked Greenwood hopefully.

Connochie, Fraser and Helmsley immediately subscribed for portions of the hide. Colonel Blacker decided his sons would appreciate crocodile belts. Pitt and Burnard thought they might pin a strip of croc to their factory walls, but it was Shepherd who pointed out the pool was now free territory and he would lead the charge to the water.

'Not so fast, Mr. Shepherd!' Percy Etherton raised his voice. 'Aren't you forgetting something?'

'And what's that?' Shepherd asked while others faltered.

'Like you, gentlemen, crocodiles appreciate their own company. Where you see one, there are generally others. Secondly, as the Chief Pilot points out, the Westlands have now been airborne for two hours. They could be back soon. In other words, you don't have time to go swimming.'

The crew's disappointment was palpable. Then the trumpet sounded to warn that an aeroplane had been sighted. Trade in crocodile fractions was suspended and dreams of cool water were put aside. Which Westland would it be?

Several minutes later Ellison and Bonnett landed in *Akbar*. Out of their flying suits, the two men began sucking up gallons of iced lemonade while Ellison made his initial report to an attentive audience.

'We approached at 34,000 feet but as we closed in, wide stratiform clouds began to bloom and multiply. We circled to admire the phenomenon and then encountered massive turbulence. So we came back to base.'

Clydesdale understood that when a pilot of Ellison's experience spoke of massive turbulence, it must have been extremely lumpy. 'And what about the Air Commodore and Fisher?'

Ellison toweled the sweat from his face. 'I lost sight of them near the mountain. *Akbar* began jumping like a mad donkey, so I imagine Fellowes was in similar conditions. That would have been around noon.'

'I thought I saw them once, just as we turned for home,' said Bonnett without much confidence. 'The clouds were working like dry ice machines. Unbelievable. Very unnerving.'

While the two men went to Dr. Bennett's tent for medical checks, Fraser dismounted the Eagle camera and magazines. Meanwhile everybody was waiting for *Lucy*.

The engineers returned to their chairs after telling Aziz to pin the reptile's skin somewhere out of sight.

'Place it downwind, near the fuel tent and latrines,' Pitt suggested. 'You did well on that deal, Sergeant. Almost fifty rupees of profit for an outlay of five rupees.'

'I like making money.' Greenwood looked at his watch. 'And they're overdue now, by five minutes.'

211

Burnard also checked his timepiece. 'Nearer ten, if you include the fuel burned during warm-up.'

Pitt shook his head and sighed loudly. 'Oh deary me. Fanny Houston is not going to like this. Not one bit.'

53. Purnea Bungalow – April 4th 1933

FROM THE AIR, ELEANOR COULD see no golfers eyeing up their shots as the Gypsy Moth side-slipped towards the fairway. With Clydesdale at the controls, it had taken a mere ten minutes to fly from Lalbalu, leaving their colleagues to follow by car. Clydesdale eased the throttle as the grass came to meet them and with a soft thump the wings surrendered their lift.

Eleanor was surprised to find herself clenching her hands. Landing was a deceptive procedure, generally safe enough, but on occasion it could go hideously wrong.

Bonnett had last seen *Lucy* over the sweeping snowfields of Kanchenjunga. She wondered if Perry might have headed to the emergency strip at Forbeganj?

Eleanor arranged her hair while Clydesdale taxied and when the engine stopped, she was the first to alight, her heart beating faster than usual. She waited till Clydesdale had placed the chocks and then said. 'You know it was the first time he flew that Westland?'

'There was a first time for me. *Lucy's* a fine machine. Nothing to it, just a larger Moth.'

Clydesdale was the perfect gentleman, thought Eleanor. And so reassuring. Or was he just being kind?

'I felt he was somewhat ambitious, heading for Kanchenjunga just like that, but I didn't like to say anything.'

'I understand,' said Clydesdale taking her arm. 'But he's no novice, Eleanor. He'll have landed somewhere safely. Now let's set about finding them. I'll inform the Raja. He'll know how to organize a search.'

Together they hurried to the bungalow where Clydesdale gave her a hug before departing for the palace. Eleanor went to her bedroom. I'll find some fresh clothing, she thought. Keep busy. But Perry's things still lay where he'd left them that morning, and now she recalled watching the Westland take off to vanish in the haze. Where on earth were they? The clammy heat was so oppressive. To bury her fears she took a shower and then sat wrapped in a towel at her dressing table. On it stood a vase of flowers and family photos in a leather travel frame. She stared at their faces. When would they need to know what was happening? How soon would it appear in the papers back home? And what about Fisher's family? They too might soon be gripped by this dreadful suspense.

She put on a dress of blue seersucker. Her reflection in the mirror looked much cooler than she felt, and now she wanted to brush her hair. Best foot forward, Eleanor, she told herself. It wouldn't do for all these men to see her losing her composure.

However her silver hairbrush was not on the dressing table where she'd left it. She looked on the floor and in her suitcase but it wasn't there. So where was it? She remembered what the Ranee had said, how some people believed the Gods would punish those who invaded their territory. She and Perry had laughed about that.

Eleanor left her room and found Golwalla sitting on a chair on the verandah. He jumped up, hands clasped together. 'Yes, Memsab?'

'I've lost my hairbrush. Have you've seen it anywhere?'

Golwalla seesawed his head. 'Oh no, Memsab. I've seen no brush.'

'It's a silver brush with a handle. Do try and find it. I'd be so grateful.'

'Very good, Memsab. A silver brush.'

'Thank you, Golwalla, and some lemonade please.'

Golwalla left to get the drink as it struck her that the brush was among several items that had gone missing. Various crewmen had also mislaid personal effects. But now she heard the cars returning from Lalbalu. She pulled her fingers through her hair to tidy it and took a seat on the verandah. Then she put on her glasses, picked up a magazine and stiffened her lip. Don't worry my dear, she told Perry in her head. I'm not going to be a hysterical wife.

Shepherd, Blacker and Etherton soon appeared, but without news. Thoughts about the missing biplane were totally speculative. Shepherd was hopping around nervously, wondering how to handle the story.

'Best to say nothing,' advised Blacker. 'Always better than wild rumor.'

'I agree,' Shepherd said. 'But I can't vouch for the others.'

'What others?'

'Other reporters have popped up. It's bad enough having Pitt broadcast his lurid tales. That at least is containable but Barkas has teamed up with a Reuter's man who's hanging around. So much for *The Times* holding the exclusive rights.'

'Forget the contractual issues, Mr. Shepherd. We need to find Fellowes and Fisher,' said Blacker. 'Once we know the facts, then write your story.'

'But it cannot be suppressed indefinitely. Missing airmen are a valid news story by any standard.'

'Maybe you can hold off till this evening?' Eleanor suggested, thinking of those carefree faces in her photographs. 'To give us a chance to locate them first?' She had come to like Shepherd. He'd been so helpful and courteous during the long flight to India. 'A fair compromise?'

'Just till this evening,' Shepherd conceded. 'But you're right. No need to involve the world prematurely.'

Etherton removed his topee to wipe his brow. 'I totally agree, Mr. Shepherd. And Pitt has promised to keep mum for the moment.'

Blacker and Shepherd went into the bungalow. Etherton took a seat beside Eleanor as the houseboy arrived with a glasses of lemonade.

Etherton took one. 'We may need reporters, just as a huntsman employs hounds to find a fox. When we alert the locals then everything will be beyond our control.'

'My husband's no fox,' said Eleanor. 'But he's certainly gone to ground. 'You know, Percy, I'm stupid to be worrying about this, but my silver hair-brush has also vanished.'

'A hairbrush?' said Etherton. 'Did your husband take it with him?'

'Definitely not. And I can't believe it's bothering me in the circumstances, It came from Asprey, a gift from my mother on my twenty-first birthday.'

'I'll make enquiries,' said Etherton who could see the Dodge pickup kicking up dust near the golf course. 'Mrs. Smith obviously in a hurry.'

The pickup came to a stop and Sally bounded over to join them. 'The Raja has put out an all-points appeal. Any reports of a downed flying machine will be relayed to him. Clydesdale will stay with the Raja for the present.'

'So that's all we can do for the moment,' said Etherton. He left the two women and went to speak with Fraser and the filmies who were now disembarking from their truck.

Sally sat down with Eleanor. 'I'm so sorry to hear the news. Bonnett says his Eagle camera worked perfectly, so you can tell that to your husband when he returns.'

'Yes. Yes.' Eleanor tried to stay positive. 'And I hear McIntyre has gone to Calcutta to see if the labs there can rescue the Everest photos.'

'Very unlikely I'm told, but Fraser has developed Blacker's work and Shepherd has already sent the best of them to *The Times*. It's amazing to think such unique pictures are being created here in this remote bungalow.'

Eleanor lowered her voice. 'Forgive me, Sally, but how can there be simply no news? If a huge lump of metal comes crashing down on this densely populated land, don't you think someone might have noticed? But if they had gone down over Kanchenjunga, then nobody would find them in a hundred years. It's the silence that worries me.'

'It's far too soon to be thinking like that.' Sally lit a cigarette. 'How about a game of cards? Let's play Rummy?'

'Rummy?' Eleanor thought for a moment. 'I suppose so.'

For an hour Eleanor and Sally traded cards. Then they were distracted by Etherton who began shouting in fluent Hindi at a houseboy named Charlie. Uncharacteristically, Etherton was growling like a regimental mastiff and apparently ordering the youth to remove his sandals and stand still.

'What on earth's going on?' asked Eleanor.

'I've no idea, but sometimes one just has to yell.' Sally shuffled the cards. 'Maybe it's not how people behave in Surrey or Mayfair, but it's quite normal in India. We shout to get the point across.'

After the inquisition subsided, Etherton strode off and the houseboy picked up his sandals and ran away. The two women continued their game while the sun slowly sank behind the distant tamarind and mango groves. Then Clydesdale arrived in the Raja's shooting brake.

Both women stood up as the Chief Pilot ran over. He was smiling broadly. 'We've found them! They're both safe on the ground.'

'That's wonderful.' Eleanor sighed. 'Thank God for that. I was about to start worrying.'

'So now you don't have to.' Clydesdale looked equally relieved as he turned to meet Blacker emerging from the bungalow. 'Yes, they're in good shape. They put down at Dinajpur, forty miles from here. No damage sustained. If I hurry, I can get there in the Gypsy Moth before dark. Tomorrow Ellison and Pitt will take over some fuel with a starting handle to get them airborne.'

'And then what?' asked Eleanor. She had stood up far too fast and was feeling strangely dizzy.

'Back to Everest of course,' said Blacker. 'That's why we came and we haven't signed off yet, have we?'

54. Harley Street – April 4rd 1933

'THE THING I MOST HATE in life is visiting the doctor,' confessed Lady Houston from the depths of her fur coat. 'I pay these Harley Street people a small fortune, but ultimately they can only give you bad news, since we're all condemned to slide into the chasm of demise.'

So morbidness was back on the menu, thought Garland who sat beside her employer in the Rolls. Her health had not been mentioned for a week or more, while Lady Houston concentrated on her expedition's progress. Today her annual medical checkup was due in Harley Street where Britain's senior consultants treated those who could afford their fees.

'But it's how we live on our journey to the chasm that matters, don't you think?' said Garland. 'Only yesterday your pilots pulled off the greatest of triumphs and today the press is brimming with praise for your role in it all. Doesn't that give you a feeling of immortal achievement?'

The silence suggested that Garland's comment had been received favorably as the Rolls cruised around Regent's Park. It was a clear morning and Londoners were enjoying the blooming season. One resident had loved it so much that he had drunk numerous bottles of beer before collapsing on a bench beside the road. Lady Houston sat up. 'Stop the car, John. Right here!'

The Rolls halted. Without waiting, Lady Houston pushed open her door and stepped out. 'My bag, please, Garland.'

Garland lifted the bulky handbag from the floor and passed it to the heiress who snapped it open to extract two five pound notes. Walking and then tiptoeing to the recumbent tramp, Lady Houston bent down to slide the notes into his coat pocket. She came back, almost scampering, to the Rolls and climbed back in.

'When he wakes up, he'll suppose an angel came to bless him!'

'A very generous angel. It's my guess,' said Garland, 'he'll then head to the pub for more beer.'

'Of course he will, but don't we all return to our follies until we really have to dismiss them? At least he'll be happy.'

Shortly the Rolls arrived in Harley Street where polished brass plaques on the doorways carried multiple acronyms of the practitioners inside. John stopped outside No. 52. The appointment was for 11.45 so they had ten minutes in hand.

'I wonder if there'll be any more news today?' said Lady Houston. 'Nobody told me yesterday the aerial cameras had failed. In fact it was the BBC who first mentioned it.'

'The flight was successful, and that's the main thing.' said Garland. 'They were so keen on their survey, that I guess they'll have the problems figured out before the next flight.'

'Surveys aren't my concern,' said Lady Houston. 'But they should have informed me. If they say they have flown over the summit then Clydesdale's word is good enough. I see no reason for a second flight just for photos.'

Garland escorted Lady Houston to the consultant's reception room and then returned to the street. John was polishing paintwork while Mungo slept on the front seat, out of harm's way.

'Do you think she'll mind if I make a quick trip to Selfridges? I don't want to get into trouble.'

'Trouble, Miss Garland?' John was in uniform today, his grey cap sporting the red RR insignia. He stopped cleaning and looked Garland in the eye. 'Secretaries are dispensable, as are radio officers, dress designers, cooks, maids, doctors, lawyers and even Prime Ministers.'

'That sounds rather ruthless. What about you then?'

'I've been with her a good many years. Chauffeurs, gamekeepers, gardeners and jockeys are generally favored by those with money.'

Garland pursed her lips. 'So, what do you think?'

'That's for you to decide, Miss.' John stooped for another run with his shammy. The sight of the Rolls was turning heads along the street. 'Did you ask her?'

'With all this Everest news, I haven't had the chance.'

John smiled. 'She won't mind if I run you to Selfridges. Hop in.'

A few minutes later, in Selfridges, Garland had found her way to the Easter egg counter and then to the hosiery section where she purchased two pairs of stockings. Next, in the tempting zone of the fashion department, she fell in love with a beautiful summer dress by Schiaparelli. Its flared shoulders and narrow waist were irresistible as was its silky cream fabric. Garland parted with several weeks' worth of wages. An extravagance? Not really, she thought. She was just celebrating her role in the Everest triumph.

With her purchases, Garland left the store and walked east down Oxford Street where news vendors were bawling at their stands. She noticed people were converging for the early edition of the *Evening Standard*. Something was afoot. 'Air Disaster!' The vendor's call resonated. 'Air Disaster! Airship Disaster! Read all about it!'

Garland immediately bought a copy and stopped to read the front page. It was all there, the uncompromising report of a major disaster. The *USS Akron*, the largest and most costly airship in the skies, had crashed, allegedly forced into the ocean by massive down draughts. Over seventy crewmen had drowned in the grey seas off New Jersey. Garland read the story from start to finish.

Garland's father had died when an airship fell onto Ohio's soil in 1925 so this was horribly poignant! Her Ladyship would be devastated.

Garland dashed back to Harley Street. Pacing along she read more about the disaster. It was, wrote the reporter, the worst air accident in history, and had come within hours of the epic flight over the Himalayas.

Back outside No. 52. Garland opened the Rolls door and was surprised to find that Lady Houston was already inside.

'Where have you been, Garland?' she said in a tone as hard as the *Liberty*'s keel, 'I've been waiting five minutes. John says you went to do some shopping.'

'I went to get you an Easter present, milady. But then I came across this.' Garland showed the newspaper's headline.

Lady Houston seized the paper and quickly read it. 'Sickening. Quite tragic. But that's not all, Garland.'

Garland reclaimed her seat beside Lady Houston as John started the engine. 'No?'

'Just as I was leaving the doctor's office, a telephone call came from Willie Graham relaying some dreadful news from Lord Peel.'

'Oh no?'

'Yes, Garland. The Air Commodore and my Westland did not return from their flight today and nobody knows what's become of them.' Lady Houston thrust the newspaper back to Garland. 'Take down this message for the Marquis of Clydesdale and send him a cable straight away.'

'Now Lady Houston?'

'You silly girl! Don't you see how urgent this is? You can send it from the first Post Office John can find.'

Garland fished in her handbag for her notebook and pencil as Lady Houston began dictating.

'The good spirit of the mountain has been kind to you and brought you success. Be content. Do not tempt the evil spirits of the mountain to bring disaster. Come home now. Intuition tells me to warn you there is danger if you linger.'

55. Lalbalu – 5pm April 5th 1933

AFTER THE RESCUED WESTLAND HAD flown from Dinajpur to Lalbalu, the ground crew began an exhaustive inspection. Like probing doctors, Greenwood and Pitt examined it thoroughly. After two forced landings, Helmsley and Burnard hunted for any damage to wings and fuselage. Young had the easier task of recharging the oxygen cylinders. No abnormalities were reported and the men sauntered to the hangar entrance where Gallimore, the fuel expert, was chatting with Fisher and Connochie.

Pitt had his own views on the event. 'I didn't know what to expect when they put me down at Dinajpur this morning. You, Mr. Fisher, you should get down on your knees and thank all your lucky stars.'

Fisher laughed but he did agree. 'Kanchenjunga was the easy bit. Then it got bumpy with clouds bursting around us like flak. I saw *Akbar* vanish near a stack of cumulus. Twice I thought the jolts would finish us. Then we were on our own, heading south over a blanket of cloud until we found a hole to drop through. The first landing by the railway was alright, but I nearly shat myself on the second.'

Pitt had seen the stricken biplane at the site. 'That was no runway. It was a wallow for water buffalo. But why take off with only enough juice for ten minutes? No wonder he got his medals. Either he's braver than brave – or totally mad. I don't know which.'

'Probably both,' suggested Fisher. 'That school scared the wits out of me. When the Peggy quit, all I heard was a whistle in the rigging as we fell. Then I saw this playground. Packed full of kids. I could hear their racket as we swept over maybe thirty feet above them. I could see the horror in their little faces. Then we hit the deck fifty yards beyond, leaped over a track, through some sugar cane, just missing two big trees to stop only feet away from two buffaloes, just like Aziz keeps here.'

'Don't talk to me about Aziz,' Gallimore said. 'I found him helping himself to some fuel today. To lend to one of the drivers, he said. I told him our fuel would explode a car's engine, but I don't think he understood. Sorry, go on Fisher.'

'We also scattered a pack of dogs,' Fisher resumed. 'When I got out I couldn't believe it. Thousands of people, not to mention all the school kids, were racing out to gape at us.'

'Did you get any footage?' Connochie asked.

'Footage? You are joking! It took us both ten minutes to stop our hands trembling. I couldn't even light a cigarette.'

Greenwood felt for the Woodbines in his shirt pocket. He flipped one to Fisher. 'Go on, mate. You deserve it.'

Fisher caught the cigarette and lit it with his much coveted new Zippo. 'But much worse was to come. We had to spend the night in a local doss house with ten million fleas for company and that was after a lethal curry for dinner which attacked us from within.'

Pitt was making plans for a vivid, firsthand story. He would write it immediately and take it to the cable office. By dawn next day the citizens of Bristol would read about Fisher's drama over breakfast.

'So do we know when they'll go back to Everest? Pitt asked. 'What else did you learn from Fellowes over your dodgy curry?'

Fisher shuddered. 'The plan remains unchanged but Gupta is predicting haze, heat and high-winds.'

Connochie felt this was an ideal moment to reveal his news. 'Barkas has dreamed up a new plan whatever the weather. We need shots of elephants, of weather balloons and you'll love this, of smoke action!'

Burnard turned to Pitt. 'I told you so. I must fix a container with stannic crystals to a wing strut. When the observer pulls its release the colors burst in the slipstream.'

Pitt was incredulous. 'Is that it? No wing-walkers in green saris? No elephants in parachutes? So what colors then?'

'Red, white and blue.'

'For a black and white film?' Pitt was speechless. 'I don't get it.'

56. Purnea – April 5th 1933

DUSK HAD FALLEN. ON THE bungalow's verandah, Blacker was observing his colleagues at the long table. He was listening to their conversation and the chink of ice in his drink when a Post Office messenger arrived on a motor bike. The man dismounted and gave an envelope to Clydesdale which he opened immediately. A startled look on the Chief Pilot's face implied it was not good news.

Blacker would not enquire initially, in case it concerned a personal matter. If it involved the expedition, Clydesdale would tell soon enough. There were no secrets between men who flew together over Everest.

Sitting back Blacker considered events were broadly going to plan. The sortie to Kanchenjunga had proved the cameras were now functioning correctly and Fraser would hopefully soon emerge from the darkroom with the results. Bonnett had canned plenty of footage on 16 mm, film for processing elsewhere. It was unlikely that the damnable Barkas would be satisfied though, keeping up his tireless clamor for sequences of dubious value.

Blacker's mind was still throbbing after his spectacular tour of the Himalayan summits. Only he and Clydesdale had looked down upon that lump of snow that comprised the highest point on Earth. But neither had seen any indications of the missing climbers Irvine and Mallory. Though disappointing, many had anticipated as much. But they weren't finished yet! They should now consolidate their achievements in a second sortie.

McIntyre and Eleanor came from the bungalow to join them. Mrs. Fellowes did not look too happy. Blacker rose to his feet. 'Panic's over, Mrs. Fellowes. Your man came back in one piece.'

'Yes, Colonel, but with the most rampant diarrhea. He's had it ever since he ate something quite ghastly in Dinajpur.'

'Oh dear. That means Delhi Belly.' said Blacker. 'Gut Destructor, or as I call it, Karachi Crouch. Best to get some bleach.'

Eleanor was not amused. 'It means he can't perform his duties for the expedition. The Doctor has confined him to bed until he recovers.'

McIntyre was sorry to hear of their leader's ill health. 'Aye, keep the khazi free and the man in bed. That's the best remedy, Eleanor. As for his duties, nobody's flying anywhere, are we? Grim weather is forecast for at least a week. I'd say the Air Commodore picked his timing well. I wish him a speedy recovery.'

Eleanor relaxed. 'Thank you Mac. You're very kind.'

The implication that he had been less so did not escape Blacker, but he had other things to think about. If Fellowes was ill, he and Percy would assume joint leadership. With dwindling funds, fuel and oxygen, they would have to use their imagination.

'So we're back where we began,' he said to McIntyre. 'Sitting out the weather until we get a second run.'

'And I'm raring to go,' said Mac. 'The last flight was a shambles thanks to Bonnett's jig. Next time I'll skim some snow from the summit.'

'Your quick thinking, Mac, saved Bonnett's life.' Eleanor held out her glass for a refill as Framjee passed by. 'Now I must get back to my patient. Good night all. See you in the morning.'

Blacker watched Eleanor enter the bungalow. Then the trio sat down as Framjee replenished their drinks while Golwalla lit paraffin flares around the verandah. In their soft glow McIntyre revealed how the engineers had rigged up a generator and electric bulbs at their camp at Lalbalu. 'An inventive lot, aren't they?'

'Personally, I can do without the endless whine of petrol generators,' said Blacker. 'Anyway, I suggest we draw up a flight plan. Etherton is dining with the Raja tonight, so we have the place to ourselves.'

Clydesdale and McIntyre agreed so Blacker continued. 'In my view Fellowes was extraordinarily lucky to survive both landings. Irresponsible, perhaps, but I couldn't say so in front of Eleanor.'

'Of course not. The poor woman had a nasty fright and now has a sick husband on her hands,' said McIntyre.

Blacker heard the unspoken message from the young pilot, and changed tack. 'You're not brimming with cheery conversation tonight, Clydesdale. Something bothering you?'

The Chief Pilot produced the recently delivered cable. 'I intended to show this to Fellowes. It's from our sponsor. *The good spirit of the mountain has been kind to you and brought you success. Be content. Do not tempt the evil spirits of the mountain to bring disaster. Come home now. Intuition tells me to warn you there is danger if you linger.*'

'Daft as ever,' Blacker decided. 'Evil spirits? Intuition? All absolute rubbish!'

'Lucy has had her moment of glory and wants to leave it at that,' said McIntyre. 'From her viewpoint, can't say I blame her.'

'But we're not going to grant her that wish, are we, gentlemen?'

'I certainly don't intend to,' said McIntyre. 'I've got my flight to make before I go home.'

Blacker nodded. 'And Clydesdale, how do you feel about it?'

The Chief Pilot was less certain. 'I'm with you both because we must complete the survey. We didn't come all this way for only half of the potential. But how do we ignore this request from Lucy in the meantime?'

'We could blame unreliable facilities at the cable office?' suggested McIntyre. 'It might work?'

'That's perfect.' Blacker beckoned Framjee. He found these two young men so much easier to deal with than certain members of the expedition. 'Time for another snifter then before dinner?'

57. Rules Restaurant, London – April 6th 1933

THE WINE WAITER POURED THREE glasses of champagne for the diners.

Blumenfeld picked up his glass. 'Happy birthday, Garland. Have a good one.'

'And I echo that,' said Willie Graham. 'And we'll save the big party until the pilots return.'

'Thank you both,' said Garland, raising her glass. 'Assuming they make it back. After the epic on empty fuel tanks, nothing will surprise me,'

Garland was wondering why she'd been invited to lunch because she hadn't mentioned her birthday to anyone. Making it to thirty was all very well, but she was happy to stay in her twenties.

Blumenfeld had called that morning and then Lady Houston suggested that Garland should have lunch with him at Rules Restaurant. Lady Houston said she'd stay at home because she was feeling chesty. They should put the bill on her account, assuming they had no objections to including her lawyer too? It was a done deal.

Leaving John to supervise life at Byron Cottage, Garland went by cab at 12.30 a.m. to Covent Garden. 'Rules is the oldest restaurant in London,' said Lady Houston. 'Charles Dickens used to eat there and Buster Keaton loves it. The allure is something that you, Garland, should definitely experience.'

Alluring, it was. But why did Willie Graham have to be present? Usually the lawyer kept in touch by phone. After ordering her food, Garland came straight to the point. 'So what's the deal then? You must have something to discuss. You didn't know it was my birthday.'

The lawyer grinned. 'I've seen your passport. But putting birthdays and Himalayan triumphs aside, Lady Houston is extremely alarmed by all the latest news from India. She's very anxious and wants to reduce any potential for further problems.'

Garland waited for Blumenfeld's opinion but the editor stayed silent, so clearly the two men wanted her views.

'I live cheek by jowl with her. Extremely alarmed and anxious is an understatement,' said Garland. 'She feels that war has broken out between the spirits on the mountain and her men in Purnea.'

'Who are all on the other side of the planet,' Blumenfeld pointed out.

'That is to say, beyond our control.'

Willie Graham understood. 'Which explains why the expedition never had my endorsement from the outset.'

Blumenfeld pursed his lips. 'So you have the moral high ground.'

'And if anyone gets blamed, it will be me,' said Garland. 'I hoped the flight might divert Lucy from her war with the Prime Minister.'

Blumenfeld shrugged. 'No one's to blame.'

'There's no question of that.' Willie Graham leaned forward. 'Nobody diverts Lucy from what she wants to do.'

Blumenfeld agreed. 'So what's Lucy's beef? Haven't they knocked off Everest and Kanchenjunga? And been applauded by the world's press into the bargain?'

'You wouldn't think so at Byron Cottage. She has been having dreams of peril and disaster ever since they lost the Fox Moth. Then it was bad weather, failed cameras and the terrible Akron disaster. When she read of Fellowes' crash landing, her fuses blew. Even the dog beat it out of there.'

Blumenfeld laughed. 'I'd pay a small fortune for that dog's story. Anyway, I see no point in ordering the pilots home. I've spoken with Lord Peel who believes Blacker is determined to complete the operation, so we can't do much about it in London, can we?'

Garland was trying to enjoy the very stylish atmosphere of Rules. It was fun to be away from the moody curtains of gloom at Byron Cottage. The waiters brought their food and no wonder the menus and chefs had stood the test of time. It was all excellent, and a very thoughtful birthday gift, decided Garland as a Medoc 1929 was poured into their wine glasses.

But now the headwaiter came to their table to report there was an urgent call for Mr. Graham. He could take it on the desk telephone. Reluctantly Willie Graham had no choice but to throw down his napkin and leave the table.

'Maybe Lucy's had another dream?' Blumenfeld wondered with a mischievous chuckle. 'Don't let her blame you, Garland. If Lucy hadn't wanted to finance Clydesdale, she could have found any number of excuses. She loves fame and we provide the oxygen.'

'That's for sure.'

Blumenfeld lent towards her. 'Now Garland, I've no idea how long you plan on staying with Lucy and you've survived for nearly a year. But if you want a return to journalism, I'll try to find you something different.'

'I hope you're not thinking about The *Saturday Review*?'

'Lucy's rag for her rants?' Blumenfeld grimaced. 'Don't touch it because it would drive you nuts in a week. No, you'd have to offer your resignation.'

'And what would she think of that?'

'Your first duty is to yourself. If you're happy with Lucy and vice versa, then stay. If you're not, then your talents and experience will take you as far as you want.'

Garland appreciated this encouragement. 'Yes, being at the centre of the action does have benefits. But you'll remember, a while back, I asked if I might write her biography?'

'A good idea,' said Blumenfeld. 'What did she say?'

'I'm still waiting for her decision.'

Blumenfeld was one of the busiest men in London, but he had the skill of always having time for others. 'So what's the problem?'

'Firstly, it's the confidentiality agreement. Secondly, she won't made up her mind. Can you say something to help her along?'

'You'll find that wealth, Garland, frequently breeds paranoia. The richer folk get, the more fretful and fearful they become. I'll bear it in mind.' The lawyer had finished his call and was returning to the table. 'At my Easter party, we'll talk about it then.'

Mr. Graham sat down and the waiter showed pudding menus to the three diners.

'Do we have time?' Blumenfeld wondered. 'No need to rush off?'

Willie Graham stared blankly at the menu. 'No, that won't be necessary. In fact, we now have an additional excuse to linger. We must consider a new twist in this Everest saga, a fait accompli.'

Blumenfeld sat up. 'Something we should know about?'

'It won't stay secret for long. so I'll tell you.' said Willie Graham. 'Lloyd's Insurance have just informed Lord Peel that if the pilots intend to make a second Everest flight the underwriters must insist on new terms.'

'The plan for two flights has never changed. It was even mentioned in today's press,' said Blumenfeld. 'So what's biting Lloyds?'

'They want an additional £600 as a premium for the next flight.'

Blumenthal blinked. 'Just to insure two biplanes for three hours in their natural habitat? That's £200 an hour!'

'Lord Peel objected immediately,' said the lawyer. 'He understood cover was provided for two flights over Everest. But the small print explicitly refers to making two high-altitude flights over the Himalayas. For Lloyds that includes Everest and Kanchenjunga. In short, the pilots have fulfilled their allotted quota.'

'And so Lloyds want more money? Ok, what's new?' said Blumenfeld with complete indifference. 'I'll have some crème brûlée as we think about it.'

'Ditto,' said Garland. She smiled at both men before adding. 'But I'll bet you anything you like that Lucy won't put up that kind of money for a second bite at the cherry.'

58. Visit to Dharbanga – April 13th 1933

AFTER TWO HIMALAYAN SORTIES THE expedition team stood down while poor weather set in. Both Westlands remained in their hangars, but other means of transport were always available. One of these was now kneeling in front of Percy Etherton.

He put his polished shoe on a folded hind leg and taking the wispy tail in one hand, pulled himself up to the howdah. Leaning down, he offered a hand to Blacker who took the same route over the animal's rump to the cushioned seat. Then with a shout from the mahout, the elephant rose with studious deliberation until all four legs were upright. From this height, both men now had a perfect view of the proceedings.

Today, the expedition leaders were on a day visit to the Maharaja of Darbhanga. It was his bungalow they'd been borrowing, his tribesmen who had located the lost Air Commodore and his friendship with Lord Peel that had secured their welcome to India. The Maharaja's hospitality also included the overnight creation of an airstrip from which this grand procession was now slowly pacing towards his palace for a lavish banquet.

'I can count forty elephants,' Etherton decided. 'But top marks go to that monster chariot drawn by four of them. What a sight!'

'It looks like a Mark IV battle tank on wheels,' Blacker said. 'And I do hope Mrs. Fellowes appreciates the honor.'

The procession moved along, each elephant painted and draped in glittering caparisons of gold, saffron and purple. Tiers of silvered bangles hung from their tusks firing kaleidoscopic colors in to the morning sunlight. Alongside each elephant strode uniformed handlers while discordant musicians, thrashing at heavy drums and cymbals, drew the cortège forward between avenues of turbaned militiamen and waving crowds.

Fellowes and Eleanor rode in the giant chariot because they were guests of honor. Percy Etherton could see that the Air Commodore was trying very hard to enjoy the experience.

'The poor man's clearly suffering,' he said to Blacker. 'But he felt obliged to attend.'

'The silly bugger should have stayed in Purnea.'

'Duty first, I suppose. But now's a good moment to discuss things in private. That cable from London about Lloyds insurance? I'm still wondering what to make of it.'

Blacker was waving his topee at hundreds of school-children ranged along the roadside. They were returning his salute with showers of confetti and shrill squeals of welcome.

'I'll tell you this, Percy. A premium of £600 is a diabolical sum to demand on top of the original premium. The Committee must try to find it but I doubt if Fanny Houston will dig a deeper hole in her purse. Maybe the Maharaja can put up the money?'

'Good heavens, no,' said Etherton quickly. 'Imagine how that would look.'

'Then we'll just have to burn any cables from London and float their ashes down the Ganges,' said Blacker. 'Quite simple.'

'If only it was.'

'But it is. Clydesdale and Mac are adamant about another flight to the big mountain. We need more photographs before we leave.'

'So, we simply ignore this insurance demand?'

'No choice.' Blacker tapped his monocle. 'Turn a blind eye like Admiral Nelson. And while we're out here in the rump of India, who in London can stop us?'

'I suppose you have a point.'

'Of course, Percy. We have enough supplies for one more flight. They are there to be used, not carted back to London. That's why you went to Kathmandu for two permits.'

'Yes. Another fair point.'

'So there it is,' Blacker decided. 'Not a word to anyone, except Clydesdale and McIntyre. All you need to do, Percy, is to send the Nepalese an advisory cable after take off.'

Etherton knew he'd have to think about this. There could be no leaks in the plan if they were to launch expensive but uninsured biplanes to the Himalayas. It could even lead to a major nightmare and a diplomatic disaster.

Strings of decorated white oxen with carts began merging with elegant horse-drawn carriages as the parade passed through the Darbhanga estate. The residents had been ordered to welcome the 'sky men' and their greeting was genuine. In the palace forecourt, each elephant halted beside a platform where guests alighted. They then entered a lavish reception room where large punkahs, driven by unseen hands, fanned an artificial breeze over all guests.

In the throat of this room stood the Maharajah himself wearing a turban and frock coat of cream silk. A stylish and generous man, he greeted each and every guest as they passed by on their way to the bar.

Having paid his own compliments, Etherton took a huge tumbler of pink gin and fell into conversation with the Maharanee and Mrs. Fellowes.

'My dear Percy,' said Eleanor. 'Do tell our lovely hostess about my silver hairbrush.'

'Ah yes,' he said. 'Mrs. Fellowes mislaid the item, her family heirloom, so I asked the houseboys to find it.'

The Maharanee was a pint-sized woman, eyes as brown as the Ganges. Wrapped in a shimmering sari, priceless jewelry sparkled on her neck. She gave Eleanor an attentive look. 'And did they?' she asked. 'Did they find it?'

Etherton smiled. 'Yes, in a manner of speaking, they did.'

'It was amazing,' explained Eleanor. 'Today my brush was back on the dressing table, bright and shiny as usual. The houseboys said a dog had borrowed it and then returned it overnight.'

Etherton recalled how the culprit had wriggled his toes with extreme nervousness during interrogation. Toe movements often gave the game away, but he saw no need to explain his methods to either lady.

'Indian dogs are in fact amazingly odd creatures,' said Etherton. 'Many have found their way to the hearts of Maharajas and their families. Isn't that so, your Highness?'

The Maharanee agreed readily. 'On your journey across India, Mrs. Fellowes, you will have flown near Junagadh. The Maharaja there owns a great number of dogs. Around eight hundred of them, I believe.'

'Eight hundred dogs!' Eleanor almost dropped her drink. 'You must be teasing me, Your Highness?'

'No, but it's true. And would you believe each dog has its own room and servant with a telephone link to a central clinic. It is staffed by an English vet who understands canine problems, including I'm sure, any temptation for larceny.'

Was the Maharanee joking? Both Etherton and Eleanor found her comments very humorous until the sounding of a gong summoned all guests to the feast.

59. Lalbalu – 14th April 1933

PITT HAD HEARD ABOUT THE thieving dog and was retelling the tale to the ground crew as they took a tea break. Some mentioned their own mislaid items. Gallimore's gripe was fuel pilferage whilst Connochie attributed his loss of *Hingi Chips* (handkerchiefs) and *Daraj* (drawers) to unidentified 'borrowers' at large.

'Hankies and panties! So that's why I've anchored the kettle with a rope,' Pitt explained. 'The monkeys can't steal it.'

Sergeant Greenwood tipped out the dregs of his tea. 'Looting apart, I find it odd that Lady Houston is trying to prevent our pilots from doing their job. Do they know something we don't?'

No one had the answer. Rumors and gossip flourished while the big biplanes stayed on the ground. Pitt was reaching for the kettle, when he saw a vehicle driving at great speed straight across the grass to their camp. It halted in a dust-raising mushroom as Ellison jumped out, clearly a worried man.

'There's been a nasty accident,' he announced to everybody. 'One of the hydrogen balloons exploded as they were filling it.'

All the men looked up. 'An explosion? Anyone hurt?'

'I'm afraid so,' Ellison continued. 'Gupta and two assistants have first-degree burns to face and arms. Dr. Bennett has taken them to the Purnea clinic.'

Pitt could sense a common shock. They all respected the young Indian meteorologist whose smiles disguised his dismal forecasts.

Pitt shook his head. 'Crocodiles, bad weather, failed Eagle cameras, snakes and emptied fuel tanks. Then it was rotten curry, missing hairbrushes and now poor young Gupta and his men. Whatever next to brighten the party?'

'This might,' said Ellison. 'Today we'll do the smoke sequences while the poor weather persists on the mountains. The pilots are on their way.'

'Very good, sir.' Greenwood stood up. 'We can't wait to see pretty clouds in fancy colors.'

'Be ready for start-up as soon as they arrive.'

An hour later the Westlands were readying for take off as the ground crew regrouped in the shade for refreshments. Pitt then noticed that Shepherd was nowhere to be seen.

'Where's the scribe from *The Times*?' he asked.

'After hearing of the balloon accident, he shot off,' said Burnard. 'Scooped your story, Pitt, while you were cranking up the engines.'

'That's what you think,' he said. 'Aziz just gave me a tip.'

'And what might that be? asked Burnard. 'Another dead croc?'

'Possibly an even better scoop. Let's wait and see, shall we?'

Pitt was weary of Burnard's gloomy views. He sat down in a canvas chair with his mug of tea as the Westlands took off passing at great speed on either side of a Movietone camera set in the centre of the field. A second camera in Bonnett's hands would shoot the air-to-air sequences. Powering up, the Westlands peeled left and right in a steep climb over the excited crowds. When Pitt turned his attention back to ground level, he saw Colonel Blacker limping over to join them.

'I imagine you've heard of Gupta's run-in with a balloon, sir?'

'Yes, Pitt. A very nasty affair. But it could have been worse.'

'We're all sad to hear it,' said Pitt. 'A cup of char, Colonel?'

'Thank you, Pitt.' Blacker pulled up a chair. 'Keep drinking rosy lee and all will be well.'

'Meanwhile we're waiting for smokes of poof?' said Pitt. He saw that both machines had leveled out at a thousand feet, the selected altitude for the sequence. 'Poofs of victory! Whatever next?'

Blacker nodded. 'I entirely agree with you, Pitt. But we'll go along with Barkas for the present. It keeps us legally airborne while we're helping to make his movie.'

In full view, the director stood isolated on the grass runway, waiting to fire his flare gun when the film crew was ready. Anticipation grew among the thronged Indians as they gazed up at the biplanes circling above.

Only when the green flare soared into the sky, did the ground crew stand to watch. Now came the howling sound of a Pegasus driving *Lucy* to her maximum speed of 200 mph. Then from the biplane issued pulses of colored smoke bursting astern. The effect was more impressive than Pitt had anticipated. First came red, then white and finally blue, all as great balls of ballooning smoke.

The biplane reared up, zooming back to the sky. However an unscripted drama had erupted on the ground. Around the airfield came screams of protest from several thousand Indians. Some were running onto the airfield, brushing past the posted militiamen.

'By God!' shouted Blacker. 'What in hell's name is this?'

Pitt immediately decided to reveal what he'd learned from Aziz. 'I heard a rumor, sir, that agitators are among the crowd today.'

'Agitators?' Blacker's features set hard. 'Look at them, man! They're all over the blessed airfield.'

Running along the grass runway, enraged numbers of tribesmen were shouting, remonstrating, banging drums and waving fists at the sky. Their clamor carried a message that grew more audible. 'British bombs, British out! British bombs, British out!'

The leading activists merged into a broad wave that continued remorselessly towards the hangars. Did they mean to overrun the base and destroy the two Moths parked there? Barkas and his filmies had lifted their equipment and were retreating from the advancing rabble.

Hurling down his tea, Colonel Blacker hurried into the sunlight passing the film crew. 'You called for action, Mr. Barkas!' he called to the director. 'Well now, you've bloody got it!'

The din of several thousand voices was becoming louder by the second. Pitt saw Blacker snatch the flare gun from the director before striding forward entirely alone towards the oncoming riot.

Swinging latti sticks, the Raja's militiamen had now rallied to move in behind Blacker who stood firm on the runway, hand on one hip, flare gun in the other. He shouted to the faltering ringleaders. 'No, no, no! These are not bombs! Just smoke. Stay where you are! It's for the cinema and you are all the greatest of actors. I thank you!'

With this burst of impromptu praise, Blacker somehow succeeded in persuading the ringleaders to halt. They soon dropped their protest and returned to the perimeter, leaving the field clear. Watching all this, the ground crew continued to stare in suspended disbelief. The riot had been disarmed by a single man wearing a monocle and a glare of warlike rage.

'The man has nerves of tungsten steel,' said Burnard. 'I never saw anything like it. Makes you proud to be British.'

Pitt had opened his notebook. 'Yes, Burnard, and that's the scoop Shepherd just missed.'

60. Hampstead – April 1933

LUCY HOUSTON WAS SPEAKING ON the phone, her eyes were glittering like graphite. 'No bloody no! I shall not be sending a single penny to Lloyds. Just to cover men pushing against the dark powers of the mountain? Never!'

In the dayroom at Byron Cottage, Garland watched Lady Houston slam the receiver down. She waited discreetly for a few seconds before enquiring. 'Dark powers, milady?'

'It's never safe to tempt the forces of Nature with the whimsical inventions of mankind. The natural world always wins in the end.'

'I guess you're right.'

'Everything should be simple, Garland. When things get complicated then dark powers flourish. Why did it take the deaths of a million men to crush the Kaiser when it was nothing more than a white hanky that actually stopped the war? It need never have started if there'd been just a simple agreement between leaders. That's what I mean by simple.'

Wondering how to comment, Garland said nothing.

Besides Lady Houston had more to add. She picked up a newspaper, turning to Garland. 'The airship disaster...They say it was the hand of Nature that forced the Akron down. No failure of engines or crew. Just a dark power that took the lives of all the victims.'

'Fifteen Americans,' said Garland. It was especially sensitive for her. 'Did you know my father was killed in an airship crash eight years ago?'

'You never told me this.'

'One day he was at home. Next day, there was his empty seat instead. All so sudden.'

Lucy Houston stared thoughtfully at Garland, her vexation melting away. 'Sit down. I promise not to shout again.'

Garland drew up a chair. She was still holding the latest bulletin, taken from a report in *the Bristol Evening Post*. 'You may be right about dark forces, Lady Houston. The latest news from India mentions a riot at Lalbalu.'

'A riot?' Lady Houston's bile reignited. 'Is there no end to this nonsense? So what's this about?'

Garland read the report aloud while Lady Houston's concern turned to horror and then to a groan of utter resignation. 'What does this tell you,

Garland? Considering it was just a harmless display of our national colors.'

'That they were making a fuss about nothing.'

'So they were. People often suffer from misplaced notions.'

Garland noticed how the heiress appeared to be less energetic this morning. While spring was ripe in Hampstead, the pulse of time was wearing her away. Too much fretting was no good for the old lady.

'Did I tell you Mr. Blumenfeld has invited me to his Easter party?'

'No, you didn't,' said Lady Houston. 'But that's no problem. Of course, you should go. Someone can cover for you.'

'Thank you, milady.'

Lady Houston's dark mood continued to soften. Perhaps that revelation about her father's death had registered?

'It's time for you to enjoy more of your life, I've seen you pacing the lawn. I've noted your false patience with my errant thinking and I've seen how a subtle allure overtakes you whenever an attractive man comes near.'

'Lady Houston, what do you mean?'

'Don't argue, dear. I can read the signs of sexual interest as easily as a nun reads the bible. The time may come for you to move on, Garland. To fly a new course, as pilots would say. I'll have to find a replacement for a close and loyal colleague who has helped me through this difficult year.'

A tear sprang to Garland's eye. She reached for the handkerchief tucked in the sleeve.

'Yes, it will be sad,' said Lady Houston. 'But you must find yourself a man. Here, in America, or wherever the wind takes you. Fill your heart with the love you need. And then do something I never achieved. Become a mother.'

Good grief, now what? Garland didn't know where to look. But Lady Houston still hadn't finished.

'But only find a man who is willing to care for you and your offspring. That's the key to it all. Now find your pencil and send Clydesdale and Co. yet another message. I want them back in London. I don't want them flying around in the mountains. Do they hear me?'

'There's a problem I gather at Purnea's cable office...'

'That's to be expected. The staff were probably out rioting. Just keep sending them telegrams. Tell them to come home now!'

61. Purnea. Easter Races – 7th April 1933

LEAVING LALBALU BASE UNDER THE custody of the Raja's militiamen, the engineers departed en masse for the Race Track. It was Easter Monday, another searing gusty day, and today's hot topic was the tale of Clydesdale and the baby elephant. Leaning on the white-washed rails of the course, Pitt eagerly persuaded Connochie to relate his own version.

'First came the mother elephant with her mahout. She arrived while we were playing tennis. I never saw the calf until I was hurled to the ground. I remember thinking it might be Sally Smith in her Dodge truck. Then looking up and gasping for air, I saw my assailant had a trunk like a didgeridoo with ears bigger than a pillow.'

'Jesus!' said Pitt. 'So what happened then?'

'I rolled under the drinks table. But this young elephant was feeling frisky and tried to flatten the table. Then, thank heavens, it caught sight of our Chief Pilot in his tennis kit and decided to hunt aristocrats instead. It went straight for him, trunk forward like a torpedo and ears trimmed for take-off.'

To those listening, this was an extraordinary story. For Pitt, it was yet another scoop coming his way. 'A great scene for your film. So did it get Clydesdale? Trample on him?'

'The mutilation of our hero would not please the audience.'

'So what happened?' asked Pitt.

'Clydesdale survived by legging it up a tree. The mahout slid down its mother's trunk to mediate, but the little blighter then knocked the mahout clean out of the tennis court. It was the best action sequence I never filmed.'

The story telling ended when trumpeters began signaling the start of a race. The meeting had attracted scores of Indians and planters to watch races of various classifications and handicaps. One was a contest for ponies and young riders, all frighteningly energetic. Another was for polo club members on their own ponies. A third had been for planters, friends of Tom Smith, who won easily and was now jumping onto a fresh mount for the final race.

This was open to any expedition member daring to try their luck on miscellaneous steeds provided by the Raja. The few volunteers had drawn lots for unknown animals. This random selection added more guesswork to the bets being placed with Connochie, their self-appointed bookmaker. He was offering 'evens' on Tom Smith the most accomplished horseman, but at four to one, there was good money going on Clydesdale to win. It was easy to shed rupees when they had little else to do with their pay packets.

The race began with the firing of a shotgun. Four horses, already startled by the blast and screaming spectators, bolted off in various directions. Smith trailed Clydesdale who led from the start on a dappled grey mare. To a cheering crowd who all admired his recent feat over Everest, Clydesdale galloped to an easy victory. Shepherd's race was spectacular. His rangy animal had been taking lessons from the baby elephant. It galloped into the crowd nearly causing another riot. Shepherd soared from his saddle and the horse cavorted erratically until captured.

It was the fourth horse that provided the most fun. The spry chestnut gelding was determined to ditch Etherton from the start. Bucking and twisting, jumping this way and that, the contest endured until Etherton too fell to the ground while his mount vanished in clouds of spurting sand.

'Horses were never my preferred means of transport,' Pitt dabbed tears of laughter. 'You can see why. Minds of their own.'

Connochie had seized Pitt's shoulder. 'When you stop laughing, shouldn't we see if Percy is in one piece?'

Together they ducked below the rails and ran to Etherton who was struggling to his feet, whip in hand, to stare after his mount.

'You all right, sir?' Pitt asked.

Etherton took a breath. In black jodhpurs, polished boots and a cream shirt with a blue cravat at his neck, he looked like a cavalry man. 'Bloody animal!'

'No bones broken?' asked Pitt.

'No, thank God, but it damn near killed me.' Etherton walked unsteadily to the rails where the crewmen applauded him. He took a cigarette from Connochie and stooped to the lighter. 'Hope you didn't have money on me?'

'No, sir. It was mostly on Clydesdale.'

'Very shrewd,' said Etherton. 'He drew the Raja's best horse.'

'So you and Shepherd had the rodeo brutes.'

Shepherd came up. He too seemed shaken. 'What a nightmare! I was in the crowd with no control whatsoever.'

''Minds of their own, that's the problem,' Pitt said.

'Horses are not alone in that respect, Mr. Pitt.' Shepherd's eyes narrowed. 'But we won't go into that now.'

A dozen teenage Indian girls were standing nearby. They giggled self-consciously when Connochie offered to take their photograph with his pocket Kodak camera. In their saris, showing slender midriffs jeweled at the navel, the girls of Purnea made a lovely sight. Soon the unseated horsemen along with engineers and filmies were posing beside the young beauties while Connochie exposed a full roll of film. Etherton then went off to find a drink while those who had bet on Clydesdale claimed their winnings. Pitt counted his rupees and then prepared to head to bar.

'Not yet, Mr. Pitt,' said Shepherd.

Pitt turned back. 'Don't we deserve a drink after all that?'

'I want a word with you first. On our own.'

'You didn't expect to win, did you?' asked Pitt.

Shepherd took off his riding hat. 'My job is to report on any news for *The Times*. They bought the exclusive rights to this expedition. News cannot be hijacked by other parties, do you understand?'

'I'm not deaf, Mr. Shepherd. I only cover the non-Himalayan elements for my Bristol readers. That's not contravening any supposed rights. Your complaint is out of order.'

Shepherd's long face remained rigid. 'Be that as it may. My point is that filing news stories carries professional responsibility.'

'Meaning what, Mr. Shepherd?'

'That stories can become distorted by the time they reach London. The expedition has suffered enough problems. We've lost the support of the Committee, Lloyds Insurance and now Lady Houston. All because of irresponsible stories.'

'So the crocodile wasn't real, then? The snake in the bungalow wasn't there and I was only dreaming when I retrieved the Westland from a buffalo wallow in Dinajpur?'

'No. All of that was true and we need to put all those incidents behind us. I don't appreciate amateur reporting when we have to move forward together. We can't afford to let the cat out of the bag.'

'What cat? You mean the Raja's man-eater?'

'Mr. Pitt. Be sensible will you? We must be very careful how we file reports from now on.'

'I'm an engineer, not a mind reader.'

'You know bloody well what I'm talking about. You manage the engines, Pitt, so you will have realized they haven't finished the flying operation yet. But we don't want all London to know that.'

'Very good. I'll forget I heard it from you.'

'No, Mr. Pitt! You haven't heard it from anyone.'

Pitt decided he should humor Shepherd with a smile and a handshake. The man had a job to do, and so did he. 'We gentlemen of the press must appreciate one another. So let me get you a drink, old son.'

62. Great Dunmow – Easter Monday April 1933

A RIPPING CRACK OF THUNDER over the village of Great Dunmow brought lunchtime conversation to a temporary halt. Guests at Ralph Blumenfeld's country home were aware of an impending storm, but it would not stop them sipping drinks and yarning about their lives and aspirations. They had enjoyed cocktails, canapés and poached salmon with infinite wine on this Easter holiday. Tomorrow they'd be back at their desks in the city, fifty miles to the south.

Unfortunately Garland had arrived late. The bank holiday trains from London were spasmodic and long distance cabs were expensive. Flustered by delays, she eventually reached the farmhouse in the Essex countryside ten minutes before lunch was served. In a flurry of introductions, she gathered that most guests came from the worlds of art and media.

Garland took her place between the pictures editor of the *Daily Express* and the travel editor of *Tatler*. Both journalists were fast-witted and knew about her role with Lady Houston, and wanted tidbits about the heiress and her Himalayan adventure. Apart the loss of one aeroplane, wasn't it lucky the whole venture had proceeded so well? The *Tatler* man, a suave socialite who knew Shepherd, felt *The Times* had been served well. Sensational action had been fairly reported.

Garland smiled. She could not reveal how her employer felt about *The Times*. The *Tatler* man rambled on about Cannes Film Festival which he would attend in May. Would Barkas be back for that? Again Garland didn't know. Strawberries came with Cornish cream and the picture editor said how impressed he was by the Himalayan photographs. But wasn't it odd, he pointed out, that *The Times* had printed a full front page photo of Makalu's ridge instead of Everest's peak? It was strange, Garland agreed, but misunderstandings occurred, didn't they?

And with the strawberries came more strident thunder. Soon isolated drops of rain began to fall faster than the anecdotes from Fleet Street. People abandoned the dining table to find sofas and comfy chairs.

Below the low ceiling beams of the farmhouse, Blumenfeld found Garland and introduced her to a stylish woman who held an absurdly long cigarette holder between gloved fingers. She was appraising his private collection of paintings on the wall.

'Someone you should meet,' Blumenfeld said. 'Elizabeth Penrose is from *Vogue*, New York. Elizabeth is the Fashion editor. And this young lady is my friend Garland Ross, from Ohio.'

Garland shook hands, desperately unsure of her appearance. Her summer dress was a rag when compared to the floral exuberance of the Fashion editor's swirling dress cut on the bias. *Vogue* magazine for Chrissake!

Blumenfeld said. 'Elizabeth, please tell Garland what's been happening in Manhattan while she's been helping Lady Houston with the Everest flight.'

The lofty look in the *Vogue* editor's eyes vanished. 'Now, isn't that exciting? That's one heck of a story.'

'Tell me about it.' Blumenfeld turned to go. 'I'll leave you to sort out the world. Please excuse me.'

Elizabeth Penrose spoke a husky tone. 'I bet you're relieved it's all over with no accidents.'

'Not quite over. The pilots are still out there, playing tennis and filming, so we understand. But they did the job and returned in one piece, though they nearly crashed on a school after leaving Kanchenjunga.'

'On a school? What a terrible thought! So is it true they're going for a second flight over Everest?'

Evidently Elizabeth Penrose had not heard of the latest flight prohibitions imposed by Lloyds. 'All we know is that we're getting no responses. Maybe they're hoping for another flight.'

'And does it matter?' Elizabeth Penrose blew smoke at the ceiling. 'Surely one flight is enough?'

Garland smiled. 'That's exactly Lady Houston's view.'

'She's a very rare woman. I'm told she was something of a trendsetter in her time?'

Garland nodded. 'Drury Lane, Monaco, Paris. She was there.'

Now the fashion editor gave Garland an American no-nonsense look. 'What if I commission you to write a piece about Lucy's dress sense?'

Garland took a sip of coffee, trying to think clearly. 'I'm not really permitted to write about her. But there may be something I could do.' Garland couldn't let this opportunity pass. 'If you can wait a month or so. My contract is due to expire and I'm going to America for a break.'

'Well, that's fine. It's just an idea.'

'I'm hoping to get her approval for a biography I'd like to write. Then I might give you the full story,' said Garland. 'When she was in Paris, back in her heyday, she'd match her outfits to suit the décor of restaurants where she dined. She knew all the maître d's and chefs by name.'

'How marvelous.'

'And this is no secret,' added Garland. 'When her steam yacht was damaged in a collision at sea, the insurance claim on her ruined lingerie was set at twenty-five thousand dollars.'

'For lingerie? That's a huge figure. Was she running a brothel?'

'Who knows?' Garland laughed. 'It was long before I met her.'

'And yet she's not going to pay the insurance for another flight?'

'Definitely not.' The high priestess of fashion must have been talking to Blumenfeld, thought Garland. 'Mind you, Lucy can change her mind whenever it suits her.'

'What woman wouldn't? Now tell me about Harald Penrose.'

'Harald Penrose?' asked Garland.

'Wasn't he the test pilot?'

'Oh, *that* Penrose.' Garland remembered. 'He didn't go to India. He stayed in Somerset, where Westland is based. What can I tell you?'

Miss Penrose stooped to scrutinize an ink drawing by Felix Topolski in their host's collection. Briefly distracted she straightened. 'Maybe you can find out if he is related to me? Wouldn't that be fun? I adore the style and the image of aviators. They're so brave, so calm, so magnetic.'

'That's another view you and Lucy share,' said Garland. 'The expedition would never have happened if that hadn't been the case.'

The fashion editor waved her cigarette holder in an arc towards an ashtray. 'If Penrose and I are relatives, I'd be so pleased. And as for the commission, when you get Lucy's approval just let me know.'

63. The Caledonian Club – April 1933

LORD PEEL, BLUMENFELD AND HINKS had been invited by John Buchan to the Caledonian Club in St. James Square. There, he hoped, they could review outstanding matters following the Easter break.

Waiting for the his colleagues to arrive, Buchan sat in the club's bar reviewing his day's achievements – or lack of them. Again he'd been assisting pre-production for The Thirty-Nine Steps. It was frustrating that screen writers had altered a story that had taken him months to create. They were pruning it to bare essentials.

Equally annoying was his other great project. The expedition was now grounded by financial edicts from London while pandering to the whims of another dragooning director under contract to the same film company. Whatever he felt about such grievances, Buchan was realistic. There was a price for everything, he reminded himself, as he stood to greet Arthur Hinks.

The geographer was in an amiable mood. 'Well, John, it's a year since you first came to the Royal Geographic. I admit, I was dubious initially but I heartily congratulate your team for advancing the sciences of geography.'

'And the RGS had a big hand in it,' said Buchan. 'Now, before the others arrive, Arthur, what news of Ruttledge and his climbers?'

'Rather negative, I fear. They're stuck in camp because of the lousy weather, just like the pilots.'

'So they'll be lucky to scale Everest before the monsoon?'

'Racing bad weather is never good practice for mountaineers or aviators. But there is some news. Ruttledge and his radio man did make contact with Purnea, meaning radio waves can transmit in the Himalaya. It's a successful byproduct of the enterprise.'

Buchan's reaction was preempted by the arrival of Lord Peel and Blumenfeld who ordered drinks before coming over to join them. Lord Peel was holding a large manila envelope. He opened it to slide a selection of prints onto a table.

'These photographs came by airmail from Blacker via Calcutta. Straight from the darkroom in Purnea. Go ahead. Help yourselves. They're not state secrets.'

For several minutes the prints were passed around allowing each man to examine the cliffs and snow gullies that tapered to the highest point on the planet.

Hinks made the first comment. 'Great pictures, but not the least hint of Irvin or Mallory.'

Lord Peel took out a pocket magnifying glass for his own inspection. 'Not so much as a pin in the pinnacle.'

'Surely we weren't expecting to see Mallory and Irvin sitting on top like frozen buddhas?' said Blumenfeld. 'I'd have sold my last drop of blood for that story.'

'Blood couldn't buy it, Ralph,' said Buchan. '*The Times* beat you to it.'

'To Lucy's lasting fury,' laughed Blumenfeld. 'Now she's forgotten MacDonald, preferring to make war on *The Times*.'

'The PM lost no sleep over her tantrums,' said Lord Peel. 'And I imagine the Astors will ignore them just as easily. Lucy, despite all her wealth, is no match for government and newspapers.'

'And it's most unlikely that *The Times* will ever publish her real reasons for backing the flight.'

'Which were?' Hinks looked up from the photographs.

'To prove Britain can still achieve great feats,' said Buchan. 'To remind the world of our Empire. All frightfully jingoistic, I agree, but that's Lucy's rationale. The scientific objectives mean less to her.'

Blumenfeld had his own view. 'Our readers see Lucy for what she does, rather than what she says. She backs British enterprise. She waves the national flag and that's our editorial policy too. We may publish some of her views in due course.'

'Whatever her motives, these photos would not exist without her.' Hinks said. 'I can't wait to see the survey strips.'

'You'll be lucky to get any survey strips,' said Lord Peel. 'The Eagle cameras failed on the first flight and now there can be no second flight due to insurance obstacles.'

'And that, my Lord, would be a real shame,' said Hinks. 'Especially, after all the effort and investment. Surely if they have a permit and logistics for a second flight, they should go up again?'

'Then maybe your Royal Geographic can stump up the premium? Or perhaps the *Daily Express* could chip in?' Buchan noticed how quickly both men shook their heads. 'Believe me, we've asked everyone. Lucy won't budge and nor will Lloyds.'

Lord Peel was gathering the photographs. 'And that's why I've sent yet another cable demanding them to pack up and return as soon as Fellowes recovers from his dysentery. Meanwhile they're restricted to making local flights for the film people. But no more surveys, I'm sorry to say. No more pictures of the Himalayas.'

'Who's in charge then? asked Hinks.

'Colonel Blacker. He's perfectly qualified. He was in charge of His Majesty's Air Force at the outbreak of war in 1914.'

'Therefore you trust him?' said Blumenfeld.

'What are you inferring?' replied Buchan. 'Blacker's totally dependable.'

'If I was a betting man...' Blumenfeld let the thought hang. 'A man like McIntyre would seize any chance to return to Everest,'

'We'll see,' said Lord Peel. 'But if something went wrong, it might lead to a diplomatic row not to mention financial horror for those of us obliged to cover the losses. As committee members we could well feature in any ensuing legal proceedings. After nearly flattening an entire school, I hope they've learned that a second flight would amount to irresponsibility of the worst kind.'

Blumenfeld cocked his head thoughtfully. 'You may be right about that, Your Lordship, but our headline writers at the *Express* probably won't see it that way.

64. Purnea Palace – April 1933

ELEANOR FELLOWES WAS NO FOOL. Surely the subtle changes in her relationship with other members of the expedition were not imagined? Geniality had turned to brief and hasty interchange. Conversations with the pilots, normally so forthcoming and amusing, now only touched on trivial matters of local gossip. No one was talking about the Himalayas, the weather or the Westland biplanes. Even Shepherd seemed less interested in flight schedules than before. Everyone wanted to discuss Barkas and his movie instead.

'No, the men don't chat to me, and rarely for a moment longer than necessary,' she explained to the Ranee and Sally Smith who sat with her in the palace reception room.

The high ceiling and spacious door arches had been designed to keep the occupants cool but did little for intimacy. Even so the ever bubbly and modern Ranee had dispensed with servants because she loved serving tea herself, using a teapot in the shape of an art deco Sadler racing car. She told Eleanor she had bought it in Harrods along with the Doulton tea service on her last trip to London.

'So I think you're experiencing a form of purdah,' the Ranee concluded. 'We do that out here, as you know.'

Earlier the Ranee had taken her two visitors on a tour which included the defunct purdah quarters. In previous years female residents lived there in rooms surrounding a dim quadrangle. Hidden from public gaze and direct sunlight, their security was enforced by a latticework on windows, spy-holes and gratings.

'Perhaps I am indeed in purdah,' said Eleanor. 'But I don't see why. Do I reek of Perry's illness? You would tell me if I were?'

Sally nodded vigorously. 'Of course I would, but you don't. Some may see you as a risk since you are nursing your husband.'

'But they're happy to socialize with Dr. Bennett. The officers are the worst. The engineers and film crew are quite willing to chat.'

'You know what men are,' said the Ranee. 'Once they have what they desire, they frequently lose interest. Your pilots have achieved their goals and must now be planning other things to do with their aeroplanes.'

Sally wore loose slacks and a turquoise cotton blouse that suited her

248

tanned face. 'My Tom will be back to work on the estate as soon as you all vanish.'

The Ranee rolled her eyes and wailed. 'Oooh! I don't want you to go. It's been so much fun having you here.'

Fans on the ceiling continued to swish cool air over the three women. The blades were powered by an elaborate system of gears and rods connected to an unseen punkah-wallah cranking a handle. Life in India, thought Eleanor, was built on infinite human cogs all interchanging to drive the national energy.

'We're not going anywhere until Perry recovers,' said Eleanor. 'He's the one to fly me home, and presently he can only just stagger to the bathroom.'

The Ranee understood. 'It's all so unfortunate.'

Sally was equally sympathetic. 'The poor man. Ever since he put down in Dinajpur he's been under the weather. He must have eaten something quite awful.'

'And he's generally so resilient,' said Eleanor. 'He even had soup made from rats once.'

Sally's squawk of disgust echoed in the room.

'It was a delicacy in the trenches so he says,' said Eleanor.

The Ranee pulled a face and Eleanor giggled. She appreciated these outings with Sally, the visits to the Ranee or the social club. She would miss this backwater of Purnea, along with the old Dodge, the buffalos, camels and elephants all clogging the roads. Indians ran their lives on so many diverse beliefs and practices thought Eleanor. India had been magical, Perry's ailment being one exception.

'My advice, Eleanor, is to get your Doctor to prescribe our local water cure,' said the Ranee. 'You mix salt with baking powder and orange juice. Give it to your husband whenever you can. There's little else to do but to wait for the illness to go its way and vanish.'

Waiting! That was another of India's specialities. Waiting for cows to move on, for trains to materialize, for documents to be delivered, for good flying conditions. Even Clydesdale had agreed to wait for Barkas to complete his shoot, a surprising change of heart after all the grumbling previously aimed at the director.

Then Raja Banaili came striding in. He was attired in a blue shirt, tweed jacket and white flannels. 'Is there something I'm missing?' he asked. 'I heard you all giggling.'

'Nothing of significance,' the Ranee giggled. 'Nothing at all.'

The Raja helped himself to a piece of almond cake. He was a stout but energetic man with a strong appetite for gossip, action, food and drama.

'Then, allow me to tell you something that will really make you chatter. I have a new plan in my sights. You can have one guess each.'

'Another man-eating tiger?' suggested Sally.

'No, Sally. One is enough and I will find him.'

It was Eleanor's turn. 'If you're working for Barkas, just ensure he doesn't blow you up like poor Mr. Gupta.'

'No, no. Nothing like that.' The Raja cocked his head and looked to his wife. 'Your turn now.'

'My hope,' said the Ranee, 'is that next time you plan races, you will provide proper horses for your guests.'

'No no.' The Raja ignored the jibe. 'But it was fun when Percy abandoned his horse, I must admit. And it gave me some ideas.'

'What do you mean? You too want to fall face first onto the soil of India? In front of all the people?'

The Raja of Banaili finished the almond cake. He raised a finger and shook his head until he had swallowed. 'No, my dear, that privilege I will leave for others. I've accepted an offer from Flight Lieutenant McIntyre. I am preparing to go up for a flight in one of his aeroplanes.'

65. Second Everest flight – April 19th 1933

IT WAS THE MOVEMENT OF air that woke him. Blacker propped himself on an elbow as the houseboy Framjee parted the mosquito netting to pass him a mug of tea.

'Chota hazri, sahib. No clouding today.'

'Thank you Framjee. That's good. Very good.' Blacker pointed to Clydesdale's dormant frame in the neighboring bed. 'Tea for him and for Mr. McIntyre and Mr. Fisher. Be very, very quiet, won't you.'

'Yes sah.' Framjee tiptoed away.

Blacker sipped the tea, looking across to the other bed. The young aristocrat slept like granite, never having learned the art for cat napping like those who fought at ground level. Blacker sipped his tea. At least the weather, so Framjee said, was clear.

He quickly reviewed the plan agreed over dinner on the previous night. The stratagem required that Fellowes' should remain afflicted by dysentery. This was an odd wish to make for a friend and fellow officer, nevertheless it was essential.

When briefed, Etherton had merely raised his eyes to the heavens and clamped his lips tight. Mum was the word. Barkas and Shepherd may have guessed that a second flight was on the cards but as each wanted footage or stories, neither man was likely to blow the whistle.

Ostensibly all flight operations were now dedicated to filming, not to Himalayan survey. This was the case presented to Dr. Bennett and Eleanor. Blacker added that in his opinion, based on years of dysentery experience, they would be well advised to keep Fellowes in bed for a few days more. Their reactions indicated they probably didn't believe him, nevertheless they agreed to do so.

After dinner Blacker had sent a message to Lalbalu requesting that both Westlands should be fully fueled and loaded with oxygen and survey cameras by 07.30 hours. The crafty lads would see through the ruse, but they weren't in direct touch with Fellowes

The priority now was a swift and silent departure from the bungalow to get airborne before Fellowes was alerted.

He felt more confident when his fellow conspirators had all tiptoed into the open air. They hurried across the maidan in the early light to waiting cars and set off at speed for Lalbalu. Local farmers, ferrying vegetables to market on their backs and heads, watched as the two Vauxhall cars raced towards the airbase.

By the time they reached Lalbalu, Ellison had already taken the Puss Moth up to assess the Himalayan skyline and on his return, his prognosis was favorable. Blacker had no qualms about giving the order to commence the operation.

The following thirty minutes involved the ponderous donning of flight suits built like medieval armor. By the time he had given the eyeglass a polish and pulled down his goggles he knew how a knight felt before battle. Around the aerodrome, crowds were again enthralled by the drama. The crew were busy, all believing high-altitude business was imminent and if the officers were giving orders, they would be blameless.

At 07.45 the two Pegasus engines gave voice and there was still no sign of the Air Commodore. Somewhere in Blacker's mind were the Field Services Regulations drafted by the Duke of Wellington. These stated that subordinates could revise an order if conditions changed between its issuance and its implementation. This would be his defense if he ever came to face an inquest.

The aircrew climbed to their cockpits in fuselages vibrating to the pulse of the engines. Fixing harnesses and tubes was a well-practiced skill and shortly the pilots' thumbs went up. The Pegasus engines raised their note and sprang forward, heading once more towards the Himalayas.

Blacker set about his work. Carefully he tested the survey camera's electric motor. It was working to order. Even better, the internal voice link with Clydesdale was also working.

'So far so good,' reported Clydesdale as they climbed through 10,000 feet. 'How are things in the back seat? Over.'

Blacker peered from the cockpit as the fields of Bihar disappeared in the haze. 'All good. Cameras, oxygen, heating and radio, all tickety-boo. Over.'

'Dammit,' said Clydesdale.

Blacker frowned. 'Problem?'

'Not with the Westland,' came the reply. 'I left something behind.'

Blacker was in no mood for mysteries. 'What did you leave?'

'My lucky charm. A medallion of St. Christopher, a gift from my mother. I must have left it with my shaving kit this morning.'

'Maybe that thieving dog is at it again? Blacker gave a gruff laugh. 'It's not a problem. Just thank the god Ganesh for removing all obstacles to our plan.'

The Westland hummed on, the altimeter rising slowly but surely.

66. Lalbalu – April 19th 1933

ON THE GRASS AT LALBALU the goats and sheep were grazing while the spectators had retreated to squat in the shade until the aeroplanes returned. Few understood how a machine as large as an elephant could leave the ground to perform exotic dances in the sky. It was so exciting and the British pilots would soon be leaving, so harvesting could be postponed.

'I'm going to miss all this,' Pitt confessed to Connochie and Burnard as they sat near the silent hangars. 'No wonder the locals don't wear watches. Time means nothing here.'

Connochie was fashioning paper darts for the two sons of Aziz. He launched a dart and the boys raced to retrieve it. 'So the question is this. When will the Air Commodore learn his pilots have departed against his orders?'

Pitt thought about this as he absorbed the atmosphere with its pervasive reek of cow-dung and the constant cries of hawks and mynah birds. From blackened stoves, where curried chapatis simmered, came the rich scent of spice and oils. All this he would miss when he went home.

'It won't be too long,' Pitt replied. 'And he may well order a court-martial. A hanging maybe? Or even a firing squad? I'm not sure what happens to officers who flagrantly break the rules.'

'Either outcome would make a very fitting end to your film.' Burnard lit a cigarette and chuckled.

'You've been in the jungle too long,' said Connochie. 'Borrowing uninsured RAF machines is not a capital offense. The ends always justify the means for the military. It's often the rule for filmmakers too.'

Pitt nodded thoughtfully. Life had its benefits in Bristol. He thought of the semi-detached house from which he cycled daily to Bristol Aviation. He knew the route so well he could do it blindfold. But now he had enough memories to provide countless anecdotes in his local pub. Rounds of free drinks were assured. Maybe his articles for the *Bristol Evening Post* would provide good pocket money. He could give lectures to the Rotarians or the Guild of Aviation Engineers? Whatever came of it, his two Peggies had performed faultlessly and that's what mattered.

Pitt checked his watch. The engines would have devoured half their fuel supply by now. He looked up as Aziz and his cart approached. A crate of live chickens sat on the cart beside the crocodile's skin. Aziz halted the oxen beside their awning.

'The crocodile, sahib, is ready for you.' Aziz held up the skin grinning with toothless satisfaction.

The engineers tried to admire the offered item. Aziz had done a fair job on the curing but the skin travelled with a thousand flies to discourage close inspection. In any case, there was no time because two cars were arriving from Purnea.

Connochie glanced at the two engineers. 'Cue the music! Fellowes is a-coming.'

The cars came rattling between the trees, through the guard post straight to the hangars. Fellowes, his wife and Dr. Bennett stepped from one vehicle. Shepherd and Percy Etherton descended with less haste from the other. After glaring at the empty hangars, the Air Commodore turned his attention to the ground crew, advancing with a bellow. 'Sergeant Greenwood!'

Greenwood was on his feet. 'Sir! Good morning, sir. Pleased to see you're on the mend, sir.'

'I may be recovered, Sergeant. But I'm decidedly not pleased!'

'Sorry to hear that sir.'

Pitt had rarely seen so much animation in an officer. Normally so courteous, Fellowes was rearing like a cobra, his eyes glaring furiously below the brim of his topee. For once, Pitt stayed silent leaving the RAF officers to resolve their spat.

'Where are the Westlands, Sergeant?' Fellowes roared again. 'I never authorized any flights today!'

Sergeant Greenwood stood at attention. 'I can't be sure, sir. None of us knew the flight plan. They just arrived at dawn and we followed orders.'

'Not my orders!'

'You weren't here to give them, sir. Colonel Blacker, Squadron Leader Clydesdale and Flight Lieutenant McIntyre said they had unfinished business. Some work for Mr. Barkas and his film crew, sir. It was a routine departure, sir.'

'There was nothing routine about it,' snapped Fellowes. 'Did they take oxygen? Were they wearing high-altitude suits?'

'I believe they were, sir.'

'Then clearly they were heading for the Himalaya! With no authorization and more to the point, with no insurance!'

Pitt now became aware of movement on the airfield. The goats were being gathered. People were leaving the shade.

'If I may, sir?' Pitt intervened between the Sergeant and the Air Commodore. 'I believe we have incoming aircraft, sir.'

The thrumming note of a Pegasus engine was audible. Eyes turned up as the airbase trumpet sounded and the sunlight caught on the wings of an incoming biplane. Fellowes stared. 'Just one machine, Mr. Pitt. That is the PV3 *Lucy*.'

'And she hasn't had enough time to reach Everest.'

'I doubt if that was ever their intention.' Shepherd shielded his eyes from the sun to watch the Westland touch down. 'Clydesdale would never have gone along with such a plan.'

'More than his career's worth,' Pitt suggested. 'From my viewpoint, the more sorties we make the better. We like testing our engines out here in nowhere land.'

'So where's *Akbar*?' demanded Fellowes, as he paced across the hangar doorway. 'Can you please tell me, Mr. Pitt?'

The Westland *Lucy* was taxiing towards them and Pitt shrugged politely. 'I haven't a clue, sir. You'll have to ask the Chief Pilot, sir. I've got work to do.'

67. Purnea Bungalow – April 19th 1933

AT 8 P.M. THE EXPOSED plates from the Eagle cameras began to yield results. In the pink glow of the darkroom, images were now emerging. Measuring five by four inches, each showed up sharp and clear. A procession of vertical shots capturing the Everest massif as square miles of mangled ice and rock had been recorded for ever.

Blacker had been assisting Fraser in this magic. On strings above the rinsing dishes, his plates from his flight that morning over the southern flanks of the mountain were drying nicely. Also featured was the magnificent evidence of McIntyre's spectacular visit to the highest peak. Blacker wiped the sweat from his mustache. It was hotter than the gorge of Hades, but worth it.

'Now that's the stuff, Fraser.' Blacker stooped over the mutating images in the tray. 'Just what we need.'

Fraser was reading a thermometer. 'I hope so, sir. They must be among the most expensive photos ever taken.'

In the dim light, Fraser appeared ghostly, a spirit held briefly in the grip of immortality. A thousand memories of similar young men heading to the trenches suddenly came to Blacker's mind.

'There are many more costly photographs, Fraser. All records of the Great War. They show mud, blood, craters, a collapsed turret or trench maybe, but mainly corpses. These pictures of the Himalaya show a land that has defied all man's follies. This is the throne of Nature herself.'

'If you put it that way, sir.'

Blacker nodded. 'Believe me. Some of these will reach the world's presses and millions will soon see what nobody has ever seen before.'

'I do hope so.' Using acrylic tongs Fraser agitated the fluids in a dish. 'It's a good thing you took these pictures, sir, whatever they may say in London.'

'Thank you, Fraser,' said Blacker. 'I appreciate that. We got what we came for. Bring along the best, when they're dry.'

Ducking through the blackout curtains, Blacker went to make his report to his team now waiting on the verandah.

'Thanks to the surveys made this morning, you'll be pleased to hear that a carpet of images covering the approaches to Everest has been recorded. Our main objective is achieved.'

Percy Etherton led a round of self-congratulation. Blacker noticed that Fellowes did not join in. Presumably the man was still festering because his orders had been ignored. Damn it. Did it matter what Fellowes thought?

'A special tribute,' Blacker suggested, 'must be made to our Air Commodore for overcoming his illness in time to see our safe return from the Himalayas. Bravo for Fellowes!'

As the team endorsed this toast, Fraser arrived with the prints. Blacker quickly selected one and held it up for all to see. 'Here's a superb image of the spume cloud, racing from the peak. You were clever to get this one, Mac. It's a unique photograph.'

McIntyre was standing with Sally Smith and Barkas. The pilot was, as usual, brimming with mischievous energy. 'Aye. Thank you Colonel, but the praise is due to Fisher. He took the picture. I was trying to hang onto *Akbar*.'

Blacker lifted a drink from Framjee's tray. 'Tricky flying in all that spume, I imagine?'

'You might say so. Chips of flying ice and snow like marbles. Nearly bust the wind shield. A wee bit bumpy over the peak itself. In fact, it felt like an ammunition factory exploding below me. All credit to Westland for their solid work. As I said, I was just the monkey in the cockpit.'

Blacker saw how quickly Clydesdale agreed with McIntyre. The Chief Pilot had been uncommunicative for some hours, no doubt pressured by the conflicting demands of his situation. Messages from Lady Houston had continued to arrive. Lloyds and the Committee were clamoring for their immediate return. As an officer, Clydesdale had disobeyed Fellowes, but to what degree? *Lucy* had not passed over the summit but had detoured to skirt the mighty peak on its southern flanks. Within the terms of obedience there was a fair rationale for their action.

'Does this mean I can finally write the full story?' asked Shepherd. Against all his journalistic passion for a scoop, he had been persuaded to conceal the second flight from the world's media.

'Mr. Shepherd,' said Etherton. 'You have served our interests with exceptional patience and skill. Of course, please take your pick of the photographs and tell the story as you see it.' He glanced at Blacker and Fellowes. 'Do we all agree?'

A muscle twitched on the Air Commodore's temple as he replied. 'I cannot predict how they'll take the news in London, and possibly like an exploding ammunition factory as far as Lady Houston is concerned. But we're all alive, in one piece and the Westlands are safe on the ground. A job well done. Yes, Mr. Shepherd, publish and be damned.'

68. Purnea – April 1933

THE ENGINEERS HAD BEEN PREPPING all aircraft for their final departure from the now world-famous strip at Lalbalu. The final take-off was scheduled for the following day, so with everything ready, the ground crew headed to Purnea for their last evening at the clubhouse. After McIntyre's decisive triumph over Everest the party was likely to be memorable.

It was 5 p.m. when Pitt and Burnard arrived at the club. Pitt noticed more Indians than usual among the planters and their wives all gathering to say farewell to the high-flyers.

Connochie met them at the bar. He pointed to the Moth parked on the rough grass of the nearby golf course. 'The Raja is about to make his first flight,' he announced. 'Mac will take him up for a joy ride, to include loop, barrel roll and stall turn. We're about to shoot the sequence.'

'I'd rather shoot Barkas,' muttered Burnard. 'He's been hopping around getting under our feet all day. I can't wait to get home.'

'Shame on you Burnard.' Pitt could see the Fellowes on the lawn, chatting with the Maharanee of Dharbanga and other Indian ladies in a dazzle of saris. 'I'm going to miss all this.'

Pitt ordered a beer and recalled all the incidents that he had relayed to the readership of Bristol. A pity this reporting was about to end. As for his rival, he would be relieved to live without Shepherd's gibes and condescension. He saw Clydesdale regaling the Maharajah of Dharbanga and his family. Fisher and Bonnett, he noted, had teamed up with Gupta who, thank goodness, had recovered sufficiently from his burns to attend. Gupta's radiant wife stood with him in a scarlet sari. Once again she was the most striking of all but tonight the crowd was interested in one thing only. Raja Banaili was about to get airborne.

Colonel Blacker came hurrying from the golf course. Cutting through the crowd, he walked straight to Pitt and almost took the beer from his hand. 'Pitt. I'm glad you're here. We've got a spot of bother with the Moth. Maybe you and Burnard would care to help?'

To both engineers this didn't sound like a request. Besides, since the Colonel had selected them personally for the expedition, they owed him a favor or two.

Pitt had some beer while he still had the chance. 'So what's the bother, Colonel?'

'Follow me and you'll understand.' Blacker turned to lead them back through the party goers onto the golf course. Once out of general earshot, Blacker explained the problem. 'Actually it's not the Moth, but the Raja himself. The poor fellow cannot get into the cockpit. He's too big to fit inside.'

'Perhaps he should eat less,' suggested Burnard.

'This is no time for thoughtless comments,' Blacker retorted. 'Our host is stuck. He can't sit down and he can't get out. And I don't want this in the press, do you hear me, Pitt?'

'Not from my pen, sir.' Trying hard not to laugh, Pitt stepped forward. 'Let's take a look.'

At the Moth, they found it difficult to keep straight faces. McIntyre stood in his lightweight flight suit, gallantly shielding the Raja from public view. Their host was squatting ignominiously in the cockpit supported by his elbows on the leather coaming.

'Perhaps a firm push on each shoulder?' McIntyre whispered. 'We could shove him in?'

'I'm like a melon in an egg cup. This is such a silly business.' The Raja could laugh at his misfortune. 'I'm so glad to see you, Mr. Pitt.'

'We'll soon have you installed, sir. First we must empty your pockets.' Pitt had noticed how a bulge in the Raja's suit had caused the problem. He opened the flap and pulled out a bag of boiled sweets.'

'I see you came well supplied, sir.'

'It was the Ranee who insisted. Mrs. Fellowes said that sucking sweets is good practice when flying.'

With pockets empty, the engineers managed to jiggle the Raja's corpulence past the leather coaming until, with a sigh of relief, he sank into the seat. 'Bless you gentlemen. Thank you so much. This is the most exciting day of my life.'

'I know that feeling.' McIntyre said, as he helped his passenger to secure the harness. 'You're going to need this.'

McIntyre then slipped into his cockpit, strapped on his harness and primed the carburetor. Pitt went to swing the propellor and the Moth fired up, ready to go. As the rescue squad returned to the club house, they passed the camera crew, where Barkas was issuing instructions to Connochie.

'When Mac comes to land,' the director was saying. 'The shot must capture a path of glittering lights on either side of the Moth. It will create a magical setting to end the greatest story.'

'You'd make a good officer, Mr. Barkas. Perhaps the Air Ministry will give you a job,' said Pitt.

'Now, now, Pitt.' The film director had a drink in one hand, a megaphone in the other. 'I'm very happy in my profession. I'm sure the film will find its way to the Academy for a nomination.'

Colonel Blacker gave Barkas an affectionate punch to the shoulder. 'I like a man who thinks big.'

'I appreciate that, Colonel,' said Barkas. 'And let me add, this is our wrap party so Gaumont-British will be picking up the tab for everything.'

'I like that even better,' said Blacker.

Leaving the filmies to their work, Blacker and the engineers made it back to the club house as the Moth revved for take-off. Soon it was scampering along the fairway towards a twilight sky.

At the bar, Blacker told Etherton how they had successfully implanted the Raja, and that Barkas was picking up the tab for the party. News of the generosity by Gaumont-British would soon be sweeping through the crowd.

'And now that the cable office is operating normally, praise has been arriving.' Etherton took several cables from his pocket. 'Lucy has forgiven us for failing to heed her demands. She says the pilots' courage and success have inspired her to invest in Supermarine engine development.'

Pitt could see the Moth biplane climbing above the palm trees where the fruit bats were also taking to the air. 'So there's an Oscar in the offing and a profitable future for Bristol and Westland? That sounds like wonderful news for all.'

Etherton opened another cable. 'And this, my friends, came from the Vatican. I've been invited to visit the Pope.'

'Just you, Percy? Don't I get to see him?' Blacker was disappointed.

'I shouldn't worry, Colonel,' said Pitt. 'You're a military man, not really a man for God, sir. And besides you've already met the Goddess.'

Climbing higher, the Moth banked in the fading rays of sunlight. Then Mac pushed down its nose and cut the throttle. Only the music from Dr. Bennett's gramophone could be heard as the Moth spiraled silently towards the ground, before leveling out over the flare-lit runway.

Some spectators wondered if Mac had left it too late to pull out. Then they saw the Raja waving joyfully and throwing fistfuls of objects from his cockpit. As the engine kicked in, streamers of red and white smoke trailed in the slipstream. The vapors hung like thin curtains in the evening air before Mac dived again weaving the Moth around and through the lingering smoke. The crowd applauded mightily, a vision none would forget.

Etherton turned to the bar crowd as the Moth turned to land. 'So that's it, gentlemen. Job well done, everyone happy.'

Colonel Blacker wanted the last word. 'And as you foresaw at the beginning, Percy, it was as easy as tying a knot in a tiger's tail.'

69. Savoy Hotel – April 21st 1933

FOR THOSE DINING IN THE Savoy Grill, the change in decibel level was distinct. Conversations paused, heads turned and eyes darted towards a new arrival now making her way with the maître d' to the table where Blumenfeld, Garland and Willie Graham had just ordered their meal.

None of them had been expecting Lady Houston.

The three diners stood as waiters introduced a fourth chair and table setting. Garland took the ebony stick from Lady Houston who sat down with a sparkling smile. 'Pink champagne, please, Felix. You know what I like.'

The maitre d' had anticipated the order. A bottle of rose champagne was already arriving with the wine waiter. Lady Houston was not wearing gloves and an opal ring glittered on her finger as she took a glass. She continued beaming as she explained.

'The doctor released me early and I'm feeling so well. I decided to pop down and join you. I hope you don't mind.'

After ten months with Her Ladyship, Garland recognized pure theater. When had Lucy ever minded what people thought about her? Nonetheless, they were all delighted to hear of the doctor's report. Lucy Houston waved their comments aside to ask Felix for a plate of fresh herrings.

'Herrings have always my favorite,' Lucy explained. 'We should do more for men who earn their living from the sea, don't you think?'

'Very true,' said Willie Graham. 'Scottish fishermen are having a poor time of it these days.'

'Not like Scottish lawyers then,' growled Lucy.

Garland saw the lawyer recoil. She would try to prevent any more insinuations like that. 'With respect, milady, this is supposed to be my leaving lunch. When I'm sailing back to America, I don't want to think of you being at war with Willie.'

Lady Houston agreed. 'How right you are, Garland. I shall miss your advice, especially now you're abandoning me for Uncle Sam. But you wisely accepted my guidance many times, which is more than my pilots did! They were sitting around all those weeks in India, pretending to work make a film, when in reality they were waiting to sneak off to Everest. It's all over the papers today! McIntyre flouted all my requests and vetoes and then confronted horrendous wind conditions over the summit, all in total contravention of my wishes.'

'But you must admit, Lucy, they took some brilliant pictures,' said Blumenfeld. He had run one such photograph in the *Daily Express* after agreeing rights with *The Times*. 'McIntyre is now the second Scot to blow the dust off Everest and the Committee is breathing a vast sigh of relief.'

Lady Houston sipped champagne, her eyes checking the tables of neighboring diners before she turned to Blumenfeld.

'We were all conned, Ralph. There's no other way of putting it. Mind you, being conned doesn't really bother me. I can ignore disobedience, but it was the refusal of Lloyds to insure the flight that had me worried. Imagine the brouhaha if McIntyre had lost his wings over Everest? My name would have been associated with a failure and that scurvy little runt in Downing Street would have forced me to pay for a replacement Westland.'

'My fears all along.' Willie Graham was anxious to reinforce the reason for his invoices.

'We see the pilots' behavior as magnificent insubordination. That's how we described it,' said Blumenfeld. 'Very British.'

'And maybe you're right, Ralph,' Lady Houston smiled. 'But I do like to insure things you know.'

'And Lloyds can breath again. No claims. No disputes. It's all irrelevant now,' said Blumenfeld.

Lady Houston accepted that recrimination for her-acclaimed pilots was a non-starter. 'But tell me, Ralph, what's next in this extravaganza? Am I to expect any more nasty surprises?'

Blumenfeld shook his head. 'On the contrary, Lucy. One of the aircrew – I think it was Fisher – may have seen an ice axe lying on a ledge, not far from the summit. Sadly he didn't get a photograph , but my news desk think it could only have belonged to Mallory or Irvine.'

'We may never know,' said Lady Houston. 'The riddle remains.'

'And you'll like this, Lucy,' Blumenfeld continued. 'In the survey photographs they discovered a lake of hot water. It never freezes and it has been named after you. They will call it Parvati Tal.'

'Parvati Tal?' Lady Houston frowned. 'What's that got to do with me?'

'In the local dialect, it means The Lady of the Mountains.'

Lady Houston clasped her hands together. 'That's very kind of them. I like that, I do. So, Ralph, have we done with surprises?'

'I hope so,' said Blumenfeld. 'Clydesdale and Ellison will fly the Westlands to Karachi for dismantling and repatriation by ship. The Fellowes and McIntyre will return in privately insured biplanes.'

'A good thing too,' said Lady Houston. 'Anyway, I'm sending them each a box of cigars from Friborg and Treyer.'

The diners all agreed that was a magnificent gesture and the conversation paused for the arrival of the main course.

Garland had chosen baked salmon. The men had ordered Dover sole. This lifestyle might soon be missing from her life, she realized. If she was lucky, she might be soon writing articles and running to a faster pulse instead of licking stamps for this endearing but contentious Dame of the British Empire.

Lady Houston had been reading Garland's thoughts. 'So, it's off on the high seas for you, young lady.' Lady Houston put down her fork to dab her lips with the napkin. 'What will I do without your charming company and your easy way with Mungo?'

Garland braced herself, fearing Lady Houston was about to air some indiscretions. 'You'll manage. So will the dog.'

Blumenfeld, bless him, steered the conversation away. 'Oh, there's something you might want to know,' he said to Garland. 'You remember meeting Elizabeth Penrose at Easter?'

'Of course I do. And I telephoned Westland to see if their test pilot had relatives in America? Sadly, I don't think there's a link.'

'Never mind. Elizabeth Penrose, called me yesterday' said Blumenfeld. 'She may have an opening for you in New York.'

'At *Vogue*! I don't believe it.'

'Believe it when it happens,' muttered Lady Houston. 'Anyway, Garland, you can always come back to me and Mungo if all else fails.'

'That's so sweet of you. I don't know how to thank you.'

'Life is about making and taking opportunities.' Lady Houston reached for her drink. 'But a girl like you can't work for ever for an old goat like me. Good heavens, when I was your age, I learned how to create more opportunities than I care to mention.'

'And you'll remember, Lady Houston,' said Garland quickly, 'that I'm still longing to write your biography.'

'That must wait for the moment.' Lady Houston cocked her head defiantly. 'Nobody needs to know my secrets. In fact, I've forgotten most of them myself, but this story makes sound advice for any young woman. I'll tell you if it goes no further. Understood?'

Before Lady Houston could begin, a bellboy came to her chair, carrying an envelope on a silver tray. She took it and placed it on the table. Since nobody wanted dessert, they ordered coffee instead.

Lucy Houston waited until the coffee cups were filled. When the waiters had withdrawn, she placed her elbows on the table and slowly pulled aside the silk scarf around her neck. Below it lay two strings of black pearls, small as marbles, and each alive with the sheen of Tahitian beauty.

'You all know my emerald is false, but these pearls are most certainly not.' Lucy Houston raised each string of pearls, displaying them with pride and grace. 'These cost more than the entire flight to Everest and, should you care to ask, without them the expedition would never have taken place.'

'How's that?' Blumenfeld asked.

'I saw them in a shop in Regent Street one day, back when Sir Robert Houston was chasing me all over town. He was like a rutting stag, desperate to get at me he was. But I wasn't going to give in easily. So I resisted his interest and especially all the jewels he offered to me. All were rubbish I told him. They weren't good enough for me.'

'That was quite a move,' Blumenfeld said. 'A risky one.'

'And I've been telling Garland to master the art, the ability to negotiate until the terms are right. Then one day, I casually mentioned to Sir Robert how the subtle beauty of these pearls was more to my liking. The price tag nearly knocked poor Robert off his feet when he reluctantly agreed to purchase them.'

'And you got them!' Garland said.

'I've kept them ever since. We were married a few months later and you know the rest.' Lady Houston replaced the scarf. 'I prefer to hide them but they remain the loveliest and most desirable pearls in London. With them came all my good fortune, the yacht, the Schneider Trophy, the help for a thousand charities and, last but not least, the aerial conquest of Everest. So, Garland, remember what I've told you – that the female of the species is more deadly than the male.'

Lucy Houston opened her bag and pulled out a sealed envelope. Then she picked up the envelope left by the bellboy and handed both to Garland.

'Time for you to go, my dear. I've promised Mr. Churchill that I will finance engines at Supermarine. They are going to build Spitfires so I hear and I must discuss all that with these two gentlemen. Here, then, are two little gifts from me, Garland. To thank you for your friendship and to open up your future.'

Lost for words with a lump creeping into her throat, Garland stood up. Both men rose and she stepped to place a kiss on Willy Graham's whiskery cheek.

'Goodbye, Willie. I'll let you know when I'm back in Britain.'

'Always at your service, Garland. And very good luck to you.'

Garland turned to Ralph Blumenfeld. She felt a tear in her eye. She hugged him and then kissed both his cheeks. 'We've come a long way since Lake Placid.'

'Haven't we just?' Blumenfeld returned her squeeze. 'You and I will keep in touch.'

'For sure we will.'

When Garland turned to the final farewell, Lucy Houston did not stand as she took Garland's kiss and gripped her outstretched hand. Lucy dabbed at her Garland's eyes with her napkin.

'Go on, Garland. John and Mungo have sent their farewells. I've reserved a room for you, here tonight. John has left your bags with the porter and has gone to buy cigars for the pilots.'

'Please thank John. Tell him I'll miss him and Mungo too.'

'Not half as much as they'll miss you,' said Lady Houston. 'Now here are the keys to some rooms upstairs. Take your pick of the Savoy's best. And in this other envelope there's a wee gift, as the Scots would say. Enjoy yourself and write to me, once in a while. That's all I ask.'

Garland picked up her handbag to leave the table. Every eye in the Grill Room was on her as Felix escorted her to the foyer where a porter ushered her towards the elevators.

By the time she reached the sixth floor, Garland had opened the envelope which contained the keys. There were two inside. Why did Lady Houston expect her to make a choice? A gesture of extravagance, Garland decided. She ran her fingers over the other envelope and recognized the rustle of bank notes. She followed the porter down the corridor. After the busy chatter of the grill, all was hushed and quiet.

So which was it to be? Room 620 or Room 622?

'Is there any difference?' she asked, as the porter hovered uncertainly between the doors. 'I wonder which has the best view?'

'They're identical, Miss. But I was told the choice is yours. I've already put the gentleman's bags inside Room 620.'

What gentleman? Oh my God, what was Lady Houston up to now?

'Then I'll take 622. Thank you.'

She tipped the porter after he had installed her bags. It wasn't his fault that he'd been included in the plot. Alone at last, Garland took a brief wander around the room, admiring its decor and its view over the Thames. She had only one final night in London before boarding next morning's boat train to Southampton. She wanted to relax and take in a night in the West End. But who was this 'gentleman' installed in the neighboring room? She decided to find out immediately.

Taking both keys, Garland returned to the corridor. At least she had an exit route if needed, and wasn't the female of the species supposedly more deadly? She slid the key into the lock of Room 622 and pushed it open.

Donal Ryan was relaxing on the bed reading *The Racing Gazette*. He was in a white linen shirt and green cravat and he seemed genuinely surprised to see her. 'And what in heck's name are you doing here?'

Ryan sprang off the bed and stood before her, hands on his hips. 'I might ask the same of you.'

The memory of Ryan's Enfield on Skegness sands came racing back, firing all her nerves. 'Lucy gave me the key to this room. But why are you here?'

'Waiting for tomorrow's boat train to Southampton,' said Ryan with a dawning smile. 'I'm off to Kentucky to buy her some fresh yearlings.'

'The wily cheek of the woman!' Garland had to laugh. 'So, she's shipping us off together, whether we like it or not?'

'Do I mind - if you don't?'

Ryan's soft voice, his charm and tactile energy made the next decision much easier. Garland knew exactly how she would like to be spending the next few weeks. Some thoughtful soul had placed a champagne bottle in an ice bucket on the side-table.

'Then let's open that bottle while we debate that question.' Garland returned Donal's smile, as she walked to the ice bucket. 'It's pink champagne, so no need to wonder who sent it.'

ABOUT THE AUTHOR

George Almond – This grandson of a Wyoming horse rancher, enjoys revisiting great adventures and was himself a cowboy in Texas and Canada, before going to St. Edmund Hall, Oxford to study modern languages.

Since then the years have provided him with many exotic adventures on land, sea and in the air. Drawn to stories of an epic nature, the author was inspired by a chance meeting with the sherpa Tenzing Norgay and Lord Hunt, who led the famous 1953 expedition. From them he learned how the aerial photos taken by Lady Houston's pilots had been studied carefully during assault planning for the first successful ascent.

This work is his personal outcome of that long distant meeting.

In researching this story, the author offers gratitude and acknowledgment to the many sources including family members, mountaineers, engineers and pilots who have all provided valuable input about the true events of the flight.

The Flight Expedition was successful because highly experienced men and women were involved. All had survived the horrendous years of the Great War and were by nature, confident, bold and determined in their various roles for the expedition.

With so many colorful characters, it seemed logical to relate events from their different viewpoints leading the reader along the many paths that the expedition followed to its lofty target.

For further information about this unique operation:
Please visit   www.evenhigherthaneverest.com